FUTURE PERFECT

Our mixture *would,* I think, be effective. I hope you are thinking of doing Mars—in some detail. Let me be in *there,* at the right moment—or in other words at an early stage.

Letter from Henry James to H. G. Wells
September 23, 1902

FUTURE PERFECT

American Science Fiction of the Nineteenth Century

H. BRUCE FRANKLIN

New York OXFORD UNIVERSITY PRESS 1966

Library of Congress Catalogue Card Number: 66-14475

Acknowledgment to Andrew R. MacAndrew and New American Library, Inc., for permission to quote from his translation of Dostoevsky's *Notes from Underground* (Signet Classic, 1961) © 1961 by Andrew R. MacAndrew.

I am grateful to all the members of my senior seminars in science fiction for all they have contributed to this book; without them it would have been impossible.

Printed in the United States of America

FOR JANE

CONTENTS

INTRODUCTION

Because the nineteenth century was the first century in which science fiction became a common form of writing, the present century is the first in which it is possible to look back at a body of science fiction created in a different age. From the perspective of the present, this science fiction of the past shows just how much an age determines and displays itself through what it sees as remote possibilities. American science fiction of the nineteenth century can now provide insights into nineteenth-century America, into the history of science and its relations to society, into the predictions, expectations, and fantasies of the present, and into the nature of science fiction, and, thereby, of all fiction.

Science, a cumulative process which exists to be superseded, and fiction, a series of individual attempts to create matter which cannot be superseded, have vastly differing relations to time. Insofar as any work of science fiction is a form of science it partakes of the temporality and impermanence of science and surrenders the timelessness of fiction. The most brilliant prognostications of the past have, ironically, little immediate relevance to the present human situation; we in 1966 may admire their brilliance but only from our superior position in later time—to look back upon them, no matter how admiringly, is to look down upon them. So that any story in this collection which has withstood time or even triumphed over it has somehow managed to span the chasm, or apparent chasm, between fiction and science.

Science fiction did not, as many still believe, begin either in the twentieth century or with Jules Verne and H. G. Wells. Half a dozen histories of science fiction now start with Lucian of Samosata and trace the development of the form through Ariosto, Kepler, Cyrano de Bergerac, Mary Shelley, and Poe to the present. But even these surveys barely hint of the extent and depth of nineteenth-century science fiction. To take its full measure it would be necessary to add up all the tales of strange psychic phenomena, utopian romances, wondrous discoveries, and extraordinary voyages in time and space to be found in all the books and periodicals of the century. But to get at least a glimpse of science fiction's importance in nineteenth-century American fiction, one has only to look directly at the works of the most important writers, something which, surprisingly enough, no one seems to have done from this angle.

There was no major ninteenth-century American writer of fiction, and indeed few in the second rank, who did not write some science fiction or at least one utopian romance. Charles Brockden Brown, often called the first professional American author, built his romances on the spontaneous combustion of a living man, almost superhuman ventriloquism, hallucinations, extraordinary plagues, and extreme somnambulism; Washington Irving's most famous story is a time-travel story; James Fenimore Cooper produced a society of monkeys who live in the polar regions in *The Monikins* (1835) and placed a utopian society on a group of islands that rises suddenly out of the ocean in *The Crater* (1848); William Gilmore Simms contributed to the lost-continent tradition in *Atalantis* (1832) and helped swell the tide of fiction about mesmerism with "Mesmerides in a Stage-coach; or Passes en Passant"; Melville's first major work of pure fiction was *Mardi,* a full-length philosophical voyage to all kinds of utopian and would-be utopian societies, and he later wrote one of the first robot stories in English; Oliver Wendell Holmes, insofar as he was a writer of fiction, was a writer of science fiction; Mark Twain's *A Connecticut Yankee in King Arthur's Court* is one of the greatest of time-travel books, and he experimented with a number of other forms of science fiction; William Dean Howells, in addition to writing two utopian romances (*A Traveler from Altruria* and *Through the Eye of the Needle*), was an editor, collector, sympathetic critic, and composer of fiction which explored the outer limits of telepathy, clairvoyance, and teleportation (see, for instance, his own *Between the Dark and the Daylight* and *Questionable Shapes* and one collection he edited and introduced, *Shapes That Haunt the Dusk*); Henry James wrote a number of ghostly stories based on strange psychic phenomena and left at his death in hundreds of pages of manuscript the unfinished *The Sense of the Past,* a tale of time travel; Stephen Crane's "The Monster" is a splendid variation on the *Frankenstein* theme; even Mary E. Wilkins Freeman left both realism and ghosts behind long enough to write "The Hall Bedroom," a story about a disappearance into "the fifth dimension"; and Hawthorne, Poe, Fitz-James O'Brien, Edward Bellamy, and Ambrose Bierce all play leading roles in the history of science fiction.

In fact, not until late in the nineteenth century did much American fiction operate in a strictly realistic mode, that is, by presenting counterfeits of common events in a society familiar to its readers. Born during the height of English gothicism and growing up during the full bloom of English romanticism, American fiction developed as its most characteristic form what its authors called the "Romance." And whenever that word Romance appears in a title or preface, the reader may expect to find something at least verging on science fiction. Slowly during the nineteenth century, writers and readers began to be aware that a new form had developed from the old Romance—something which began to be called the scientific romance. The term "science fiction" may have first been used in the twentieth century, but that may be simply because of the earlier taboo against using nouns to modify nouns; as early as 1876 (as pointed out by Thomas D. Clareson) an introduction to William Henry Rhodes's collection of fantasy and science fiction entitled *Caxton's Book* discussed "scientific fiction" as a distinct genre.

The same crowds that jammed the lecture halls when scientists spoke and that supported dozens of popularizing scientific journals insatiably yearned for any conceivable kind of fictional marvel. Specialized magazines of fantasy and science fiction did not appear until late in the century simply because a very high percentage of the fiction published in the leading periodicals (*United States Magazine and Democratic Review, The Southern Literary Messenger, Graham's, Godey's, Harper's Monthly, Putnam's, Scribner's, The Atlantic Monthly, Cosmopolitan*) was fantasy and science fiction. This fiction appeared often, just as it does in several of today's science-fiction magazines, alongside factual popularizations of scientific progress and theories. It was not until the last years of the century that the so-called "rise of realism" tended to make science fiction seem a lowbrow and puerile entertainment. The incredible career of the science-fiction "dime" novel helped solidify this abject position, a position from which science fiction, most people would think, has yet to emerge completely. But those who find science fiction "subliterary" fail to see that:

1. Most twentieth-century science fiction, like most nineteenth-century science fiction, like most realistic fiction of the nineteenth and twentieth centuries, like most fiction of any variety of any human time and place, must of necessity be ordinary rather than extraordinary.

2. Much science fiction is based on ancient literary assumptions—such as the premise that literature teaches and delights by

being delightful teaching, and the Platonic premise that the creative artist should imitate ideal forms rather than actualities —that happen today to be at the bottom of the wheel of fashion.

3. A different kind of literature from realistic fiction, science fiction demands a different kind of reading.

HAWTHORNE AND POE

NATHANIEL HAWTHORNE AND SCIENCE FICTION

All fiction presumably seeks to describe present reality, which includes the history of that reality, its implicit possibilities, and its ideals and nightmares, that is, everything conceivable. One may think of realistic fiction, historical fiction, science fiction, and fantasy as theoretically distinct strategies for describing what is real. Realistic fiction seeks to describe present reality in terms of a counterfeit of that reality; historical fiction seeks to describe present reality in terms of a counterfeit of that reality's history; science fiction seeks to describe present reality in terms of a credible hypothetical invention—past, present, or, most usually, future—extrapolated from that reality; fantasy seeks to describe present reality in terms of an impossible alternative to that reality. Realistic fiction views what is by projecting what may seem to be; historical fiction views what is by projecting what may seem to have been; science fiction views what is by projecting what not inconceivably could be; fantasy views what is by projecting what could not be. To put the matter in the simplest terms, realistic fiction tries to imitate actualities, historical fiction past probabilities, science fiction possibilities, fantasy impossibilities.

Of course pure examples of realistic fiction, historical fiction, science fiction, or fantasy do not exist. The most fantastic story must still compound even its most fanciful and monstrous creations out of physical and psychological actualities; the most realistic fiction must still be composed of verbal dreams; all historical fiction in one sense is clearly a kind of fantasy; science fiction contains the ambivalent elements of both realistic fiction and fantasy. In practice every piece of fiction is a combination of all four theoretical modes, deriving what we may call its nature from the proportions and arrangements of its elements.

When a writer chooses among these four modes and their possible combinations, his choice determines certain limitations and potentialities. A writer who chooses to imitate only present actualities has the most limited range, but he has available to him the force of the here and now. A writer who chooses to imitate purely past probabilities or future possibilities may make another world available to the reader but in so doing may cut himself off from much of the reader's world. A writer who plunges into pure fantasy goes much further; he comes close to insisting openly that the reader find a higher kind of reality in the writer's invention *qua* invention than in the real world. This demand may be implicit in most fiction, but it is usually veiled carefully; it is one made openly only by the insane, and by them not usually with consciousness.

Of course such an insistence is really the hidden hubris of any writer who would be—to use that revealing term—creative. Hawthorne recognized this throughout his writing career and expressed his horror at his chosen role in many ways in many places. He saw himself as a fantasy-maker like the inept showman in "Main Street," a mere romancer like that *voyeur* Coverdale, a fiendish displayer of fantastic psychological horrors like Satan himself in "Young Goodman Brown." For, after all, as he wrote in "Fancy's Show Box," "a novel writer or a dramatist, in creating a villain of romance and fitting him with evil deeds" is hard to distinguish from the actual villain, whose villainy largely consists in his "projecting" crimes.

Despite his constant attempts to escape the fantastical and grasp the realistic, Hawthorne persisted in seeing symbolic marvels wherever he looked. Within the realistic main plots of "My Kinsman, Major Molineux," "Roger Malvin's Burial," "The Minister's Black Veil," *The Scarlet Letter, The Blithedale Romance,* and *The Marble Faun* occur, or apparently occur, such fantastic events as Satan directing a crucifixion, a supernatural monster being created out of guilt, the entire earth assuming a symbolic black veil, the heavens themselves commenting in a blazing letter on human affairs, a veil dissolving time and space, and a prehistoric faun in the shape of an Italian count re-enacting all of human history. But as Dorville Libby astutely pointed out in 1869 (in "The Supernatural in Hawthorne," *Overland Monthly*): "Hawthorne's are not fairy stories. In dealing with either nature or art he never violates physical laws."

Hawthorne does not offer his fiction as either a counterfeit of actuality or an impossible alternative to it. He presents both marvels and more or less plausible explanations of them. Aware of all the issues of the modes of fiction, he even makes some of his works turn upon the question: To which category of fiction does this belong? The most obvious example is "Young Goodman Brown," which provides several alternative explanations of its dramatized historical action, ranging from realistic-historical fiction (the apparently fantastic events are merely a Puritan dream) through science fiction (psychological processes have actually given different shape to external reality) to fantasy (the Devil and witches' sabbath have had objective reality). To call a story such as "Young Goodman Brown" science fiction would be to stretch that term beyond any usefulness and raise fruitless problems of definition. A great deal of Hawthorne's work, however, not only fits almost any definition of science fiction, but actually itself defines that mode.

Hawthorne's notebooks display the archetypal science fictionist at work, finding in the extension of accepted science and its methods the formulas for parabolic fiction:

> Questions as to unsettled points of History, and Mysteries of Nature, to be asked of a mesmerized person.
>
> Imaginary diseases to be cured by impossible remedies—as, a dose of the Grand Elixir, in the yolk of a Phoenix's egg. The diseases may be either moral or physical.
>
> A physician for the cure of moral diseases.
>
> A moral philosopher to buy a slave, or otherwise get possession of a human being, and to use him for the sake of experiment, by trying the operation of a certain vice on him.
>
> Madame Calderon de la B (in Life in Mexico) speaks of persons who have been inoculated with the venom of rattlesnakes, by pricking them in various places with the tooth. These persons are thus secured forever against the bite of any venomous reptile. They have the power of calling snakes, and feel great pleasure in playing with and handling them. Their own bite becomes poisonous to people not inoculated in the same manner. Thus a part of the serpent's nature appears to be transfused into them.*

As can be seen here and throughout the notebooks, one typical genesis for Hawthorne's fiction is the genesis which typifies science fiction—a speculation generated immediately out of a brush with science.

Although Hawthorne's science fiction may seem to us fantastical, he usually extrapolated it with care from scientific and medical theory accepted by his contemporaries or their predecessors. "The Man of Adamant," a rather thin little sketch about a misanthrope who literally turns into stone, illustrates some of

* *The American Notebooks*, Randall Stewart, ed. (New Haven, 1932), pp. 93-8.

Hawthorne's methods. The symbolic petrifaction is given a more or less scientific explanation: the man of adamant has a rare disease, "a deposition of calculous particles within his heart, caused by an obstructed circulation of the blood"; he lives in a cave, drinking the water which otherwise "would have been congealed into a pebble"; his stone corpse, found more than a century after his death, may be due to "the moisture of the cave," which "possessed a petrifying quality." But Hawthorne equivocates the plausibility of the physical events by making them seem really beyond physical explanation. No reader of this sketch could guess that Hawthorne just the year before (1836) had written, as editor of *The American Magazine of Useful and Entertaining Knowledge,* a straightforward account of "a new method of preserving the dead" found in "the last American Journal of Science"—"converting animal substances into stone."

The long line of doctors, chemists, botanists, mesmerists, physicists, and inventors who parade the wonders of their skills throughout Hawthorne's fiction rarely strays far from historically accepted achievements or theories. The mechanical marvels of "The Artist of the Beautiful," the scientific creations of "The Birthmark," and the medical theories of "Rappaccini's Daughter" are not original concoctions.

Only in his obsession with the elixir of life did Hawthorne disdain rooting his science fiction in science, and this proved costly. The elixir of life, which Randall Stewart has called "a topic of major importance in the study of Hawthorne's work," * adequately dramatizes the coherent but relatively simple fable of "Dr. Heidegger's Experiment" and adequately fulfills a subordinate role in "The Birthmark." But Hawthorne was never able to make it do what he wanted it to. At the end of his life, unable to put together a coherent fictional speculation, Hawthorne moved pseudo-scientists and their elixir of life through an endless series of meaningless combinations, resulting in such

* See his discussion in *The American Notebooks,* pp. lxxxii-lxxxviii.

unfinished documents as *Septimius Felton; or, The Elixir of Life* and *The Dolliver Romance.*

In only a few works did Hawthorne let science fiction predominate. Yet in three of the four major romances, science-fictional elements run as a defining and controlling undercurrent beneath the realistic surface action. Chillingworth's secret experiment on Dimmesdale controls the center of *The Scarlet Letter* and defines the roles of the two men; the action in *The House of the Seven Gables* derives from and is symbolized by the hypnotic powers of the Maules and the perhaps consequent peculiar physiology of the Pyncheons; all of the major events in *The Blithedale Romance* flow out of the exhibition of hypnotic control that symbolically defines them.

Of these, *The Blithedale Romance* may seem to contain the most questionable example of science fiction, but that is only if one forgets the status of hypnotism in 1852. In fact, Priscilla's actions as a mesmeric subject are carefully modeled on findings of the French Academy as presented with wonder in "Animal Magnetism" in *The American Magazine of Useful and Entertaining Knowledge* for December 1835, four months before Hawthorne became editor of that magazine. The following description of *The Blithedale Romance,* which constituted the entire preface to the 1899 Henry Altemus edition, locates the book with reference to contemporaneous and subsequent scientific theory:

> *The Blithedale Romance* opened up a new phase of romantic literature. Psychology, with its mysteries so little appreciated, so slightly explored, so often quite undiscovered, furnished the basis for those elements of the marvellous which made that tale a Romance. So wonderful are the recent developments in psychology that it is but natural that much of the work of the modern romancer should take him into the same field. Hawthorne in this story anticipated many of the recent disclosures in hypnotism.

These words bear a surprising likeness to those familiar accolades given to the science fiction that predicted television, space flight, and atomic power. But Hawthorne's three great complete works of science fiction demonstrate that such an accolade obscures more than it reveals.

'The perfect future in the present': "The Birthmark"

"The Birthmark" is both an intricately wrought science fiction and an intricately wrought commentary on the fiction of science. Science in "The Birthmark" appears in many different forms: in the particular experiment which constitutes almost the entire action and in the psychology of the experimenter, both of which Hawthorne derives in part from a standard text on physiology; in the relation of that experimenter's science to science at the date of the story's action (late eighteenth century) and of its publication (half a century later); in an allegory of science as idea, ideal, and process.

The kind of experiment, as Randall Stewart notes, is adumbrated in two entries in the journal, entries which suggest the moral ambivalence of the story itself:

> A person to be in the possession of something as perfect as mortal man has a right to expect; he tries to make it better, and ruins it entirely. [1837]
>
> A person to be the death of his beloved in trying to raise her to more than mortal perfection; yet this should be a comfort to him for having aimed so highly and holily. [1840]

The psychology of the experimenter, as Stewart also notes, is suggested in an entry referring to Dr. Andrew Combe's *The Principles of Physiology*:

> The case quoted in Combe's Physiology, from Pinel, of a young man of great talents and profound knowl-

> edge of chemistry, who had in view some new discovery of importance. In order to put his mind into the highest possible activity, he shut himself up, for several successive days, and used various methods of excitement; he had a singing girl with him; he drank spirits; smelled penetrating odors, sprinkled cologne-water round the room &c. &c. Eight days thus passed, when he was seized with a fit of frenzy, which terminated in mania. [1842]

The particular experiment seems to have been suggested by another passage in Combe's *Physiology*. In a section entitled "Reciprocal Action between the Skin and Other Organs," Combe warns:

> Nothing, indeed, can be more delusive than the rash application of merely physical laws to the explanation of the phenomena of living beings. Vitality is a principle superior to, and in continual warfare with, the laws which regulate the actions of inanimate bodies; and it is only after life has become extinct that these laws regain the mastery, and lead to the rapid decomposition of the animal machine. In studying the functions of the human body, therefore, we must be careful not to hurry to conclusions, before taking time to examine the influence of the vital principle in modifying the expected results.
>
> It is in consequence of the sympathy and reciprocity of action existing between the skin and the internal organs that burns and even scalds of no very great extent prove fatal, by inducing internal, generally intestinal, inflammation.

The main lines of "The Birthmark" are, or should be, quite clear. Aylmer the scientist, in attempting to remove his wife Georgiana's birthmark, her only defect apparent to him, makes her perfect in death. Aylmer, who represents the Faustian, overreaching, overintellectualized, and overspiritualized aspects of science, sacrifices his nearly angelic but real wife Georgiana to the ideal of perfection. He is to be pitied for his folly, abhorred for his heartlessness, and admired for his aspirations. As Robert Heilman has pointed out in "Hawthorne's 'The Birthmark': Science as Religion" (*South Atlantic Quarterly*, 1949), the tale turns on Aylmer's mistaking science for religion, a mistake in which Georgiana follows him and which leads them to pervert the language and actions of religion. Georgiana stands throughout the action as surrogate or synecdoche for the entire nonscientific world.

Of course there is much more in the story, and the admirable unity of its complex elements has been much discussed. What has been overlooked is its explicit allegory of science in time, an allegory which culminates in the final punning words of the story: "the perfect future in the present."

The very first words of the story firmly locate the action in a particular period of the history of science: "In the latter part of the last century there lived a man of science . . ." The fairy-tale tone of this opening suits a time when fairy tales were becoming historic fact: "In those days, when the comparatively recent discovery of electricity and other kindred mysteries of Nature seemed to open paths into the region of miracle . . ."

"The Birthmark" shows the ways in which science may be entertaining knowledge, glorious entertainment. While science is offering to Aylmer the scientist an apparent path to the Ideal, it is offering primarily entertainment, though imperfect, to his audience, patient, model, and victim:

> To dispel the tedium of the hours which her husband found it necessary to devote to the processes of combination and analysis, Georgiana turned over the volumes of his scientific library. In many dark old tomes she met with chapters full of romance and poetry. They were the works of the philosophers of the middle ages, such as Albertus Magnus, Cornelius Agrippa, Paracelsus, and the famous friar who created the prophetic Brazen Head. All these antique naturalists stood in advance of their centuries, yet were imbued with some of

> their credulity, and therefore were believed, and perhaps imagined themselves to have acquired from the investigation of Nature a power above Nature, and from physics a sway over the spiritual world. Hardly less curious and imaginative were the early volumes of the Transactions of the Royal Society, in which the members, knowing little of the limits of natural possibility, were continually recording wonders or proposing methods whereby wonders might be wrought.

These early scientists have become—through the actions of their successors—creators of romance, poetry, curious and imaginative volumes. But even these alchemists, pseudo-scientists, and proto-scientists are measured and assessed in terms of their times: they "stood in advance of their centuries."

Aylmer almost disdains these early dreams of science:

> He gave a history of the long dynasty of the alchemists, who spent so many ages in quest of the universal solvent by which the golden principle might be elicited from all things vile and base. Aylmer appeared to believe that, by the plainest scientific logic, it was altogether within the limits of possibility to discover this long-sought medium; "but," he added, "a philosopher who should go deep enough to acquire the power would attain too lofty a wisdom to stoop to the exercise of it." Not less singular were his opinions in regard to the elixir vitae. He more than intimated that it was at his option to concoct a liquid that should prolong life for years, perhaps interminably; but that it would produce a discord in Nature which all the world, and chiefly the quaffer of the immortal nostrum, would find cause to curse.

How should we apply Aylmer's theory of wisdom to our own transmuters of the atoms of metals and miracle-workers in geriatrics? For us, Aylmer's assertions about the practical powers of the scientist must point to the nightmarish fairy-tale qualities of the world in which we live:

> "[This] is the most precious poison that ever was concocted in this world. By its aid I could apportion the lifetime of any mortal at whom you might point your finger. The strength of the dose would determine whether he were to linger out years, or drop dead in the midst of a breath. No king on his guarded throne could keep his life if I, in my private station, should deem that the welfare of millions justified me in depriving him of it."
>
> "Why do you keep such a terrific drug?" inquired Georgiana in horror.
>
> "Do not mistrust me, dearest," said her husband, smiling; "its virtuous potency is yet greater than its harmful one."

But Aylmer's science may not be under such great control as he pretends. When Georgiana, in part representing the non-scientific world, touches a flower which Aylmer has created for her, "the whole plant suffered a blight, its leaves turning coal-black as if by the agency of fire."

Despite these seemingly radioactive ashes, the heart of the problem of science in "The Birthmark" does not lie in the ultimate effects of science. It lies in the fictional and momentary nature of science itself. Hawthorne dramatizes the problem in two parts of Aylmer's amusing scientific show. First:

> In order to soothe Georgiana, and, as it were, to release her mind from the burden of actual things, Aylmer now put in practice some of the light and playful secrets which science had taught him among its profounder lore. Airy figures, absolutely bodiless ideas, and forms of unsubstantial beauty came and danced before her, imprinting their momentary footsteps on beams of light. Though she had some indistinct idea of the method of these optical phenomena, still the illusion was almost perfect enough to warrant the belief that her husband possessed sway over the spiritual world. Then again, when she felt a wish to look forth from her seclusion, immediately, as if her thoughts were

> answered, the procession of external existence flitted across a screen. The scenery and the figures of actual life were perfectly represented, but with that bewitching, yet indescribable difference which always makes a picture, an image, or a shadow so much more attractive than the original.

This last sentence contains a paradigm of the whole story. After it comes the devastation of the plant, and then this:

> To make up for this abortive experiment, he proposed to take her portrait by a scientific process of his own invention. It was to be effected by rays of light striking upon a polished plate of metal. Georgiana assented; but, on looking at the result, was affrighted to find the features of the portrait blurred and indefinable; while the minute figure of a hand appeared where the cheek should have been. Aylmer snatched the metallic plate and threw it into a jar of corrosive acid.

The impressive symbolic relations between what Aylmer displays and what he is in the process of doing to Georgiana should not blind us to a further significance in his show. What Aylmer shows to Georgiana in the latter part of the eighteenth century is a trinity of miracles; what Aylmer shows to the mid-nineteenth-century reader are three recent inventions, the diorama, the stereoscope, and the daguerreotype, each still imbued with a certain amount of wonder; what Aylmer shows to us are three primitive gadgets, now not even commonplace but superseded by motion pictures, television, and close-up photographs of Mars. The alert mid-nineteenth-century reader would recognize Aylmer's anticipation of Daguerre's co-invention of the diorama in 1822 and daguerreotype in 1835 and Sir Charles Wheatstone's invention of the stereoscope in 1832; he presumably would see evidence of two things: Aylmer's marvelous inventiveness and the ephemeral achievement of that inventiveness. We, even more than the mid-nineteenth-century reader, are in a good position to see that one age's wonders are commonplaces for the next and relics for the following. And thus we are ready to apprehend fully the final sentence of "The Birthmark," which describes in a pun based on verb tenses the myopia of Aylmer and the science he represents:

> The momentary circumstance was too strong for him; he failed to look beyond the shadowy scope of time, and, living once for all in eternity, to find the perfect future in the present.

To find the perfect future in the present is both a central function of science fiction and one of its principal dangers. "The Birthmark" may show us some traps—dramatic, psychological, and moral—in the airplane, submarine, and moon-flight fiction of the day before yesterday, the spaceship and atomic-bomb fiction of yesterday, and perhaps even the matter-displacement fiction of today. Science fiction may show us the perfect future—that is, the epilogue of the present—but it should not mislead us into confusing realities.

"'Well, that does beat all nature!'": "The Artist of the Beautiful"

One of the peculiarities of science fiction is the extraordinary attention it pays to the natural physical world and man's relations to that world. In a way this would seem to be paradoxical, for science fiction focuses on a physical object or phenomenon which does not now seem to have existence. Yet it is this very focus which brings into view so much of the physical world. By denying a part of present existence or substituting something new, science fiction calls attention to the physical status quo. By extrapolating from known natural laws or scientific theory, it makes the worlds of nature and science an essential part of its subject. Just as a violation of civil law throws a citizen into the legal world and intimately involves him in that world's concerns, a violation of accepted natural law throws a fiction into the scientific world and intimately involves it in that world's concerns. Realistic fiction, with its commitment to imitating actualities, cannot deeply explore improbable cosmic possibilities; fantasy, with its conception in impossibilities, cannot explore scientific probabilities with precision. Science fiction by definition is a fiction radically intertwined with the physical world, and in practice is generally a fiction which grants to the physical world an extraordinary prominence in the human condition. To ask "What if physical event A should happen?" is to suggest that physical event A is of great importance.

But Hawthorne was prepared to answer his speculative questions in ways which in turn questioned the questions. Most science fiction writers tend to believe that material things are of great concern; Hawthorne tended to suggest that material things were of value only insofar as they symbolized the immaterial. His science fiction thus tends to become a kind of anti-science fiction, only exalting the scientist insofar as he transcends both his science and the matter with which it deals.

In "The Artist of the Beautiful" the relations among man, the physical cosmos in which he exists, and the ideal world which defines his identity become manifest in a mechanical butterfly. The appropriately named creator of this enormously symbolic toy, Owen Warland, is so great a technician and technologist as to be at once both Artist and Scientist. Which, in Hawthorne's terms, is to say that he must aspire to transcend all of space and all of time. Or, as a less sympathetic observer puts it, " 'He would turn the sun out of its orbit and derange the whole course of time, if . . . his ingenuity could grasp anything bigger than a child's toy!' "

As would-be original creator, Warland is in conflict with both the physical and social worlds, can form no earthly attachments, and remains locked, "full of little petulances," within the circle of his aspirations. Like Aylmer, Warland could if he would produce enormous practical benefits for mankind. When for a brief period he steps aside from his appointed cosmic task, he sets the pace for all the life of his small world; commerce, medicine, love, and even eating run on his time:

> In consequence of the good report thus acquired, Owen Warland was invited by the proper authorities to regulate the clock in the church steeple. He succeeded so admirably in this matter of public interest that the merchants gruffly acknowledged his merits on 'Change; the nurse whispered his praises as she gave the potion in the sick chamber; the lover blessed him at the hour of appointed interview; and the town in general thanked Owen for the punctuality of dinner time.

But Warland gives up time and the world for one ambition: "to spiritualize machinery" by creating in the form of a mechanism "Nature's ideal butterfly." Warland surrenders all to the classic symbol of the soul, Psyche's form.

When Warland succeeds, Hawthorne is able to build into that butterfly a tremendous variety of paradoxes, ironies, and glories; for in that mechanism man, matter, and the Ideal ineluctably meet. The blacksmith who has married Warland's beloved asserts, " 'There is more real use in one downright blow of my sledge hammer than in the whole five years' labor that our friend Owen has wasted on this butterfly,' " but he can make this assertion only after "bestowing the heartiest praise that he could find expression for": " 'Well, that does beat all nature!' "

In the "perfect beauty" of the butterfly, "the consideration of size was entirely lost"; "Had its wings overreached the firmament, the mind could not have been more filled or satisfied." But when Warland himself asks, " 'Wherefore ask who created it, so it be beautiful?' " he gives voice to a fatal question. For it is only the unnatural that can beat all Nature.

And it is the natural which ultimately beats, at least physically, anything which momentarily triumphs over it. While Warland has been conceiving, creating, and delivering the offspring of his spirit, organic nature has passed him by. His beloved Annie Hovenden and her earth-and-fire blacksmith husband have been fashioning a child of nature. What his father calls "the little monkey" is the alternative to the butterfly. He is alive, whereas the butterfly only, as Warland puts it, " 'may well be said to possess life, for it has absorbed my own being into itself.' " The child is greater in space, and is therefore able to destroy the butterfly physically. He is greater in time, carrying on the physical being of his earthy father and the moral being of his worldly grandfather while snuffing out in the material butterfly whatever spiritual being Warland had placed in it. When Annie is "admiring her own infant . . . far more than the artistic butterfly," it is "with good reason." It is good reason in this story of paternity and creation, but when the natural child destroys the artificial butterfly Warland can look "placidly at what seemed the ruin of his life's labor" because it "was yet no ruin":

> He had caught a far other butterfly than this. When the artist rose high enough to achieve the beautiful, the symbol by which he made it perceptible to mortal senses became of little value in his eyes while his spirit possessed itself in the enjoyment of the reality.

Nature does indeed surpass the Ideal in being, in space, and in time—but not in reality.

So here we have a fiction obsessively concerned with a unique, small, useless, ephemeral, physical object simultaneously asserting the object's transcendence of Nature and the insignificance of the object. This is science fiction with a vengeance, for it makes all of science an inferior kind of fiction. But, we may ask, if objects are merely symbols, then why turn to the objective world for meaningful, that is, symbolic, relationships? "The

Artist of the Beautiful" poses, but does not answer, this question—unless the only answer consists of dramatizing tensions among natural creation, artistic creation, and purely symbolic creation.

"Too real an existence" or "'Surely it is a dream'": "Rappaccini's Daughter"

An obvious alternative to pure creation is useful creation, and one form of useful creation quite obvious to us is dangerous creation. The scientist in "The Birthmark" makes an "unwilling recognition of the truth" that Nature "permits us, indeed, to mar, but seldom to mend, and like a jealous patentee, on no account to make"; then, in trying merely to mend, he fatally mars. The scientist in "The Artist of the Beautiful" rejects this "truth" and for the moment makes something that transcends moments; but what he makes is a physical trifle. In "Rappaccini's Daughter" there are two scientists; one creates a poisonous new Eden, and the other becomes the marplot of this brave new world.

Rather than drawing a line between Art and Science or Artist and Scientist, Hawthorne points to their ultimate identity. A primary distinction between Warland and Rappaccini is not that one is an artist and the other a scientist, but that one is an artist-scientist working on a "microscopic" scale while the other is an artist-scientist working on a microcosmic scale. When Rappaccini sees what seems to be his perfect creation, his science appears the triumph of art: "the pale man of science seemed to gaze with a triumphant expression at the beautiful youth and maiden, as might an artist who should spend his life in achieving a picture or a group of statuary and finally be satisfied with his success."

Both scientists create artistic alternatives to nature. But Warland's scientific art is merely unworldly and subversive by indirection; Rappaccini's artistic science is actively anti-worldly and revolutionary in intent. Warland wishes his creation to be an ideal improvement on nature; Rappaccini wishes his creation to be an impervious affront to nature.

The basic allegory in "Rappaccini's Daughter" is clear. Rappaccini, creator of the poisonous apparent "Eden of the present world," in trying to be God exposes his created daughter Beatrice, the Adam of this inverted Eden, to the destructive machinations of a modern snake in the grass, Baglioni, who persuades the Eve-like Giovanni, created in part out of Beatrice, to introduce the fatal food into the learned fool's paradise. Rappaccini has made Beatrice, whose soul is perfection, into a creature of physical poisons; Baglioni makes Giovanni, in whose soul "the lurid intermixture" of emotions "produces the illuminating blaze of the infernal regions," into a creature of jealous revenge. Hawthorne moves this set of basic symbols through an increasingly complex pattern, vastly extending the referential range of the story. The theological and moral allegory forms a framework which upholds, incorporates, and becomes part of fertility myth (Vertumnus and Pomona); other versions of creation and perversion (*The Tempest* and *Othello*); and the elementary but ever-recurring problems of epistemology. Suffice it to say here that while every biblical, mythical, and literary reference in the story meaningfully juxtaposes the context in which it appears and the context to which it refers, the narrative itself is an arrangement of magic mirrors directly calculated to deceive—egregiously deceive—the superficial skimmer of pages. Unless the reader is extremely careful, he is likely to find himself drunkenly staring at a grotesque image of himself. At the center of this wicked display is Giovanni's view of Beatrice.

Hawthorne's primary trick on the reader is leading him to think that the principal issue of the story, like that of the narrative itself, revolves around the problems of perception. The question which moves the narrative is: Is Giovanni's vision of Beatrice accurate, that is, is she really poisonous? The reader is strenuously encouraged to pose this question in Giovanni's terms.

Baglioni gives Giovanni wine "which caused his brain to swim with strange fantasies in reference to Dr. Rappaccini and the beautiful Beatrice." Then follow the ambiguous visions of the garden:

> But now, *unless Giovanni's draughts of wine had bewildered his senses,* a singular incident occurred. A small orange-colored reptile, of the lizard or chameleon species, chanced to be creeping along the path, just at the feet of Beatrice. It appeared to Giovanni,—*but, at the distance from which he gazed, he could scarcely have seen anything so minute,—it appeared to him,* however, that a drop or two of moisture from the broken stem of the flower descended upon the lizard's head. For an instant the reptile contorted itself violently, and then lay motionless in the sunshine.
>
> Now, here *it could not be but that Giovanni Guasconti's eyes deceived him.* Be that as it might, he *fancied* that, while Beatrice was gazing at the insect with childish delight, it grew faint and fell at her feet; its bright wings shivered; it was dead—from no cause that he could discern, unless it were the atmosphere of her breath.
>
> . . . few as the moments were, it seemed to Giovanni, when she was on the point of vanishing beneath the sculptured portal, that his beautiful bouquet was already beginning to wither in her grasp. *It was an idle thought; there could be no possibility of distinguishing a faded flower from a fresh one at so great a distance.* [All italics mine, H.B.F.]

At this point Giovanni's responses to this show seem perfectly appropriate: " 'Am I awake? Have I my senses?' said he to himself. 'What is this being? Beautiful shall I call her, or inexpressibly terrible?' " But these are dangerously misleading questions, and gradually the perceptive reader, unlike Giovanni, comes to the awareness that the eyes may deceive by seeing rather than fancying.

Is Giovanni's vision of Beatrice accurate? Of course, but it is entirely inadequate. Is she really poisonous? In fact she is, but not in reality. What is real in the world of "Rappaccini's Daughter" is not what Rappaccini, Baglioni, and Giovanni think and act upon, for they mistake the actual for the real. Despite the emanations from Beatrice which have "too real an existence to be at once shaken off," Giovanni remains malevolently fixed in his "earthly illusion." Beatrice's final words ring true: " 'Oh, was there not, from the first, more poison in thy nature than in mine?' "

But "nature" here is a complicated pun, for the motherless Beatrice is not entirely a natural creature. When she talks of the poisonous shrub, she hints at the unnaturalness of not only her nurture but even her genesis:

> "It has qualities that you little dream of. But I, dearest Giovanni,—I grew up and blossomed with the plant and was nourished with its breath. It was my sister, and I loved it with a human affection; for, alas!—hast thou not suspected it?—there was an awful doom."
>
> . . .
>
> "There was an awful doom," she continued, "the effect of my father's fatal love of science, which estranged me from all society of my kind."

And these words have qualities that Beatrice little dreams of, leading, by way of the word "dream," to the inmost realities of "Rappaccini's Daughter."

In a world in which objective reality may be merely delusive, dreams advance strong claims to being the truest expression of one of the truest realities—hidden psychological reality. Immediately after Giovanni's very first view of Beatrice, he "dreamed of a rich flower and beautiful girl"; "Flower and maiden were different, and yet the same, and fraught with some strange peril in either shape." This dream, arising within Giovanni's mind from the conjunction of that mind with Beatrice's external reality, determines the reality of that mind and fashions Beatrice's physical fate. This is the poison which makes Beatrice's "earthly part," so "radically" fashioned by Rappaccini, perish "at the feet of her father and Giovanni." Earth returns to earth, and the last word of the story, in the unfeeling mouth of the significantly named *Pietro* Baglioni, is "experiment."

Baglioni had previously evoked the central dramatic irony from the mouth of Giovanni. " 'Rappaccini, with what he calls the interest of science before his eyes,' " asserts Baglioni, " 'will hesitate at nothing.' " Giovanni's response tells us much more than it tells him: " 'It is a dream,' muttered Giovanni to himself; 'surely it is a dream.' " Giovanni's ambiguous words apply equally to the world in which he finds himself and the world of Rappaccini's science.

But this leaves us in a curious position, for what are we to make of the conjunction of an objective world of mere dreams, such as Giovanni's psychological horrors, and a world that merely dreams about objects, such as Rappaccini's pure science? Perhaps the answer to this question is precisely what Hawthorne's science fiction seeks. By making a fiction in which science is itself a kind of fiction about a delusory world, Hawthorne suggests that what is real is that which is only possible.

NATHANIEL HAWTHORNE
The Birthmark *

In the latter part of the last century there lived a man of science, an eminent proficient in every branch of natural philosophy, who not long before our story opens had made experience of a spiritual affinity more attractive than any chemical one. He had left his laboratory to the care of an assistant, cleared his fine countenance from the furnace smoke, washed the stain of acids from his fingers, and persuaded a beautiful woman to become his wife. In those days, when the comparatively recent discovery of electricity and other kindred mysteries of Nature seemed to open paths into the region of miracle, it was not unusual for the love of science to rival the love of woman in its depth and absorbing energy. The higher intellect, the imagination, the spirit, and even the heart might all find their congenial aliment in pursuits which, as some of their ardent votaries believed, would ascend from one step of powerful intelligence to another, until the philosopher should lay his hand on the secret of creative force and perhaps make new worlds for himself. We know not whether Aylmer possessed this degree of faith in man's ultimate control over Nature. He had devoted himself, however, too unreservedly to scientific studies ever to be weaned from them by any second passion. His love for his young wife might prove the stronger of the two; but it could only be by intertwining itself with his love of science and uniting the strength of the latter to his own.

Such a union accordingly took place, and was attended with

* *The Pioneer*, March 1843.

truly remarkable consequences and a deeply impressive moral. One day, very soon after their marriage, Aylmer sat gazing at his wife with a trouble in his countenance that grew stronger until he spoke.

"Georgiana," said he, "has it never occurred to you that the mark upon your cheek might be removed?"

"No, indeed," said she, smiling; but, perceiving the seriousness of his manner, she blushed deeply. "To tell you the truth, it has been so often called a charm that I was simple enough to imagine it might be so."

"Ah, upon another face perhaps it might," replied her husband; "but never on yours. No, dearest Georgiana, you came so nearly perfect from the hand of Nature that this slightest possible defect, which we hesitate whether to term a defect or a beauty, shocks me, as being the visible mark of earthly imperfection."

"Shocks you, my husband!" cried Georgiana, deeply hurt; at first reddening with momentary anger, but then bursting into tears. "Then why did you take me from my mother's side? You cannot love what shocks you!"

To explain this conversation, it must be mentioned that in the centre of Georgiana's left cheek there was a singular mark, deeply interwoven, as it were, with the texture and substance of her face. In the usual state of her complexion—a healthy though delicate bloom—the mark wore a tint of deeper crimson, which imperfectly defined its shape amid the surrounding rosiness. When she blushed it gradually became more indistinct, and finally vanished amid the triumphant rush of blood that bathed the whole cheek with its brilliant glow. But if any shifting motion caused her to turn pale there was the mark again, a crimson stain upon the snow, in what Aylmer sometimes deemed an almost fearful distinctness. Its shape bore not a little similarity to the human hand, though of the smallest pygmy size. Georgiana's lovers were wont to say that some fairy at her birth hour had laid her tiny hand upon the infant's cheek, and left this impress there in token of the magic endowments that were to give her such sway over all hearts. Many a desperate swain would have risked life for the privilege of pressing his lips to the mysterious hand. It must not be concealed, however, that the impression wrought by this fairy sign manual varied exceedingly according to the difference of temperament in the beholders. Some fastidious persons—but they were exclusively of her own sex—affirmed that the bloody hand, as they chose to call it, quite destroyed the effect of Georgiana's beauty and rendered her countenance even hideous. But it would be as reasonable to say that one of those small blue stains which sometimes occur in the purest statuary marble would convert the Eve of Powers to a monster. Masculine observers, if the birthmark did not heighten their admiration, contented themselves with wishing it away, that the world might possess one living specimen of ideal loveliness without the semblance of a flaw. After his marriage,—for he thought little or nothing of the matter before,—Aylmer discovered that this was the case with himself.

Had she been less beautiful,—if Envy's self could have found aught else to sneer at,—he might have felt his affection heightened by the prettiness of this mimic hand, now vaguely portrayed, now lost, now stealing forth again and glimmering to and fro with every pulse of emotion that throbbed within her heart; but, seeing her otherwise so perfect, he found this one defect grow more and more intolerable with every moment of their united lives. It was the fatal flaw of humanity which Nature, in one shape or another, stamps ineffaceably on all her productions, either to imply that they are temporary and finite, or that their perfection must be wrought by toil and pain. The crimson hand expressed the ineludible gripe in which mortality clutches the highest and purest of earthly mould, degrading them into kindred with the lowest, and even with the very brutes, like whom their visible frames return to dust. In this manner, selecting it as the symbol of his wife's liability to sin, sorrow, decay, and death, Aylmer's sombre imagination was not long in rendering the birthmark a frightful object, causing him more trouble and horror than ever Georgiana's beauty, whether of soul or sense, had given him delight.

At all the seasons which should have been their happiest he invariably, and without intending it, nay, in spite of a purpose to the contrary, reverted to this one disastrous topic. Trifling as it at first appeared, it so connected itself with innumerable trains of thought and modes of feeling that it became the central point of all. With the morning twilight Aylmer opened his eyes upon his wife's face and recognized the symbol of imperfection;

and when they sat together at the evening hearth his eyes wandered stealthily to her cheek, and beheld, flickering with the blaze of the wood fire, the spectral hand that wrote mortality where he would fain have worshipped. Georgiana soon learned to shudder at his gaze. It needed but a glance with the peculiar expression that his face often wore to change the roses of her cheek into a deathlike paleness, amid which the crimson hand was brought strongly out, like a bass relief of ruby on the whitest marble.

Late one night, when the lights were growing dim so as hardly to betray the stain on the poor wife's cheek, she herself, for the first time, voluntarily took up the subject.

"Do you remember, my dear Aylmer," said she, with a feeble attempt at a smile, "have you any recollection, of a dream last night about this odious hand?"

"None! none whatever!" replied Aylmer, starting; but then he added, in a dry, cold tone, affected for the sake of concealing the real depth of his emotion, "I might well dream of it; for, before I fell asleep, it had taken a pretty firm hold of my fancy."

"And you did dream of it?" continued Georgiana, hastily; for she dreaded lest a gush of tears should interrupt what she had to say. "A terrible dream! I wonder that you can forget it. Is it possible to forget this one expression?—'It is in her heart now; we must have it out!' Reflect, my husband; for by all means I would have you recall that dream."

The mind is in a sad state when Sleep, the all-involving, cannot confine her spectres within the dim region of her sway, but suffers them to break forth, affrighting this actual life with secrets that perchance belong to a deeper one. Aylmer now remembered his dream. He had fancied himself with his servant Aminadab, attempting an operation for the removal of the birthmark; but the deeper went the knife, the deeper sank the hand, until at length its tiny grasp appeared to have caught hold of Georgiana's heart; whence, however, her husband was inexorably resolved to cut or wrench it away.

When the dream had shaped itself perfectly in his memory Aylmer sat in his wife's presence with a guilty feeling. Truth often finds its way to the mind close muffled in robes of sleep, and then speaks with uncompromising directness of matters in regard to which we practise an unconscious self-deception during our waking moments. Until now he had not been aware of the tyrannizing influence acquired by one idea over his mind, and of the lengths which he might find in his heart to go for the sake of giving himself peace.

"Aylmer," resumed Georgiana, solemnly, "I know not what may be the cost to both of us to rid me of this fatal birthmark. Perhaps its removal may cause cureless deformity; or it may be the stain goes as deep as life itself. Again: do we know that there is a possibility, on any terms, of unclasping the firm gripe of this little hand which was laid upon me before I came into the world?"

"Dearest Georgiana, I have spent much thought upon the subject," hastily interrupted Aylmer. "I am convinced of the perfect practicability of its removal."

"If there be the remotest possibility of it," continued Georgiana, "let the attempt be made, at whatever risk. Danger is nothing to me; for life, while this hateful mark makes me the object of your horror and disgust,—life is a burden which I would fling down with joy. Either remove this dreadful hand, or take my wretched life! You have deep science. All the world bears witness of it. You have achieved great wonders. Cannot you remove this little, little mark, which I cover with the tips of two small fingers? Is this beyond your power, for the sake of your own peace, and to save your poor wife from madness?"

"Noblest, dearest, tenderest wife," cried Aylmer, rapturously, "doubt not my power. I have already given this matter the deepest thought—thought which might almost have enlightened me to create a being less perfect than yourself. Georgiana, you have led me deeper than ever into the heart of science. I feel myself fully competent to render this dear cheek as faultless as its fellow; and then, most beloved, what will be my triumph when I shall have corrected what Nature left imperfect in her fairest work! Even Pygmalion, when his sculptured woman assumed life, felt not greater ecstasy than mine will be."

"It is resolved, then," said Georgiana, faintly smiling. "And, Aylmer, spare me not, though you should find the birthmark take refuge in my heart at last."

Her husband tenderly kissed her cheek—her right cheek—not that which bore the impress of the crimson hand.

The next day Aylmer apprised his wife of a plan that he had

formed whereby he might have opportunity for the intense thought and constant watchfulness which the proposed operation would require; while Georgiana, likewise, would enjoy the perfect repose essential to its success. They were to seclude themselves in the extensive apartments occupied by Aylmer as a laboratory, and where, during his toilsome youth, he had made discoveries in the elemental powers of Nature that had roused the admiration of all the learned societies in Europe. Seated calmly in this laboratory, the pale philosopher had investigated the secrets of the highest cloud region and of the profoundest mines; he had satisfied himself of the causes that kindled and kept alive the fires of the volcano; and had explained the mystery of fountains, and how it is that they gush forth, some so bright and pure, and others with such rich medicinal virtues, from the dark bosom of the earth. Here, too, at an earlier period, he had studied the wonders of the human frame, and attempted to fathom the very process by which Nature assimilates all her precious influences from earth and air, and from the spiritual world, to create and foster man, her masterpiece. The latter pursuit, however, Aylmer had long laid aside in unwilling recognition of the truth—against which all seekers sooner or later stumble—that our great creative Mother, while she amuses us with apparently working in the broadest sunshine, is yet severely careful to keep her own secrets, and, in spite of her pretended openness, shows us nothing but results. She permits us, indeed, to mar, but seldom to mend, and, like a jealous patentee, on no account to make. Now, however, Aylmer resumed these half-forgotten investigations; not, of course, with such hopes or wishes as first suggested them; but because they involved much physiological truth and lay in the path of his proposed scheme for the treatment of Georgiana.

As he led her over the threshold of the laboratory, Georgiana was cold and tremulous. Aylmer looked cheerfully into her face, with intent to reassure her, but was so startled with the intense glow of the birthmark upon the whiteness of her cheek that he could not restrain a strong convulsive shudder. His wife fainted.

"Aminadab! Aminadab!" shouted Aylmer, stamping violently on the floor.

Forthwith there issued from an inner apartment a man of low stature, but bulky frame, with shaggy hair hanging about his visage, which was grimed with the vapors of the furnace. This personage had been Aylmer's underworker during his whole scientific career, and was admirably fitted for that office by his great mechanical readiness, and the skill with which, while incapable of comprehending a single principle, he executed all the details of his master's experiments. With his vast strength, his shaggy hair, his smoky aspect, and the indescribable earthiness that incrusted him, he seemed to represent man's physical nature; while Aylmer's slender figure, and pale, intellectual face, were no less apt a type of the spiritual element.

"Throw open the door of the boudoir, Aminadab," said Aylmer, "and burn a pastil."

"Yes, master," answered Aminadab, looking intently at the lifeless form of Georgiana; and then he muttered to himself, "If she were my wife, I'd never part with that birthmark."

When Georgiana recovered consciousness she found herself breathing an atmosphere of penetrating fragrance, the gentle potency of which had recalled her from her deathlike faintness. The scene around her looked like enchantment. Aylmer had converted those smoky, dingy, sombre rooms, where he had spent his brightest years in recondite pursuits, into a series of beautiful apartments not unfit to be the secluded abode of a lovely woman. The walls were hung with gorgeous curtains, which imparted the combination of grandeur and grace that no other species of adornment can achieve; and, as they fell from the ceiling to the floor, their rich and ponderous folds, concealing all angles and straight lines, appeared to shut in the scene from infinite space. For aught Georgiana knew, it might be a pavilion among the clouds. And Aylmer, excluding the sunshine, which would have interfered with his chemical processes, had supplied its place with perfumed lamps, emitting flames of various hue, but all uniting in a soft, impurpled radiance. He now knelt by his wife's side, watching her earnestly, but without alarm; for he was confident in his science, and felt that he could draw a magic circle round her within which no evil might intrude.

"Where am I? Ah, I remember," said Georgiana, faintly; and she placed her hand over her cheek to hide the terrible mark from her husband's eyes.

"Fear not, dearest!" exclaimed he. "Do not shrink from me!

Believe me, Georgiana, I even rejoice in this single imperfection, since it will be such a rapture to remove it."

"O, spare me!" sadly replied his wife. "Pray do not look at it again. I never can forget that convulsive shudder."

In order to soothe Georgiana, and, as it were, to release her mind from the burden of actual things, Aylmer now put in practice some of the light and playful secrets which science had taught him among its profounder lore. Airy figures, absolutely bodiless ideas, and forms of unsubstantial beauty came and danced before her, imprinting their momentary footsteps on beams of light. Though she had some indistinct idea of the method of these optical phenomena, still the illusion was almost perfect enough to warrant the belief that her husband possessed sway over the spiritual world. Then again, when she felt a wish to look forth from her seclusion, immediately, as if her thoughts were answered, the procession of external existence flitted across a screen. The scenery and the figures of actual life were perfectly represented, but with that bewitching yet indescribable difference which always makes a picture, an image, or a shadow so much more attractive than the original. When wearied of this, Aylmer bade her cast her eyes upon a vessel containing a quantity of earth. She did so, with little interest at first; but was soon startled to perceive the germ of a plant shooting upward from the soil. Then came the slender stalk; the leaves gradually unfolded themselves; and amid them was a perfect and lovely flower.

"It is magical!" cried Georgiana. "I dare not touch it."

"Nay, pluck it," answered Aylmer,—"pluck it, and inhale its brief perfume while you may. The flower will wither in a few moments and leave nothing save its brown seed vessels; but thence may be perpetuated a race as ephemeral as itself."

But Georgiana had no sooner touched the flower than the whole plant suffered a blight, its leaves turning coal-black as if by the agency of fire.

"There was too powerful a stimulus," said Aylmer, thoughtfully.

To make up for this abortive experiment, he proposed to take her portrait by a scientific process of his own invention. It was to be effected by rays of light striking upon a polished plate of metal. Georgiana assented; but, on looking at the result, was affrighted to find the features of the portrait blurred and indefinable; while the minute figure of a hand appeared where the cheek should have been. Aylmer snatched the metallic plate and threw it into a jar of corrosive acid.

Soon, however, he forgot these mortifying failures. In the intervals of study and chemical experiment he came to her flushed and exhausted, but seemed invigorated by her presence, and spoke in glowing language of the resources of his art. He gave a history of the long dynasty of the alchemists, who spent so many ages in quest of the universal solvent by which the golden principle might be elicited from all things vile and base. Aylmer appeared to believe that, by the plainest scientific logic, it was altogether within the limits of possibility to discover this long-sought medium; "but," he added, "a philosopher who should go deep enough to acquire the power would attain too lofty a wisdom to stoop to the exercise of it." Not less singular were his opinions in regard to the elixir vitae. He more than intimated that it was at his option to concoct a liquid that should prolong life for years, perhaps interminably; but that it would produce a discord in Nature which all the world, and chiefly the quaffer of the immortal nostrum, would find cause to curse.

"Aylmer, are you in earnest?" asked Georgiana, looking at him with amazement and fear. "It is terrible to possess such power, or even to dream of possessing it."

"O, do not tremble, my love," said her husband. "I would not wrong either you or myself by working such inharmonious effects upon our lives; but I would have you consider how trifling, in comparison, is the skill requisite to remove this little hand."

At the mention of the birthmark, Georgiana, as usual, shrank as if a redhot iron had touched her cheek.

Again Aylmer applied himself to his labors. She could hear his voice in the distant furnace room giving directions to Aminadab, whose harsh, uncouth, misshapen tones were audible in response, more like the grunt or growl of a brute than human speech. After hours of absence, Aylmer reappeared and proposed that she should now examine his cabinet of chemical products and natural treasures of the earth. Among the former he showed her a small vial, in which, he remarked, was contained a gentle yet most powerful fragrance, capable of impregnating all the breezes that blow across a kingdom. They were of inestimable value, the contents of that little vial; and, as he said so, he threw some of the perfume into the air and filled the room with piercing and invigorating delight.

"And what is this?" asked Georgiana, pointing to a small crystal globe containing a gold-colored liquid. "It is so beautiful to the eye that I could imagine it the elixir of life."

"In one sense it is," replied Aylmer; "or rather, the elixir of immortality. It is the most precious poison that ever was concocted in this world. By its aid I could apportion the lifetime of any mortal at whom you might point your finger. The strength of the dose would determine whether he were to linger out years, or drop dead in the midst of a breath. No king on his guarded throne could keep his life if I, in my private station, should deem that the welfare of millions justified me in depriving him of it."

"Why do you keep such a terrific drug?" inquired Georgiana in horror.

"Do not mistrust me, dearest," said her husband, smiling; "its virtuous potency is yet greater than its harmful one. But see! here is a powerful cosmetic. With a few drops of this in a vase of water, freckles may be washed away as easily as the hands are cleansed. A stronger infusion would take the blood out of the cheek, and leave the rosiest beauty a pale ghost."

"Is it with this lotion that you intend to bathe my cheek?" asked Georgiana, anxiously.

"O, no," hastily replied her husband; "this is merely superficial. Your case demands a remedy that shall go deeper."

In his interviews with Georgiana, Aylmer generally made minute inquiries as to her sensations, and whether the confinement of the rooms and the temperature of the atmosphere agreed with her. These questions had such a particular drift that Georgiana began to conjecture that she was already subjected to certain physical influences, either breathed in with the fragrant air or taken with her food. She fancied likewise, but it might be altogether fancy, that there was a stirring up of her system—a strange, indefinite sensation creeping through her veins, and tingling, half painfully, half pleasurably, at her heart. Still, whenever she dared to look into the mirror, there she beheld herself pale as a white rose and with the crimson birthmark stamped upon her cheek. Not even Aylmer now hated it so much as she.

To dispel the tedium of the hours which her husband found it necessary to devote to the processes of combination and analysis, Georgiana turned over the volumes of his scientific library. In many dark old tomes she met with chapters full of romance and poetry. They were the works of the philosophers of the middle ages, such as Albertus Magnus, Cornelius Agrippa, Paracelsus, and the famous friar who created the prophetic Brazen Head. All these antique naturalists stood in advance of their centuries, yet were imbued with some of their credulity, and therefore were believed, and perhaps imagined themselves to have acquired from the investigation of Nature a power above Nature, and from physics a sway over the spiritual world. Hardly less curious and imaginative were the early volumes of the Transactions of the Royal Society, in which the members, knowing little of the limits of natural possibility, were continually recording wonders or proposing methods whereby wonders might be wrought.

But, to Georgiana, the most engrossing volume was a large folio from her husband's own hand, in which he had recorded every experiment of his scientific career, its original aim, the methods adopted for its development, and its final success or failure, with the circumstances to which either event was attributable. The book, in truth, was both the history and emblem of his ardent, ambitious, imaginative, yet practical and laborious life. He handled physical details as if there were nothing beyond them; yet spiritualized them all and redeemed himself from materialism by his strong and eager aspiration towards the infinite. In his grasp the veriest clod of earth assumed a soul. Georgiana, as she read, reverenced Aylmer and loved him more profoundly than ever, but with a less entire dependence on his judgment than heretofore. Much as he had accomplished, she could not but observe that his most splendid successes were almost invariably failures, if compared with the ideal at which he aimed. His brightest diamonds were the merest pebbles, and felt to be so by himself, in comparison with the inestimable gems which lay hidden beyond his reach. The volume, rich with achievements that had won renown for its author, was yet as melancholy a record as ever mortal hand had penned. It was the sad confession and continual exemplification of the shortcomings of the composite man, the spirit burdened with clay and working in matter, and of the despair that assails the higher nature at finding itself so miserably thwarted by the earthly part. Perhaps every man of genius, in whatever sphere, might recognize the image of his own experience in Aylmer's journal.

So deeply did these reflections affect Georgiana that she laid her face upon the open volume and burst into tears. In this situation she was found by her husband.

"It is dangerous to read in a sorcerer's books," said he with a smile, though his countenance was uneasy and displeased. "Georgiana, there are pages in that volume which I can scarcely glance over and keep my senses. Take heed lest it prove as detrimental to you."

"It has made me worship you more than ever," said she.

"Ah, wait for this one success," rejoined he, "then worship me if you will. I shall deem myself hardly unworthy of it. But come, I have sought you for the luxury of your voice. Sing to me, dearest."

So she poured out the liquid music of her voice to quench the thirst of his spirit. He then took his leave with a boyish exuberance of gayety, assuring her that her seclusion would endure but a little longer, and that the result was already certain. Scarcely had he departed when Georgiana felt irresistibly impelled to follow him. She had forgotten to inform Aylmer of a symptom which for two or three hours past had begun to excite her attention. It was a sensation in the fatal birthmark, not painful, but which induced a restlessness throughout her system. Hastening after her husband, she intruded for the first time into the laboratory.

The first thing that struck her eye was the furnace, that hot and feverish worker, with the intense glow of its fire, which by the quantities of soot clustered above it seemed to have been burning for ages. There was a distilling apparatus in full operation. Around the room were retorts, tubes, cylinders, crucibles, and other apparatus of chemical research. An electrical machine stood ready for immediate use. The atmosphere felt oppressively close, and was tainted with gaseous odors which had been tormented forth by the processes of science. The severe and homely simplicity of the apartment, with its naked walls and brick pavement, looked strange, accustomed as Georgiana had become to the fantastic elegance of her boudoir. But what chiefly, indeed almost solely, drew her attention, was the aspect of Aylmer himself.

He was pale as death, anxious and absorbed, and hung over the furnace as if it depended upon his utmost watchfulness whether the liquid which it was distilling should be the draught of immortal happiness or misery. How different from the sanguine and joyous mien that he had assumed for Georgiana's encouragement!

"Carefully now, Aminadab; carefully, thou human machine; carefully, thou man of clay," muttered Aylmer, more to himself than his assistant. "Now, if there be a thought too much or too little, it is all over."

"Ho! ho!" mumbled Aminadab. "Look, master! look!"

Aylmer raised his eyes hastily, and at first reddened, then grew paler than ever, on beholding Georgiana. He rushed towards her and seized her arm with a gripe that left the print of his fingers upon it.

"Why do you come hither? Have you no trust in your husband?" cried he, impetuously. "Would you throw the blight of that fatal birthmark over my labors? It is not well done. Go, prying woman! go!"

"Nay, Aylmer," said Georgiana with the firmness of which she possessed no stinted endowment, "it is not you that have a right to complain. You mistrust your wife; you have concealed the anxiety with which you watch the development of this experiment. Think not so unworthily of me, my husband. Tell me all the risk we run, and fear not that I shall shrink; for my share in it is far less than your own."

"No, no, Georgiana!" said Aylmer, impatiently; "it must not be."

"I submit," replied she, calmly. "And, Aylmer, I shall quaff whatever draught you bring me; but it will be on the same principle that would induce me to take a dose of poison if offered by your hand."

"My noble wife," said Aylmer, deeply moved, "I knew not the height and depth of your nature until now. Nothing shall be concealed. Know, then, that this crimson hand, superficial as it seems, has clutched its grasp into your being with a strength of which I had no previous conception. I have already administered agents powerful enough to do aught except to change your entire physical system. Only one thing remains to be tried. If that fail us we are ruined."

"Why did you hesitate to tell me this?" asked she.

"Because, Georgiana," said Aylmer, in a low voice, "there is danger."

"Danger? There is but one danger—that this horrible stigma shall be left upon my cheek!" cried Georgiana. "Remove it, remove it, whatever be the cost, or we shall both go mad!"

"Heaven knows your words are too true," said Aylmer, sadly. "And now, dearest, return to your boudoir. In a little while all will be tested."

He conducted her back and took leave of her with a solemn tenderness which spoke far more than his words how much was now at stake. After his departure Georgiana became rapt in musings. She considered the character of Aylmer and did it completer justice than at any previous moment. Her heart exulted, while it trembled, at his honorable love—so pure and lofty that it would accept nothing less than perfection nor miserably make itself contented with an earthlier nature than he had dreamed of. She felt how much more precious was such a sentiment than that meaner kind which would have borne with the imperfection for her sake, and have been guilty of treason to holy love by degrading its perfect idea to the level of the actual; and with her whole spirit she prayed that, for a single moment, she might satisfy his highest and deepest conception. Longer than one moment she well knew it could not be; for his spirit was ever on the march, ever ascending, and each instant required something that was beyond the scope of the instant before.

The sound of her husband's footsteps aroused her. He bore a crystal goblet containing a liquor colorless as water, but bright enough to be the draught of immortality. Aylmer was pale; but it seemed rather the consequence of a highly-wrought state of mind and tension of spirit than of fear or doubt.

"The concoction of the draught has been perfect," said he, in answer to Georgiana's look. "Unless all my science have deceived me, it cannot fail."

"Save on your account, my dearest Aylmer," observed his wife, "I might wish to put off this birthmark of mortality by relinquishing mortality itself in preference to any other mode. Life is but a sad possession to those who have attained precisely the degree of moral advancement at which I stand. Were I weaker and blinder, it might be happiness. Were I stronger, it might be endured hopefully. But, being what I find myself, methinks I am of all mortals the most fit to die."

"You are fit for heaven without tasting death!" replied her husband. "But why do we speak of dying? The draught cannot fail. Behold its effect upon this plant."

On the window seat there stood a geranium diseased with yellow blotches which had overspread all its leaves. Aylmer poured a small quantity of the liquid upon the soil in which it grew. In a little time, when the roots of the plant had taken up the moisture, the unsightly blotches began to be extinguished in a living verdure.

"There needed no proof," said Georgiana, quietly. "Give me the goblet. I joyfully stake all upon your word."

"Drink, then, thou lofty creature!" exclaimed Aylmer, with fervid admiration. "There is no taint of imperfection on thy spirit. Thy sensible frame, too, shall soon be all perfect."

She quaffed the liquid and returned the goblet to his hand.

"It is grateful," said she, with a placid smile. "Methinks it is like water from a heavenly fountain; for it contains I know not what of unobtrusive fragrance and deliciousness. It allays a feverish thirst that had parched me for many days. Now, dearest, let me sleep. My earthly senses are closing over my spirit like the leaves around the heart of a rose at sunset."

She spoke the last words with a gentle reluctance, as if it required almost more energy than she could command to pronounce the faint and lingering syllables. Scarcely had they loitered through her lips ere she was lost in slumber. Aylmer sat by her side, watching her aspect with the emotions proper to a man the whole value of whose existence was involved in the process now to be tested. Mingled with this mood, however, was the philosophic investigation characteristic of the man of science. Not the minutest symptom escaped him. A heightened flush of the cheek, a slight irregularity of breath, a quiver of the eyelid, a hardly perceptible tremor through the frame,—such were the details which, as the moments passed, he wrote down in his folio volume. Intense thought had set its stamp upon every previous page of that volume; but the thoughts of years were all concentrated upon the last.

While thus employed, he failed not to gaze often at the fatal hand, and not without a shudder. Yet once, by a strange and unaccountable impulse, he pressed it with his lips. His spirit recoiled, however, in the very act; and Georgiana, out of the midst of her deep sleep, moved uneasily and murmured as if in remonstrance. Again Aylmer resumed his watch. Nor was it without avail. The crimson hand, which at first had been strongly visible upon the marble paleness of Georgiana's cheek, now grew more faintly outlined. She remained not less pale than ever; but the birthmark, with every breath that came and went, lost somewhat of its former distinctness. Its presence had been awful; its departure was more awful still. Watch the stain of the rainbow fading out of the sky, and you will know how that mysterious symbol passed away.

"By Heaven! it is well nigh gone!" said Aylmer to himself, in almost irrepressible ecstasy. "I can scarcely trace it now. Success! success! And now it is like the faintest rose color. The lightest flush of blood across her cheek would overcome it. But she is so pale!"

He drew aside the window curtain and suffered the light of natural day to fall into the room and rest upon her cheek. At the same time he heard a gross, hoarse chuckle, which he had long known as his servant Aminadab's expression of delight.

"Ah, clod! ah, earthly mass!" cried Aylmer, laughing in a sort of frenzy, "you have served me well! Matter and spirit—earth and heaven—have both done their part in this! Laugh, thing of the senses! You have earned the right to laugh."

These exclamations broke Georgiana's sleep. She slowly unclosed her eyes and gazed into the mirror which her husband had arranged for that purpose. A faint smile flitted over her lips when she recognized how barely perceptible was now that crimson hand which had once blazed forth with such disastrous brilliancy as to scare away all their happiness. But then her eyes sought Aylmer's face with a trouble and anxiety that he could by no means account for.

"My poor Aylmer!" murmured she.

"Poor? Nay, richest, happiest, most favored!" exclaimed he. "My peerless bride, it is successful! You are perfect!"

"My poor Aylmer," she repeated, with a more than human tenderness, "you have aimed loftily; you have done nobly. Do not repent that, with so high and pure a feeling, you have rejected the best the earth could offer. Aylmer, dearest Aylmer, I am dying!"

Alas! it was too true! The fatal hand had grappled with the mystery of life, and was the bond by which an angelic spirit kept itself in union with a mortal frame. As the last crimson tint of the birth-mark—that sole token of human imperfection—faded from her cheek, the parting breath of the now perfect woman passed into the atmosphere, and her soul, lingering a moment near her husband, took its heavenward flight. Then a hoarse, chuckling laugh was heard again! Thus ever does the gross fatality of earth exult in its invariable triumph over the immortal essence which, in this dim sphere of half development, demands the completeness of a higher state. Yet, had Aylmer reached a profounder wisdom, he need not thus have flung away the happiness which would have woven his mortal life of the selfsame texture with the celestial. The momentary circumstance was too strong for him; he failed to look beyond the shadowy scope of time, and, living once for all in eternity, to find the perfect future in the present.

NATHANIEL HAWTHORNE

The Artist of the Beautiful *

An elderly man, with his pretty daughter on his arm, was passing along the street, and emerged from the gloom of the cloudy evening into the light that fell across the pavement from the window of a small shop. It was a projecting window; and on the inside were suspended a variety of watches, pinchbeck, silver, and one or two of gold, all with their faces turned from the street, as if churlishly disinclined to inform the wayfarers what o'clock it was. Seated within the shop, sidelong to the window, with his pale face bent earnestly over some delicate piece of mechanism on which was thrown the concentrated lustre of a shade lamp, appeared a young man.

"What can Owen Warland be about?" muttered old Peter Hovenden, himself a retired watchmaker and the former master of this same young man whose occupation he was now wondering at. "What can the fellow be about? These six months past I have never come by his shop without seeing him just as steadily at work as now. It would be a flight beyond his usual foolery to seek for the perpetual motion; and yet I know enough of my old business to be certain that what he is now so busy with is no part of the machinery of a watch."

"Perhaps, father," said Annie, without showing much interest in the question, "Owen is inventing a new kind of timekeeper. I am sure he has ingenuity enough."

"Poh, child! He has not the sort of ingenuity to invent any

* *Democratic Review,* June 1844.

thing better than a Dutch toy," answered her father, who had formerly been put to much vexation by Owen Warland's irregular genius. "A plague on such ingenuity! All the effect that ever I knew of it was, to spoil the accuracy of some of the best watches in my shop. He would turn the sun out of its orbit and derange the whole course of time, if, as I said before, his ingenuity could grasp any thing bigger than a child's toy!"

"Hush, father! He hears you!" whispered Annie, pressing the old man's arm. "His ears are as delicate as his feelings; and you know how easily disturbed they are. Do let us move on."

So Peter Hovenden and his daughter Annie plodded on without further conversation, until in a by-street of the town they found themselves passing the open door of a blacksmith's shop. Within was seen the forge, now blazing up and illuminating the high and dusky roof, and now confining its lustre to a narrow precinct of the coal-strewn floor, according as the breath of the bellows was puffed forth or again inhaled into its vast leathern lungs. In the intervals of brightness it was easy to distinguish objects in remote corners of the shop and the horseshoes that hung upon the wall; in the momentary gloom the fire seemed to be glimmering amidst the vagueness of unenclosed space. Moving about in this red glare and alternate dusk was the figure of the blacksmith, well worthy to be viewed in so picturesque an aspect of light and shade, where the bright blaze struggled with the black night, as if each would have snatched his comely strength from the other. Anon he drew a whitehot bar of iron from the coals, laid it on the anvil, uplifted his arm of might, and was soon enveloped in the myriads of sparks which the strokes of his hammer scattered into the surrounding gloom.

"Now, that is a pleasant sight," said the old watchmaker. "I know what it is to work in gold; but give me the worker in iron after all is said and done. He spends his labor upon a reality. What say you, daughter Annie?"

"Pray don't speak so loud, father," whispered Annie. "Robert Danforth will hear you."

"And what if he should hear me?" said Peter Hovenden. "I say again, it is a good and a wholesome thing to depend upon main strength and reality, and to earn one's bread with the bare and brawny arm of a blacksmith. A watchmaker gets his brain puzzled by his wheels within a wheel, or loses his health or the nicety of his eyesight, as was my case, and finds himself at middle age, or a little after, past labor at his own trade, and fit for nothing else, yet too poor to live at his ease. So I say once again, give me main strength for my money. And then, how it takes the nonsense out of a man! Did you ever hear of a blacksmith being such a fool as Owen Warland yonder?"

"Well said, uncle Hovenden!" shouted Robert Danforth from the forge, in a full, deep, merry voice, that made the roof reëcho. "And what says Miss Annie to that doctrine? She, I suppose, will think it a genteeler business to tinker up a lady's watch than to forge a horseshoe or make a gridiron."

Annie drew her father onward without giving him time for reply.

But we must return to Owen Warland's shop, and spend more meditation upon his history and character than either Peter Hovenden, or probably his daughter Annie, or Owen's old schoolfellow, Robert Danforth, would have thought due to so slight a subject. From the time that his little fingers could grasp a penknife, Owen had been remarkable for a delicate ingenuity, which sometimes produced pretty shapes in wood, principally figures of flowers and birds, and sometimes seemed to aim at the hidden mysteries of mechanism. But it was always for purposes of grace, and never with any mockery of the useful. He did not, like the crowd of schoolboy artisans, construct little windmills on the angle of a barn or watermills across the neighboring brook. Those who discovered such peculiarity in the boy as to think it worth their while to observe him closely, sometimes saw reason to suppose that he was attempting to imitate the beautiful movements of Nature as exemplified in the flight of birds or the activity of little animals. It seemed, in fact, a new development of the love of the beautiful, such as might have made him a poet, a painter, or a sculptor, and which was as completely refined from all utilitarian coarseness as it could have been in either of the fine arts. He looked with singular distaste at the stiff and regular processes of ordinary machinery. Being once carried to see a steam engine, in the expectation that his intuitive comprehension of mechanical principles would be gratified, he turned pale and grew sick, as if something monstrous and unnatural had been presented to him. This horror was partly owing to the size and terrible energy of the iron laborer; for the character of Owen's mind was microscopic, and tended naturally to the minute, in accordance with his diminutive frame and the marvellous smallness and delicate power of his fingers. Not that his sense of beauty was thereby diminished into a sense of prettiness. The beautiful idea has no relation to size, and may be as perfectly developed in a space too minute for any but microscopic investigation as within the ample verge that is measured by the arc of the rainbow. But, at all events, this characteristic minuteness in his objects and accomplishments made the world even more incapable than it might otherwise have been of appreciating Owen Warland's genius. The boy's relatives saw nothing better to be done—as perhaps there was not—than to bind him apprentice to a watchmaker, hoping that his strange ingenuity might thus be regulated and put to utilitarian purposes.

Peter Hovenden's opinion of his apprentice has already been expressed. He could make nothing of the lad. Owen's apprehension of the professional mysteries, it is true, was inconceivably quick; but he altogether forgot or despised the grand object of a watchmaker's business, and cared no more for the measurement of time than if it had been merged into eternity. So long, however, as he remained under his old master's care, Owen's lack of sturdiness made it possible, by strict injunctions and sharp oversight, to restrain his creative eccentricity within bounds; but when his apprenticeship was served out, and he had taken the little shop which Peter Hovenden's failing eyesight compelled him to relinquish, then did people recognize how unfit a person was Owen Warland to lead old blind Father Time along his daily course. One of his most rational projects was to connect a musical operation with the machinery of his watches, so that all the harsh dissonances of life might be rendered tuneful, and each flitting moment fall into the abyss of the past in golden drops of harmony. If a family clock was intrusted to him for repair,—one of those tall, ancient clocks that have grown nearly allied to human nature by measuring out the lifetime of many generations,—he would take upon himself to arrange a dance or funeral procession of figures across its venerable face, representing twelve mirthful or melancholy hours. Several freaks of this kind quite destroyed the young watchmaker's credit with that steady and matter-of-fact class of people who hold the opinion that time is not to be trifled with, whether considered as the medium of advancement and prosperity in this world or preparation for the next. His custom rapidly diminished—a misfortune, however, that was probably reckoned among his better accidents by Owen Warland, who was becoming more and more absorbed in a secret occupation which drew all his science and manual dexterity into itself, and likewise gave full employment to the characteristic tendencies of his genius. This pursuit had already consumed many months.

After the old watchmaker and his pretty daughter had gazed at him out of the obscurity of the street, Owen Warland was seized with a fluttering of the nerves, which made his hand tremble too violently to proceed with such delicate labor as he was now engaged upon.

"It was Annie herself!" murmured he. "I should have known it, by this throbbing of my heart, before I heard her father's voice. Ah, how it throbs! I shall scarcely be able to work again on this exquisite mechanism to-night. Annie! dearest Annie! thou shouldst give firmness to my heart and hand, and not shake them thus; for, if I strive to put the very spirit of beauty into form and give it motion, it is for thy sake alone. O throbbing heart, be quiet! If my labor be thus thwarted, there will come vague and unsatisfied dreams, which will leave me spiritless to-morrow."

As he was endeavoring to settle himself again to his task, the shop door opened and gave admittance to no other than the stalwart figure which Peter Hovenden had paused to admire, as seen amid the light and shadow of the blacksmith's shop. Robert Danforth had brought a little anvil of his own manufacture, and peculiarly constructed, which the young artist had recently bespoken. Owen examined the article, and pronounced it fashioned according to his wish.

"Why, yes," said Robert Danforth, his strong voice filling the shop as with the sound of a bass viol, "I consider myself equal to any thing in the way of my own trade; though I should have made but a poor figure at yours with such a fist as this," added he, laughing, as he laid his vast hand beside the delicate one of Owen. "But what then? I put more main strength into one blow of my sledge hammer than all that you have expended since you were a 'prentice. Is not that the truth?"

"Very probably," answered the low and slender voice of Owen.

"Strength is an earthly monster. I make no pretensions to it. My force, whatever there may be of it, is altogether spiritual."

"Well, but, Owen, what are you about?" asked his old school-fellow, still in such a hearty volume of tone that it made the artist shrink, especially as the question related to a subject so sacred as the absorbing dream of his imagination. "Folks do say that you are trying to discover the perpetual motion."

"The perpetual motion? Nonsense!" replied Owen Warland, with a movement of disgust; for he was full of little petulances. "It can never be discovered. It is a dream that may delude men whose brains are mystified with matter, but not me. Besides, if such a discovery were possible, it would not be worth my while to make it only to have the secret turned to such purposes as are now effected by steam and water power. I am not ambitious to be honored with the paternity of a new kind of cotton machine."

"That would be droll enough!" cried the blacksmith, breaking out into such an uproar of laughter that Owen himself and the bell glasses on his workboard quivered in unison. "No, no, Owen! No child of yours will have iron joints and sinews. Well, I won't hinder you any more. Good night, Owen, and success; and if you need any assistance, so far as a downright blow of hammer upon anvil will answer the purpose, I'm your man."

And with another laugh the man of main strength left the shop.

"How strange it is," whispered Owen Warland to himself, leaning his head upon his hand, "that all my musings, my purposes, my passion for the beautiful, my consciousness of power to create it—a finer, more ethereal power, of which this earthly giant can have no conception,—all, all, look so vain and idle whenever my path is crossed by Robert Danforth! He would drive me mad were I to meet him often. His hard, brute force darkens and confuses the spiritual element within me; but I, too, will be strong in my own way. I will not yield to him."

He took from beneath a glass a piece of minute machinery, which he set in the condensed light of his lamp, and, looking intently at it through a magnifying glass, proceeded to operate with a delicate instrument of steel. In an instant, however, he fell back in his chair and clasped his hands, with a look of horror on his face that made its small features as impressive as those of a giant would have been.

"Heaven! What have I done?" exclaimed he. "The vapor, the influence of that brute force,—it has bewildered me and obscured my perception. I have made the very stroke—the fatal stroke—that I have dreaded from the first. It is all over—the toil of months, the object of my life. I am ruined!"

And there he sat, in strange despair, until his lamp flickered in the socket and left the Artist of the Beautiful in darkness.

Thus it is that ideas, which grow up within the imagination and appear so lovely to it and of a value beyond whatever men call valuable, are exposed to be shattered and annihilated by contact with the practical. It is requisite for the ideal artist to possess a force of character that seems hardly compatible with its delicacy; he must keep his faith in himself while the incredulous world assails him with its utter disbelief; he must stand up against mankind and be his own sole disciple, both as respects his genius and the objects to which it is directed.

For a time Owen Warland succumbed to this severe but inevitable test. He spent a few sluggish weeks with his head so continually resting in his hands that the townspeople had scarcely an opportunity to see his countenance. When at last it was again uplifted to the light of day, a cold, dull, nameless change was perceptible upon it. In the opinion of Peter Hovenden, however, and that order of sagacious understandings who think that life should be regulated, like clockwork, with leaden weights, the alteration was entirely for the better. Owen now, indeed, applied himself to business with dogged industry. It was marvellous to witness the obtuse gravity with which he would inspect the wheels of a great, old silver watch; thereby delighting the owner, in whose fob it had been worn till he deemed it a portion of his own life, and was accordingly jealous of its treatment. In consequence of the good report thus acquired, Owen Warland was invited by the proper authorities to regulate the clock in the church steeple. He succeeded so admirably in this matter of public interest that the merchants gruffly acknowledged his merits on 'Change; the nurse whispered his praises as she gave the potion in the sick chamber; the lover blessed him at the hour of appointed interview; and the town in general thanked Owen for the punctuality of dinner time. In a word, the heavy weight upon his spirits kept every thing in order, not merely within his own system, but wheresoever the iron accents of the church clock were audible. It was a circumstance, though minute yet characteristic of his present state, that, when employed to engrave names or initials on silver spoons, he now wrote the requisite letters in the plainest possible style, omitting a variety of fanciful flourishes that had heretofore distinguished his work in this kind.

One day, during the era of this happy transformation, old Peter Hovenden came to visit his former apprentice.

"Well, Owen," said he, "I am glad to hear such good accounts of you from all quarters, and especially from the town clock yonder, which speaks in your commendation every hour of the twenty-four. Only get rid altogether of your nonsensical trash about the beautiful, which I nor nobody else, nor yourself to boot, could ever understand,—only free yourself of that, and your success in life is as sure as daylight. Why, if you go on in this way, I should even venture to let you doctor this precious old watch of mine; though, except my daughter Annie, I have nothing else so valuable in the world."

"I should hardly dare touch it, sir," replied Owen, in a depressed tone; for he was weighed down by his old master's presence.

"In time," said the latter,—"in time, you will be capable of it."

The old watchmaker, with the freedom naturally consequent on his former authority, went on inspecting the work which Owen had in hand at the moment, together with other matters that were in progress. The artist, meanwhile, could scarcely lift his head. There was nothing so antipodal to his nature as this man's cold, unimaginative sagacity, by contact with which every thing was converted into a dream except the densest matter of the physical world. Owen groaned in spirit and prayed fervently to be delivered from him.

"But what is this?" cried Peter Hovenden abruptly, taking up a dusty bell glass, beneath which appeared a mechanical something, as delicate and minute as the system of a butterfly's anatomy. "What have we here? Owen! Owen! there is witchcraft in these little chains, and wheels, and paddles. See! with one pinch of my finger and thumb I am going to deliver you from all future peril."

"For Heaven's sake," screamed Owen Warland, springing up with wonderful energy, "as you would not drive me mad, do not touch it! The slightest pressure of your finger would ruin me forever."

"Aha, young man! And is it so?" said the old watchmaker, looking at him with just enough of penetration to torture Owen's soul with the bitterness of worldly criticism. "Well, take your own course; but I warn you again that in this small piece of mechanism lives your evil spirit. Shall I exorcise him?"

"You are my evil spirit," answered Owen, much excited,—"you and the hard, coarse world! The leaden thoughts and the despondency that you fling upon me are my clogs, else I should long ago have achieved the task that I was created for."

Peter Hovenden shook his head, with the mixture of contempt and indignation which mankind, of whom he was partly a representative, deem themselves entitled to feel towards all simpletons who seek other prizes than the dusty one along the highway. He then took his leave, with an uplifted finger and a sneer upon his face that haunted the artist's dreams for many a night afterwards. At the time of his old master's visit, Owen was probably on the point of taking up the relinquished task; but, by this sinister event, he was thrown back into the state whence he had been slowly emerging.

But the innate tendency of his soul had only been accumulating fresh vigor during its apparent sluggishness. As the summer advanced he almost totally relinquished his business, and permitted Father Time, so far as the old gentleman was represented by the clocks and watches under his control, to stray at random through human life, making infinite confusion among the train of bewildered hours. He wasted the sunshine, as people said, in wandering through the woods and fields and along the banks of streams. There, like a child, he found amusement in chasing butterflies or watching the motions of water insects. There was something truly mysterious in the intentness with which he contemplated these living playthings as they sported on the breeze or examined the structure of an imperial insect whom he had imprisoned. The chase of butterflies was an apt emblem of the ideal pursuit in which he had spent so many golden hours; but would the beautiful idea ever be yielded to his hand like the butterfly that symbolized it? Sweet, doubtless, were these days, and congenial to the artist's soul. They were full of bright conceptions, which gleamed through his intellectual world as the butterflies gleamed through the outward atmosphere, and were real to him, for the instant, without the toil, and perplexity, and many disappointments of attempting to make them visible to the sensual eye. Alas that the artist, whether in poetry or whatever other material, may not content himself with the inward enjoyment of the beautiful, but must chase the flitting mystery beyond the verge of his ethereal domain, and crush its frail being in seizing it with a material grasp. Owen Warland felt the impulse to give external reality to his ideas as irresistibly as any of the poets or painters who have arrayed the world in a dimmer and fainter beauty, imperfectly copied from the richness of their visions.

The night was now his time for the slow progress of re-creating the one idea to which all his intellectual activity referred itself. Always at the approach of dusk he stole into the town, locked himself within his shop, and wrought with patient delicacy of touch for many hours. Sometimes he was startled by the rap of the watchman, who, when all the world should be asleep, had caught the gleam of lamplight through the crevices of Owen Warland's shutters. Daylight, to the morbid sensibility of his mind, seemed to have an intrusiveness that interfered with his pursuits. On cloudy and inclement days, therefore, he sat with his head upon his hands, muffling, as it were, his sensitive brain in a mist of indefinite musings; for it was a relief to escape from the sharp distinctness with which he was compelled to shape out his thoughts during his nightly toil.

From one of these fits of torpor he was aroused by the entrance of Annie Hovenden, who came into the shop with the freedom of a customer and also with something of the familiarity of a childish friend. She had worn a hole through her silver thimble, and wanted Owen to repair it.

"But I don't know whether you will condescend to such a task," said she, laughing, "now that you are so taken up with the notion of putting spirit into machinery."

"Where did you get that idea, Annie?" said Owen, starting in surprise.

"O, out of my own head," answered she, "and from something that I heard you say, long ago, when you were but a boy

and I a little child. But come; will you mend this poor thimble of mine?"

"Any thing for your sake, Annie," said Owen Warland,—"any thing, even were it to work at Robert Danforth's forge."

"And that would be a pretty sight!" retorted Annie, glancing with imperceptible slightness at the artist's small and slender frame. "Well; here is the thimble."

"But that is a strange idea of yours," said Owen, "about the spiritualization of matter."

And then the thought stole into his mind that this young girl possessed the gift to comprehend him better than all the world besides. And what a help and strength would it be to him in his lonely toil if he could gain the sympathy of the only being whom he loved! To persons whose pursuits are insulated from the common business of life—who are either in advance of mankind or apart from it—there often comes a sensation of moral cold that makes the spirit shiver as if it had reached the frozen solitudes around the pole. What the prophet, the poet, the reformer, the criminal, or any other man with human yearnings, but separated from the multitude by a peculiar lot, might feel, poor Owen Warland felt.

"Annie," cried he, growing pale as death at the thought, "how gladly would I tell you the secret of my pursuit! You, methinks, would estimate it rightly. You, I know, would hear it with a reverence that I must not expect from the harsh, material world."

"Would I not? to be sure I would!" replied Annie Hovenden, lightly laughing. "Come; explain to me quickly what is the meaning of this little whirligig, so delicately wrought that it might be a plaything for Queen Mab. See! I will put it in motion."

"Hold!" exclaimed Owen, "hold!"

Annie had but given the slightest possible touch, with the point of a needle, to the same minute portion of complicated machinery which has been more than once mentioned, when the artist seized her by the wrist with a force that made her scream aloud. She was affrighted at the convulsion of intense rage and anguish that writhed across his features. The next instant he let his head sink upon his hands.

"Go, Annie," murmured he; "I have deceived myself, and

must suffer for it. I yearned for sympathy, and thought, and fancied, and dreamed that you might give it me; but you lack the talisman, Annie, that should admit you into my secrets. That touch has undone the toil of months and the thought of a lifetime! It was not your fault, Annie; but you have ruined me!"

Poor Owen Warland! He had indeed erred, yet pardonably; for if any human spirit could have sufficiently reverenced the processes so sacred in his eyes, it must have been a woman's. Even Annie Hovenden, possibly, might not have disappointed him had she been enlightened by the deep intelligence of love.

The artist spent the ensuing winter in a way that satisfied any persons who had hitherto retained a hopeful opinion of him that he was, in truth, irrevocably doomed to inutility as regarded the world, and to an evil destiny on his own part. The decease of a relative had put him in possession of a small inheritance. Thus freed from the necessity of toil, and having lost the steadfast influence of a great purpose,—great, at least, to him,—he abandoned himself to habits from which it might have been supposed the mere delicacy of his organization would have availed to secure him. But, when the ethereal portion of a man of genius is obscured, the earthly part assumes an influence the more uncontrollable, because the character is now thrown off the balance to which Providence had so nicely adjusted it, and which, in coarser natures, is adjusted by some other method. Owen Warland made proof of whatever show of bliss may be found in riot. He looked at the world through the golden medium of wine, and contemplated the visions that bubble up so gayly around the brim of the glass, and that people the air with shapes of pleasant madness, which so soon grow ghostly and forlorn. Even when this dismal and inevitable change had taken place, the young man might still have continued to quaff the cup of enchantments, though its vapor did but shroud life in gloom and fill the gloom with spectres that mocked at him. There was a certain irksomeness of spirit, which, being real, and the deepest sensation of which the artist was now conscious, was more intolerable than any fantastic miseries and horrors that the abuse of wine could summon up. In the latter case he could remember, even out of the midst of his trouble, that all was but a delusion; in the former, the heavy anguish was his actual life.

From this perilous state he was redeemed by an incident which

more than one person witnessed, but of which the shrewdest could not explain or conjecture the operation on Owen Warland's mind. It was very simple. On a warm afternoon of spring, as the artist sat among his riotous companions with a glass of wine before him, a splendid butterfly flew in at the open window and fluttered about his head.

"Ah," exclaimed Owen, who had drank freely, "are you alive again, child of the sun and playmate of the summer breeze, after your dismal winter's nap? Then it is time for me to be at work!"

And, leaving his unemptied glass upon the table, he departed, and was never known to sip another drop of wine.

And now, again, he resumed his wanderings in the woods and fields. It might be fancied that the bright butterfly, which had come so spirit-like into the window as Owen sat with the rude revellers, was indeed a spirit commissioned to recall him to the pure, ideal life that had so etherealized him among men. It might be fancied that he went forth to seek this spirit in its sunny haunts; for still, as in the summer time gone by, he was seen to steal gently up wherever a butterfly had alighted, and lose himself in contemplation of it. When it took flight his eyes followed the winged vision, as if its airy track would show the path to heaven. But what could be the purpose of the unseasonable toil, which was again resumed, as the watchman knew by the lines of lamplight through the crevices of Owen Warland's shutters? The townspeople had one comprehensive explanation of all these singularities. Owen Warland had gone mad! How universally efficacious—how satisfactory, too, and soothing to the injured sensibility of narrowness and dulness—is this easy method of accounting for whatever lies beyond the world's most ordinary scope! From St. Paul's days down to our poor little Artist of the Beautiful, the same talisman had been applied to the elucidation of all mysteries in the words or deeds of men who spoke or acted too wisely or too well. In Owen Warland's case the judgment of his townspeople may have been correct. Perhaps he was mad. The lack of sympathy—that contrast between himself and his neighbors which took away the restraint of example—was enough to make him so. Or possibly he had caught just so much of ethereal radiance as served to bewilder him, in an earthly sense, by its intermixture with the common daylight.

One evening, when the artist had returned from a customary

ramble and had just thrown the lustre of his lamp on the delicate piece of work so often interrupted, but still taken up again, as if his fate were imbodied in its mechanism, he was surprised by the entrance of old Peter Hovenden. Owen never met this man without a shrinking of the heart. Of all the world he was most terrible, by reason of a keen understanding which saw so distinctly what it did see, and disbelieved so uncompromisingly in what it could not see. On this occasion the old watchmaker had merely a gracious word or two to say.

"Owen, my lad," said he, "we must see you at my house to-morrow night."

The artist began to mutter some excuse.

"O, but it must be so," quoth Peter Hovenden, "for the sake of the days when you were one of the household. What, my boy! don't you know that my daughter Annie is engaged to Robert Danforth? We are making an entertainment, in our humble way, to celebrate the event."

"Ah!" said Owen.

That little monosyllable was all he uttered; its tone seemed cold and unconcerned to an ear like Peter Hovenden's; and yet there was in it the stifled outcry of the poor artist's heart, which he compressed within him like a man holding down an evil spirit. One slight outbreak, however, imperceptible to the old watchmaker, he allowed himself. Raising the instrument with which he was about to begin his work, he let it fall upon the little system of machinery that had, anew, cost him months of thought and toil. It was shattered by the stroke!

Owen Warland's story would have been no tolerable representation of the troubled life of those who strive to create the beautiful, if, amid all other thwarting influences, love had not interposed to steal the cunning from his hand. Outwardly he had been no ardent or enterprising lover; the career of his passion had confined its tumults and vicissitudes so entirely within the artist's imagination that Annie herself had scarcely more than a woman's intuitive perception of it; but, in Owen's view, it covered the whole field of his life. Forgetful of the time when she had shown herself incapable of any deep response, he had persisted in connecting all his dreams of artistical success with Annie's image; she was the visible shape in which the spiritual power that he worshipped, and on whose altar he hoped to lay a not unworthy offering, was made manifest to him. Of course he had deceived himself; there were no such attributes in Annie Hovenden as his imagination had endowed her with. She, in the aspect which she wore to his inward vision, was as much a creature of his own as the mysterious piece of mechanism would be were it ever realized. Had he become convinced of his mistake through the medium of successful love,—had he won Annie to his bosom, and there beheld her fade from angel into ordinary woman,—the disappointment might have driven him back, with concentrated energy, upon his sole remaining object. On the other hand, had he found Annie what he fancied, his lot would have been so rich in beauty that out of its mere redundancy he might have wrought the beautiful into many a worthier type than he had toiled for; but the guise in which his sorrow came to him, the sense that the angel of his life had been snatched away and given to a rude man of earth and iron, who could neither need nor appreciate her ministrations,—this was the very perversity of fate that makes human existence appear too absurd and contradictory to be the scene of one other hope or one other fear. There was nothing left for Owen Warland but to sit down like a man that had been stunned.

He went through a fit of illness. After his recovery his small and slender frame assumed an obtuser garniture of flesh than it had ever before worn. His thin cheeks became round; his delicate little hand, so spiritually fashioned to achieve fairy taskwork, grew plumper than the hand of a thriving infant. His aspect had a childishness such as might have induced a stranger to pat him on the head—pausing, however, in the act, to wonder what manner of child was here. It was as if the spirit had gone out of him, leaving the body to flourish in a sort of vegetable existence. Not that Owen Warland was idiotic. He could talk, and not irrationally. Somewhat of a babbler, indeed, did people begin to think him; for he was apt to discourse at wearisome length of marvels of mechanism that he had read about in books, but which he had learned to consider as absolutely fabulous. Among them he enumerated the Man of Brass, constructed by Albertus Magnus, and the Brazen Head of Friar Bacon; and, coming down to later times, the automata of a little coach and horses, which it was pretended had been manufactured for the Dauphin of France; together with an insect that buzzed about the ear like a living fly, and yet was but a contrivance of minute steel springs. There was a story, too, of a duck that waddled, and quacked, and ate; though, had any honest citizen purchased it for dinner, he would have found himself cheated with the mere mechanical apparition of a duck.

"But all these accounts," said Owen Warland, "I am now satisfied are mere impositions."

Then, in a mysterious way, he would confess that he once thought differently. In his idle and dreamy days he had considered it possible, in a certain sense, to spiritualize machinery, and to combine with the new species of life and motion thus produced a beauty that should attain to the ideal which Nature has proposed to herself in all her creatures, but has never taken pains to realize. He seemed, however, to retain no very distinct perception either of the process of achieving this object or of the design itself.

"I have thrown it all aside now," he would say. "It was a dream such as young men are always mystifying themselves with. Now that I have acquired a little common sense, it makes me laugh to think of it."

Poor, poor and fallen Owen Warland! These were the symptoms that he had ceased to be an inhabitant of the better sphere that lies unseen around us. He had lost his faith in the invisible, and now prided himself, as such unfortunates invariably do, in the wisdom which rejected much that even his eye could see, and trusted confidently in nothing but what his hand could touch. This is the calamity of men whose spiritual part dies out of them and leaves the grosser understanding to assimilate them more and more to the things of which alone it can take cognizance; but in Owen Warland the spirit was not dead nor passed away; it only slept.

How it awoke again is not recorded. Perhaps the torpid slumber was broken by a convulsive pain. Perhaps, as in a former instance, the butterfly came and hovered about his head and reinspired him,—as indeed this creature of the sunshine had always a mysterious mission for the artist,—reinspired him with the former purpose of his life. Whether it were pain or happiness that thrilled through his veins, his first impulse was to thank Heaven for rendering him again the being of thought, imagination, and keenest sensibility that he had long ceased to be.

"Now for my task," said he. "Never did I feel such strength for it as now."

Yet, strong as he felt himself, he was incited to toil the more diligently by an anxiety lest death should surprise him in the midst of his labors. This anxiety, perhaps, is common to all men who set their hearts upon any thing so high, in their own view of it, that life becomes of importance only as conditional to its accomplishment. So long as we love life for itself, we seldom dread the losing it. When we desire life for the attainment of an object, we recognize the frailty of its texture. But, side by side with this sense of insecurity, there is a vital faith in our invulnerability to the shaft of death while engaged in any task that seems assigned by Providence as our proper thing to do, and which the world would have cause to mourn for should we leave it unaccomplished. Can the philosopher, big with the inspiration of an idea that is to reform mankind, believe that he is to be beckoned from this sensible existence at the very instant when he is mustering his breath to speak the word of light? Should he perish so, the weary ages may pass away—the world's whole life sand may fall, drop by drop—before another intellect is prepared to develop the truth that might have been uttered then. But history affords many an example where the most precious spirit, at any particular epoch manifested in human shape, has gone hence untimely, without space allowed him, so far as mortal judgment could discern, to perform his mission on the earth. The prophet dies, and the man of torpid heart and sluggish brain lives on. The poet leaves his song half sung, or finishes it beyond the scope of mortal ears, in a celestial choir. The painter—as Allston did—leaves half his conception on the canvas to sadden us with its imperfect beauty, and goes to picture forth the whole, if it be no irreverence to say so, in the hues of heaven. But rather such incomplete designs of this life will be perfected nowhere. This so frequent abortion of man's dearest projects must be taken as a proof that the deeds of earth, however etherealized by piety or genius, are without value, except as exercises and manifestations of the spirit. In heaven, all ordinary thought is higher and more melodious than Milton's song. Then, would he add another verse to any strain that he had left unfinished here?

But to return to Owen Warland. It was his fortune, good or ill, to achieve the purpose of his life. Pass we over a long space of intense thought, yearning effort, minute toil, and wasting anxiety, succeeded by an instant of solitary triumph: let all this be imagined; and then behold the artist, on a winter evening, seeking admittance to Robert Danforth's fireside circle. There he found the man of iron, with his massive substance, thoroughly warmed and attempered by domestic influences. And there was Annie, too, now transformed into a matron, with much of her husband's plain and sturdy nature, but imbued, as Owen Warland still believed, with a finer grace, that might enable her to be the interpreter between strength and beauty. It happened, likewise, that old Peter Hovenden was a guest this evening at his daughter's fireside; and it was his well-remembered expression of keen, cold criticism that first encountered the artist's glance.

"My old friend Owen!" cried Robert Danforth, starting up, and compressing the artist's delicate fingers within a hand that was accustomed to gripe bars of iron. "This is kind and neighborly to come to us at last. I was afraid your perpetual motion had bewitched you out of the remembrance of old times."

"We are glad to see you," said Annie, while a blush reddened her matronly cheek. "It was not like a friend to stay from us so long."

"Well, Owen," inquired the old watchmaker, as his first greeting, "how comes on the beautiful? Have you created it at last?"

The artist did not immediately reply, being startled by the apparition of a young child of strength that was tumbling about on the carpet—a little personage who had come mysteriously out of the infinite, but with something so sturdy and real in his composition that he seemed moulded out of the densest substance which earth could supply. This hopeful infant crawled towards the new comer, and setting himself on end, as Robert Danforth expressed the posture, stared at Owen with a look of such sagacious observation that the mother could not help exchanging a proud glance with her husband. But the artist was disturbed by the child's look, as imagining a resemblance between it and Peter Hovenden's habitual expression. He could have fancied that the old watchmaker was compressed into this baby shape, and looking out of those baby eyes, and repeating, as he now did, the malicious question:—

"The beautiful, Owen! How comes on the beautiful? Have you succeeded in creating the beautiful?"

"I have succeeded," replied the artist, with a momentary light of triumph in his eyes and a smile of sunshine, yet steeped in such depth of thought that it was almost sadness. "Yes, my friends, it is the truth. I have succeeded."

"Indeed!" cried Annie, a look of maiden mirthfulness peeping out of her face again. "And is it lawful, now, to inquire what the secret is?"

"Surely; it is to disclose it that I have come," answered Owen Warland. "You shall know, and see, and touch, and possess the secret! For, Annie,—if by that name I may still address the friend of my boyish years,—Annie, it is for your bridal gift that I have wrought this spiritualized mechanism, this harmony of motion, this mystery of beauty. It comes late indeed; but it is as we go onward in life, when objects begin to lose their freshness of hue and our souls their delicacy of perception, that the spirit of beauty is most needed. If,—forgive me, Annie,—if you know how to value this gift, it can never come too late."

He produced, as he spoke, what seemed a jewel box. It was carved richly out of ebony by his own hand, and inlaid with a fanciful tracery of pearl, representing a boy in pursuit of a butterfly, which, elsewhere, had become a winged spirit, and was flying heavenward; while the boy, or youth, had found such efficacy in his strong desire that he ascended from earth to cloud, and from cloud to celestial atmosphere, to win the beautiful. This case of ebony the artist opened, and bade Annie place her finger on its edge. She did so, but almost screamed as a butterfly fluttered forth, and, alighting on her finger's tip, sat waving the ample magnificence of its purple and gold-speckled wings, as if in prelude to a flight. It is impossible to express by words the glory, the splendor, the delicate gorgeousness which were softened into the beauty of this object. Nature's ideal butterfly was here realized in all its perfection; not in the pattern of such faded insects as flit among earthly flowers, but of those which hover across the meads of paradise for child-angels and the spirits of departed infants to disport themselves with. The rich down was visible upon its wings; the lustre of its eyes seemed instinct with spirit. The firelight glimmered around this wonder—the candles gleamed upon it; but it glistened apparently by its own radiance, and illuminated the finger and outstretched hand on which it rested with a white gleam like that of precious stones.

In its perfect beauty, the consideration of size was entirely lost. Had its wings overreached the firmament, the mind could not have been more filled or satisfied.

"Beautiful! beautiful!" exclaimed Annie. "Is it alive? Is it alive?"

"Alive? To be sure it is," answered her husband. "Do you suppose any mortal has skill enough to make a butterfly, or would put himself to the trouble of making one, when any child may catch a score of them in a summer's afternoon? Alive? Certainly! But this pretty box is undoubtedly of our friend Owen's manufacture; and really it does him credit."

At this moment the butterfly waved its wings anew, with a motion so absolutely lifelike that Annie was startled, and even awestricken; for, in spite of her husband's opinion, she could not satisfy herself whether it was indeed a living creature or a piece of wondrous mechanism.

"Is it alive?" she repeated, more earnestly than before.

"Judge for yourself," said Owen Warland, who stood gazing in her face with fixed attention.

The butterfly now flung itself upon the air, fluttered round Annie's head, and soared into a distant region of the parlor, still making itself perceptible to sight by the starry gleam in which the motion of its wings enveloped it. The infant on the floor followed its course with his sagacious little eyes. After flying about the room, it returned in a spiral curve and settled again on Annie's finger.

"But is it alive?" exclaimed she again; and the finger on which the gorgeous mystery had alighted was so tremulous that the butterfly was forced to balance himself with his wings. "Tell me if it be alive, or whether you created it."

"Wherefore ask who created it, so it be beautiful?" replied Owen Warland. "Alive? Yes, Annie; it may well be said to possess life, for it has absorbed my own being into itself; and in the secret of that butterfly, and in its beauty,—which is not merely outward, but deep as its whole system,—is represented the intellect, the imagination, the sensibility, the soul of an Artist of the Beautiful! Yes; I created it. But"—and here his countenance somewhat changed—"this butterfly is not now to me what it was when I beheld it afar off in the daydreams of my youth."

"Be it what it may, it is a pretty plaything," said the blacksmith, grinning with childlike delight. "I wonder whether it would condescend to alight on such a great clumsy finger as mine? Hold it hither, Annie."

By the artist's direction, Annie touched her finger's tip to that of her husband; and, after a momentary delay, the butterfly fluttered from one to the other. It preluded a second flight by a similar, yet not precisely the same, waving of wings as in the first experiment; then, ascending from the blacksmith's stalwart finger, it rose in a gradually enlarging curve to the ceiling, made one wide sweep around the room, and returned with an undulating movement to the point whence it had started.

"Well, that does beat all nature!" cried Robert Danforth, bestowing the heartiest praise that he could find expression for; and, indeed, had he paused there, a man of finer words and nicer perception could not easily have said more. "That goes beyond me, I confess. But what then? There is more real use in one downright blow of my sledge hammer than in the whole five years' labor that our friend Owen has wasted on this butterfly."

Here the child clapped his hands and made a great babble of indistinct utterance, apparently demanding that the butterfly should be given him for a plaything.

Owen Warland, meanwhile, glanced sidelong at Annie, to discover whether she sympathized in her husband's estimate of the comparative value of the beautiful and the practical. There was, amid all her kindness towards himself, amid all the wonder and admiration with which she contemplated the marvellous work of his hands and incarnation of his idea, a secret scorn—too secret, perhaps, for her own consciousness, and perceptible only to such intuitive discernment as that of the artist. But Owen, in the latter stages of his pursuit, had risen out of the region in which such a discovery might have been torture. He knew that the world, and Annie as the representative of the world, whatever praise might be bestowed, could never say the fitting word nor feel the fitting sentiment which should be the perfect recompense of an artist who, symbolizing a lofty moral by a material trifle,—converting what was earthly to spiritual gold,—had won the beautiful into his handiwork. Not at this latest moment was he to learn that the reward of all high performance must be sought within itself, or sought in vain. There was, however, a view of the matter which Annie and her husband, and even

Peter Hovenden, might fully have understood, and which would have satisfied them that the toil of years had here been worthily bestowed. Owen Warland might have told them that this butterfly, this plaything, this bridal gift of a poor watchmaker to a blacksmith's wife, was, in truth, a gem of art that a monarch would have purchased with honors and abundant wealth, and have treasured it among the jewels of his kingdom as the most unique and wondrous of them all. But the artist smiled and kept the secret to himself.

"Father," said Annie, thinking that a word of praise from the old watchmaker might gratify his former apprentice, "do come and admire this pretty butterfly."

"Let us see," said Peter Hovenden, rising from his chair, with a sneer upon his face that always made people doubt, as he himself did, in every thing but a material existence. "Here is my finger for it to alight upon. I shall understand it better when once I have touched it."

But, to the increased astonishment of Annie, when the tip of her father's finger was pressed against that of her husband, on which the butterfly still rested, the insect drooped its wings and seemed on the point of falling to the floor. Even the bright spots of gold upon its wings and body, unless her eyes deceived her, grew dim, and the glowing purple took a dusky hue, and the starry lustre that gleamed around the blacksmith's hand became faint and vanished.

"It is dying! it is dying!" cried Annie, in alarm.

"It has been delicately wrought," said the artist, calmly. "As I told you, it has imbibed a spiritual essence—call it magnetism, or what you will. In an atmosphere of doubt and mockery its exquisite susceptibility suffers torture, as does the soul of him who instilled his own life into it. It has already lost its beauty; in a few moments more its mechanism would be irreparably injured."

"Take away your hand, father!" entreated Annie, turning pale. "Here is my child; let it rest on his innocent hand. There, perhaps, its life will revive and its colors grow brighter than ever."

Her father, with an acrid smile, withdrew his finger. The butterfly then appeared to recover the power of voluntary motion, while its hues assumed much of their original lustre, and the gleam of starlight, which was its most ethereal attribute, again formed a halo round about it. At first, when transferred from Robert Danforth's hand to the small finger of the child, this radiance grew so powerful that it positively threw the little fellow's shadow back against the wall. He, meanwhile, extended his plump hand as he had seen his father and mother do, and watched the waving of the insect's wings with infantine delight. Nevertheless, there was a certain odd expression of sagacity that made Owen Warland feel as if here were old Peter Hovenden, partially, and but partially, redeemed from his hard scepticism into childish faith.

"How wise the little monkey looks!" whispered Robert Danforth to his wife.

"I never saw such a look on a child's face," answered Annie, admiring her own infant, and with good reason, far more than the artistic butterfly. "The darling knows more of the mystery than we do."

As if the butterfly, like the artist, were conscious of something not entirely congenial in the child's nature, it alternately sparkled and grew dim. At length it arose from the small hand of the infant with an airy motion that seemed to bear it upward without an effort, as if the ethereal instincts with which its master's spirit had endowed it impelled this fair vision involuntarily to a higher sphere. Had there been no obstruction, it might have soared into the sky and grown immortal. But its lustre gleamed upon the ceiling; the exquisite texture of its wings brushed against that earthly medium; and a sparkle or two, as of stardust, floated downward and lay glimmering on the carpet. Then the butterfly came fluttering down, and, instead of returning to the infant, was apparently attracted towards the artist's hand.

"Not so! not so!" murmured Owen Warland, as if his handiwork could have understood him. "Thou hast gone forth out of thy master's heart. There is no return for thee."

With a wavering movement, and emitting a tremulous radiance, the butterfly struggled, as it were, towards the infant, and was about to alight upon his finger; but, while it still hovered in the air, the little child of strength, with his grandsire's sharp and shrewd expression in his face, made a snatch at the marvellous insect and compressed it in his hand. Annie screamed. Old

Peter Hovenden burst into a cold and scornful laugh. The blacksmith, by main force, unclosed the infant's hand, and found within the palm a small heap of glittering fragments, whence the mystery of beauty had fled forever. And as for Owen Warland, he looked placidly at what seemed the ruin of his life's labor, and which was yet no ruin. He had caught a far other butterfly than this. When the artist rose high enough to achieve the beautiful, the symbol by which he made it perceptible to mortal senses became of little value in his eyes while his spirit possessed itself in the enjoyment of the reality.

NATHANIEL HAWTHORNE
Rappaccini's Daughter *

A young man, named Giovanni Guasconti, came, very long ago, from the more southern region of Italy, to pursue his studies at the University of Padua. Giovanni, who had but a scanty supply of gold ducats in his pocket, took lodgings in a high and gloomy chamber of an old edifice which looked not unworthy to have been the palace of a Paduan noble, and which, in fact, exhibited over its entrance the armorial bearings of a family long since extinct. The young stranger, who was not unstudied in the great poem of his country, recollected that one of the ancestors of this family, and perhaps an occupant of this very mansion, had been pictured by Dante as a partaker of the immortal agonies of his Inferno. These reminiscences and associations, together with the tendency to heartbreak natural to a young man for the first time out of his native sphere, caused Giovanni to sigh heavily as he looked around the desolate and ill-furnished apartment.

"Holy Virgin, signor!" cried old Dame Lisabetta, who, won by the youth's remarkable beauty of person, was kindly endeavoring to give the chamber a habitable air, "what a sigh was that to come out of a young man's heart! Do you find this old mansion gloomy? For the love of Heaven, then, put your head out of the window, and you will see as bright sunshine as you have left in Naples."

Guasconti mechanically did as the old woman advised, but could not quite agree with her that the Paduan sunshine was as

* *Democratic Review,* December 1844.

cheerful as that of southern Italy. Such as it was, however, it fell upon a garden beneath the window and expended its fostering influences on a variety of plants, which seemed to have been cultivated with exceeding care.

"Does this garden belong to the house?" asked Giovanni.

"Heaven forbid, signor, unless it were fruitful of better pot herbs than any that grow there now," answered old Lisabetta. "No; that garden is cultivated by the own hands of Signor Giacomo Rappaccini, the famous doctor, who, I warrant him, has been heard of as far as Naples. It is said that he distils these plants into medicines that are as potent as a charm. Oftentimes you may see the signor doctor at work, and perchance the signora, his daughter, too, gathering the strange flowers that grow in the garden."

The old woman had now done what she could for the aspect of the chamber; and, commending the young man to the protection of the saints, took her departure.

Giovanni still found no better occupation than to look down into the garden beneath his window. From its appearance, he judged it to be one of those botanic gardens which were of earlier date in Padua than elsewhere in Italy or in the world. Or, not improbably, it might once have been the pleasure-place of an opulent family; for there was the ruin of a marble fountain in the centre, sculptured with rare art, but so wofully shattered that it was impossible to trace the original design from the chaos of remaining fragments. The water, however, continued to gush and sparkle into the sunbeams as cheerfully as ever. A little gurgling sound ascended to the young man's window and made him feel as if the fountain were an immortal spirit, that sung its song unceasingly and without heeding the vicissitudes around it, while one century imbodied it in marble and another scattered the perishable garniture on the soil. All about the pool into which the water subsided grew various plants, that seemed to require a plentiful supply of moisture for the nourishment of gigantic leaves, and, in some instances, flowers gorgeously magnificent. There was one shrub in particular, set in a marble vase in the midst of the pool, that bore a profusion of purple blossoms, each of which had the lustre and richness of a gem; and the whole together made a show so resplendent that it seemed enough to illuminate the garden, even had there been no sunshine. Every portion of the soil was peopled with plants and herbs, which, if less beautiful, still bore tokens of assiduous care, as if all had their individual virtues, known to the scientific mind that fostered them. Some were placed in urns, rich with old carving, and others in common garden pots; some crept serpent-like along the ground or climbed on high, using whatever means of ascent was offered them. One plant had wreathed itself round a statue of Vertumnus, which was thus quite veiled and shrouded in a drapery of hanging foliage, so happily arranged that it might have served a sculptor for a study.

While Giovanni stood at the window he heard a rustling behind a screen of leaves, and became aware that a person was at work in the garden. His figure soon emerged into view, and showed itself to be that of no common laborer, but a tall, emaciated, sallow, and sickly-looking man, dressed in a scholar's garb of black. He was beyond the middle term of life, with gray hair, a thin, gray beard, and a face singularly marked with intellect and cultivation, but which could never, even in his more youthful days, have expressed much warmth of heart.

Nothing could exceed the intentness with which this scientific gardener examined every shrub which grew in his path: it seemed as if he was looking into their inmost nature, making observations in regard to their creative essence, and discovering why one leaf grew in this shape and another in that, and wherefore such and such flowers differed among themselves in hue and perfume. Nevertheless, in spite of this deep intelligence on his part, there was no approach to intimacy between himself and these vegetable existences. On the contrary, he avoided their actual touch or the direct inhaling of their odors with a caution that impressed Giovanni most disagreeably; for the man's demeanor was that of one walking among malignant influences, such as savage beasts, or deadly snakes, or evil spirits, which, should he allow them one moment of license, would wreak upon him some terrible fatality. It was strangely frightful to the young man's imagination to see this air of insecurity in a person cultivating a garden, that most simple and innocent of human toils, and which had been alike the joy and labor of the unfallen parents of the race. Was this garden, then, the Eden of the present world? And this man, with such a perception of harm in what his own hands caused to grow,—was he the Adam?

The distrustful gardener, while plucking away the dead leaves or pruning the too luxuriant growth of the shrubs, defended his hands with a pair of thick gloves. Nor were these his only armor. When, in his walk through the garden, he came to the magnificent plant that hung its purple gems beside the marble fountain, he placed a kind of mask over his mouth and nostrils, as if all this beauty did but conceal a deadlier malice; but, finding his task still too dangerous, he drew back, removed the mask, and called loudly, but in the infirm voice of a person affected with inward disease,—

"Beatrice! Beatrice!"

"Here am I, my father. What would you?" cried a rich and youthful voice from the window of the opposite house—a voice as rich as a tropical sunset, and which made Giovanni, though he knew not why, think of deep hues of purple or crimson and of perfumes heavily delectable. "Are you in the garden?"

"Yes, Beatrice," answered the gardener; "and I need your help."

Soon there emerged from under a sculptured portal the figure of a young girl, arrayed with as much richness of taste as the most splendid of the flowers, beautiful as the day, and with a bloom so deep and vivid that one shade more would have been too much. She looked redundant with life, health, and energy; all of which attributes were bound down and compressed, as it were, and girdled tensely, in their luxuriance, by her virgin zone. Yet Giovanni's fancy must have grown morbid while he looked down into the garden; for the impression which the fair stranger made upon him was as if here were another flower, the human sister of those vegetable ones, as beautiful as they, more beautiful than the richest of them, but still to be touched only with a glove, nor to be approached without a mask. As Beatrice came down the garden path, it was observable that she handled and inhaled the odor of several of the plants which her father had most sedulously avoided.

"Here, Beatrice," said the latter, "see how many needful offices require to be done to our chief treasure. Yet, shattered as I am, my life might pay the penalty of approaching it so closely as circumstances demand. Henceforth, I fear, this plant must be consigned to your sole charge."

"And gladly will I undertake it," cried again the rich tones of the young lady, as she bent towards the magnificent plant and opened her arms as if to embrace it. "Yes, my sister, my splendor, it shall be Beatrice's task to nurse and serve thee; and thou shalt reward her with thy kisses and perfumed breath, which to her is as the breath of life."

Then, with all the tenderness in her manner that was so strikingly expressed in her words, she busied herself with such attentions as the plant seemed to require; and Giovanni, at his lofty window, rubbed his eyes, and almost doubted whether it were a girl tending her favorite flower, or one sister performing the duties of affection to another. The scene soon terminated. Whether Dr. Rappaccini had finished his labors in the garden, or that his watchful eye had caught the stranger's face, he now took his daughter's arm and retired. Night was already closing in; oppressive exhalations seemed to proceed from the plants and steal upward past the open window; and Giovanni, closing the lattice, went to his couch and dreamed of a rich flower and beautiful girl. Flower and maiden were different, and yet the same, and fraught with some strange peril in either shape.

But there is an influence in the light of morning that tends to rectify whatever errors of fancy, or even of judgment, we may have incurred during the sun's decline, or among the shadows of the night, or in the less wholesome glow of moonshine. Giovanni's first movement, on starting from sleep, was to throw open the window and gaze down into the garden which his dreams had made so fertile of mysteries. He was surprised, and a little ashamed, to find how real and matter-of-fact an affair it proved to be, in the first rays of the sun which gilded the dewdrops that hung upon leaf and blossom, and, while giving a brighter beauty to each rare flower, brought every thing within the limits of ordinary experience. The young man rejoiced that, in the heart of the barren city, he had the privilege of overlooking this spot of lovely and luxuriant vegetation. It would serve, he said to himself, as a symbolic language to keep him in communion with Nature. Neither the sickly and thoughtworn Dr. Giacomo Rappaccini, it is true, nor his brilliant daughter, were now visible; so that Giovanni could not determine how much of the singularity which he attributed to both was due to their own qualities and how much to his wonder-working fancy; but he was inclined to take a most rational view of the whole matter.

In the course of the day he paid his respects to Signor Pietro Baglioni, professor of medicine in the university, a physician of eminent repute, to whom Giovanni had brought a letter of introduction. The professor was an elderly personage, apparently of genial nature and habits that might almost be called jovial. He kept the young man to dinner, and made himself very agreeable by the freedom and liveliness of his conversation, especially when warmed by a flask or two of Tuscan wine. Giovanni, conceiving that men of science, inhabitants of the same city, must needs be on familiar terms with one another, took an opportunity to mention the name of Dr. Rappaccini. But the professor did not respond with so much cordiality as he had anticipated.

"Ill would it become a teacher of the divine art of medicine," said Professor Pietro Baglioni, in answer to a question of Giovanni, "to withhold due and well-considered praise of a physician so eminently skilled as Rappaccini; but, on the other hand, I should answer it but scantily to my conscience were I to permit a worthy youth like yourself, Signor Giovanni, the son of an ancient friend, to imbibe erroneous ideas respecting a man who might hereafter chance to hold your life and death in his hands. The truth is, our worshipful Dr. Rappaccini has as much science as any member of the faculty—with perhaps one single exception—in Padua, or all Italy; but there are certain grave objections to his professional character."

"And what are they?" asked the young man.

"Has my friend Giovanni any disease of body or heart, that he is so inquisitive about physicians?" said the professor, with a smile. "But as for Rappaccini, it is said of him—and I, who know the man well, can answer for its truth—that he cares infinitely more for science than for mankind. His patients are interesting to him only as subjects for some new experiment. He would sacrifice human life, his own among the rest, or whatever else was dearest to him, for the sake of adding so much as a grain of mustard seed to the great heap of his accumulated knowledge."

"Methinks he is an awful man indeed," remarked Guasconti, mentally recalling the cold and purely intellectual aspect of Rappaccini. "And yet, worshipful professor, is it not a noble spirit? Are there many men capable of so spiritual a love of science?"

"God forbid," answered the professor, somewhat testily; "at least, unless they take sounder views of the healing art than those adopted by Rappaccini. It is his theory that all medicinal virtues are comprised within those substances which we term vegetable poisons. These he cultivates with his own hands, and is said even to have produced new varieties of poison, more horribly deleterious than Nature, without the assistance of this learned person, would ever have plagued the world withal. That the signor doctor does less mischief than might be expected with such dangerous substances, is undeniable. Now and then, it must be owned, he has effected, or seemed to effect, a marvellous cure; but, to tell you my private mind, Signor Giovanni, he should receive little credit for such instances of success,—they being probably the work of chance,—but should be held strictly accountable for his failures, which may justly be considered his own work."

The youth might have taken Baglioni's opinions with many grains of allowance had he known that there was a professional warfare of long continuance between him and Dr. Rappaccini, in which the latter was generally thought to have gained the advantage. If the reader be inclined to judge for himself, we refer him to certain black-letter tracts on both sides, preserved in the medical department of the University of Padua.

"I know not, most learned professor," returned Giovanni, after musing on what had been said of Rappaccini's exclusive zeal for science,—"I know not how dearly this physician may love his art; but surely there is one object more dear to him. He has a daughter."

"Aha!" cried the professor, with a laugh. "So now our friend Giovanni's secret is out. You have heard of this daughter, whom all the young men in Padua are wild about, though not half a dozen have ever had the good hap to see her face. I know little of the Signora Beatrice save that Rappaccini is said to have instructed her deeply in his science, and that, young and beautiful as fame reports her, she is already qualified to fill a professor's chair. Perchance her father destines her for mine! Other absurd rumors there be, not worth talking about or listening to. So now, Signor Giovanni, drink off your glass of lachryma."

Guasconti returned to his lodgings somewhat heated with the wine he had quaffed, and which caused his brain to swim with strange fantasies in reference to Dr. Rappaccini and the beautiful Beatrice. On his way, happening to pass by a florist's, he bought a fresh bouquet of flowers.

Ascending to his chamber, he seated himself near the window, but within the shadow thrown by the depth of the wall, so that he could look down into the garden with little risk of being discovered. All beneath his eye was a solitude. The strange plants were basking in the sunshine, and now and then nodding gently to one another, as if in acknowledgment of sympathy and kindred. In the midst, by the shattered fountain, grew the magnificent shrub, with its purple gems clustering all over it; they glowed in the air, and gleamed back again out of the depths of the pool, which thus seemed to overflow with colored radiance from the rich reflection that was steeped in it. At first, as we have said, the garden was a solitude. Soon, however,—as Giovanni had half hoped, half feared, would be the case,—a figure appeared beneath the antique sculptured portal, and came down between the rows of plants, inhaling their various perfumes as if she were one of those beings of old classic fable that lived upon sweet odors. On again beholding Beatrice, the young man was even startled to perceive how much her beauty exceeded his recollection of it; so brilliant, so vivid, was its character, that she glowed amid the sunlight, and, as Giovanni whispered to himself, positively illuminated the more shadowy intervals of the garden path. Her face being now more revealed than on the former occasion, he was struck by its expression of simplicity and sweetness—qualities that had not entered into his idea of her character, and which made him ask anew what manner of mortal she might be. Nor did he fail again to observe, or imagine, an analogy between the beautiful girl and the gorgeous shrub that hung its gemlike flowers over the fountain—a resemblance which Beatrice seemed to have indulged a fantastic humor in heightening, both by the arrangement of her dress and the selection of its hues.

Approaching the shrub, she threw open her arms, as with a passionate ardor, and drew its branches into an intimate embrace—so intimate that her features were hidden in its leafy bosom and her glistening ringlets all intermingled with the flowers.

"Give me thy breath, my sister," exclaimed Beatrice; "for I am faint with common air. And give me this flower of thine, which I separate with gentlest fingers from the stem and place it close beside my heart."

With these words the beautiful daughter of Rappaccini plucked one of the richest blossoms of the shrub, and was about to fasten it in her bosom. But now, unless Giovanni's draughts of wine had bewildered his senses, a singular incident occurred. A small orange-colored reptile, of the lizard or chameleon species, chanced to be creeping along the path, just at the feet of Beatrice. It appeared to Giovanni,—but, at the distance from which he gazed, he could scarcely have seen any thing so minute,—it appeared to him, however, that a drop or two of moisture from the broken stem of the flower descended upon the lizard's head. For an instant the reptile contorted itself violently, and then lay motionless in the sunshine. Beatrice observed this remarkable phenomenon, and crossed herself, sadly, but without surprise; nor did she therefore hesitate to arrange the fatal flower in her bosom. There it blushed, and almost glimmered with the dazzling effect of a precious stone, adding to her dress and aspect the one appropriate charm which nothing else in the world could have supplied. But Giovanni, out of the shadow of his window, bent forward and shrank back, and murmured and trembled.

"Am I awake? Have I my senses?" said he to himself. "What is this being? Beautiful shall I call her, or inexpressibly terrible?"

Beatrice now strayed carelessly through the garden, approaching closer beneath Giovanni's window, so that he was compelled to thrust his head quite out of its concealment in order to gratify the intense and painful curiosity which she excited. At this moment there came a beautiful insect over the garden wall: it had, perhaps, wandered through the city, and found no flowers or verdure among those antique haunts of men until the heavy perfumes of Dr. Rappaccini's shrubs had lured it from afar. Without alighting on the flowers, this winged brightness seemed to be attracted by Beatrice, and lingered in the air and fluttered about her head. Now, here it could not be but that Giovanni Guasconti's eyes deceived him. Be that as it might, he fancied that, while Beatrice was gazing at the insect with childish delight, it grew faint and fell at her feet; its bright wings shivered; it was dead—from no cause that he could discern, unless it were the atmosphere of her breath. Again Beatrice crossed herself and sighed heavily as she bent over the dead insect.

An impulsive movement of Giovanni drew her eyes to the window. There she beheld the beautiful head of the young man —rather a Grecian than an Italian head, with fair, regular features, and a glistening of gold among his ringlets—gazing down upon her like a being that hovered in mid air. Scarcely knowing what he did, Giovanni threw down the bouquet which he had hitherto held in his hand.

"Signora," said he, "there are pure and healthful flowers. Wear them for the sake of Giovanni Guasconti."

"Thanks, signor," replied Beatrice, with her rich voice, that came forth as it were like a gush of music, and with a mirthful expression half childish and half womanlike. "I accept your gift, and would fain recompense it with this precious purple flower; but, if I toss it into the air, it will not reach you. So Signor Guasconti must even content himself with my thanks."

She lifted the bouquet from the ground, and then, as if inwardly ashamed at having stepped aside from her maidenly reserve to respond to a stranger's greeting, passed swiftly homeward through the garden. But, few as the moments were, it seemed to Giovanni, when she was on the point of vanishing beneath the sculptured portal, that his beautiful bouquet was already beginning to wither in her grasp. It was an idle thought; there could be no possibility of distinguishing a faded flower from a fresh one at so great a distance.

For many days after this incident the young man avoided the window that looked into Dr. Rappaccini's garden, as if something ugly and monstrous would have blasted his eyesight had he been betrayed into a glance. He felt conscious of having put himself, to a certain extent, within the influence of an unintelligible power by the communication which he had opened with Beatrice. The wisest course would have been, if his heart were in any real danger, to quit his lodgings and Padua itself at once; the next wiser, to have accustomed himself, as far as possible, to the familiar and daylight view of Beatrice—thus bringing her rigidly and systematically within the limits of ordinary experience. Least of all, while avoiding her sight, ought Giovanni to have remained so near this extraordinary being that the proximity and possibility even of intercourse should give a kind of substance and reality to the wild vagaries which his imagination ran riot continually in producing. Guasconti had not a deep heart—or, at all events, its depths were not sounded now; but he had a quick fancy, and an ardent southern temperament, which rose every instant to a higher fever pitch. Whether or no Beatrice possessed those terrible attributes, that fatal breath, the affinity with those so beautiful and deadly flowers which were indicated by what Giovanni had witnessed, she had at least instilled a fierce and subtle poison into his system. It was not love, although her rich beauty was a madness to him; nor horror, even while he fancied her spirit to be imbued with the same baneful essence that seemed to pervade her physical frame; but a wild offspring of both love and horror that had each parent in it, and burned like one and shivered like the other. Giovanni knew not what to dread; still less did he know what to hope; yet hope and dread kept a continual warfare in his breast, alternately vanquishing one another and starting up afresh to renew the contest. Blessed are all simple emotions, be they dark or bright! It is the lurid intermixture of the two that produces the illuminating blaze of the infernal regions.

Sometimes he endeavored to assuage the fever of his spirit by a rapid walk through the streets of Padua or beyond its gates: his footsteps kept time with the throbbings of his brain, so that the walk was apt to accelerate itself to a race. One day he found himself arrested; his arm was seized by a portly personage, who had turned back on recognizing the young man and expended much breath in overtaking him.

"Signor Giovanni! Stay, my young friend!" cried he. "Have you forgotten me? That might well be the case if I were as much altered as yourself."

It was Baglioni, whom Giovanni had avoided ever since their first meeting, from a doubt that the professor's sagacity would look too deeply into his secrets. Endeavoring to recover himself, he stared forth wildly from his inner world into the outer one and spoke like a man in a dream.

"Yes; I am Giovanni Guasconti. You are Professor Pietro Baglioni. Now let me pass!"

"Not yet, not yet, Signor Giovanni Guasconti," said the professor, smiling, but at the same time scrutinizing the youth with an earnest glance. "What! did I grow up side by side with your father? and shall his son pass me like a stranger in these old streets of Padua? Stand still, Signor Giovanni; for we must have a word or two before we part."

"Speedily, then, most worshipful professor, speedily," said Giovanni, with feverish impatience. "Does not your worship see that I am in haste?"

Now, while he was speaking there came a man in black along the street, stooping and moving feebly like a person in inferior health. His face was all overspread with a most sickly and sallow hue, but yet so pervaded with an expression of piercing and active intellect that an observer might easily have overlooked the merely physical attributes and have seen only this wonderful energy. As he passed, this person exchanged a cold and distant salutation with Baglioni, but fixed his eyes upon Giovanni with an intentness that seemed to bring out whatever was within him worthy of notice. Nevertheless, there was a peculiar quietness in the look, as if taking merely a speculative, not a human, interest in the young man.

"It is Dr. Rappaccini!" whispered the professor when the stranger had passed. "Has he ever seen your face before?"

"Not that I know," answered Giovanni, starting at the name.

"He *has* seen you! he must have seen you!" said Baglioni, hastily. "For some purpose or other, this man of science is making a study of you. I know that look of his! It is the same that coldly illuminates his face as he bends over a bird, a mouse, or a butterfly; which, in pursuance of some experiment, he has killed by the perfume of a flower; a look as deep as Nature itself, but without Nature's warmth of love. Signor Giovanni, I will stake my life upon it, you are the subject of one of Rappaccini's experiments!"

"Will you make a fool of me?" cried Giovanni, passionately. "*That*, signor professor, were an untoward experiment."

"Patience! patience!" replied the imperturbable professor. "I tell thee, my poor Giovanni, that Rappaccini has a scientific interest in thee. Thou hast fallen into fearful hands! And the Signora Beatrice,—what part does she act in this mystery?"

But Guasconti, finding Baglioni's pertinacity intolerable, here broke away, and was gone before the professor could again seize his arm. He looked after the young man intently and shook his head.

"This must not be," said Balgioni to himself. "The youth is the son of my old friend, and shall not come to any harm from which the arcana of medical science can preserve him. Besides, it is too insufferable an impertinence in Rappaccini thus to snatch the lad out of my own hands, as I may say, and make use of him for his infernal experiments. This daughter of his! It shall be looked to. Perchance, most learned Rappaccini, I may foil you where you little dream of it!"

Meanwhile Giovanni had pursued a circuitous route, and at length found himself at the door of his lodgings. As he crossed the threshold he was met by old Lisabetta, who smirked and smiled, and was evidently desirous to attract his attention; vainly, however, as the ebullition of his feelings had momentarily subsided into a cold and dull vacuity. He turned his eyes full upon the withered face that was puckering itself into a smile, but seemed to behold it not. The old dame, therefore, laid her grasp upon his cloak.

"Signor! signor!" whispered she, still with a smile over the whole breadth of her visage, so that it looked not unlike a grotesque carving in wood, darkened by centuries. "Listen, signor! There is a private entrance into the garden!"

"What do you say?" exclaimed Giovanni, turning quickly about, as if an inanimate thing should start into feverish life. "A private entrance into Dr. Rappaccini's garden?"

"Hush! hush! not so loud!" whispered Lisabetta, putting her hand over his mouth. "Yes; into the worshipful doctor's garden, where you may see all his fine shrubbery. Many a young man in Padua would give gold to be admitted among those flowers."

Giovanni put a piece of gold into her hand.

"Show me the way," said he.

A surmise, probably excited by his conversation with Baglioni, crossed his mind, that this interposition of old Lisabetta might perchance be connected with the intrigue, whatever were its nature, in which the professor seemed to suppose that Dr. Rappaccini was involving him. But such a suspicion, though it disturbed Giovanni, was inadequate to restrain him. The instant that he was aware of the possibility of approaching Beatrice, it seemed an absolute necessity of his existence to do so. It mattered not whether she were angel or demon; he was irrevocably within her sphere, and must obey the law that whirled him onward, in everlessening circles, towards a result which he did not attempt to foreshadow; and yet, strange to say, there came across him a sudden doubt whether this intense interest on his part were not delusory; whether it were really of so deep and positive a nature as to justify him in now thrusting himself into an incalculable position; whether it were not merely the fantasy of a young man's brain, only slightly or not at all connected with his heart.

He paused, hesitated, turned half about, but again went on. His withered guide led him along several obscure passages, and finally undid a door, through which, as it was opened, there came the sight and sound of rustling leaves, with the broken sunshine glimmering among them. Giovanni stepped forth, and, forcing himself through the entanglement of a shrub that wreathed its tendrils over the hidden entrance, stood beneath his own window in the open area of Dr. Rappaccini's garden.

How often is it the case that, when impossibilities have come to pass and dreams have condensed their misty substance into tangible realities, we find ourselves calm, and even coldly self-possessed, amid circumstances which it would have been a delirium of joy or agony to anticipate! Fate delights to thwart us thus. Passion will choose his own time to rush upon the scene, and lingers sluggishly behind when an appropriate adjustment of events would seem to summon his appearance. So was it now with Giovanni. Day after day his pulses had throbbed with feverish blood at the improbable idea of an interview with Beatrice, and of standing with her, face to face, in this very garden, basking in the Oriental sunshine of her beauty, and snatching from her full gaze the mystery which he deemed the riddle of his own existence. But now there was a singular and untimely equanimity within his breast. He threw a glance around the garden to discover if Beatrice or her father were present, and, perceiving that he was alone, began a critical observation of the plants.

The aspect of one and all of them dissatisfied him; their gorgeousness seemed fierce, passionate, and even unnatural. There was hardly an individual shrub which a wanderer, straying by himself through a forest, would not have been startled to find growing wild, as if an unearthly face had glared at him out of the thicket. Several also would have shocked a delicate instinct by an appearance of artificialness indicating that there had been such commixture, and, as it were, adultery of various vegetable species, that the production was no longer of God's making, but the monstrous offspring of man's depraved fancy, glowing with only an evil mockery of beauty. They were probably the result of experiment, which in one or two cases had succeeded in mingling plants individually lovely into a compound possessing the questionable and ominous character that distinguished the whole growth of the garden. In fine, Giovanni recognized but two or three plants in the collection, and those of a kind that he well knew to be poisonous. While busy with these contemplations he heard the rustling of a silken garment, and, turning, beheld Beatrice emerging from beneath the sculptured portal.

Giovanni had not considered with himself what should be his deportment; whether he should apologize for his intrusion into the garden, or assume that he was there with the privity at least, if not by the desire, of Dr. Rappaccini or his daughter; but Beatrice's manner placed him at his ease, though leaving him still in doubt by what agency he had gained admittance. She came lightly along the path and met him near the broken fountain. There was surprise in her face, but brightened by a simple and kind expression of pleasure.

"You are a connoisseur in flowers, signor," said Beatrice, with a smile, alluding to the bouquet which he had flung her from the window. "It is no marvel, therefore, if the sight of my father's rare collection has tempted you to take a nearer view. If he were here, he could tell you many strange and interesting facts as to the nature and habits of these shrubs; for he has spent a lifetime in such studies, and this garden is his world."

"And yourself, lady," observed Giovanni, "if fame says true, —you likewise are deeply skilled in the virtues indicated by these rich blossoms and these spicy perfumes. Would you deign to be my instructress, I should prove an apter scholar than if taught by Signor Rappaccini himself."

"Are there such idle rumors?" asked Beatrice, with the music of a pleasant laugh. "Do people say that I am skilled in my father's science of plants? What a jest is there! No; though I have grown up among these flowers, I know no more of them than their hues and perfume; and sometimes methinks I would fain rid myself of even that small knowledge. There are many flowers here, and those not the least brilliant, that shock and offend me when they meet my eye. But pray, signor, do not believe these stories about my science. Believe nothing of me save what you see with your own eyes."

"And must I believe all that I have seen with my own eyes?" asked Giovanni, pointedly, while the recollection of former scenes made him shrink. "No, signora; you demand too little of me. Bid me believe nothing save what comes from your own lips."

It would appear that Beatrice understood him. There came a

deep flush to her cheek; but she looked full into Giovanni's eyes, and responded to his gaze of uneasy suspicion with a queenlike haughtiness.

"I do so bid you, signor," she replied. "Forget whatever you may have fancied in regard to me. If true to the outward senses, still it may be false in its essence; but the words of Beatrice Rappaccini's lips are true from the depths of the heart outward. Those you may believe."

A fervor glowed in her whole aspect and beamed upon Giovanni's consciousness like the light of truth itself; but while she spoke there was a fragrance in the atmosphere around her, rich and delightful, though evanescent, yet which the young man, from an indefinable reluctance, scarcely dared to draw into his lungs. It might be the odor of the flowers. Could it be Beatrice's breath which thus embalmed her words with a strange richness, as if by steeping them in her heart? A faintness passed like a shadow over Giovanni and flitted away; he seemed to gaze through the beautiful girl's eyes into her transparent soul, and felt no more doubt or fear.

The tinge of passion that had colored Beatrice's manner vanished; she became gay, and appeared to derive a pure delight from her communion with the youth not unlike what the maiden of a lonely island might have felt conversing with a voyager from the civilized world. Evidently her experience of life had been confined within the limits of that garden. She talked now about matters as simple as the daylight or summer clouds, and now asked questions in reference to the city, or Giovanni's distant home, his friends, his mother, and his sisters—questions indicating such seclusion, and such lack of familiarity with modes and forms, that Giovanni responded as if to an infant. Her spirit gushed out before him like a fresh rill that was just catching its first glimpse of the sunlight and wondering at the reflections of earth and sky which were flung into its bosom. There came thoughts, too, from a deep source, and fantasies of a gemlike brilliancy, as if diamonds and rubies sparkled upward among the bubbles of the fountain. Ever and anon there gleamed across the young man's mind a sense of wonder that he should be walking side by side with the being who had so wrought upon his imagination, whom he had idealized in such hues of terror, in whom he had positively witnessed such manifestations of dreadful attributes—that he should be conversing with Beatrice like a brother, and should find her so human and so maidenlike. But such reflections were only momentary; the effect of her character was too real not to make itself familiar at once.

In this free intercourse they had strayed through the garden, and now, after many turns among its avenues, were come to the shattered fountain, beside which grew the magnificent shrub, with its treasury of glowing blossoms. A fragrance was diffused from it which Giovanni recognized as identical with that which he had attributed to Beatrice's breath, but incomparably more powerful. As her eyes fell upon it, Giovanni beheld her press her hand to her bosom as if her heart were throbbing suddenly and painfully.

"For the first time in my life," murmured she, addressing the shrub, "I had forgotten thee."

"I remember, signora," said Giovanni, "that you once promised to reward me with one of these living gems for the bouquet which I had the happy boldness to fling to your feet. Permit me now to pluck it as a memorial of this interview."

He made a step towards the shrub with extended hand; but Beatrice darted forward, uttering a shriek that went through his heart like a dagger. She caught his hand and drew it back with the whole force of her slender figure. Giovanni felt her touch thrilling through his fibres. "Touch it not!" exclaimed she, in a voice of agony. "Not for thy life! It is fatal!"

Then, hiding her face, she fled from him and vanished beneath the sculptured portal. As Giovanni followed her with his eyes, he beheld the emaciated figure and pale intelligence of Dr. Rappaccini, who had been watching the scene, he knew not how long, within the shadow of the entrance.

No sooner was Guasconti alone in his chamber than the image of Beatrice came back to his passionate musings, invested with all the witchery that had been gathering around it ever since his first glimpse of her, and now likewise imbued with a tender warmth of girlish womanhood. She was human; her nature was endowed with all gentle and feminine qualities; she was worthiest to be worshipped; she was capable, surely, on her part, of the height and heroism of love. Those tokens which he had hitherto considered as proofs of a frightful peculiarity in her physical and moral system were now either forgotten or by the subtle sophistry of passion transmitted into a golden crown of enchantment, rendering Beatrice the more admirable by so much as she was the more unique. Whatever had looked ugly was now beautiful; or, if incapable of such a change, it stole away and hid itself among those shapeless half ideas which throng the dim region beyond the daylight of our perfect consciousness. Thus did he spend the night, nor fell asleep until the dawn had begun to awake the slumbering flowers in Dr. Rappaccini's garden, whither Giovanni's dreams doubtless led him. Up rose the sun in his due season, and, flinging his beams upon the young man's eyelids, awoke him to a sense of pain. When thoroughly aroused, he became sensible of a burning and tingling agony in his hand—in his right hand—the very hand which Beatrice had grasped in her own when he was on the point of plucking one of the gemlike flowers. On the back of that hand there was now a purple print like that of four small fingers, and the likeness of a slender thumb upon his wrist.

O, how stubbornly does love,—or even that cunning semblance of love which flourishes in the imagination, but strikes no depth of root into the heart,—how stubbornly does it hold its faith until the moment comes when it is doomed to vanish into thin mist! Giovanni wrapped a handkerchief about his hand and wondered what evil thing had stung him, and soon forgot his pain in a revery of Beatrice.

After the first interview, a second was in the inevitable course of what we call fate. A third; a fourth; and a meeting with Beatrice in the garden was no longer an incident in Giovanni's daily life, but the whole space in which he might be said to live; for the anticipation and memory of that ecstatic hour made up the remainder. Nor was it otherwise with the daughter of Rappaccini. She watched for the youth's appearance and flew to his side with confidence as unreserved as if they had been playmates from early infancy—as if they were such playmates still. If, by any unwonted chance, he failed to come at the appointed moment, she stood beneath the window and sent up the rich sweetness of her tones to float around him in his chamber and echo and reverberate throughout his heart: "Giovanni! Giovanni! Why tarriest thou? Come down!" And down he hastened into that Eden of poisonous flowers.

But, with all this intimate familiarity, there was still a reserve in Beatrice's demeanor, so rigidly and invariably sustained that the idea of infringing it scarcely occurred to his imagination. By all appreciable signs, they loved; they had looked love with eyes that conveyed the holy secret from the depths of one soul into the depths of the other, as if it were too sacred to be whispered by the way; they had even spoken love in those gushes of passion when their spirits darted forth in articulated breath like tongues of long hidden flame; and yet there had been no seal of lips, no clasp of hands, nor any slightest caress such as love claims and hallows. He had never touched one of the gleaming ringlets of her hair; her garment—so marked was the physical barrier between them—had never been waved against him by a breeze. On the few occasions when Giovanni had seemed tempted to overstep the limit, Beatrice grew so sad, so stern, and withal wore such a look of desolate separation, shuddering at itself, that not a spoken word was requisite to repel him. At such time he was startled at the horrible suspicions that rose, monsterlike, out of the caverns of his heart and stared him in the face; his love grew thin and faint as the morning mist; his doubts alone had substance. But, when Beatrice's face brightened again after the momentary shadow, she was transformed at once from the mysterious, questionable being whom he had watched with so much awe and horror; she was now the beautiful and unsophisticated girl whom he felt that his spirit knew with a certainty beyond all other knowledge.

A considerable time had now passed since Giovanni's last meeting with Baglioni. One morning, however, he was disagreeably surprised by a visit from the professor, whom he had scarcely thought of for whole weeks, and would willingly have forgotten still longer. Given up as he had long been to a pervading excitement, he could tolerate no companions except upon condition of their perfect sympathy with his present state of feeling. Such sympathy was not to be expected from Professor Baglioni.

The visitor chatted carelessly for a few moments about the gossip of the city and the university, and then took up another topic.

"I have been reading an old classic author lately," said he, "and met with a story that strangely interested me. Possibly you may remember it. It is of an Indian prince, who sent a beautiful woman as a present to Alexander the Great. She was as lovely as the dawn and gorgeous as the sunset; but what especially distinguished her was a certain rich perfume in her breath—richer than a garden of Persian roses. Alexander, as was natural to a youthful conqueror, fell in love at first sight with this magnificent stranger; but a certain sage physician, happening to be present, discovered a terrible secret in regard to her."

"And what was that?" asked Giovanni, turning his eyes downward to avoid those of the professor.

"That this lovely woman," continued Baglioni, with emphasis, "had been nourished with poisons from her birth upward, until her whole nature was so imbued with them that she herself had become the deadliest poison in existence. Poison was her element of life. With that rich perfume of her breath she blasted the very air. Her love would have been poison—her embrace death. Is not this a marvellous tale?"

"A childish fable," answered Giovanni, nervously starting from his chair. "I marvel how your worship finds time to read such nonsense among your graver studies."

"By the by," said the professor, looking uneasily about him, "what singular fragrance is this in your apartment? Is it the perfume of your gloves? It is faint, but delicious; and yet, after all, by no means agreeable. Were I to breathe it long, methinks it would make me ill. It is like the breath of a flower; but I see no flowers in the chamber."

"Nor are there any," replied Giovanni, who had turned pale as the professor spoke; "nor, I think, is there any fragrance except in your worship's imagination. Odors, being a sort of element combined of the sensual and the spiritual, are apt to deceive us in this manner. The recollection of a perfume, the bare idea of it, may easily be mistaken for a present reality."

"Ay; but my sober imagination does not often play such tricks," said Baglioni; "and, were I to fancy any kind of odor, it would be that of some vile apothecary drug, wherewith my fingers are likely enough to be imbued. Our worshipful friend Rappaccini, as I have heard, tinctures his medicaments with odors richer than those of Araby. Doubtless, likewise, the fair and learned Signora Beatrice would minister to her patients with draughts as sweet as a maiden's breath; but woe to him that sips them!"

Giovanni's face evinced many contending emotions. The tone

in which the professor alluded to the pure and lovely daughter of Rappaccini was a torture to his soul; and yet the intimation of a view of her character, opposite to his own, gave instantaneous distinctness to a thousand dim suspicions, which now grinned at him like so many demons. But he strove hard to quell them and to respond to Baglioni with a true lover's perfect faith.

"Signor professor," said he, "you were my father's friend; perchance, too, it is your purpose to act a friendly part towards his son. I would fain feel nothing towards you save respect and deference; but I pray you to observe, signor, that there is one subject on which we must not speak. You know not the Signora Beatrice. You cannot, therefore, estimate the wrong—the blasphemy, I may even say—that is offered to her character by a light or injurious word."

"Giovanni! my poor Giovanni!" answered the professor, with a calm expression of pity, "I know this wretched girl far better than yourself. You shall hear the truth in respect to the poisoner Rappaccini and his poisonous daughter; yes, poisonous as she is beautiful. Listen; for, even should you do violence to my gray hairs, it shall not silence me. That old fable of the Indian woman has become a truth by the deep and deadly science of Rappaccini and in the person of the lovely Beatrice."

Giovanni groaned and hid his face.

"Her father," continued Baglioni, "was not restrained by natural affection from offering up his child in this horrible manner as the victim of his insane zeal for science; for, let us do him justice, he is as true a man of science as ever distilled his own heart in an alembic. What, then, will be your fate? Beyond a doubt you are selected as the material of some new experiment. Perhaps the result is to be death; perhaps a fate more awful still. Rappaccini, with what he calls the interest of science before his eyes, will hesitate at nothing."

"It is a dream," muttered Giovanni to himself; "surely it is a dream."

"But," resumed the professor, "be of good cheer, son of my friend. It is not yet too late for the rescue. Possibly we may even succeed in bringing back this miserable child within the limits of ordinary nature, from which her father's madness has estranged her. Behold this little silver vase! It was wrought by the hands of the renowned Benvenuto Cellini, and is well worthy to be a love gift to the fairest dame in Italy. But its contents are invaluable. One little sip of this antidote would have rendered the most virulent poisons of the Borgias innocuous. Doubt not that it will be as efficacious against those of Rappaccini. Bestow the vase, and the precious liquid within it, on your Beatrice, and hopefully await the result."

Baglioni laid a small, exquisitely wrought silver vial on the table and withdrew, leaving what he had said to produce its effect upon the young man's mind.

"We will thwart Rappaccini yet," thought he, chuckling to himself, as he descended the stairs; "but, let us confess the truth of him, he is a wonderful man—a wonderful man indeed; a vile empiric, however, in his practice, and therefore not to be tolerated by those who respect the good old rules of the medical profession."

Throughout Giovanni's whole acquaintance with Beatrice, he had occasionally, as we have said, been haunted by dark surmises as to her character; yet so thoroughly had she made herself felt by him as a simple, natural, most affectionate, and guileless creature, that the image now held up by Professor Baglioni looked as strange and incredible as if it were not in accordance with his own original conception. True, there were ugly recollections connected with his first glimpses of the beautiful girl; he could not quite forget the bouquet that withered in her grasp, and the insect that perished amid the sunny air, by no ostensible agency save the fragrance of her breath. These incidents, however, dissolving in the pure light of her character, had no longer the efficacy of facts, but were acknowledged as mistaken fantasies, by whatever testimony of the senses they might appear to be substantiated. There is something truer and more real than what we can see with the eyes and touch with the finger. On such better evidence had Giovanni founded his confidence in Beatrice, though rather by the necessary force of her high attributes than by any deep and generous faith on his part. But now his spirit was incapable of sustaining itself at the height to which the early enthusiasm of passion had exalted it; he fell down, grovelling among earthly doubts, and defiled therewith the pure whiteness of Beatrice's image. Not that he gave her up; he did but distrust. He resolved to institute some decisive test that should satisfy him, once for all, whether there were those dreadful peculiarities in her physical nature which could not be supposed to exist without some corresponding monstrosity of soul. His eyes, gazing down afar, might have deceived him as to the lizard, the insect, and the flowers; but if he could witness, at the distance of a few paces, the sudden blight of one fresh and healthful flower in Beatrice's hand, there would be room for no further question. With this idea he hastened to the florist's and purchased a bouquet that was still gemmed with the morning dewdrops.

It was now the customary hour of his daily interview with Beatrice. Before descending into the garden, Giovanni failed not to look at his figure in the mirror—a vanity to be expected in a beautiful young man, yet, as displaying itself at that troubled and feverish moment, the token of a certain shallowness of feeling and insincerity of character. He did gaze, however, and said to himself that his features had never before possessed so rich a grace, nor his eyes such vivacity, nor his cheeks so warm a hue of superabundant life.

"At least," thought he, "her poison has not yet insinuated itself into my system. I am no flower to perish in her grasp."

With that thought he turned his eyes on the bouquet, which he had never once laid aside from his hand. A thrill of indefinable horror shot through his frame on perceiving that those dewy flowers were already beginning to droop; they wore the aspect of things that had been fresh and lovely yesterday. Giovanni grew white as marble, and stood motionless before the mirror, staring at his own reflection there as at the likeness of something frightful. He remembered Baglioni's remark about the fragrance that seemed to pervade the chamber. It must have been the poison in his breath! Then he shuddered—shuddered at himself. Recovering from his stupor, he began to watch with curious eye a spider that was busily at work hanging its web from the antique cornice of the apartment, crossing and recrossing the artful system of interwoven lines—as vigorous and active a spider as ever dangled from an old ceiling. Giovanni bent towards the insect, and emitted a deep, long breath. The spider suddenly ceased its toil; the web vibrated with a tremor originating in the body of the small artisan. Again Giovanni sent forth a breath, deeper, longer, and imbued with a venomous feeling out of his heart: he knew not whether he were wicked, or only desperate.

The spider made a convulsive gripe with his limbs and hung dead across the window.

"Accursed! accursed!" muttered Giovanni, addressing himself. "Hast thou grown so poisonous that this deadly insect perishes by thy breath?"

At that moment a rich, sweet voice came floating up from the garden.

"Giovanni! Giovanni! It is past the hour! Why tarriest thou? Come down!"

"Yes," muttered Giovanni again. "She is the only being whom my breath may not slay! Would that it might!"

He rushed down, and in an instant was standing before the bright and loving eyes of Beatrice. A moment ago his wrath and despair had been so fierce that he could have desired nothing so much as to wither her by a glance; but with her actual presence there came influences which had too real an existence to be at once shaken off; recollections of the delicate and benign power of her feminine nature, which had so often enveloped him in a religious calm; recollections of many a holy and passionate outgush of her heart, when the pure fountain had been unsealed from its depths and made visible in its transparency to his mental eye; recollections which, had Giovanni known how to estimate them, would have assured him that all this ugly mystery was but an earthly illusion, and that, whatever mist of evil might seem to have gathered over her, the real Beatrice was a heavenly angel. Incapable as he was of such high faith, still her presence had not utterly lost its magic. Giovanni's rage was quelled into an aspect of sullen insensibility. Beatrice, with a quick spiritual sense, immediately felt that there was a gulf of blackness between them which neither he nor she could pass. They walked on together, sad and silent, and came thus to the marble fountain and to its pool of water on the ground, in the midst of which grew the shrub that bore gemlike blossoms. Giovanni was affrighted at the eager enjoyment—the appetite, as it were—with which he found himself inhaling the fragrance of the flowers.

"Beatrice," asked he, abruptly, "whence came this shrub?"

"My father created it," answered she, with simplicity.

"Created it! created it!" repeated Giovanni. "What mean you, Beatrice?"

"He is a man fearfully acquainted with the secrets of Nature," replied Beatrice; "and, at the hour when I first drew breath, this plant sprang from the soil, the offspring of his science, of his intellect, while I was but his earthly child. Approach it not!" continued she, observing with terror that Giovanni was drawing nearer to the shrub. "It has qualities that you little dream of. But I, dearest Giovanni,—I grew up and blossomed with the plant and was nourished with its breath. It was my sister, and I loved it with a human affection; for, alas!—hast thou not suspected it?—there was an awful doom."

Here Giovanni frowned so darkly upon her that Beatrice paused and trembled. But her faith in his tenderness reassured her, and made her blush that she had doubted for an instant.

"There was an awful doom," she continued, "the effect of my father's fatal love of science, which estranged me from all society of my kind. Until Heaven sent thee, dearest Giovanni, O, how lonely was thy poor Beatrice!"

"Was it a hard doom?" asked Giovanni, fixing his eyes upon her.

"Only of late have I known how hard it was," answered she, tenderly. "O, yes; but my heart was torpid, and therefore quiet."

Giovanni's rage broke forth from his sullen gloom like a lightning flash out of a dark cloud.

"Accursed one!" cried he, with venomous scorn and anger. "And, finding thy solitude wearisome, thou hast severed me likewise from all the warmth of life and enticed me into thy region of unspeakable horror!"

"Giovanni!" exclaimed Beatrice, turning her large bright eyes upon his face. The force of his words had not found its way into her mind; she was merely thunderstruck.

"Yes, poisonous thing!" repeated Giovanni, beside himself with passion. "Thou hast done it! Thou hast blasted me! Thou hast filled my veins with poison! Thou hast made me as hateful, as ugly, as loathsome and deadly a creature as thyself—a world's wonder of hideous monstrosity! Now, if our breath be happily as fatal to ourselves as to all others, let us join our lips in one kiss of unutterable hatred, and so die!"

"What has befallen me?" murmured Beatrice, with a low moan out of her heart. "Holy Virgin, pity me, a poor heart-broken child!"

"Thou,—dost thou pray?" cried Giovanni, still with the same fiendish scorn. "Thy very prayers, as they come from thy lips, taint the atmosphere with death. Yes, yes; let us pray! Let us to church and dip our fingers in the holy water at the portal! They that come after us will perish as by a pestilence! Let us sign crosses in the air! It will be scattering curses abroad in the likeness of holy symbols!"

"Giovanni," said Beatrice, calmly, for her grief was beyond passion, "why dost thou join thyself with me thus in those terrible words? I, it is true, am the horrible thing thou namest me. But thou,—what hast thou to do, save with one other shudder at my hideous misery to go forth out of the garden and mingle with thy race, and forget that there ever crawled on earth such a monster as poor Beatrice?"

"Dost thou pretend ignorance?" asked Giovanni, scowling upon her. "Behold! this power have I gained from the pure daughter of Rappaccini."

There was a swarm of summer insects flitting through the air in search of the food promised by the flower odors of the fatal garden. They circled round Giovanni's head, and were evidently attracted towards him by the same influence which had drawn them for an instant within the sphere of several of the shrubs. He sent forth a breath among them, and smiled bitterly at Beatrice as at least a score of the insects fell dead upon the ground.

"I see it! I see it!" shrieked Beatrice. "It is my father's fatal science! No, no, Giovanni; it was not I! Never! never! I dreamed only to love thee and be with thee a little time, and so to let thee pass away, leaving but thine image in mine heart; for, Giovanni, believe it, though my body be nourished with poison, my spirit is God's creature, and craves love as its daily food. But my father,—he has united us in this fearful sympathy. Yes; spurn me, tread upon me, kill me! O, what is death after such words as thine? But it was not I. Not for a world of bliss would I have done it."

Giovanni's passion had exhausted itself in its outburst from his lips. There now came across him a sense, mournful, and not without tenderness, of the intimate and peculiar relationship between Beatrice and himself. They stood, as it were, in an utter solitude, which would be made none the less solitary by the densest throng of human life. Ought not, then, the desert of humanity around them to press this insulated pair closer togther? If they should be cruel to one another, who was there to be kind to them? Besides, thought Giovanni, might there not still be a hope of his returning within the limits of ordinary nature, and leading Beatrice, the redeemed Beatrice, by the hand? O, weak, and selfish, and unworthy spirit, that could dream of an earthly union and earthly happiness as possible, after such deep love had been so bitterly wronged as was Beatrice's love by Giovanni's blighting words! No, no; there could be no such hope. She must pass heavily, with that broken heart, across the borders of Time—she must bathe her hurts in some fount of paradise, and forget her grief in the light of immortality, and *there* be well.

But Giovanni did not know it.

"Dear Beatrice," said he, approaching her, while she shrank away as always at his approach, but now with a different impulse, "dearest Beatrice, our fate is not yet so desperate. Behold! there is a medicine, potent, as a wise physician has assured me, and almost divine in its efficacy. It is composed of ingredients the most opposite to those by which thy awful father has brought this calamity upon thee and me. It is distilled of blessed herbs. Shall we not quaff it together, and thus be purified from evil?"

"Give it me!" said Beatrice, extending her hand to receive the little silver vial which Giovanni took from his bosom. She added, with a peculiar emphasis, "I will drink; but do thou await the result."

She put Baglioni's antidote to her lips; and, at the same moment, the figure of Rappaccini emerged from the portal and came slowly towards the marble fountain. As he drew near, the pale man of science seemed to gaze with a triumphant expression at the beautiful youth and maiden, as might an artist who should spend his life in achieving a picture or a group of statuary and finally be satisfied with his success. He paused; his bent form grew erect with conscious power; he spread out his hands over them in the attitude of a father imploring a blessing upon his children; but those were the same hands that had thrown poison into the stream of their lives. Giovanni trembled. Beatrice shuddered nervously, and pressed her hand upon her heart.

"My daughter," said Rappaccini, "thou art no longer lonely in the world. Pluck one of those precious gems from thy sister shrub and bid thy bridegroom wear it in his bosom. It will not harm him now. My science and the sympathy between thee and him have so wrought within his system that he now stands apart from common men, as thou dost, daughter of my pride and triumph, from ordinary women. Pass on, then, through the world, most dear to one another and dreadful to all besides!"

"My father," said Beatrice, feebly,—and still as she spoke she kept her hand upon her heart,—"wherefore didst thou inflict this miserable doom upon thy child?"

"Miserable!" exclaimed Rappaccini. "What mean you, foolish girl? Dost thou deem it misery to be endowed with marvellous gifts against which no power nor strength could avail an enemy—misery, to be able to quell the mightiest with a breath—misery, to be as terrible as thou art beautiful? Wouldst thou, then, have preferred the condition of a weak woman, exposed to all evil and capable of none?"

"I would fain have been loved, not feared," murmured Beatrice, sinking down upon the ground. "But now it matters not. I am going, father, where the evil which thou hast striven to mingle with my being will pass away like a dream—like the fragrance of these poisonous flowers, which will no longer taint my breath among the flowers of Eden. Farewell, Giovanni! Thy words of hatred are like lead within my heart; but they, too, will fall away as I ascend. O, was there not, from the first, more poison in thy nature than in mine?"

To Beatrice,—so radically had her earthly part been wrought upon by Rappaccini's skill,—as poison had been life, so the powerful antidote was death; and thus the poor victim of man's ingenuity and of thwarted nature, and of the fatality that attends all such efforts of perverted wisdom, perished there, at the feet of her father and Giovanni. Just at that moment Professor Pietro Baglioni looked forth from the window, and called loudly, in a tone of triumph mixed with horror, to the thunder-stricken man of science,—

"Rappaccini! Rappaccini! and is *this* the upshot of your experiment?"

EDGAR ALLAN POE AND SCIENCE FICTION

Whereas Hawthorne has been rarely, and then only in passing, mentioned in relation to science fiction, Poe has continually been called, both in America and Europe, the father of the genre. As early as 1858 in Spain, Poe was designated "the first to exploit the marvelous in the field of science." * Jules Verne's indebtedness to Poe was acknowledged by Verne himself and several nineteenth-century French critics. In 1905, "Science in Romance," an anonymous article in *The Saturday Review,* cited Poe (accusingly) as "probably the father" of that "pseudo-science" fiction "which still has its living practitioners in Dr. Conan Doyle and Mr. H. G. Wells." In 1909, Maurice Renard in "Du merveilleux scientifique et son action sur l'intelligence du progrès" (*Le Spectateur, Revue Critique*) called Poe the true founder of the marvelous-scientific romance and cited "The Facts in the Case of M. Valdemar" and "A Tale of the Ragged Mountains" as the prototypic stories. This view was echoed by Hubert Matthey in *Essai sur le merveilleux dans la littérature française depuis 1800* (1915), which claimed that Poe's "mixture of logic and narrative" made him "the creator of the marvelous-scientific romance" and offered "The Facts in the Case of M. Valdemar," "A Tale

* C. Alphonso Smith, *Edgar A. Poe, How to Know Him,* Indianapolis, 1923, p. 12.

of the Ragged Mountains," and "A Descent into the Maelström" as "the prototypes of a genre which had to develop after him." Peter Penzoldt in *The Supernatural in Fiction* (1952) asserts that before Verne "Poe alone wrote true science fiction." Olney Clarke, in an article in *The Georgia Review* (1958) entitled "Edgar Allan Poe—Science-Fiction Pioneer," states unequivocally that Poe was "the originator" of the genre and says why: "Poe's role in the creation of the modern science-fiction genre was of primary importance. He was the first writer of science-centered fiction to base his stories firmly on a rational kind of extrapolation, avoiding the supernatural." Or, as Sam Moskowitz asserted in *Explorers of the Infinite* (1963): "The full range of Poe's influence upon science fiction is incalculable, but his greatest contribution to the advancement of the genre was the precept that every departure from norm must be explained *scientifically*."

The argument for Poe's importance in the development of science fiction rests mainly on his concern with the details of physical process. Weight, volume, chemical composition, precise medical symptoms, temperature, mechanical details—reasonably accurate and coherent—do, it is quite true, constitute a large portion of such stories as "Hans Pfaall," "The Balloon-Hoax," and "The Facts in the Case of M. Valdemar." But thanks to the research of Walter B. Norris (*Nation*, 1910), Meredith Neill Posey (*Modern Language Notes*, 1930), Sidney E. Lind (*PMLA*, 1947), J. O. Bailey in *Pilgrims through Space and Time* (1947), Harold H. Scudder (*American Literature*, 1949), and Ronald S. Wilkinson (*American Literature*, 1960) we now know that Poe borrowed about eight pages of "Hans Pfaall" from "Joseph Atterley's" [George Tucker] *A Voyage to the Moon*, Sir John Herschel's *A Treatise on Astronomy*, and Abraham Rees's *Cyclopedia;* that over one-fourth of "The Balloon-Hoax" comes virtually unchanged from Monck Mason's *Account of the Late Aeronautical Expedition from London to Weilburg* and the anonymous (probably also Mason's) *Remarks on the Ellipsoidal*

Balloon, propelled by the Archimedean Screw, described as the New Aerial Machine; and that the details of mesmerism in "The Facts in the Case of M. Valdemar" and "A Tale of the Ragged Mountains" are transcribed from the Reverend Chauncey Hare Townshend's *Facts of Mesmerism.* Poe tends to present all this kind of detail not as acquired information but as his own original discovery. "Maelzel's Chess Player" illustrates his method and how it misleads anyone ignorant of his sources. This piece, which has very recently (1963) been called Poe's "brilliant exposé," an example of his "superlatively logical mind" operating "with nothing to go on except the manner in which the game was conducted," was actually lifted outright from a readily available publication.*

Perhaps it is no important qualification of the seriousness of Poe's interest in physical process that his facts and figures are unacknowledged paraphrases or quotations from popularized scientific writings. After all, one function of science fiction has been traditionally, particularly since Verne, to offer sugar-coated popularizations of current scientific theory and process. If a reader in 1844 discovers that "The Balloon-Hoax" is after all not so far-fetched, has he not gotten Poe's message? Perhaps so, but if so, that is the problem with much of Poe's science fiction and the science fiction written in what might be called the Poe tradition.

One question which must be asked of those who champion Poe as the father of science fiction, bequeathing to his heirs the great values overlooked by his progenitors, is this: Does the ultimate meaning of Poe's science fiction mislead one as to the ultimate possibilities of the form? Rarely in Poe's science fiction does one find science itself as a subject and nowhere does one find any kind of true scientist as a consequential figure. Poe tends to

* See W. K. Wimsatt, Jr., "Poe and the Chess Automaton," *American Literature*, 1939, for an account of Poe's theft and his effort to cover his tracks by disparaging his source.

present technological details about an aerial voyage across the Atlantic or to the moon with little attention to the significance of technology; enumeration of mesmeric passes with little evaluation of scientific as opposed, say, to dramatic psychology; measurement itself rather than the measurement of measurement. Now of course Poe sometimes resisted this tendency, and when we look at "Mesmeric Revelation," *Eureka*, and "Mellonta Tauta" we shall see one reason why Poe did not take existing science seriously: he has an alternative kind of science to offer. Furthermore, much—probably most—other science fiction is even less seriously concerned with science. And there are those—such as Maxim Gorki, Hugo Gernsback, the 1940 Soviet conference on science fiction, and the sympathetic nineteenth-century reviewers of Verne—who argue that the chief value of science fiction is to make available with a sugar-coating of drama some scientific facts and figures. But if science fiction is merely a popularizer of science rather than the literature which, growing with science, evaluates it and relates it meaningfully to the rest of existence, it is hardly worth serious attention. The anonymous author of that 1905 article "Science in Romance" may then have the wisest words about both what he calls "pseudo-science" fiction and its probable "father" Poe:

> On the whole it is better when we want science to read science; and when we want fiction not to read a composite thing in which the science diverts us from the fiction, and the fiction is not more imaginary than the pseudo-science. The scientific romance is therefore crude and we do not think it has much of a future. We hope not.

At this point the other line maintained by partisans of Poe's contribution to science fiction might interpose. Poe is hailed by them as the artistic welder of gothicism to science, creator not only of both the tale of terror and the tale of ratiocination but of their fusion as well. Poe's short fiction is then acclaimed in terms of Poe's own arguments about the short story, expressed best in the famous passage from his review of Hawthorne's *Twice-Told Tales*:

> A skilful literary artist has constructed a tale. If wise, he has not fashioned his thoughts to accommodate his incidents; but having conceived, with deliberate care, a certain unique or single *effect* to be wrought out, he then invents such incidents—he then combines such events as may best aid him in establishing this preconceived effect. If his very initial sentence tend not to the outbringing of this effect, then he has failed in his first step. In the whole composition there should be no word written, of which the tendency, direct or indirect, is not to the one preestablished design.

This is the line that brings Hawthorne and Poe into direct confrontation. The key word in Poe's argument, as his italics indicate, is "effect." The argument that fiction should be evaluated for its effectiveness, its success in achieving the objective correlative which the author desires, slides around the question as to what it should effect. To say that the tale of terror is "effective" may not necessarily, in the long run, be to praise it.

Unlike Hawthorne's, Poe's science fiction emotionally exploits or, alternatively, in a sense scientifically explores strange physical phenomena in and of themselves. Both authors write tales abounding in gothic apparatus and strange emotional effects, but no one would call Hawthorne a purveyor of the tale of terror; for Hawthorne's effects are incidental to a much larger design, whereas Poe's effects are either ends in themselves or means to involve the reader in explorations of physical phenomena *per se*. The two categories of Poe's science fiction are distinguished in Moskowitz's *Explorers of the Infinite* in these terms:

> Basically, Poe's science fiction stories can be divided into two major categories. The first, including such tales as *Ms. Found in a Bottle, A Descent into the Mael-*

> *ström*, and *A Tale of the Ragged Mountains*, comprises artistic science fiction in which the mood or effect is primary and the scientific rationality serves merely to strengthen the aesthetic aspect.
>
> In the other group, examples of which are *Mellonta Tauta, Hans Phaal—A Tale*, and *The Thousand-and-Second Tale of Scheherazade*, the idea was paramount and the style was modulated to provide an atmospheric background which would remain unobtrusive, and not take the spotlight from the scientific concept.

These terms describe what is missing from both the tale contrived like an electric coil to induce particular emotions in the reader and the tale contrived as a wheelbarrow to bring to the reader some scientific notion or knickknack. In the first, the science is merely a device; in the other, the fiction is merely a device. Each uses either the science or the fiction for ulterior purposes; neither brings the science and the fiction into a meaningful unity.

Poe, then, may be the father not of science fiction but rather of what is so often associated with the term science fiction—fiction which popularizes science for boys and girls of all ages while giving them the creeps. But perhaps we should not let Poe mislead us with either his rhetorically directed theories about the short story or his extended quibbles about scientific accuracy in fiction (as in the statement affixed to "The Balloon-Hoax"). By ignoring both, one may be able to perceive that the tale of terror can be more than a mere tale of terror and the science in the tales can be more than mere pseudo-science.

"The Facts in the Case of M. Valdemar" exemplifies perfectly Poe's science-fiction tale of terror. Of all Poe's stories, this one seems to fit his formula most closely; every sentence and every detail seem contrived to move the reader toward the horrible effect which reaches its climax in the last sentence. Yet surely anyone who finds "The Facts in the Case of M. Valdemar" of enduring value does not do so merely because the story horrifies him or merely because he admires Poe for making a story which can horrify him. Would anyone who wants to be as horrified as possible turn to fiction rather than to the countless horrors of his own external and internal worlds? And if a horror story merely offers a safe escape from the terrors of the rest of the world, indulgence in it may be mere cowardice. Any enduring value in a story like "The Facts in the Case of M. Valdemar" comes not from the horror itself, but from something which the story dramatizes in the horror or with the horror. It comes not from the demonstration that man can make physical horror—this we already know far too well—but that man can make order even out of both physical and psychological horror. The reader's experience is not that of the student who "swooned" or the nurses who "immediately left the chamber, and could not be induced to return" but of the mind that stays. "The Facts in the Case" is effective then not so much as a tale of physical terror but as a tale about the terror of the physical. The physical details of M. Valdemar's condition and the mesmeric science which brings them about may then turn out to be as much subject of the fiction as devices to subject us to the fiction. To the extent that this is true, "The Facts in the Case of M. Valdemar" falls into the other category of Poe's science fiction, science fiction as physical speculation.

Science fiction as a form of physical (as distinguished from utopian, moral, psychological, or religious) speculation is what Poe may have provided with significant new dimensions, though by no means giving it birth. This is not a fiction which seeks to popularize scientific ideas but a fiction which seeks to formulate ideas that could not be formulated in any other way, certainly in no "non-fictional" way. It is a fiction concerned not with actual physical details but with hypothetical possibilities which may have physical existence or which may only be represented metaphorically as physical things. This is the fiction which merges indistinguishably into the new scientific hypothesis, and its value must be determined in the same ways—by pragmatic tests and proof of its internal design. One might say that insofar as it can be pragmatically tested as true it is scientifically sound, and insofar as its internal design is true it is mathematically sound. Poe's obscure statement of a theory of this kind of imaginative fiction may be far more valuable than his well-known theories about the short story. The statement appears in the one work which seeks to practice the theory, *Eureka—A Prose Poem*, and, in a somewhat more dramatized version, in "Mellonta Tauta," published a few months later, in the year of Poe's death.

According to the narrator of "Mellonta Tauta" (and of a mysterious document presented in *Eureka*) the scientists of 2848 have scorn for what they call the only two paths of thought open to "ancient" times: the deductive (from Aries Tottle) and the inductive (or Baconian, from Hog). These modern theorists operate by the only way to great advances in knowledge—intuitive leaps; the great leap of imagination takes place, and the product of this leap is then made as self-consistent as possible. This process—which the narrator offers as the one fruitful path of scientific speculation—perfectly describes an ideal form of science fiction as physical speculation. It also defines science as a kind of fiction. When Hawthorne dramatizes science as a kind of fiction he is principally dramatizing its dangers; when Poe dramatizes his kind of science as a kind of fiction, he is principally dramatizing its glorious potential. For Poe science and fiction could by coming together approach what he saw as the ultimate kind of meaningfulness, described in these terms in *Eureka*:

> . . . *the Universe* . . . in the supremeness of its symmetry, is but the most sublime of poems. Now symmetry and consistency are convertible terms:—thus Poetry and Truth are one. A thing is consistent in the ratio of its truth—true in the ratio of its consistency. *A perfect consistency, I repeat, can be nothing but an absolute truth.* We may take it for granted, then, that Man can-

> not long or widely err, if he suffer himself to be guided by his poetical, which I have maintained to be his truthful, in being his symmetrical, instinct. He must have a care, however, lest, in pursuing too heedlessly the superficial symmetry of forms and motions, he leave out of sight the really essential symmetry of the principles which determine and control them.

The great intuitive speculation made self-consistent is thus for Poe the creation which nullifies all distinctions between kinds of verbal constructs.

Whether Poe ever achieved his ideal of a great intuitive speculation made self-consistent is certainly dubious. Probably the closest he came is *Eureka,* pointedly entitled *A Prose Poem* and accurately described by Charles O'Donnell * as "an abstract fiction." Attempts have been made to demonstrate that *Eureka* really constitutes a great scientific speculation which anticipates modern conceptions of the universe, but they demonstrate little more than an ignorance of modern physics (and of Poe's sources).† The value of *Eureka* does not reside in its scientific accuracy but in the fascination and internal consistency of its metaphors. That is, one reads *Eureka* as one reads, say, Isaac Asimov's "The Last Question," which describes the universe's passing by entropy through inconceivable periods of time into the form of a single computer which then issues the command, "Let there be light."

Poe's marriage of science and fiction may be viewed from another vantage point. Here *Eureka,* "Mesmeric Revelation," and "The Fall of the House of Usher" appear as a continuum. At one end is *Eureka,* a straight "non-fictional" speculation; in the middle is "Mesmeric Revelation," in which one character mesmerizes another, who then gives forth a straight "non-fictional"

* In "From Earth to Ether: Poe's Flight into Space," *PMLA,* 1962.

† See Clayton Hoagland, "The Universe of *Eureka:* A Comparison of the Theories of Eddington and Poe," *Southern Literary Messenger,* 1939, and George Nordstedt, "Poe and Einstein," *Open Court,* 1930.

speculation which has been called a rough draft of *Eureka* (*cf.* Hawthorne's earlier notebook entry, "Questions as to . . . Mysteries of Nature, to be asked of a mesmerized person"); and at the other end is "The Fall of the House of Usher," which dramatizes part of the speculation engaged in by the other two works. *Eureka* and "Mesmeric Revelation" speculate that inanimate matter may be sentient; "The Fall of the House of Usher" presents a universe in which sentient inanimate matter plays a major role in the dramatic action.* The three forms may be called pure speculation, pure speculation in a dramatic frame, and dramatized speculation. As the speculation takes these three forms each form makes it less a matter of "science" and more a matter of "fiction." Perhaps it is no coincidence that hardly anybody reads *Eureka,* few read "Mesmeric Revelation," and everybody reads "The Fall of the House of Usher" (but hardly anybody reads it as scientific speculation).

A pure scientific speculation can be incredible, new and credible, or old and credible. That is, one can reject it as unbelievable, accept it as believable, or dismiss it as already believed. Confronted with *Eureka,* one may say "Hogwash!" or "Eureka!" or "Ho hum." And if *Eureka's* speculations were ever to be widely accepted, that would be the historical order of the three reactions. That is, paradoxically, *Eureka* would become less interesting if read as commonly accepted science rather than imaginative fiction. For science, unlike fiction, exists to be superseded. So one returns to Hawthorne's insight into the fiction which, by tying itself to matter, ties itself to the moment and momentary destructibility. It is no wonder then that the circulation of the major science-fiction magazines was suddenly cut in half by the first Sputnik.

Poe dramatizes the paradox-laden temporality and provincialism of our attitudes toward science in "The Thousand-and-

* See Arthur E. Robinson, "Order and Sentience in 'The Fall of the House of Usher,'" *PMLA,* 1961.

Second Tale of Scheherazade," in which the actual creations of technology and the actual discoveries of science seem to the king incredibly fantastic (so much more fantastic than Scheherazade's first thousand and one tales that he has her throttled). This is the kind of insight that Hawthorne had dealt with two years earlier in "The Birthmark" in the brief passage which dramatizes some of the wildest fantasies of the late eighteenth century as the technological commonplaces of the mid-nineteenth century. Besides the lighthearted jocularity of Poe's work and the wild seriousness of Hawthorne's, perhaps the chief difference between them is that Hawthorne subordinates this kind of insight into a highly complex moral allegory whereas Poe is able to sum up his nine-thousand-word demonstration in its epigraph: "Truth is stranger than fiction." This and the fact that Hawthorne's stories need and get volumes of explication, Poe's stories practically none, point to the most essential difference between Hawthorne's science fiction and Poe's.

Hawthorne's science fiction at its best is nothing if not complete. Poe's science fiction—experimental, exploratory, pointed, tremendously incomplete even when highly finished, turning simply toward the physical world or the emotions of the reader and away from complexity—presents a series of plane surfaces which call for little explication because they infold few meanings. It can be used and used well by many kinds of subsequent writers, who may follow out the varied experiments, appropriate the new materials, follow the points into areas where they become less pointed, move in the dimensions which these plane surfaces suggest lie beyond themselves.

EDGAR ALLAN POE

A Tale of the Ragged Mountains *

During the fall of the year 1827, while residing near Charlottesville, Virginia, I casually made the acquaintance of Mr. Augustus Bedloe. This young gentleman was remarkable in every respect, and excited in me a profound interest and curiosity. I found it impossible to comprehend him either in his moral or his physical relations. Of his family I could obtain no satisfactory account. Whence he came, I never ascertained. Even about his age—although I call him a young gentleman—there was something which perplexed me in no little degree. He certainly *seemed* young—and he made a point of speaking about his youth—yet there were moments when I should have had little trouble in imagining him a hundred years of age. But in no regard was he more peculiar than in his personal appearance. He was singularly tall and thin. He stooped much. His limbs were exceedingly long and emaciated. His forehead was broad and low. His complexion was absolutely bloodless. His mouth was large and flexible, and his teeth were more wildly uneven, although sound, than I had ever before seen teeth in a human head. The expression of his smile, however, was by no means unpleasing, as might be supposed; but it had no variation whatever. It was one of profound melancholy—of a phaseless and unceasing gloom. His eyes were abnormally large, and round like those of a cat. The pupils, too, upon any accession or diminution of light, underwent contraction or dilation, just such as is observed in the feline tribe. In

* *Godey's Lady's Book,* April 1844.

moments of excitement the orbs grew bright to a degree almost inconceivable; seeming to emit luminous rays, not of a reflected, but of an intrinsic lustre, as does a candle or the sun; yet their ordinary condition was so totally vapid, filmy and dull, as to convey the idea of the eyes of a long-interred corpse.

These peculiarities of person appeared to cause him much annoyance, and he was continually alluding to them in a sort of half explanatory, half apologetic strain, which, when I first heard it, impressed me very painfully. I soon, however, grew accustomed to it, and my uneasiness wore off. It seemed to be his design rather to insinuate than directly to assert that, physically, he had not always been what he was—that a long series of neuralgic attacks had reduced him from a condition of more than usual personal beauty, to that which I saw. For many years past he had been attended by a physician, named Templeton—an old gentleman, perhaps seventy years of age—whom he had first encountered at Saratoga, and from whose attention, while there, he either received, or fancied that he received, great benefit. The result was that Bedloe, who was wealthy, had made an arrangement with Doctor Templeton, by which the latter, in consideration of a liberal annual allowance, had consented to devote his time and medical experience exclusively to the care of the invalid.

Doctor Templeton had been a traveller in his younger days, and, at Paris, had become a convert, in great measure, to the doctrines of Mesmer. It was altogether by means of magnetic remedies that he had succeeded in alleviating the acute pains of his patient; and this success had very naturally inspired the latter with a certain degree of confidence in the opinions from which the remedies had been educed. The Doctor, however, like all enthusiasts, had struggled hard to make a thorough convert of his pupil, and finally so far gained his point as to induce the sufferer to submit to numerous experiments.—By a frequent repetition of these, a result had arisen, which of late days has become so common as to attract little or no attention, but which, at the period of which I write, had very rarely been known in America. I mean to say, that between Doctor Templeton and Bedloe there had grown up, little by little, a very distinct and strongly marked *rapport,* or magnetic relation. I am not prepared to assert, however, that this *rapport* extended beyond the limits of the simple sleep-producing power; but this power itself had attained great intensity. At the first attempt to induce the magnetic somnolency, the mesmerist entirely failed. In the fifth or sixth he succeeded very partially, and after long continued effort. Only at the twelfth was the triumph complete. After this the will of the patient succumbed rapidly to that of the physician, so that, when I first became acquainted with the two, sleep was brought about almost instantaneously, by the mere volition of the operator, even when the invalid was unaware of his presence. It is only now, in the year 1845, when similar miracles are witnessed daily by thousands, that I dare venture to record this apparent impossibility as a matter of serious fact.

The temperament of Bedloe was, in the highest degree, sensitive, excitable, enthusiastic. His imagination was singularly vigorous and creative; and no doubt it derived additional force from the habitual use of morphine, which he swallowed in great quantity, and without which he would have found it impossible to exist. It was his practice to take a very large dose of it immediately after breakfast, each morning—or rather immediately after a cup of strong coffee, for he ate nothing in the forenoon—and then set forth alone, or attended only by a dog, upon a long ramble among the chain of wild and dreary hills that lie westward and southward of Charlottesville, and are there dignified by the title of the Ragged Mountains.

Upon a dim, warm, misty day, towards the close of November, and during the strange *interregnum* of the seasons which in America is termed the Indian Summer Mr. Bedloe departed, as usual, for the hills. The day passed, and still he did not return.

About eight o'clock at night, having become seriously alarmed at his protracted absence, we were about setting out in search of him, when he unexpectedly made his appearance, in health no worse than usual, and in rather more than ordinary spirits. The account which he gave of his expedition, and of the events which had detained him, was a singular one indeed.

"You will remember," said he, "that it was about nine in the morning when I left Charlottesville. I bent my steps immediately to the mountains, and, about ten, entered a gorge which was entirely new to me. I followed the windings of this pass with much interest.—The scenery which presented itself on all sides, although scarcely entitled to be called grand, had about it an indescribable, and to me, a delicious aspect of dreary desolation.

The solitude seemed absolutely virgin. I could not help believing that the green sods and the gray rocks upon which I trod, had been trodden never before by the foot of a human being. So entirely secluded, and in fact inaccessible, except through a series of accidents, is the entrance of the ravine, that it is by no means impossible that I was indeed the first adventurer—the very first and sole adventurer who had ever penetrated its recesses.

"The thick and peculiar mist, or smoke, which distinguishes the Indian Summer, and which now hung heavily over all objects, served, no doubt, to deepen the vague impressions which these objects created. So dense was this pleasant fog, that I could at no time see more than a dozen yards of the path before me. This path was excessively sinuous, and as the sun could not be seen, I soon lost all idea of the direction in which I journeyed. In the meantime the morphine had its customary effect—that of enduing all the external world with an intensity of interest. In the quivering of a leaf—in the hue of a blade of grass—in the shape of a trefoil—in the humming of a bee—in the gleaming of a dew-drop—in the breathing of the wind—in the faint odors that came from the forest—there came a whole universe of suggestion—a gay and motly train of rhapsodical and immethodical thought.

"Busied in this, I walked on for several hours, during which the mist deepened around me to so great an extent, that at length I was reduced to an absolute groping of the way. And now an indescribable uneasiness possessed me—a species of nervous hesitation and tremor.—I feared to tread, lest I should be precipitated into some abyss. I remembered, too, strange stories told about these Ragged Hills, and of the uncouth and fierce races of men who tenanted their groves and caverns. A thousand vague fancies oppressed and disconcerted me—fancies the more distressing because vague. Very suddenly my attention was arrested by the loud beating of a drum.

"My amazement was, of course, extreme. A drum in these hills was a thing unknown. I could not have been more surprised at the sound of the trump of the Archangel. But a new and still more astounding source of interest and perplexity arose. There came a wild rattling or jingling sound, as if of a bunch of large keys—and upon the instant a dusky-visaged and half-naked man rushed past me with a shriek. He came so close to my person that I felt his hot breath upon my face. He bore in one hand an instrument composed of an assemblage of steel rings, and shook them vigorously as he ran. Scarcely had he disappeared in the mist, before, panting after him, with open mouth and glaring eyes, there darted a huge beast. I could not be mistaken in its character. It was a hyena.

"The sight of this monster rather relieved than heightened my terrors—for I now made sure that I dreamed, and endeavored to arouse myself to waking consciousness. I stepped boldly and briskly forward. I rubbed my eyes. I called aloud. I pinched my limbs. A small spring of water presented itself to my view, and here, stooping, I bathed my hands and my head and neck. This seemed to dissipate the equivocal sensations which had hitherto annoyed me. I arose, as I thought, a new man, and proceeded steadily and complacently on my unknown way.

"At length, quite overcome by exertion, and by a certain oppressive closeness of the atmosphere, I seated myself beneath a tree. Presently there came a feeble gleam of sunshine, and the shadow of the leaves of the tree fell faintly but definitely upon the grass. At this shadow I gazed wonderingly for many minutes. Its character stupified me with astonishment. I looked upward. The tree was a palm.

"I now arose hurriedly, and in a state of fearful agitation—for the fancy that I dreamed would serve me no longer. I saw—I felt that I had perfect command of my senses—and these senses now brought to my soul a world of novel and singular sensation. The heat became all at once intolerable. A strange odor loaded the breeze.—A low continuous murmur, like that arising from a full, but gently-flowing river, came to my ears, intermingled with the peculiar hum of multitudinous human voices.

"While I listened in an extremity of astonishment which I need not attempt to describe, a strong and brief gust of wind bore off the incumbent fog as if by the wand of an enchanter.

"I found myself at the foot of a high mountain, and looking down into a vast plain, through which wound a majestic river. On the margin of this river stood an Eastern-looking city, such as we read of in the Arabian Tales, but of a character even more singular than any there described. From my position, which was far above the level of the town, I could perceive its every nook and corner, as if delineated on a map. The streets seemed innumerable, and crossed each other irregularly in all directions, but were rather long winding alleys than streets, and absolutely swarmed with inhabitants. The houses were wildly picturesque. On every hand was a wilderness of balconies, of verandahs, of minarets, of shrines, and fantastically carved oriels. Bazaars abounded; and in these were displayed rich wares in infinite variety and profusion—silks, muslins, the most dazzling cutlery, the most magnificent jewels and gems. Besides these things, were seen, on all sides, banners and palanquins, litters with stately dames close veiled, elephants gorgeously caparisoned, idols grotesquely hewn, drums, banners and gongs, spears, silver and gilded maces. And amid the crowd, and the clamor, and the general intricacy and confusion—amid the million of black and yellow men, turbaned and robed, and of flowing beard, there roamed a countless multitude of holy filleted bulls, while vast legions of the filthy but sacred ape clambered, chattering and shrieking, about the cornices of the mosques, or clung to the minarets and oriels. From the swarming streets to the banks of the river, there descended innumerable flights of steps leading to bathing places, while the river itself seemed to force a passage with difficulty through the vast fleets of deeply-burthened ships that far and wide encumbered its surface. Beyond the limits of the city arose, in frequent majestic groups, the palm and the cocoa, with other gigantic and weird trees of vast age; and here and there might be seen a field of rice, the thatched hut of a peasant, a tank, a stray temple, a gypsy camp, or a solitary graceful maiden taking her way, with a pitcher upon her head, to the banks of the magnificent river.

"You will say now, of course, that I dreamed; but not so. What I saw—what I heard—what I felt—what I thought—had about it nothing of the unmistakeable idiosyncrasy of the dream. All was rigorously self-consistent. At first, doubting that I was really awake, I entered into a series of tests, which soon convinced me that I really was. Now, when one dreams, and, in the dream, suspects that he dreams, the suspicion *never fails to confirm itself*, and the sleeper is almost immediately aroused.—Thus Novalis errs not in saying that 'we are near waking when we dream that we dream.' Had the vision occurred to me as I describe it, without my suspecting it as a dream, then a dream it might absolutely have been, but, occurring as it did, and suspected and tested as it was, I am forced to class it among other phenomena."

"In this I am not sure that you are wrong," observed Dr. Templeton, "but proceed. You arose and descended into the city."

"I arose," continued Bedloe, regarding the Doctor with an air of profound astonishment, "I arose, as you say, and descended into the city. On my way, I fell in with an immense populace, crowding, through every avenue, all in the same direction, and exhibiting in every action the wildest excitement. Very suddenly, and by some inconceivable impulse, I became intensely imbued with personal interest in what was going on. I seemed to feel that I had an important part to play, without exactly understanding what it was. Against the crowd which environed me, however, I experienced a deep sentiment of animosity. I shrank from amid them, and, swiftly, by a circuitous path, reached and entered the city. Here all was the wildest tumult and contention. A small party of men, clad in garments half-Indian, half-European, and officered by gentlemen in a uniform partly British, were engaged, at great odds, with the swarming rabble of the alleys. I joined the weaker party, arming myself with the weapons of a fallen officer, and fighting I knew not whom with the nervous ferocity of despair. We were soon overpowered by numbers, and driven to seek refuge in a species of kiosk. Here we barricaded ourselves, and, for the present, were secure. From a loop-hole near the summit of the kiosk, I perceived a vast crowd, in furious agitation, surrounding and assaulting a gay palace that overhung the river. Presently, from an upper window of this palace, there descended an effeminate-looking person, by means of a string made of the turbans of his attendants. A boat was at hand, in which he escaped to the opposite bank of the river.

"And now a new object took possession of my soul. I spoke a few hurried but energetic words to my companions, and, having succeeded in gaining over a few of them to my purpose, made a frantic sally from the kiosk. We rushed amid the crowd that surrounded it. They retreated, at first, before us. They rallied, fought madly, and retreated again. In the mean time we were borne far from the kiosk, and became bewildered and entangled among the narrow streets of tall overhanging houses, into the recesses of which the sun had never been able to shine.

The rabble pressed impetuously upon us, harassing us with their spears, and overwhelming us with flights of arrows. These latter were very remarkable, and resembled in some respects the writhing creese of the Malay. They were made to imitate the body of a creeping serpent, and were long and black, with a poisoned barb. One of them struck me upon the right temple. I reeled and fell. An instantaneous and dreadful sickness seized me. I struggled—I gasped—I died."

"You will hardly persist *now*," said I, smiling, "that the whole of your adventure was not a dream. You are not prepared to maintain that you are dead?"

When I said these words, I of course expected some lively sally from Bedloe in reply; but, to my astonishment, he hesitated, trembled, became fearfully pallid, and remained silent. I looked towards Templeton. He sat erect and rigid in his chair—his teeth chattered, and his eyes were starting from their sockets. "Proceed!" he at length said hoarsely to Bedloe.

"For many minutes," continued the latter, "my sole sentiment—my sole feeling—was that of darkness and nonentity, with the consciousness of death. At length, there seemed to pass a violent and sudden shock through my soul, as if of electricity. With it came the sense of elasticity and of light. This latter I felt—not saw. In an instant I seemed to rise from the ground. But I had no bodily, no visible, audible, or palpable presence. The crowd had departed. The tumult had ceased. The city was in comparative repose. Beneath me lay my corpse, with the arrow in my temple, the whole head greatly swollen and disfigured. But all these things I felt—not saw. I took interest in nothing. Even the corpse seemed a matter in which I had no concern. Volition I had none, but appeared to be impelled into motion, and flitted buoyantly out of the city, retracing the circuitous path by which I had entered it. When I had attained that point of the ravine in the mountains, at which I had encountered the hyena, I again experienced a shock as of a galvanic battery; the sense of weight, of volition, of substance, returned. I became my original self, and bent my steps eagerly homewards—but the past had not lost the vividness of the real—and not now, even for an instant, can I compel my understanding to regard it as a dream."

"Nor was it," said Templeton, with an air of deep solemnity, "yet it would be difficult to say how otherwise it should be termed. Let us suppose only, that the soul of the man of to-day is upon the verge of some stupendous psychal discoveries. Let us content ourselves with this supposition. For the rest I have some explanation to make. Here is a water-colour drawing, which I should have shown you before, but which an unaccountable sentiment of horror has hitherto prevented me from showing."

We looked at the picture which he presented. I saw nothing in it of an extraordinary character; but its effect upon Bedloe was prodigious. He nearly fainted as he gazed. And yet it was but a miniature portrait—a miraculously accurate one, to be sure—of his own very remarkable features. At least this was my thought as I regarded it.

"You will perceive," said Templeton, "the date of this picture—it is here, scarcely visible, in this corner—1780. In this year was the portrait taken. It is the likeness of a dead friend—a Mr. Oldeb—to whom I became much attached at Calcutta, during the administration of Warren Hastings. I was then only twenty years old.—When I first saw you, Mr. Bedloe, at Saratoga, it was the miraculous similarity which existed between yourself and the painting, which induced me to accost you, to seek your friendship, and to bring about those arrangements which resulted in my becoming your constant companion. In accomplishing this point, I was urged partly, and perhaps principally, by a regretful memory of the deceased, but also, in part, by an uneasy, and not altogether horrorless curiosity respecting yourself.

"In your detail of the vision which presented itself to you amid the hills, you have described, with the minutest accuracy, the Indian city of Benares, upon the Holy River. The riots, the combats, the massacre, were the actual events of the insurrection of Cheyte Sing, which took place in 1780, when Hastings was put in imminent peril of his life. The man escaping by the string of turbans, was Cheyte Sing himself. The party in the kiosk were sepoys and British officers, headed by Hastings. Of this party I was one, and did all I could to prevent the rash and fatal sally of the officer who fell, in the crowded alleys, by the poisoned arrow of a Bengalee. That officer was my dearest friend. It was Oldeb. You will perceive by these manuscripts," (here the speaker produced a note-book in which several pages appeared to have been freshly written) "that at the very period in which you fancied these things amid the hills, I was engaged in detailing them upon paper here at home."

In about a week after this conversation, the following paragraphs appeared in a Charlottesville paper.

"We have the painful duty of announcing the death of Mr. AUGUSTUS BEDLO, a gentleman whose amiable manners and many virtues have long endeared him to the citizens of Charlottesville.

"Mr. B., for some years past, has been subject to neuralgia, which has often threatened to terminate fatally, but this can be regarded only as the mediate cause of his decease. The proximate cause was one of especial singularity. In an excursion to the Ragged Mountains, a few days since, a slight cold and fever were contracted, attended with great determination of blood to the head. To relieve this, Dr. Templeton resorted to topical bleeding. Leeches were applied to the temples. In a fearfully brief period the patient died, when it appeared that, in the jar containing the leeches, had been introduced, by accident, one of the venomous vermicular sangsues which are now and then found in the neighboring ponds. This creature fastened itself upon a small artery in the right temple. Its close resemblance to the medicinal leech caused the mistake to be overlooked until too late.

"N.B. The poisonous sangsue of Charlottesville may always be distinguished from the medicinal leech by its blackness, and especially by its writhing or vermicular motions, which very nearly resemble those of a snake."

I was speaking with the editor of the paper in question, upon the topic of this remarkable accident, when it occurred to me to ask how it happened that the name of the deceased had been given as Bedlo.

"I presume," said I, "you have authority for this spelling, but I have always supposed the name to be written with an *e* at the end."

"Authority?—no," he replied. "It is a mere typographical error. The name is Bedlo with an *e*, all the world over, and I never knew it to be spelt otherwise in my life."

"Then," said I mutteringly, as I turned upon my heel, "then indeed has it come to pass that one truth is stranger than any fiction—for Bedlo, without the *e*, what is it but Oldeb conversed? And this man tells me it is a typographical error."

EDGAR ALLAN POE

The Facts in the Case of M. Valdemar *

Of course I shall not pretend to consider it any matter for wonder, that the extraordinary case of M. Valdemar has excited discussion. It would have been a miracle had it not—especially under the circumstances. Through the desire of all parties concerned, to keep the affair from the public, at least for the present, or until we had farther opportunities for investigation—through our endeavors to effect this—a garbled or exaggerated account made its way into society, and became the source of many unpleasant misrepresentations, and, very naturally, of a great deal of disbelief.

It is now rendered necessary that I give the *facts*—as far as I comprehend them myself. They are, succinctly, these:

My attention, for the last three years, had been repeatedly drawn to the subject of Mesmerism; and, about nine months ago, it occurred to me, quite suddenly, that in the series of experiments made hitherto, there had been a very remarkable and most unaccountable omission:—no person had as yet been mesmerized *in articulo mortis*. It remained to be seen, first, whether, in such condition, there existed in the patient any susceptibility to the magnetic influence; secondly, whether, if any existed, it was impaired or increased by the condition; thirdly, to what extent, or for how long a period, the encroachments of Death might be arrested by the process. There were other points to be ascertained, but these most excited my curiosity—the last in

* *American Whig Review*, December 1845.

especial, from the immensely important character of its consequences.

In looking around me for some subject by whose means I might test these particulars, I was brought to think of my friend, M. Ernest Valdemar, the well-known compiler of the "Bibliotheca Forensica," and author (under the *nom de plume* of Issachar Marx) of the Polish versions of "Wallenstein" and "Gargantua." M. Valdemar, who has resided principally at Harlaem, N. Y., since the year 1839, is (or was) particularly noticeable for the extreme spareness of his person—his lower limbs much resembling those of John Randolph; and, also, for the whiteness of his whiskers, in violent contrast to the blackness of his hair—the latter, in consequence, being very generally mistaken for a wig. His temperament was markedly nervous, and rendered him a good subject for mesmeric experiment. On two or three occasions I had put him to sleep with little difficulty, but was disappointed in other results which his peculiar constitution had naturally led me to anticipate. His will was at no period positively, or thoroughly, under my control, and in regard to *clairvoyance,* I could accomplish with him nothing to be relied upon. I always attributed my failure at these points to the disordered state of his health. For some months previous to my becoming acquainted with him, his physicians had declared him in a confirmed phthisis. It was his custom, indeed, to speak calmly of his approaching dissolution, as of a matter neither to be avoided nor regretted.

When the ideas to which I have alluded first occurred to me, it was of course very natural that I should think of M. Valdemar. I knew the steady philosophy of the man too well to apprehend any scruples from *him;* and he had no relatives in America who would be likely to interfere. I spoke to him frankly upon the subject; and, to my surprise, his interest seemed vividly excited. I say to my surprise; for, although he had always yielded his person freely to my experiments, he had never before given me any tokens of sympathy with what I did. His disease was of that character which would admit of exact calculation in respect to the epoch of its termination in death; and it was finally arranged between us that he would send for me about twenty-four hours before the period announced by his physicians as that of his decease.

It is now rather more than seven months since I received, from M. Valdemar himself, the subjoined note:

My dear P——,

You may as well come *now*. D—— and F—— are agreed that I cannot hold out beyond to-morrow midnight; and I think they have hit the time very nearly.

Valdemar.

I received this note within half an hour after it was written, and in fifteen minutes more I was in the dying man's chamber. I had not seen him for ten days, and was appalled by the fearful alteration which the brief interval had wrought in him. His face wore a leaden hue; the eyes were utterly lustreless; and the emaciation was so extreme that the skin had been broken through by the cheek-bones. His expectoration was excessive. The pulse was barely perceptible. He retained, nevertheless, in a very remarkable manner, both his mental power and a certain degree of physical strength. He spoke with distinctness—took some palliative medicines without aid—and, when I entered the room, was occupied in penciling memoranda in a pocket-book. He was propped up in the bed by pillows. Doctors D—— and F—— were in attendance.

After pressing Valdemar's hand, I took these gentlemen aside, and obtained from them a minute account of the patient's condition. The left lung had been for eighteen months in a semi-osseous or cartilaginous state, and was, of course, entirely useless for all purposes of vitality. The right, in its upper portion, was also partially, if not thoroughly, ossified, while the lower region was merely a mass of purulent tubercles, running one into another. Several extensive perforations existed; and, at one point, permanent adhesion to the ribs had taken place. These appearances in the right lobe were of comparatively recent date. The ossification had proceeded with very unusual rapidity; no sign of it had been discovered a month before, and the adhesion had only been observed during the three previous days. Independently of the phthisis, the patient was suspected of aneurism of the aorta; but on this point the osseous symptoms rendered an exact diagnosis impossible. It was the opinion of both physicians that M. Valdemar would die about midnight on the morrow (Sunday). It was then seven o'clock on Saturday evening.

On quitting the invalid's bed-side to hold conversation with myself, Doctors D—— and F—— had bidden him a final farewell. It had not been their intention to return; but, at my request, they agreed to look in upon the patient about ten the next night.

When they had gone, I spoke freely with M. Valdemar on the subject of his approaching dissolution, as well as, more particularly, of the experiment proposed. He still professed himself quite willing and even anxious to have it made, and urged me to commence it at once. A male and a female nurse were in attendance; but I did not feel myself altogether at liberty to engage in a task of this character with no more reliable witnesses than these people, in case of sudden accident, might prove. I therefore postponed operations until about eight the next night, when the arrival of a medical student with whom I had some acquaintance (Mr. Theodore L——l,) relieved me from farther embarrassment. It had been my design, originally, to wait for the physicians; but I was induced to proceed, first by the urgent entreaties of M. Valdemar, and secondly, by my convinction that I had not a moment to lose, as he was evidently sinking fast.

Mr. L——l was so kind as to accede to my desire that he would take notes of all that occurred; and it is from his memoranda that what I now have to relate is, for the most part, either condensed or copied *verbatim*.

It wanted about five minutes of eight when, taking the patient's hand, I begged him to state, as distinctly as he could, to Mr. L——l, whether he (M. Valdemar) was entirely willing that I should make the experiment of mesmerizing him in his then condition.

He replied feebly, yet quite audibly, "Yes, I wish to be mesmerized"—adding immediately afterwards, "I fear you have deferred it too long."

While he spoke thus, I commenced the passes which I had already found most effectual in subduing him. He was evidently influenced with the first lateral stroke of my hand across his forehead; but although I exerted all my powers, no farther perceptible effect was induced until some minutes after ten o'clock, when Doctors D—— and F—— called, according to appointment. I explained to them, in a few words, what I designed, and as they opposed no objection, saying that the patient was already in the death agony, I proceeded without hesitation—exchanging, however, the lateral passes for downward ones, and directing my gaze entirely into the right eye of the sufferer.

By this time his pulse was imperceptible and his breathing was stertorous, and at intervals of half a minute.

This condition was nearly unaltered for a quarter of an hour. At the expiration of this period, however, a natural although a very deep sigh escaped the bosom of the dying man, and the stertorous breathing ceased—that is to say, its stertorousness was no longer apparent; the intervals were undiminished. The patient's extremities were of an icy coldness.

At five minutes before eleven I perceived unequivocal signs of the mesmeric influence. The glassy roll of the eye was changed for that expression of uneasy *inward* examination which is never seen except in cases of sleep-waking, and which it is quite impossible to mistake. With a few rapid lateral passes I made the lids quiver, as in incipient sleep, and with a few more I closed them altogether. I was not satisfied, however, with this, but continued the manipulations vigorously, and with the fullest exertion of the will, until I had completely stiffened the limbs of the slumberer, after placing them in a seemingly easy position. The legs were at full length; the arms were nearly so, and reposed on the bed at a moderate distance from the loins. The head was very slightly elevated.

When I had accomplished this, it was fully midnight, and I requested the gentlemen present to examine M. Valdemar's condition. After a few experiments, they admitted him to be in an unusually perfect state of mesmeric trance. The curiosity of both the physicians was greatly excited. Dr. D—— resolved at once to remain with the patient all night, while Dr. F—— took leave with a promise to return at daybreak. Mr. L——l and the nurses remained.

We left M. Valdemar entirely undisturbed until about three o'clock in the morning, when I approached him and found him in precisely the same condition as when Dr. F—— went away—that is to say, he lay in the same position; the pulse was imperceptible; the breathing was gentle (scarcely noticeable, unless through the application of a mirror to the lips); the eyes were closed naturally; and the limbs were as rigid and as cold as marble. Still, the general appearance was certainly not that of death.

As I approached M. Valdemar I made a kind of half effort to influence his right arm into pursuit of my own, as I passed the latter gently to and fro above his person. In such experiments with this patient I had never perfectly succeeded before, and assuredly I had little thought of succeeding now; but to my astonishment, his arm very readily, although feebly, followed every direction I assigned it with mine. I determined to hazard a few words of conversation.

"M. Valdemar," I said, "are you asleep?" He made no answer, but I perceived a tremor about the lips, and was thus induced to repeat the question, again and again. At its third repetition, his whole frame was agitated by a very slight shivering; the eyelids unclosed themselves so far as to display a white line of the ball; the lips moved sluggishly, and from between them, in a barely audible whisper, issued the words:

"Yes;—asleep now. Do not wake me!—let me die so!"

I here felt the limbs and found them as rigid as ever. The right arm, as before, obeyed the direction of my hand. I questioned the sleep-waker again:

"Do you still feel pain in the breast, M. Valdemar?"

The answer now was immediate, but even less audible than before:

"No pain—I am dying."

I did not think it advisable to disturb him farther just then, and nothing more was said or done until the arrival of Dr. F——, who came a little before sunrise, and expressed unbounded astonishment at finding the patient still alive. After feeling the pulse and applying a mirror to the lips, he requested me to speak to the sleep-waker again. I did so, saying:

"M. Valdemar, do you still sleep?"

As before, some minutes elapsed ere a reply was made; and during the interval the dying man seemed to be collecting his energies to speak. At my fourth repetition of the question, he said very faintly, almost inaudibly:

"Yes; still asleep—dying."

It was now the opinion, or rather the wish, of the physicians, that M. Valdemar should be suffered to remain undisturbed in his present apparently tranquil condition, until death should supervene—and this, it was generally agreed, must now take place within a few minutes. I concluded, however, to speak to him once more, and merely repeated my previous question.

While I spoke, there came a marked change over the countenance of the sleep-waker. The eyes rolled themselves slowly open, the pupils disappearing upwardly; the skin generally assumed a cadaverous hue, resembling not so much parchment as white paper; and the circular hectic spots which, hitherto, had been strongly defined in the centre of each cheek, *went out* at once. I use this expression, because the suddenness of their departure put me in mind of nothing so much as the extinguishment of a candle by a puff of the breath. The upper lip, at the same time, writhed itself away from the teeth, which it had previously covered completely; while the lower jaw fell with an audible jerk, leaving the mouth widely extended, and disclosing in full view the swollen and blackened tongue. I presume that no member of the party then present had been unaccustomed to deathbed horrors; but so hideous beyond conception was the appearance of M. Valdemar at this moment, that there was a general shrinking back from the region of the bed.

I now feel that I have reached a point of this narrative at which every reader will be startled into positive disbelief. It is my business, however, simply to proceed.

There was no longer the faintest sign of vitality in M. Valdemar; and concluding him to be dead, we were consigning him to the charge of the nurses, when a strong vibratory motion was observable in the tongue. This continued for perhaps a minute. At the expiration of this period, there issued from the distended and motionless jaws a voice—such as it would be madness in me to attempt describing. There are, indeed, two or three epithets which might be considered as applicable to it in part; I might say, for example, that the sound was harsh, and broken and hollow; but the hideous whole is indescribable, for the simple reason that no similar sounds have ever jarred upon the ear of humanity. There were two particulars, nevertheless, which I thought then, and still think, might fairly be stated as characteristic of the intonation—as well adapted to convey some idea of its unearthly peculiarity. In the first place, the voice seemed to reach our ears—at least mine—from a vast distance, or from some deep cavern within the earth. In the second place, it impressed me (I fear, indeed, that it will be impossible to make myself comprehended) as gelatinous or glutinous matters impress the sense of touch.

I have spoken both of "sound" and of "voice." I mean to say that the sound was one of distinct—of even wonderfully, thrillingly distinct—syllabification. M. Valdemar *spoke*—obviously in reply to the question I had propounded to him a few minutes before. I had asked him, it will be remembered, if he still slept. He now said:

"Yes;—no;—I *have been* sleeping—and now—now—*I am dead*."

No person present even affected to deny, or attempted to repress, the unutterable, shuddering horror which these few words, thus uttered, were so well calculated to convey. Mr. L——l (the student) swooned. The nurses immediately left the chamber, and could not be induced to return. My own impressions I would not pretend to render intelligible to the reader. For nearly an hour, we busied ourselves, silently—without the utterance of a word—in endeavors to revive Mr. L——l. When he came to himself, we addressed ourselves again to an investigation of M. Valdemar's condition.

It remained in all respects as I have last described it, with the exception that the mirror no longer afforded evidence of respiration. An attempt to draw blood from the arm failed. I should mention, too, that this limb was no farther subject to my will. I endeavored in vain to make it follow the direction of my hand. The only real indication, indeed, of the mesmeric influence, was now found in the vibratory movement of the tongue, whenever I addressed M. Valdemar a question. He seemed to be making an effort to reply, but had no longer sufficient volition. To queries put to him by any other person than myself he seemed utterly insensible—although I endeavored to place each member of the company in mesmeric *rapport* with him. I believe that I have now related all that is necessary to an understanding of the sleep-waker's state at this epoch. Other nurses were procured; and at ten o'clock I left the house in company with the two physicians and Mr. L——l.

In the afternoon we all called again to see the patient. His condition remained precisely the same. We had now some discussion as to the propriety and feasibility of awakening him; but we had little difficulty in agreeing that no good purpose would be served by so doing. It was evident that, so far, death (or what is usually termed death) had been arrested by the mesmeric process. It seemed clear to us all that to awaken M. Valdemar would be merely to insure his instant, or at least his speedy dissolution.

From this period until the close of last week—*an interval of nearly seven months*—we continued to make daily calls at M. Valdemar's house, accompanied, now and then, by medical and other friends. All this time the sleeper-waker remained *exactly* as I have last described him. The nurses' attentions were continual.

It was on Friday last that we finally resolved to make the experiment of awakening, or attempting to awaken him; and it is the (perhaps) unfortunate result of this latter experiment which has given rise to so much discussion in private circles—to so much of what I cannot help thinking unwarranted popular feeling.

For the purpose of relieving M. Valdemar from the mesmeric trance, I made use of the customary passes. These, for a time, were unsuccessful. The first indication of revival was afforded by a partial descent of the iris. It was observed, as especially remarkable, that this lowering of the pupil was accompanied by the profuse out-flowing of a yellowish ichor (from beneath the lids) of a pungent and highly offensive odor.

It was now suggested that I should attempt to influence the patient's arm, as heretofore. I made the attempt and failed. Dr. F—— then intimated a desire to have me put a question. I did so, as follows:

"M. Valdemar, can you explain to us what are your feelings or wishes now?"

There was an instant return of the hectic circles on the cheeks; the tongue quivered, or rather rolled violently in the mouth (although the jaws and lips remained rigid as before;) and at length the same hideous voice which I have already described, broke forth:

"For God's sake!—quick!—quick!—put me to sleep—or, quick!—waken me!—quick!—*I say to you that I am dead!*"

I was thoroughly unnerved, and for an instant remained undecided what to do. At first I made an endeavor to re-compose the patient; but, failing in this through total abeyance of the will, I retraced my steps and as earnestly struggled to awaken him. In this attempt I soon saw that I should be successful—or at least I soon fancied that my success would be complete—and I am sure that all in the room were prepared to see the patient awaken.

For what really occurred, however, it is quite impossible that any human being could have been prepared.

As I rapidly made the mesmeric passes, amid ejaculations of "dead! dead!" absolutely *bursting* from the tongue and not from the lips of the sufferer, his whole frame at once—within the space of a single minute, or even less, shrunk—crumbled—absolutely *rotted* away beneath my hands. Upon the bed, before that whole company, there lay a nearly liquid mass of loathsome—of detestable putridity.

EDGAR ALLAN POE

Mellonta Tauta *

ON BOARD BALLOON "SKYLARK,"

April 1, 2848.

Now, my dear friend—now, for your sins, you are to suffer the infliction of a long gossiping letter. I tell you distinctly that I am going to punish you for all your impertinences by being as tedious, as discursive, as incoherent and as unsatisfactory as possible. Besides, here I am, cooped up in a dirty balloon, with some one or two hundred of the *canaille*, all bound on a *pleasure* excursion (what a funny idea some people have of pleasure!), and I have no prospect of touching *terra firma* for a month at least. Nobody to talk to. Nothing to do. When one has nothing to do, then is the time to correspond with one's friends. You perceive, then, why it is that I write you this letter—it is on account of my *ennui* and your sins.

Get ready your spectacles and make up your mind to be annoyed. I mean to write at you every day during this odious voyage.

Heigho! when will any *Invention* visit the human pericranium? Are we forever to be doomed to the thousand inconveniences of the balloon? Will *nobody* contrive a more expeditious mode of progress? This jog-trot movement, to my thinking, is little less than positive torture. Upon my word we have not made more than a hundred miles the hour since leaving home! The very birds beat us—at least some of them. I assure you that I do not exaggerate at all. Our motion, no doubt, seems slower than it actually is—this on account of our having no objects about us

* *Godey's Lady's Book,* February 1849.

by which to estimate our velocity, and on account of our going *with* the wind. To be sure, whenever we meet a balloon we have a chance of perceiving our rate, and then, I admit, things do not appear so very bad. Accustomed as I am to this mode of traveling, I cannot get over a kind of giddiness whenever a balloon passes us in a current directly overhead. It always seems to me like an immense bird of prey about to pounce upon us and carry us off in its claws. One went over us this morning about sunrise, and so nearly overhead that its drag-rope actually brushed the net-work suspending our car, and caused us very serious apprehension. Our captain said that if the material of the bag had been the trumpery varnished "silk" of five hundred or a thousand years ago, we should inevitably have been damaged. This silk, as he explained it to me, was a fabric composed of the entrails of a species of earthworm. The worm was carefully fed on mulberries—a kind of fruit resembling a water-melon—and, when sufficiently fat, was crushed in a mill. The paste thus arising was called *papyrus* in its primary state, and went through a variety of processes until it finally became "silk." Singular to relate, it was once much admired as an article of *female dress!* Balloons were also very generally constructed from it. A better kind of material, it appears, was subsequently found in the down surrounding the seed-vessels of a plant vulgarly called *euphorbium,* and at that time botanically termed milkweed. This latter kind of silk was designated as silk-buckingham, on account of its superior durability, and was usually prepared for use by being varnished with a solution of gum caoutchouc—a substance which in some respects must have resembled the *gutta percha* now in common use. This caoutchouc was occasionally called India rubber or rubber of whist, and was no doubt one of the numerous *fungi.* Never tell me again that I am not at heart an antiquarian.

Talking of drag-ropes—our own, it seems, has this moment knocked a man overboard from one of the small magnetic propellers that swarm in the ocean below us—a boat of about six thousand tons, and, from all accounts, shamefully crowded. These diminutive barques should be prohibited from carrying more than a definite number of passengers. The man, of course, was not permitted to get on board again, and was soon out of sight, he and his life-preserver. I rejoice, my dear friend, that we live in an age so enlightened that no such a thing as an individual is supposed to exist. It is the mass for which the true Humanity cares. By the by, talking of Humanity, do you know that our immortal Wiggins is not so original in his views of the Social Condition and so forth, as his contemporaries are inclined to suppose? Pundit assures me that the same ideas were put, nearly in the same way, about a thousand years ago, by an Irish philosopher called Furrier, on account of his keeping a retail shop for cat-peltries and other furs. Pundit *knows*, you know; there can be no mistake about it. How very wonderfully do we see verified, every day, the profound observation of the Hindoo Aries Tottle (as quoted by Pundit)—"Thus must we say that, not once or twice, or a few times, but with almost infinite repetitions, the same opinions come round in a circle among men."

April 2.—Spoke to-day the magnetic cutter in charge of the middle section of floating telegraph wires. I learn that when this species of telegraph was first put into operation by Horse, it was considered quite impossible to convey the wires over sea; but now we are at a loss to comprehend where the difficulty lay! So wags the world. *Tempora mutantur*—excuse me for quoting the Etruscan. What *would* we do without the Atalantic telegraph? (Pundit says Atlantic was the ancient adjective.) We lay to a few minutes to ask the cutter some questions, and learned, among other glorious news, that civil war is raging in Africa, while the plague is doing its good work beautifully both in Yurope and Ayesher. Is it not truly remarkable that, before the magnificent light shed upon philosophy by Humanity, the world was accustomed to regard War and Pestilence as calamities? Do you know that prayers were actually offered up in the ancient temples to the end that these *evils* (!) might not be visited upon mankind? Is it not really difficult to comprehend upon what principle of interest our forefathers acted? Were they so blind as not to perceive that the destruction of a myriad of individuals is only so much positive advantage to the mass!

April 3.—It is really a very fine amusement to ascend the rope-ladder leading to the summit of the balloon-bag and thence survey the surrounding world. From the car below, you know, the prospect is not so comprehensive—you can see little vertically. But seated here (where I write this) in the luxuriously-cushioned open piazza of the summit, one can see everything that is going on in all directions. Just now, there is quite a crowd of balloons in sight, and they present a very animated appearance, while the air is resonant with the hum of so many millions of human voices. I have heard it asserted that when Yellow or (as Pundit *will* have it) Violet, who is supposed to have been the first æronaut, maintained the practicability of traversing the atmosphere in all directions, by merely ascending or descending until a favorable current was attained, he was scarcely hearkened to at all by his cotemporaries, who looked upon him as merely an ingenious sort of madman, because the philosophers (?) of the day declared the thing impossible. Really now it does seem to me *quite* unaccountable how anything so obviously feasible could have escaped the sagacity of the ancient *savans*. But in all ages the great obstacles to advancement in Art have been opposed by the so-called men of science. To be sure, *our* men of science are not quite so bigoted as those of old:—oh, I have something *so* queer to tell you on this topic. Do you know that it is not more than a thousand years ago since the metaphysicians consented to relieve the people of the singular fancy that there existed but *two possible roads for the attainment of Truth!* Believe it if you can! It appears that long, long ago, in the night of Time, there lived a Turkish philosopher (or Hindoo possibly) called Aries Tottle. This person introduced, or at all events propagated what was termed the deductive or *à priori* mode of investigation. He started with what he maintained to be *axioms* or "self-evident truths," and thence proceeded "logically" to results. His greatest disciples were one Neuclid and one Cant. Well, Aries Tottle flourished supreme until the advent of one Hog, surnamed the "Ettrick Shepherd," who preached an entirely different system, which he called the *à posteriori* or *in*ductive. His plan referred altogether to Sensation. He proceeded by observing, analyzing and classifying facts—*instantiae naturae*, as they were affectedly called—into general laws. Aries Tottle's mode, in a word, was based on *noumena;* Hog's on *phenomena*. Well, so great was the admiration excited by this latter system that, at its first introduction, Aries Tottle fell into disrepute; but finally he recovered ground, and was permitted to divide the realm of Truth with his more modern rival. The *savans* now maintained that the Aristotelian and *Baconian* roads were the sole possible avenues to knowledge. "Baconian," you must know, was an adjective invented as equivalent to Hog-ian and more euphonious and dignified.

Now, my dear friend, I do assure you, most positively, that I represent this matter fairly, on the soundest authority; and you can easily understand how a notion so absurd on its very face must have operated to retard the progress of all true knowledge—which makes its advances almost invariably by intuitive bounds. The ancient idea confined investigation to *crawling;* and for hundreds of years so great was the infatuation about Hog especially, that a virtual end was put to all thinking properly so called. No man dared utter a truth to which he felt himself indebted to his *Soul* alone. It mattered not whether the truth was even *demonstrably* a truth, for the bullet-headed *savans* of the time regarded only *the road* by which he had attained it. They would not even *look* at the end. "Let us see the means," they cried, "the means!" If, upon investigation of the means, it was found to come neither under the category Aries (that is to say Ram) nor under the category Hog, why then the savans went no farther, but pronounced the "theorist" a fool, and would have nothing to do with him or his truth.

Now, it cannot be maintained, even, that by the crawling system the greatest amount of truth would be attained in any long series of ages, for the repression of *imagination* was an evil not to be compensated for by any superior *certainty* in the ancient modes of investigation. The error of these Jurmains, these Vrinch, these Inglitch and these Amriccans, (the later, by the way, were our own immediate progenitors,) was an error quite analogous with that of the wiseacre who fancies that he must necessarily see an object the better the more closely he holds it to his eyes. These people blinded themselves by details. When they proceeded Hoggishly, their "facts" were by no means always facts—a matter of little consequence had it not been for assuming that they *were* facts and must be facts because they appeared to be such. When they proceeded on the path of the Ram, their course was scarcely as straight as a ram's horn, for they *never had* an axiom which was an axiom at all. They must have been very blind not to see this, even in their own day; for even in their own day many of the long "established" axioms had been rejected. For example—"*Ex nihilo nihil fit;*" "a body cannot act where it is not;" "there cannot exist antipodes;" "darkness cannot come out of light"—all these, and a dozen other similar propositions, formerly admitted without hesitation as axioms, were, even at the period of which I speak, seen to be untenable. How absurd in these people, then, to persist in putting faith in "axioms" as immutable bases of Truth! But even out of the mouths of their soundest reasoners it is easy to demonstrate the futility, the impalpability of their axioms in general. Who *was* the soundest of their logicians? Let me see! I will go and ask Pundit and be back in a minute . . . Ah, here we have it! Here is a book written nearly a thousand years ago and lately translated from the Inglitch—which, by the way, appears to have been the rudiment of the Amriccan. Pundit says it is decidedly the cleverest ancient work on its topic, Logic. The author (who was much thought of in his day) was one Miller, or Mill; and we find it recorded of him, as a point of some importance, that he had a mill-horse called Bentham. But let us glance at the treatise!

Ah!—"Ability or inability to conceive," says Mr. Mill, very properly, "is in no case to be received as a criterion of axiomatic truth." What *modern* in his senses would ever think of disputing this truism? The only wonder with us must be, how it happened that Mr. Mill conceived it necessary even to hint at any thing so obvious. So far good—but let us turn over another page. What have we here?—"Contradictories cannot both be true—that is, cannot co-exist in nature." Here Mr. Mill means, for example, that a tree must be either a tree or not a tree—that it cannot be at the same time a tree and not a tree. Very well; but I ask him *why*. His reply is this—and never pretends to be any thing else than this—"Because it is impossible to conceive that contradictories can both be true." But this is no answer at all, by his own showing; for has he not just admitted as a truism that "ability or inability to conceive is *in no case* to be received as a criterion of axiomatic truth."

Now I do not complain of these ancients so much because their logic is, by their own showing, utterly baseless, worthless and fantastic altogether, as because of their pompous and imbecile proscription of all *other* roads of Truth, of all *other* means for its attainment than the two preposterous paths—the one of creeping and the one of crawling—to which they have dared to confine the Soul that loves nothing so well as to *soar*.

By the by, my dear friend, do you not think it would have puzzled these ancient dogmaticians to have determined by *which* of their two roads it was that the most important and most sublime of *all* their truths was, in effect, attained? I mean the truth of Gravitation. Newton owed it to Kepler. Kepler admitted that his three laws were *guessed at*—these three laws of all laws which led the great Inglitch mathematician to his principle, the basis of all physical principle—to go behind which we must enter the Kingdom of Metaphysics. Kepler guessed—that is to say, *imagined*. He was essentially a "theorist"—that word now of so much sanctity, formerly an epithet of contempt. Would it not have puzzled these old moles, too, to have explained by which of the two "roads" a cryptographist unriddles a cryptograph of more than usual secrecy, or by which of the two roads Champollion directed mankind to those enduring and almost innumerable truths which resulted from his deciphering the Hieroglyphics?

One word more on this topic and I will be done boring you. Is it not *passing* strange that, with their eternal prating about *roads* to Truth, these bigoted people missed what we now so clearly perceive to be the great highway—that of Consistency? Does it not seem singular how they should have failed to deduce from the works of God the vital fact that a perfect consistency *must be* an absolute truth! How plain has been our progress since the late announcement of this proposition! Investigation has been taken out of the hands of the ground-moles and given, as a task, to the true and only true thinkers, the men of ardent imagination. These latter *theorize*. Can you not fancy the shout of scorn with which my words would be received by our progenitors were it possible for them to be now looking over my shoulder? These men, I say, *theorize;* and their theories are simply corrected, reduced, systematized—cleared, little by little, of their dross of inconsistency—until, finally, a perfect consistency stands apparent which even the most stolid admit, because it *is* a consistency, to be an absolute and an unquestionable *truth*.

April 4.—The new gas is doing wonders, in conjunction with the new improvement with gutta percha. How very safe, commodious, manageable, and in every respect convenient are our modern balloons! Here is an immense one approaching us at the rate of at least a hundred and fifty miles an hour. It seems to be crowded with people—perhaps there are three or four hundred passengers—and yet it soars to an elevation of nearly a mile, looking down upon poor us with sovereign contempt. Still a hundred or even two hundred miles an hour is slow traveling, after all. *Do* you remember our flight on the railroad across the Kanadaw continent?—fully three hundred miles the hour—*that* was traveling. Nothing to be seen, though—nothing to be done but flirt, feast and dance in the magnificent saloons. Do you remember what an odd sensation was experienced when, by chance, we caught a glimpse of external objects while the cars were in full flight? Everything seemed unique—in one mass. For my part, I cannot say but that I preferred the traveling by the slow train of a hundred miles the hour. Here we were permitted to have glass windows—even to have them open—and something like a distinct view of the country was attainable. . . . Pundit says that *the route* for the great Kanadaw railroad must have been in some measure marked out about nine hundred years ago! In fact, he goes so far as to assert that actual traces of a road are still discernible—traces referable to a period quite as remote as that mentioned. The track, it appears, was *double* only; ours, you know, has twelve paths; and three or four new ones are in preparation. The ancient rails were very slight, and placed so close together as to be, according to modern notions, quite frivolous, if not dangerous in the extreme. The present width of track—fifty feet—is considered, indeed, scarcely secure enough. For my part, I make no doubt that a track of some sort *must* have existed in very remote times, as Pundit asserts; for nothing can be clearer, to my mind, than that, at some period—not less than seven centuries ago, certainly—the Northern and Southern Kanadaw continents were *united;* the Kanawdians, then, would have been driven, by necessity, to a great railroad across the continent.

April 5.—I am almost devoured by *ennui*. Pundit is the only conversible person on board; and he, poor soul! can speak of nothing but antiquities. He has been occupied all the day in the attempt to convince me that the ancient Amriccans *governed themselves!*—did ever anybody hear of such an absurdity?—that they existed in a sort of every-man-for-himself confederacy, after the fashion of the "prairie dogs" that we read of in fable. He says that they started with the queerest idea conceivable, viz: that all men are born free and equal—this in the very teeth of the laws of *gradation* so visibly impressed upon all things both in the moral and physical universe. Every man "voted," as they called it—that is to say, meddled with public affairs—until, at length, it was discovered that what is everybody's business is nobody's, and that the "Republic" (so the absurd thing was called) was without a government at all. It is related, however, that the first circumstance which disturbed, very particularly, the self-complacency of the philosophers who constructed this "Republic," was the startling discovery that universal suffrage gave opportunity for fraudulent schemes, by means of which any desired number of votes might at any time be polled, without the possibility of prevention or even detection, by any party which should be merely villanous enough not to be ashamed of the fraud. A little reflection upon this discovery sufficed to render evident the consequences, which were that rascality *must* predominate—in a word, that a republican government *could* never be anything but a rascally one. While the philosophers, however, were busied in blushing at their stupidity in not have foreseen these inevitable evils, and intent upon the invention of new theories, the matter was put to an abrupt issue by a fellow of the name of *Mob,* who took everything into his own hands and set up a despotism, in comparison with which those of the fabulous Zeros and Hellofagabaluses were respectable and delectable. This Mob (a foreigner, by the by), is said to have been the most odious of all men that ever encumbered the earth. He was a giant in stature—insolent, rapacious, filthy; had the gall of a bullock with the heart of an hyena and the brains of a peacock. He died, at length, by dint of his own energies, which exhausted him. Nevertheless, he had his uses, as everything has, however vile, and taught mankind a lesson which to this day it is in no danger of forgetting—never to run directly contrary to the natural analogies. As for Republicanism, no analogy could be found for it upon the face of the earth—unless we except the case of the "prairie dogs," an exception which seems to demonstrate, if anything, that democracy is a very admirable form of government —for dogs.

April 6.—Last night had a fine view of Alpha Lyræ, whose

disk, through our captain's spy-glass, subtends an angle of half a degree, looking very much as our sun does to the naked eye on a misty day. Alpha Lyræ, although so *very* much larger than our sun, by the by, resembles him closely as regards its spots, its atmosphere, and in many other particulars. It is only within the last century, Pundit tells me, that the binary relation existing between these two orbs began even to be suspected. The evident motion of our system in the heavens was (strange to say!) referred to an orbit about a prodigious star in the centre of the galaxy. About this star, or at all events about a centre of gravity common to all the globes of the Milky Way and supposed to be near Alcyome in the Pleiades, every one of these globes was declared to be revolving, our own performing the circuit in a period of 117,000,000 of years! *We,* with our present lights, our vast telescopic improvements and so forth, of course find it difficult to comprehend *the ground* of an idea such as this. Its first propagator was one Mudler. He was led, we must presume, to this wild hypothesis by mere analogy in the first instance; but, this being the case, he should have at least adhered to analogy in its development. A great central orb *was,* in fact, suggested; so far Mudler was consistent. This central orb, however, dynamically, should have been greater than all its surrounding orbs taken together. The question might then have been asked—"Why do we not see it?"—*we,* especially, who occupy the mid region of the cluster—the very locality *near* which, at least, must be situated this inconceivable central sun. The astronomer, perhaps, at this point, took refuge in the suggestion of non-luminosity; and here analogy was suddenly let fall. But even admitting the central orb non-luminous, how did he manage to explain its falure to be rendered visible by the incalculable host of glorious suns glaring in all directions about it? No doubt what he finally maintained was merely a centre of gravity common to all the revolving orbs—but here again analogy must have been let fall. Our system revolves, it is true, about a common centre of gravity, but it does this in connection with and in consequence of a material sun whose mass more than counterbalances the rest of the system. The mathematical circle is a curve composed of an infinity of straight lines; but this idea of the circle—this idea of it which, in regard to all earthly geometry, we consider as merely the mathematical, in contradistinction from the practical, idea

—is, in sober fact, the *practical* conception which alone we have any right to entertain in respect to those Titanic circles with which we have to deal, at least in fancy, when we suppose our system, with its fellows, revolving about a point in the centre of the galaxy. Let the most vigorous of human imaginations but attempt to take a single step towards the comprehension of a circuit so unutterable! It would scarcely be paradoxical to say that a flash of lightning itself, traveling *forever* upon the circumference of this inconceivable circle, would still *forever* be traveling in a straight line. That the path of our sun along such a circumference—that the direction of our system in such an orbit—would, to any human perception, deviate in the slightest degree from a straight line even in a million of years, is a proposition not to be entertained; and yet these ancient astronomers were absolutely cajoled, it appears, into believing that a decisive curvature had become apparent during the brief period of their astronomical history—during the mere point—during the utter nothingness of two or three thousand years! How incomprehensible, that considerations such as this did not at once indicate to them the true state of affairs—that of the binary revolution of our sun and Alpha Lyræ around a common centre of gravity!

April 7.—Continued last night our astronomical amusements. Had a fine view of the five Nepturian asteroids, and watched with much interest the putting up of a huge impost on a couple of lintels in the new temple at Daphnis in the moon. It was amusing to think that creatures so diminutive as the lunarians, and bearing so little resemblance to humanity, yet evinced a mechanical ingenuity so much superior to our own. One finds it difficult, too, to conceive the vast masses which these people handle so easily, to be as light as our reason tells us they actually are.

April 8.—Eureka! Pundit is in his glory. A balloon from Kanadaw spoke us to-day and threw on board several late papers: they contain some exceedingly curious information relative to Kanawdian or rather to Amriccan antiquities. You know, I presume, that laborers have for some months been employed in preparing the ground for a new fountain at Paradise, the emperor's principal pleasure garden. Paradise, it appears, has been, *literally* speaking, an island time out of mind—that is to say, its northern boundary was always (as far back as any records extend) a rivulet, or rather a very narrow arm of the sea. This arm was gradually widened until it attained its present breadth—a mile. The whole length of the island is nine miles; the breadth varies materially. The entire area (so Pundit says) was, about eight hundred years ago, densely packed with houses, some of them twenty stories high; land (for some most unaccountable reason) being considered as especially precious just in this vicinity. The disastrous earthquake, however, of the year 2050, so totally uprooted and overwhelmed the town (for it was almost too large to be called a village) that the most indefatigable of our antiquarians have never yet been able to obtain from the site any sufficient data (in the shape of coins, medals or inscriptions) wherewith to build up even the ghost of a theory concerning the manners, customs, &c. &c. &c., of the aboriginal inhabitants. Nearly all that we have hitherto known of them is, that they were a portion of the Knickerbocker tribe of savages infesting the continent at its first discovery by Recorder Riker, a knight of the Golden Fleece. They were by no means uncivilized, however, but cultivated various arts and even sciences after a fashion of their own. It is related of them that they were acute in many respects, but were oddly afflicted with a monomania for building what, in the ancient Amriccan, was denominated "churches"—a kind of pagoda instituted for the worship of two idols that went by the names of Wealth and Fashion. In the end, it is said, the island became, nine-tenths of it, church. The women, too, it appears, were oddly deformed by a natural protuberance of the region just below the small of the back—although, most unaccountably, this deformity was looked upon altogether in the light of a beauty. One or two pictures of these singular women have, in fact, been miraculously preserved. They look very odd, *very*—like something between a turkey-cock and a dromedary.

Well, these few details are nearly all that have descended to us respecting the ancient Knickerbockers. It seems, however, that while digging in the centre of the emperor's garden, (which, you know, covers the whole island,) some of the workmen unearthed a cubical and evidently chiseled block of granite, weighing several hundred pounds. It was in good preservation, having received, apparently, little injury from the convulsion which entombed it. On one of its surfaces was a marble slab with (only think of it!) *an inscription—a legible inscription.* Pundit is in ecstasies. Upon detaching the slab, a cavity appeared, containing a leaden box filled with various coins, a long scroll of names, several documents which appear to resemble newspapers, with other matters of intense interest to the antiquarian! There can be no doubt that all these are genuine Amriccan relics belonging to the tribe called Knickerbocker. The papers thrown on board our balloon are filled with fac similes of the coins, MSS., typography, &c. &c. I copy for your amusement the Knickerbocker inscription on the marble slab:—

THIS CORNER STONE OF A MONUMENT TO THE
MEMORY OF
GEORGE WASHINGTON,
WAS LAID WITH APPROPRIATE CEREMONIES ON THE
19TH DAY OF OCTOBER, 1847,
THE ANNIVERSARY OF THE SURRENDER OF
LORD CORNWALLIS
TO GENERAL WASHINGTON AT YORKTOWN,
A. D. 1781,
UNDER THE AUSPICES OF THE
WASHINGTON MONUMENT ASSOCIATION OF THE
CITY OF NEW YORK

This, as I give it, is a verbatim translation done by Pundit himself, so there *can* be no mistake about it. From the few words thus preserved, we glean several important items of knowledge, not the least interesting of which is the fact that a thousand years ago *actual* monuments had fallen into disuse—as was all very proper—the people contenting themselves, as we do now, with a mere indication of the design to erect a monument at some future time; a corner-stone being cautiously laid by itself "solitary and alone" (excuse me for quoting the great Amriccan poet Benton!) as a guarantee of the magnanimous *intention.* We ascertain, too, very distinctly, from this admirable inscription, the how, as well as the where and the what, of the great surrender in question. As to the *where,* it was

Yorktown (wherever that was), and as to the *what*, it was General Cornwallis (no doubt some wealthy dealer in corn). *He* was surrendered. The inscription commemorates the surrender of—what?—why, "of Lord Cornwallis." The only question is what could the savages wish him surrendered for. But when we remember that these savages were undoubtedly cannibals, we are led to the conclusion that they intended him for sausage. As to the *how* of the surrender, no language can be more explicit. Lord Cornwallis was surrendered (for sausage) "under the auspices of the Washington Monument Association"—no doubt a charitable institution for the depositing of corner-stones.—But, Heaven bless me! what is the matter? Ah! I see—the balloon has collapsed, and we shall have a tumble into the sea. I have, therefore, only time enough to add that, from a hasty inspection of facsimiles of newspapers, &c., I find that *the* great men in those days among the Amriccans were one John, a smith, and one Zacchary, a tailor.

Good bye, until I see you again. Whether you ever get this letter or not is a point of little importance, as I write altogether for my own amusement. I shall cork the MS. up in a bottle however, and throw it into the sea.

Yours everlastingly,
PUNDITA.

EXPLORATIONS

AUTOMATA

The impact of the machine on nineteenth-century economy, culture, political structure, and psychology has recently been studied from many different angles. As the machine turned country into city, serf-like peasants into slave-like workers, distance into time, hours into minutes, land into capital, and the ideal of a primitive arcadia into the idea of a highly-industrialized utopia, it loomed huge in the everyday consciousness of almost everybody. It moved into work, into the home, into domestic politics, into international and civil war, and into all kinds of fiction.

The first major work of science fiction in the century, Mary Shelley's *Frankenstein; Or the Modern Prometheus* (1817), while itself not concerned with machines, bequeathed two splendid symbols of the relations between man and machine. One of the symbols appears in the monster created by the title character, the other in the subtitle. One metaphor for the automaton-maker is Frankenstein, the other is the modern Prometheus.

Throughout the century, fiction about automata provided a means of dramatizing the relations between these two metaphors. (By 1874 mechanical men had become so commonplace that an "android" appears as parody in Edward Page Mitchell's dream spoof "The Tachypomp.") Whether the relative position of the two metaphors changed I have been unable to determine. Certainly either a story such as H. D. Jenkins's "Automaton of Dobello" (*Lakeside*, 1872), in which the "automaton" is the source of awe and terror, or a story such as William Douglas O'Connor's "The Brazen Android" (*Atlantic Monthly*, 1891), in which the "android" almost brings democracy into thirteenth-century England, would not have been out of place in any decade of nineteenth-century America.

The issues involved in the relations between man and machine are varied and far-reaching. The two stories included here dramatize all but the economic issue which is so familiar today, and which is presented in an earlier story entitled "Recollection of Six Days' Journey in the Moon" by "An Aerio-Nautical Man" (*Southern Literary Messenger*, 1844). After arriving on the moon, the "Aerio-Nautical" author voyages to "The Isle of Engines" via "a magnetic steamboat, which progressed at the rate of an hundred miles an hour." This is what he finds on the island:

> Every thing is done there by machinery; and the men themselves, if not machines, are as much their slaves, as the genius of Aladdin's lamp. These machines have in a great measure taken the place of men, and snatched the bread from their mouths, because they work so much cheaper and faster. I saw several which I was assured by the proprietor of a manufactory who was reckoned worth millions, could do the work of a thousand men. I asked what became of the thousand in the mean time; upon which he entered into a long dissertation to prove, that they were infinitely benefitted by the cheapness of every thing occasioned by these labor-saving machines. I took the liberty of observing that if they could get no work, or were deprived of its adequate rewards, it was of little consequence to them that things were cheap, as they would have no money to purchase them.

We, living in the era of "The Triple Revolution," need no fantastic voyage to witness the pertinence of this lunar argument. The "Aerio-Nautical Man" follows this discussion with a description of people, including a great number of young girls, tending machines and wretchedly enslaved to them. This scene brings us close to issues which are not so familiar.

Dr. Robert Plank, the psychiatrist who has made some brilliant orthopsychiatric studies of science fiction, in a recent paper entitled "The Golem and the Robot" (presented at the 1964 Modern Language Association meeting), showed the continuity of symbols from the medieval golem legends to the robots of modern science fiction. According to Dr. Plank's argument, there are three basic motives which would lead someone to create an automaton: an aspiration to be godlike; a need for the usefulness of the machine; a desire to avoid sexual reproduction. Focusing on this last motive, Dr. Plank points out that in tales of automata from the medieval golem to the modern robot one pattern is almost invariably present: the automaton-maker is either a man working in isolation or with another man as an assistant, and the automaton turns out in at least one way to be an alternative to natural organic production. (The sexual symbolism is perhaps most obvious in the homunculus which, according to legend, Paracelsus made from sperm nourished in horsedung.) The automaton often turns out to be monstrous and is usually in some important ways destructive.

As we have seen, Hawthorne's "The Artist of the Beautiful" provides some fine insights into the psychology of creating an automaton. Warland gives up sexual creation to make a mechanical image of his own psyche; the organic creation which he has thus denied himself, in the form of the child of his would-be mate, then destroys his automaton. Melville explores the matter further, providing insights both into manufactory scenes like the one observed by the "Aerio-Nautical Man" and into private scenes of automatism unobserved by anyone.

HERMAN MELVILLE AND SCIENCE FICTION

Although something of a scientist himself (as anthropolgist in *Typee* and classifying naturalist in *Mardi, Moby-Dick,* and *The Encantadas*), Melville was too skeptical about the significance of science to admit many scientific marvels into his work and too overwhelmed by the physical universe as it is to invent any new marvels in the natural world—except for that Whale.

This is not to say that Melville did not write at length in modes often categorized with science fiction (modes which Robert Plank includes with science fiction under the designation "heteratopias")—the marvelous voyage, utopian and dystopian fiction,* fantasy which could but should not be explained in terms of natural phenomena. In fact he created a unique fusion of these modes—the world of a ship serving as a symbolic microcosm in which apparently fantastic business takes place. The movement from his first major full-length fiction, *Mardi,* a fantastic voyage which explores innumerable eutopias and dystopias, through *Moby-Dick,* to his last full-length fiction, *The Confidence-Man,*

* As the significance of utopian fiction has become more emphatic, it has become necessary to go beyond Sir Thomas More's brilliant pun, "Utopia," i.e. the good (*eu-*) place (*topia*) which is no (*ou-*) place. One form of anti-utopian writing takes the main institutions of a eutopian society and displays them forming a dystopia (bad place). Dr. Plank's term, heteratopia (different place), is an attempt to form a category to fit all those fictional worlds offered as radically different from any actual one.

a fantastic voyage which explores the totality of existence, is, to say the least, a major contribution to the literature of created societies. But except for the scene in *Redburn* which describes the spontaneous combustion of a shanghaied drunk, Ahab's lordship over the loadstone, the extraordinary natural components of Moby Dick, and the possible effects of mesmerism and the Omni-Balsamic Reinvigorator in *The Confidence-Man,* there is practically no science fiction in the full-length works.

Of his nineteen or so pieces of short fiction, only one besides the one included here looks at all like science fiction. That story, "The Happy Failure," presents the "Great Hydraulic-Hydrostatic Apparatus" for draining inland bodies of water. But since the marvelous machine not only does not do what it is supposed to do but fails to do anything, one can hardly call "The Happy Failure" science fiction. A story about a marvelous invention can only be science fiction if its author assumes enough tentative faith in technology to let it produce something which can work in one marvelous way or another, even a catastrophic one. "The Bell-Tower" is just such a story.

Melville's only complete science fiction, "The Bell-Tower" represents an important event in the history of the genre. For here is what may be the first fully developed story in English about a man-like automaton. Melville includes all the elements which were soon to become conventional—the automaton as destroyer; the creator as a being cut off from normal organic creation; society as a possible beneficiary, possible victim of the automaton.

As anyone who has read much of his late fiction knows, Melville in this period was constructing extremely elaborate, multi-layered, multi-dimensional kinds of fiction. To read "The Bell-Tower" with understanding, one must first analyze its extraordinarily complex elements and then see how Melville synthesizes them. That is, "The Bell-Tower" must receive the same kind of reading so far reserved for "Bartleby," "Benito Cereno," and one or two other stories. That it might repay this kind of attention is suggested by the facts that Melville made it the final story in *The Piazza Tales*, his only selection of his short fiction, and that it was twice anthologized while Melville was in almost total obscurity, once as the only representation of his prose in an eleven-volume edition of the *Library of American Literature*.

One should notice first that Melville probes deeply with his automaton-creation into the psycho-sexual meaning of the creation of automata. Melville, like Dr. Robert Plank and like Hawthorne in "The Artist of the Beautiful," sees the creation of an automaton as a narcissistic act unconsciously intended to bypass the normal means of procreation. And like E. T. A. Hoffman in "Der Sandmann," Melville uses a tower as a symbolic expression of what is involved between an automaton and a man who desires it.

That the sexual symbols of "The Bell-Tower" are not primarily an unconscious revelation of Melville's psyche but a conscious revelation of some psychological relations between man and the automatic machines he creates is made clear by a comparison with Melville's carefully contrived sexual symbolism in *Mardi*, *Moby-Dick*, "I and My Chimney," and in "The Paradise of Bachelors" and "The Tartarus of Maids," a pair of sketches he published in the same year as "The Bell-Tower."

In "The Tartarus of Maids," the narrator travels into a paper factory which bodies forth an alternative to normal reproductive processes. The factory and its setting represent the female reproductive and excretory organs penetrated by a grotesque mechanical maleness. In it a boy named Cupid shows the process by which—in exactly nine minutes—"White, wet, woolly-looking stuff not unlike the albuminous part of an egg, soft-boiled" from "two great round vats" becomes finished paper—with a name. The enslaved maidens who work in this strange environment tend such machines as a "vertical thing like a piston periodically rising and falling." In this story Melville uses these sexual symbols to display the peculiar perversion and sterility of the factory system:

> Machinery—that vaunted slave of humanity—here stood menially served by human beings, who served mutely and cringingly as the slave serves the Sultan. The girls did not so much seem accessory wheels to the general machinery as mere cogs to the wheels.

These girls are not even as fortunate as the "twelve figures of gay girls, garlanded, hand-in-hand," who, as chiseled designs in the great bell of "The Bell-Tower," "danced in a choral ring."

"The Paradise of Bachelors," the other part of the dyptich published with "The Tartarus of Maids" on All-Fools Day, is the other side of the coin. The factory to which the maidens are enslaved is owned by "Old Bach"; "The Paradise of Bachelors" displays the perversion of bachelors, carousing in a sublimated orgiastic hideaway not far from Temple Bar and reached by turning from a street "soiled with mud" to "glide down a dim, monastic way, flanked by dark, sedate, and solemn piles."

The sexual symbolism of "The Bell-Tower" has still more designs. Bannadonna ("With him, common sense was theurgy; machinery, miracle; Prometheus, the heroic name for machinist; man, the true God.") is the archetypal mechanic. He constructs a gigantic tower which "in one erection" unites "bell-tower and clock-tower." "The climax-stone" is hoisted and laid with "the sound of viols" and "the firing of ordnance," but "the groined belfry" eventually crashes down with "naught but a broken and disastrous sound." On the very top of this intensely symbolic tower Bannadonna constructs the archetypal automaton, which is repeatedly called the "domino."

Bannadonna, conjoined with his bell ringed by gay girls, becomes Belladonna, the feminine form masking as the master (*cf.* the sexual transformation of Bella-Bello in the Nighttown sequence in *Ulysses*). "Domino," a word in masculine form, derives from *dominus* (lord, master) and, because of ecclesiastical usages, had come to signify a robe or mask (and thereby giving its name to the game of dominoes, a significance which we shall shortly explore). The climax of this sexual masquerade comes when the domino strikes Bannadonna as Bannadonna is trying to change the features of one of the gay girls on the bell from what they are to what he thinks they should be, from actual to ideal. Aiming at the hand of the girl, the automaton smashes the brain of the man who had created both the graven feminine beauty and the mechanical masculine strength. After this climax, "Bannadonna lay, prostrate and bleeding," revealing dramatically the perversion of the attempt to escape from the human world into the mechanical.

The coherent sexual level of the story supports and is supported by a complicated political allegory about the ante-bellum United States of America and all the republics, kingdoms, and empires which stand behind it, casting their shadows upon it in the light of history. In this allegory, the automaton stands for all kinds of slaves, from the Negroes in the South to the machines and their slaves in the North, from Balaam's ass to Talus.

What are the first words of the story?—"Like negroes, these powers own man sullenly. . . ." "Benito Cereno," included with "The Bell-Tower" in *The Piazza Tales*, shows a shipload of Negro slaves who are in fact the brutal masters of the Spanish crew, who represent all kinds of broken-down, grand, inhuman, human empire. The "white" crew is like Bannadonna, apparent master of its creature, really both its creature's slave and the unwitting agent of the self-destruction which ensues from manacling the hands and feet of others. This is one reason why the automaton is called "Haman." Negroes were, according to various arguments about slavery, the children of Ham. Hence in *Mardi*, Melville designates Africa as Hamora and refers to its enslaved American children as the "tribe of Hamo." In that earlier work, Melville handles one of the central issues of this story with more directness but much less art. Two characters, encountering for the first time Negro slaves and their white overseers, respond like this:

"Are these men?" asked Babbalanja.
"Which mean you?" asked Mohi.

Here one sees other meanings in the veiled sexual relationship of Bannadonna and his symbol of chained maleness, who is in ironic fact his domino.

Dominoes are so called because their white upper surface masks the blackness below. Melville uses the image of dominoes in almost precisely the same way Conrad was later to use it in *Heart of Darkness*. In both works the apparent mastery of white over black is no more a lie than is their apparent self-contained identities. White is, as it turns out, black; black is only another form of white. The sequel of these facts in Melville's fiction is *The Confidence-Man: His Masquerade*, in which Black Guinea appears as the second avatar of the lamb-like man, and *Billy Budd*, in which the blond handsome sailor appears as another form of the black handsome sailor; the sequel of these facts in American history is the Civil War and the consequences with which we live.

In this allegory, the bell, which becomes cracked because of its flaw, caused by the blood of a worker, is the Liberty Bell, which was rung to celebrate—and here is a fine Melvillean irony—the Declaration of Independence. By 1855 the kind of liberty bell tolling was the abolitionist gift book called *The Liberty Bell*. As the third part of "The Bell-Tower" 's epigraph proclaims, "Seeking to conquer a larger liberty, man but extends the empire of necessity."

"The great state-bell" is much like the masses whose independence it supposedly symbolizes: "limit should be set to the dependent weight of its swaying masses." When, at the climax, "no bell-stroke from the tower" could be heard, "The multitude became tumultuous" (or, in Melvillean punning, too-multuous). After the slave proves too good at his job, he is replaced by "a powerful peasant," who, "wishing to test at once the full glory of the bell," yanks it from its glorious height "in one sheer fall, three hundred feet" to lie buried, "inverted and half out of sight."

Melville's brilliant perceptions about the technological, sociological, and political conditions in the United States half a dozen years before the Civil War, like his perceptions about the sexual significance of automata, are only part of the story. The reader who wishes to see what else the story brings into its system of orbiting symbolic mirrors must examine all the metaphors which juxtapose art and nature as well as every Biblical, mythological, and historical reference in the story, particularly noting: Cronus and his children; Vulcan and his two falls; Deborah, Jael, and Sisera; Esther, Haman, and Mordecai; the tower of Babel; Babylon (see Melville's two main sources, the 1846 edition of John Kitto's *Cyclopædia of Biblical Literature* and the Book of Daniel); and the interrelations of Babel, Babylon, and Rome.

The merging of Melville's later technique with what was to become a conventional kind of science fiction produced a strange compound, one which hints of a largely unrealized potential in science fiction. "The Bell-Tower" stands as an example of a fiction which can have at least as many dimensions as its subject. Melville shows how a technological creation, the immediate subject of "The Bell-Tower," involves: the sexual nature of man; the difference between art and nature; all acts of creation; the relation between all creatures and their creators; the political, social, and economic relations deriving from these relations; the myths spun out of all these relations; and the total design of all.

HERMAN MELVILLE

The Bell-Tower *

> "Like negroes, these powers own man sullenly; mindful of their higher master; while serving, plot revenge."
>
> "The world is apoplectic with high-living of ambition; and apoplexy has its fall."
>
> "Seeking to conquer a larger liberty, man but extends the empire of necessity."
>
> FROM A PRIVATE MS.

In the south of Europe, nigh a once frescoed capital, now with dank mould cankering its bloom, central in a plain, stands what, at distance, seems the black mossed stump of some immeasurable pine, fallen, in forgotten days, with Anak and the Titan.

As all along where the pine tree falls, its dissolution leaves a mossy mound—last-flung shadow of the perished trunk; never lengthening, never lessening; unsubject to the fleet falsities of the sun; shade immutable, and true gauge which cometh by prostration—so westward from what seems the stump, one steadfast spear of lichened ruin veins the plain.

From that tree-top, what birded chimes of silver throats had rung. A stone pine; a metallic aviary in its crown: the Bell-Tower, built by the great mechanician, the unblest foundling, Bannadonna.

Like Babel's, its base was laid in a high hour of renovated earth, following the second deluge, when the waters of the Dark Ages had dried up, and once more the green appeared. No wonder that, after so long and deep submersion, the jubilant expectation of the race should, as with Noah's sons, soar into Shinar aspiration.

In firm resolve, no man in Europe at that period went beyond Bannadonna. Enriched through commerce with the Levant, the state in which he lived voted to have the noblest Bell-Tower in Italy. His repute assigned him to be architect.

* *Putnam's Monthly Magazine*, 1855; *The Piazza Tales*, 1856.

Stone by stone, month by month, the tower rose. Higher, higher; snail-like in pace, but torch or rocket in its pride.

After the masons would depart, the builder, standing alone upon its ever-ascending summit, at close of every day, saw that he overtopped still higher walls and trees. He would tarry till a late hour there, wrapped in schemes of other and still loftier piles. Those who of saints' days thronged the spot—hanging to the rude poles of scaffolding, like sailors on yards, or bees on boughs, unmindful of lime and dust, and falling chips of stone—their homage not the less inspired him to self-esteem.

At length the holiday of the Tower came. To the sound of viols, the climax-stone slowly rose in air, and, amid the firing of ordnance, was laid by Bannadonna's hands upon the final course. Then mounting it, he stood erect, alone, with folded arms, gazing upon the white summits of blue inland Alps, and whiter crests of bluer Alps off-shore—sights invisible from the plain. Invisible, too, from thence was that eye he turned below, when, like the cannon booms, came up to him the people's combustions of applause.

That which stirred them so was, seeing with what serenity the builder stood three hundred feet in air, upon an unrailed perch. This none but he durst do. But his periodic standing upon the pile, in each stage of its growth—such discipline had its last result.

Little remained now but the bells. These, in all respects, must correspond with their receptacle.

The minor ones were prosperously cast. A highly enriched one followed, of a singular make, intended for suspension in a manner before unknown. The purpose of this bell, its rotary motion, and connection with the clock-work, also executed at the time, will, in the sequel, receive mention.

In the one erection, bell-tower and clock-tower were united, though, before that period, such structures had commonly been built distinct; as the Campanile and Torre del 'Orologio of St. Mark to this day attest.

But it was upon the great state-bell that the founder lavished his more daring skill. In vain did some of the less elated magistrates here caution him; saying that though truly the tower was Titanic, yet limit should be set to the dependent weight of its swaying masses. But undeterred, he prepared his mammoth mould, dented with mythological devices; kindled his fires of balsamic firs; melted his tin and copper; and, throwing in much plate, contributed by the public spirit of the nobles, let loose the tide.

The unleashed metals bayed like hounds. The workmen shrunk. Through their fright, fatal harm to the bell was dreaded. Fearless as Shadrach, Bannadonna, rushing through the glow, smote the chief culprit with his ponderous ladle. From the smitten part, a splinter was dashed into the seething mass, and at once was melted in.

Next day a portion of the work was heedfully uncovered. All seemed right. Upon the third morning, with equal satisfaction, it was bared still lower. At length, like some old Theban king, the whole cooled casting was disinterred. All was fair except in one strange spot. But as he suffered no one to attend him in these inspections, he concealed the blemish by some preparation which none knew better to devise.

The casting of such a mass was deemed no small triumph for the caster; one, too, in which the state might not scorn to share. The homicide was overlooked. By the charitable that deed was but imputed to sudden transports of esthetic passion, not to any flagitious quality. A kick from an Arabian charger; not sign of vice, but blood.

His felony remitted by the judge, absolution given him by the priest, what more could even a sickly conscience have desired.

Honoring the tower and its builder with another holiday, the republic witnessed the hoisting of the bells and clockwork amid shows and pomps superior to the former.

Some months of more than usual solitude on Bannadonna's part ensued. It was not unknown that he was engaged upon something for the belfry, intended to complete it, and surpass all that had gone before. Most people imagined that the design would involve a casting like the bells. But those who thought they had some further insight, would shake their heads, with hints, that not for nothing did the mechanician keep so secret. Meantime, his seclusion failed not to invest his work with more or less of that sort of mystery pertaining to the forbidden.

Ere long he had a heavy object hoisted to the belfry, wrapped in a dark sack or cloak—a procedure sometimes had in the case of an elaborate piece of sculpture, or statue, which, being intended to grace the front of a new edifice, the architect does not desire exposed to critical eyes, till set up, finished, in its appointed place. Such was the impression now. But, as the object rose, a statuary present observed, or thought he did, that it was not entirely rigid, but was, in a manner, pliant. At last, when the hidden thing had attained its final height, and, obscurely seen from below, seemed almost of itself to step into the belfry, as if with little assistance from the crane, a shrewd old blacksmith present ventured the suspicion that it was but a living man. This surmise was thought a foolish one, while the general interest failed not to augment.

Not without demur from Bannadonna, the chief-magistrate of the town, with an associate—both elderly men—followed what seemed the image up the tower. But, arrived at the belfry, they had little recompense. Plausibly entrenching himself behind the conceded mysteries of his art, the mechanician withheld present explanation. The magistrates glanced toward the cloaked object, which, to their surprise, seemed now to have changed its attitude, or else had before been more perplexingly concealed by the violent muffling action of the wind without. It seemed now seated upon some sort of frame, or chair, contained within the domino. They observed that nigh the top, in a sort of square, the web of the cloth, either from accident or design, had its warp partly withdrawn, and the cross threads plucked out here and there, so as to form a sort of woven grating. Whether it were the low wind or no, stealing through the stone lattice-work, or only their own perturbed imaginations, is uncertain, but they thought they discerned a slight sort of fitful, spring-like motion, in the domino. Nothing, however incidental or insignificant, escaped their uneasy eyes. Among other things, they pried out, in a corner, an earthen cup, partly corroded and partly encrusted, and one whispered to the other, that this cup was just such a one as might, in mockery, be offered to the lips of some brazen statue, or, perhaps, still worse.

But, being questioned, the mechanician said, that the cup was simply used in his founder's business, and described the purpose; in short, a cup to test the condition of metals in fusion. He added, that it had got into the belfry by the merest chance.

Again, and again, they gazed at the domino, as at some suspicious incognito—at a Venetian mask. All sorts of vague apprehensions stirred them. They even dreaded lest, when they should descend, the mechanician, though without a flesh and blood companion, for all that, would not be left alone.

Affecting some merriment at their disquietude, he begged to relieve them, by extending a coarse sheet of workman's canvas between them and the object.

Meantime he sought to interest them in his other work; nor, now that the domino was out of sight, did they long remain insensible to the artistic wonders lying round them; wonders hitherto beheld but in their unfinished state; because, since hoisting the bells, none but the caster had entered within the belfry. It was one trait of his, that, even in details, he would not let another do what he could, without too great loss of time, accomplish for himself. So, for several preceding weeks, whatever hours were unemployed in his secret design, had been devoted to elaborating the figures on the bells.

The clock-bell, in particular, now drew attention. Under a patient chisel, the latent beauty of its enrichments, before obscured by the cloudings incident to casting, that beauty in its shyest grace, was now revealed. Round and round the bell, twelve figures of gay girls, garlanded, hand-in-hand, danced in a choral ring—the embodied hours.

"Bannadonna," said the chief, "this bell excels all else. No added touch could here improve. Hark!" hearing a sound, "was that the wind?"

"The wind, Excellenza," was the light response. "But the figures, they are not yet without their faults. They need some touches yet. When those are given, and the——block yonder," pointing towards the canvas screen, "when Haman there, as I merrily call him,—him? *it,* I mean——when Haman is fixed on this, his lofty tree, then, gentlemen, will I be most happy to receive you here again."

The equivocal reference to the object caused some return of restlessness. However, on their part, the visitors forbore further allusion to it, unwilling, perhaps, to let the foundling see how easily it lay within his plebeian art to stir the placid dignity of nobles.

"Well, Bannadonna," said the chief, "how long ere you are ready to set the clock going, so that the hour shall be sounded? Our interest in you, not less than in the work itself, makes us anxious to be assured of your success. The people, too,—why, they are shouting now. Say the exact hour when you will be ready."

"To-morrow, Excellenza, if you listen for it,—or should you not, all the same—strange music will be heard. The stroke of one shall be the first from yonder bell," pointing to the bell adorned with girls and garlands, "that stroke shall fall there, where the hand of Una clasps Dua's. The stroke of one shall sever that loved clasp. To-morrow, then, at one o'clock, as struck here, precisely here," advancing and placing his finger upon the clasp, "the poor mechanic will be most happy once more to give you liege audience, in this his littered shop. Farewell till then, illustrious magnificoes, and hark ye for your vassal's stroke."

His still, Vulcanic face hiding its burning brightness like a forge, he moved with ostentatious deference towards the scuttle, as if so far to escort their exit. But the junior magistrate, a kind-hearted man, troubled at what seemed to him a certain sardonical disdain, lurking beneath the foundling's humble mien, and in Christian sympathy more distressed at it on his account than on his own, dimly surmising what might be the final fate of such a cynic solitaire, nor perhaps uninfluenced by the general strangeness of surrounding things, this good magistrate had glanced sadly, sideways from the speaker, and thereupon his foreboding eye had started at the expression of the unchanging face of the Hour Una.

"How is this, Bannadonna?" he lowly asked, "Una looks unlike her sisters."

"In Christ's name, Bannadonna," impulsively broke in the chief, his attention, for the first attracted to the figure, by his associate's remark, "Una's face looks just like that of Deborah, the prophetess, as painted by the Florentine, Del Fonca."

"Surely, Bannadonna," lowly resumed the milder magistrate, "you meant the twelve should wear the same jocundly abandoned air. But see, the smile of Una seems but a fatal one. 'Tis different."

While his mild associate was speaking, the chief glanced, inquiringly, from him to the caster, as if anxious to mark how the discrepancy would be accounted for. As the chief stood, his advanced foot was on the scuttle's curb.

Bannadonna spoke:

"Excellenza, now that, following your keener eye, I glance upon the face of Una, I do, indeed, perceive some little variance. But look all round the bell, and you will find no two faces entirely correspond. Because there is a law in art——but the cold wind is rising more; these lattices are but a poor defense. Suffer me, magnificoes, to conduct you, at least, partly on your way. Those in whose well-being there is a public stake, should be heedfully attended."

"Touching the look of Una, you were saying, Bannadonna, that there was a certain law in art," observed the chief, as the three now descended the stone shaft, "pray, tell me, then——."

"Pardon; another time, Excellenza;—the tower is damp."

"Nay, I must rest, and hear it now. Here,—here is a wide landing, and through this leeward slit, no wind, but ample light. Tell us of your law; and at large."

"Since, Excellenza, you insist, know that there is a law in art, which bars the possibility of duplicates. Some years ago, you may remember, I graved a small seal for your republic, bearing, for its chief device, the head of your own ancestor, its illustrious founder. It becoming necessary, for the customs' use, to have innumerable impressions for bales and boxes, I graved an entire plate, containing one hundred of the seals. Now, though, indeed, my object was to have those hundred heads identical, and though, I dare say, people think them so, yet, upon closely scanning an uncut impression from the plate, no two of those five-score faces, side by side, will be found alike. Gravity is the air of all; but, diversified in all. In some, benevolent; in some, ambiguous; in two or three, to a close scrutiny, all but incipiently malign, the variation of less than a hair's breadth in the linear shadings round the mouth sufficing to all this. Now, Excellenza, transmute that general gravity into joyousness, and subject it to twelve of those variations I have described, and tell me, will you not have my hours here, and Una one of them? But I like——."

"Hark! is that——a footfall above?"

"Mortar, Excellenza; sometimes it drops to the belfry-floor from the arch where the stone-work was left undressed. I must have it seen to. As I was about to say: for one, I like this law forbidding duplicates. It evokes fine personalities. Yes, Excellenza, that strange, and—to you—uncertain smile, and those fore-looking eyes of Una, suit Bannadonna very well."

"Hark!—sure we left no soul above?"

"No soul, Excellenza; rest assured, no *soul*.—Again the mortar."

"It fell not while we were there."

"Ah, in your presence, it better knew its place, Excellenza," blandly bowed Bannadonna.

"But, Una," said the milder magistrate, "she seemed intently gazing on you; one would have almost sworn that she picked you out from among us three."

"If she did, possibly, it might have been her finer apprehension, Excellenza."

"How, Bannadonna? I do not understand you."

"No consequence, no consequence, Excellenza—but the shifted wind is blowing through the slit. Suffer me to escort you on; and then, pardon, but the toiler must to his tools."

"It may be foolish, Signor," said the milder magistrate, as, from the third landing, the two now went down unescorted, "but, somehow, our great mechanician moves me strangely. Why, just now, when he so superciliously replied, his look seemed Sisera's, God's vain foe, in Del Fonca's painting. And that young, sculptured Deborah, too. Ay, and that——."

"Tush, tush, Signor!" returned the chief. "A passing whim. Deborah?—Where's Jael, pray?"

"Ah," said the other, as they now stepped upon the sod, "Ah, Signor, I see you leave your fears behind you with the chill and gloom; but mine, even in this sunny air, remain. Hark!"

It was a sound from just within the tower door, whence they had emerged. Turning, they saw it closed.

"He has slipped down and barred us out," smiled the chief; "but it is his custom."

Proclamation was now made, that the next day, at one hour after meridian, the clock would strike, and—thanks to the mechanician's powerful art—with unusual accompaniments. But what those should be, none as yet could say. The announcement was received with cheers.

By the looser sort, who encamped about the tower all night, lights were seen gleaming through the topmost blind-work, only disappearing with the morning sun. Strange sounds, too, were heard, or were thought to be, by those whom anxious watching might not have left mentally undisturbed—sounds, not only of some ringing implement, but also—so they said—half-suppressed screams and plainings, such as might have issued from some ghostly engine, overplied.

Slowly the day drew on; part of the concourse chasing the weary time with songs and games, till, at last, the great blurred sun rolled, like a football, against the plain.

At noon, the nobility and principal citizens came from the town in cavalcade, a guard of soldiers, also, with music, the more to honor the occasion.

Only one hour more. Impatience grew. Watches were held in hands of feverish men, who stood, now scrutinizing their small dial-plates, and then, with neck thrown back, gazing toward the belfry, as if the eye might foretell that which could only be made sensible to the ear; for, as yet, there was no dial to the tower-clock.

The hour hands of a thousand watches now verged within a hair's breadth of the figure 1. A silence, as of the expectation of some Shiloh, pervaded the swarming plain. Suddenly a dull, mangled sound—naught ringing in it; scarcely audible, indeed, to the outer circles of the people—that dull sound dropped heavily from the belfry. At the same moment, each man stared at his neighbor blankly. All watches were upheld. All hour-hands were at—had passed—the figure 1. No bell-stroke from the tower. The multitude became tumultuous.

Waiting a few moments, the chief magistrate, commanding silence, hailed the belfry, to know what thing unforeseen had happened there.

No response.

He hailed again and yet again.

All continued hushed.

By his order, the soldiers burst in the tower-door; when, stationing guards to defend it from the now surging mob, the chief, accompanied by his former associate, climbed the winding stairs. Half-way up, they stopped to listen. No sound. Mounting faster, they reached the belfry; but, at the threshold, started at the spectacle disclosed. A spaniel, which, unbeknown to them, had followed them thus far, stood shivering as before some unknown monster in a brake: or, rather, as if it snuffed footsteps leading to some other world. Bannadonna lay, prostrate and bleeding, at the base of the bell which was adorned with girls and garlands. He lay at the feet of the hour Una; his head coinciding, in a vertical line, with her left hand, clasped by the hour Dua. With downcast face impending over him, like Jael over nailed Sisera in the tent, was the domino; now no more becloaked.

It had limbs, and seemed clad in a scaly mail, lustrous as a dragon-beetle's. It was manacled, and its clubbed arms were uplifted, as if, with its manacles, once more to smite its already smitten victim. One advanced foot of it was inserted beneath the dead body, as if in the act of spurning it.

Uncertainty falls on what now followed.

It were but natural to suppose that the magistrates would, at first, shrink from immediate personal contact with what they saw. At the least, for a time, they would stand in involuntary doubt; it may be, in more or less of horrified alarm. Certain it is, that an arquebuss was called for from below. And some add, that its report, followed by a fierce whiz, as of the sudden snapping of a main-spring, with a steely din, as if a stack of sword-blades should be dashed upon a pavement, these blended sounds came ringing to the plain, attracting every eye far upward to the belfry, whence, through the lattice-work, thin wreaths of smoke were curling.

Some averred that it was the spaniel, gone mad by fear, which was shot. This, others denied. True it was, the spaniel never more was seen; and, probably, for some unknown reason, it shared the burial now to be related of the domino. For, whatever the preceding circumstances may have been, the first instinctive panic over, or else all ground of reasonable fear removed, the two magistrates, by themselves, quickly rehooded the figure in the dropped cloak wherein it had been hoisted. The same night, it was secretly lowered to the ground, smuggled to the beach, pulled far out to sea, and sunk. Nor to any after urgency, even in free convivial hours, would the twain ever disclose the full secrets of the belfry.

From the mystery unavoidably investing it, the popular solution of the foundling's fate involved more or less of supernatural agency. But some few less unscientific minds pretended to find little difficulty in otherwise accounting for it. In the chain of circumstantial inferences drawn, there may, or may not, have been some absent or defective links. But, as the explanation in question is the only one which tradition has explicitly preserved, in dearth of better, it will here be given. But, in the first place, it is requisite to present the supposition entertained as to the entire motive and mode, with their origin, of the secret design of Bannadonna; the minds above-mentioned assuming to penetrate as well into his soul as into the event. The disclosure will indirectly involve reference to peculiar matters, none of the clearest, beyond the immediate subject.

At that period, no large bell was made to sound otherwise than as at present, by agitation of a tongue within, by means of ropes, or percussion from without, either from cumbrous machinery, or stalwart watchmen, armed with heavy hammers, stationed in the belfry, or in sentry-boxes on the open roof, according as the bell was sheltered or exposed.

It was from observing these exposed bells, with their watchmen, that the foundling, as was opined, derived the first suggestion of his scheme. Perched on a great mast or spire, the human figure, viewed from below, undergoes such a reduction in its apparent size, as to obliterate its intelligent features. It evinces no personality. Instead of bespeaking volition, its gestures rather resemble the automatic ones of the arms of a telegraph.

Musing, therefore, upon the purely Punchinello aspect of the human figure thus beheld, it had indirectly occurred to Bannadonna to devise some metallic agent, which should strike the hour with its mechanic hand, with even greater precision than the vital one. And, moreover, as the vital watchman on the roof, sallying from his retreat at the given periods, walked to the bell with uplifted mace, to smite it, Bannadonna had resolved that his invention should likewise possess the power of locomotion, and, along with that, the appearance, at least, of intelligence and will.

If the conjectures of those who claimed acquaintance with the intent of Bannadonna be thus far correct, no unenterprising spirit could have been his. But they stopped not here; intimating that though, indeed, his design had, in the first place, been prompted by the sight of the watchman, and confined to the devising of a subtle substitute for him: yet, as is not seldom the case with projectors, by insensible gradations, proceeding from comparatively pigmy aims to Titanic ones, the original scheme had, in its anticipated eventualities, at last, attained to an unheard of degree of daring. He still bent his efforts upon the locomotive figure for the belfry, but only as a partial type of an ulterior creature, a sort of elephantine helot, adapted to further, in a degree scarcely to be imagined, the universal conveniences and glories of humanity; supplying nothing less than a supplement to the Six Days' Work; stocking the earth with a new serf, more useful than the ox, swifter than the dolphin, stronger than the lion, more cunning than the ape, for industry an ant, more fiery than serpents, and yet, in patience, another ass. All excellences of all God-made creatures, which served man, were here to receive advancement, and then to be combined in one. Talus was to have been the all-accomplished helot's name. Talus, iron slave to Bannadonna, and, through him, to man.

Here, it might well be thought that, were these last conjectures as to the foundling's secrets not erroneous, then must he have been hopelessly infected with the craziest chimeras of his age; far outgoing Albert Magus and Cornelius Agrippa. But the contrary was averred. However marvelous his design, however apparently transcending not alone the bounds of human invention, but those of divine creation, yet the proposed means to be employed were alleged to have been confined within the sober forms of sober reason. It was affirmed that, to a degree of more than skeptic scorn, Bannadonna had been without sympathy for any of the vain-glorious irrationalities of his time. For example, he had not concluded, with the visionaries among the metaphysicians, that between the finer mechanic forces and the ruder animal vitality some germ of correspondence might prove discoverable. As little did his scheme partake of the enthusiasm of some natural philosophers, who hoped, by physiological and chemical inductions, to arrive at a knowledge of the source of life, and so qualify themselves to manufacture and improve upon it. Much less had he aught in common with the tribe of alchemists, who sought, by a species of incantations, to evoke some surprising vitality from the laboratory. Neither had he imagined, with certain sanguine theosophists, that, by faithful adoration of the Highest, unheard-of powers would be vouchsafed to man. A practical materialist, what Bannadonna had aimed at was to have been reached, not by logic, not by crucible, not by conjuration, not by altars; but by plain vice-bench and hammer. In short, to solve nature, to steal into her, to intrigue beyond her, to procure some one else to bind her to his hand;—these, one and all, had not been his objects; but, asking no favors from any element or any being, of himself, to rival her, outstrip her, and rule her. He stooped to conquer. With him, common sense was theurgy; machinery, miracle; Prometheus, the heroic name for machinist; man, the true God.

Nevertheless, in his initial step, so far as the experimental automaton for the belfry was concerned, he allowed fancy some little play; or, perhaps, what seemed his fancifulness was but his utilitarian ambition collaterally extended. In figure, the creature for the belfry should not be likened after the human pattern, nor any animal one, nor after the ideals, however wild, of ancient fable, but equally in aspect as in organism be an original production; the more terrible to behold, the better.

Such, then, were the suppositions as to the present scheme, and the reserved intent. How, at the very threshold, so unlooked for a catastrophe overturned all, or rather, what was the conjecture here, is now to be set forth.

It was thought that on the day preceding the fatality, his visitors having left him, Bannadonna had unpacked the belfry image, adjusted it, and placed it in the retreat provided—a sort of sentry-box in one corner of the belfry; in short, throughout the night, and for some part of the ensuing morning, he had been engaged in arranging everything connected with the domino: the issuing from the sentry-box each sixty minutes; sliding along a grooved way, like a railway; advancing to the clock-bell, with uplifted manacles; striking it at one of the twelve junctions of the four-and-twenty hands; then wheeling, circling the bell, and retiring to its post, there to bide for another sixty minutes, when the same process was to be repeated; the bell, by a cunning mechanism, meantime turning on its vertical axis, so as to present, to the descending mace, the clasped hands of the next two figures, when it would strike two, three, and so on, to the end. The musical metal in this time-bell being so managed in the fusion, by some art, perishing with its originator, that each of the clasps of the four-and-twenty hands should give forth its own peculiar resonance when parted.

But on the magic metal, the magic and metallic stranger never struck but that one stroke, drove but that one nail, severed but that one clasp, by which Bannadonna clung to his ambitious life.

For, after winding up the creature in the sentry-box, so that, for the present, skipping the intervening hours, it should not emerge till the hour of one, but should then infallibly emerge, and, after deftly oiling the grooves whereon it was to slide, it was surmised that the mechanician must then have hurried to the bell, to give his final touches to its sculpture. True artist, he here became absorbed; and absorption still further intensified, it may be, by his striving to abate that strange look of Una; which, though, before others, he had treated with such unconcern, might not, in secret, have been without its thorn.

And so, for the interval, he was oblivious of his creature; which, not oblivious of him, and true to its creation, and true to its heedful winding up, left its post precisely at the given moment; along its well-oiled route, slid noiselessly towards its mark; and, aiming at the hand of Una, to ring one clangorous note, dully smote the intervening brain of Bannadonna, turned backwards to it; the manacled arms then instantly up-springing to their hovering poise. The falling body clogged the thing's return; so there it stood, still impending over Bannadonna, as if whispering some post-mortem terror. The chisel lay dropped from the hand, but beside the hand; the oil-flask spilled across the iron track.

In his unhappy end, not unmindful of the rare genius of the mechanician, the republic decreed him a stately funeral. It was resolved that the great bell—the one whose casting had been jeopardized through the timidity of the ill-starred workman—should be rung upon the entrance of the bier into the cathedral. The most robust man of the country round was assigned the office of bell-ringer.

But as the pall-bearers entered the cathedral porch, naught but a broken and disastrous sound, like that of some lone Alpine land-slide, fell from the tower upon their ears. And then, all was hushed.

Glancing backwards, they saw the groined belfry crashed sideways in. It afterwards appeared that the powerful peasant, who had the bell-rope in charge, wishing to test at once the full glory of the bell, had swayed down upon the rope with one concentrate jerk. The mass of quaking metal, too ponderous for its frame, and strangely feeble somewhere at its top, loosed from its fastening, tore sideways down, and tumbling in one sheer fall, three hundred feet to the soft sward below, buried itself inverted and half out of sight.

Upon its disinterment, the main fracture was found to have started from a small spot in the ear; which, being scraped, revealed a defect, deceptively minute, in the casting; which defect must subsequently have been pasted over with some unknown compound.

The remolten metal soon reassumed its place in the tower's repaired superstructure. For one year the metallic choir of birds sang musically in its belfry-bough-work of sculptured blinds and traceries. But on the first anniversary of the tower's completion —at early dawn, before the concourse had surrounded it—an earthquake came; one loud crash was heard. The stone-pine, with all its bower of songsters, lay overthrown upon the plain.

So the blind slave obeyed its blinder lord; but, in obedience, slew him. So the creator was killed by the creature. So the bell was too heavy for the tower. So the bell's main weakness was where man's blood had flawed it. And so pride went before the fall.

MAN AS MACHINE

> A slight congestion or softening of the brain shows the least materialistic of philosophers that he must recognize the strict dependence of mind upon its organ in the only condition of life with which we are experimentally acquainted.
>
> The more we examine the mechanism of thought, the more we shall see that the automatic, unconscious action of the mind enters largely into all its processes.
>
> OLIVER WENDELL HOLMES,
> "Mechanism in Thought and Morals"
> (1870)

> Mental and physical events are, on all hands, admitted to present the strongest contrast in the entire field of being. The chasm which yawns between them is less easily bridged over by the mind than any interval we know. Why then not call it an absolute chasm? And say not only that the two worlds are different, but that they are independent?
>
> WILLIAM JAMES,
> "Are We Automata?"
> (*Mind*, 1879)

Frederic Jessup Stimson is one of those brilliant amateurs one finds writing fiction in the nineteenth century. Noted more for his work in constitutional law, which he taught at Harvard and about which he wrote many books, and his diplomatic service (he was the first United States ambassador to Argentina), he somehow found time to write a number of novels and volumes of short fiction under the pen name J. S. of Dale.

Stimson's "Dr. Materialismus," published thirty-five years after "The Bell-Tower," is more peculiarly modern, for its main concern is that central modern question: What precisely *is* the difference between man and mechanism? "The Bell-Tower" does not directly ask this question, at least not in precise physical or physiological terms. Of the stories I know, the one that most clearly resembles "Dr. Materialismus"—and the resemblance is startling—is "The Maxwell Equations" (in *Destination: Amaltheia*, Moscow, n.d.) by Anatoly Dnieprov, a contemporary Soviet physicist working in cybernetics.

Both "Dr. Materialismus" and "The Maxwell Equations" place a narrator in a situation in which he has the experience of becoming something very close to a machine; in each story the narrator is subjected by a complete materialist to varying ranges of physical frequencies which produce, as automatic responses, all the kinds of emotions man is capable of feeling. And the central issue of the difference between man and machine is precisely the same in both stories. Of course Dnieprov has available to him a more convincing kind of physical apparatus, but if Dnieprov's electromagnetic field switched places with Stimson's physical vibrations neither story would in essence be changed. The most important differences between the two stories are ancillary to the central theme. For Dnieprov's narrator, man's relationship to industry and to man depends on the question, Can man be reduced to a machine? For Stimson's narrator, man's relationship to God and to woman depends on the same question. But Dnieprov and Stimson see more than their narrators. For Dnieprov himself, man's relationship to the state also depends (in a thinly veiled political allegory) on that same question. And for Stimson, humanism's relationship to Christianity also depends on the question, as he explicitly suggests in the introduction to another story collected in an 1893 volume with "Dr. Materialismus" (the relevant part of this introduction is reprinted here as a postscript). Of course, in a larger sense—and both Dnieprov and Stimson are dramatizing this—everything about modern human experience depends on the possibility that man can be considered a machine.

FREDERIC JESSUP STIMSON
Dr. Materialismus *

I should like some time to tell how Tetherby came to his end; he, too, was a victim of materialism, as his father had been before him; but when he died, he left this story, addressed among his papers to me; and I am sure he meant that all the world (or such part of it as cares to think) should know it. He had told it, or partly told it, to us before; in fragments, in suggestions, in those midnight talks that earnest young men still have in college, or had, in 1870.

Tetherby came from that strange, cold, Maine coast, washed in its fjords and beaches by a clear, cold sea, which brings it fogs of winter but never haze of summer; where men eat little, think much, drink only water, and yet live intense lives; where the village people, in their long winters away from the world, in an age of revivals had their waves of atheism, and would transform, in those days, their pine meeting-houses into Shakspere clubs, and logically make a cult of infidelity; now, with railways, I suppose all that has ceased; they read Shakspere as little as the scriptures, and the Sunday newspaper replaces both. Such a story —such an imagination—as Tetherby's, could not happen now—perhaps. But they take life earnestly in that remote, ardent province; they think coldly; and, when you least expect it, there comes in their lives, so hard and sharp and practical, a burst of passion.

He came to Newbridge to study law, and soon developed a

* *Scribner's,* 1890; *In the Three Zones,* 1893.

strange faculty for debate. The first peculiarity was his name—which first appeared and was always spelled, C. S. J. J. Tetherby in the catalogue, despite the practice, which was to spell one's name in full. Of course, speculation was rife as to the meaning of this portentous array of initials; and soon, after his way of talk was known, arose a popular belief that they stood for nothing less than Charles Stuart Jean Jacques. Nothing less would justify the intense leaning of his mind, radical as it was, for all that was mystical, ideal, old. But afterwards we learned that he had been so named by his curious father, Colonel Sir John Jones, after a supposed loyalist ancestor, who had flourished in the time of the Revolution, and had gone to Maine to get away from it; Tetherby's father being evidently under the impression that the two titles formed a component part of the ancestor's identity.

Rousseau Tetherby, as he continued to be called, was a tall, thin, broad-shouldered fellow, of great muscular strength and yet with feeble health, given to hallucinations and morbid imaginations which he would recount to you in that deep monotone of twang that seemed only fit to sell a horse in. The boys made fun of Tetherby; he bore it with a splendid smile and a twinkle in his ice-blue eye, until one day it went too far, and then he tackled the last offender and chucked him off the boat-house float into the river. He would have rowed upon the university crew, but that his digestion gave out; strong as he was in mind and body, nothing, that went for the nutrition and fostering of life, was well with him. Such men as he are repellent to the sane, and are willed by the world to die alone.

Some one on that night, I remember, had said something derogatory about Goethe's theory of colors. A dry subject, an abstruse subject, a useless subject—as one might think—but it roused Tetherby to sudden fury. He made a vehement defence of the great poet-philosopher against the dry, barren mathematics of the Newtonian science.

"Do you cipherers think all that is is reducible to numbers? to so many beats per second, like your own dry hearts? Sound may be nothing but a quicker rattle—is it but a rattle, the music in your souls? If light is but the impact of more rapid molecules, does MAN bring nothing else, when he worships the glory of the dawn? You say, tones are a few thousand beats per second, and colors a few billion beats per second—what becomes of all the numbers left between? If colored lights count all these billions, up from red to violet, and white light is the sum of all the colors, what can be its number but infinity? But is a white light GOD? Or would you cipherers make of God a cipher? Smoke looks yellow against the sky, and blue against the forest—but how can its *number* change? You, who make all to a number, as governments do to convicts in a prison! I tell you, this rage for machinery will bear Dead Sea fruit. You confound man's highest emotions with the tickling of the gray matter in his brain; that way lies death and suicide of the soul——"

We stared; we thought he had gone crazy.

"Goethe and Dante still know more about this universe than any cipherer," he said, more calmly. And then he told us this story; we fancied it a nightmare, or a morbid dream; but earnestly he told it, and slowly, surely, he won our hearts at least to some believing in the terror of the tale.

When he was through, we parted, with few words, thinking poor Tetherby mad. But when he died it was found among his papers, addressed to me. Materialism had conquered him, but not subdued him; "say not the struggle naught availed him" though he left but this one tract behind. It is only as a sermon that it needs preserving, though the story of poor Althea Hardy was, I believe, in all essentials true.

I was born and lived, until I came to this university, in a small town in Maine. My father was a graduate of B—— College, and had never wholly dissolved his connection with that place; probably because he was there not unfavorably known to more acquaintances, and better people, than he elsewhere found. The town is one of those gentle-mannered, ferocious-minded, white wooden villages, common to Maine; with two churches, a brick town-hall, a stucco lyceum, a narrow railway station, and a spacious burying-ground. It is divided into two classes of society: one which institutes church-sociables, church-dances, church-sleighing parties; which twice a week, and critically, listens to a long and ultra-Protestant, almost mundane, essay-sermon; and which comes to town with, and takes social position from, pastoral letters of introduction, that are dated in other places and exhibited like marriage certificates. I have known the husbands at times to get their business employments on the strength of such encyclicals (but the ventures of these were not rarely attended with financial disaster, as passports only hinder honest travellers); the other class falling rather into Shakespeare clubs, intensely free-thinking, but calling Sabbath Sunday, and pretending to the slightly higher social position of the two. This is Maine, as I knew it; it may have changed since. Both classes were in general Prohibitionists, but the latter had wine to drink at home.

In this town were many girls with pretty faces; there, under that cold, concise sky of the North, they grew up; their intellects preternaturally acute, their nervous systems strung to breaking pitch, their physical growth so backward that at twenty their figures would be flat. We were intimate with them in a mental fellowship. Not that we boys of twenty did not have our preferences, but they were preferences of mere companionship; so that the magnanimous confidence of English America was justified; and anyone of us could be alone with her he preferred from morn to midnight, if he chose, and no one be the wiser or the worse. But there was one exceptional girl in B——, Althea Hardy. Her father was a rich ship-builder; and his father, a sea-captain, had married her grandmother in Catania, island of Sicily. With Althea Hardy, I think, I was in love.

In the winter of my second year at college there came to town a certain Dr. Materialismus—a German professor, scientist, socialist—ostensibly seeking employment as a German instructor at the college; practising hypnotism, magnetism, mesmerism, and mysticism; giving lectures on Hegel, believing in Hartmann, and in the indestructibility of matter and the destructibility of the soul; and his soul was a damned one, and he cared not for the loss of it.

Not that I knew this, then; I also was fascinated by him, I suppose. There was something so bold about his intellectuality, that excited my admiration. Althea and I used to dispute about it; she said she did not like the man. In my enthusiasm, I raved to her of him; and then, I suppose, I talked to him of her more than I should have done. Mind you, I had no thought of marriage then; nor, of course, of love. Althea was my most intimate friend—as a boy might have been. Sex differences were fused in the clear flame of the intellect. And B—— College itself was a co-educational institution.

The first time they met was at a coasting party; on a night of glittering cold, when the sky was dusty azure and the stars burned like blue fires. I had a double-runner, with Althea; and I asked the professor to come with us, as he was unused to the sport, and I feared lest he should be laughed at. I, of course, sat in front and steered the sled; then came Althea; then he; and it was his duty to steady her, his hands upon her waist.

We went down three times with no word spoken. The girls upon the other sleds would cry with exultation as they sped down the long hill; but Althea was silent. On the long walk up —it was nearly a mile—the professor and I talked; but I remember only one thing he said. Pointing to a singularly red star, he told us that two worlds were burning there, with people in them; they had lately rushed together, and, from planets, had become one burning sun. I asked him how he knew; it was all chemistry, he said. Althea said, how terrible it was to think of such a day of judgment on that quiet night; and he laughed a little, in his silent way, and said she was rather too late with her pity, for it had all happened some eighty years ago. "I don't see that you cry for Marie Antoinette," he said; "but that red ray you see left the star in 1789."

We left Althea at her home, and the professor asked me down to his. He lived in a strange place; the upper floor of a warehouse, upon a business street, low down in the town, above the Kennebec. He told me that he had hired it for the power; and I remembered to have noticed there a sign "To Let—One Floor, with Power." And sure enough, below the loud rush of the river, and the crushing noise made by the cakes of ice that passed over the falls, was a pulsing tremor in the house, more striking than a noise; and in the loft of his strange apartment rushed an endless band of leather, swift and silent. "It's furnished by the river," he said, "and not by steam. I thought it might be useful for some physical experiments."

The upper floor, which the doctor had rented, consisted mainly of a long loft for manufacturing, and a square room beyond it, formerly the counting-room. We had passed through the loft first (through which ran the spinning leather band), and I had noticed a forest of glass rods along the wall, but massed together like the pipes of an organ, and opposite them a row of steel bars like levers. "A mere physical experiment," said the doctor, as we sank into couches covered with white fur, in his inner apartment. Strangely disguised, the room in the old factory loft, hung with silk and furs, glittering with glass and gilding; there was no mirror, however, but, in front of me, one large picture. It represented a fainting anchorite, wan and yellow beneath his single sheepskin cloak, his eyes closing, the crucifix he was bearing just fallen in the desert sand; supporting him, the arms of a beautiful woman, roseate with perfect health, with laughing, red lips, and bold eyes resting on his wearied lids. I never had seen such a room; it realized what I had fancied of those sensuous, evil Trianons of the older and corrupt world. And yet I looked upon this picture; and as I looked, some tremor in the air, some evil influence in that place, dissolved all my intellect in wild desire.

"You admire the picture?" said Materialismus. "I painted it; she was my model." I am conscious to-day that I looked at him with a jealous envy, like some hungry beast. I had never seen such a woman. He laughed silently, and going to the wall touched what I supposed to be a bell. Suddenly my feelings changed.

"Your Althea Hardy," went on the doctor, "who is she?"

"She is not *my* Althea Hardy," I replied, with an indignation that I then supposed unreasoning. "She is the daughter of a retired sea-captain, and I see her because she alone can rank me in the class. Our minds are sympathetic. And Miss Hardy has a noble soul."

"She has a fair body," answered he; "of that much we are sure."

I cast a fierce look upon the man; my eye followed his to that picture on the wall; and some false shame kept me foolishly silent. I should have spoken then. . . . But many such fair carrion must strew the path of so lordly a vulture as this doctor was; unlucky if they thought (as he knew better) that aught of soul they bore entangled in their flesh.

"You do not strain a morbid consciousness about a chemical reaction," said he. "Two atoms rush together to make a world, or burn one, as we saw last night; it may be pleasure or it may be pain; conscious organs choose the former."

My distaste for the man was such that I hurried away, and went to sleep with a strange sadness, in the mood in which, as I suppose, believers pray; but that I was none. Dr. Materialismus had had a plum-colored velvet smoking-jacket on, with a red fez (he was a sort of beau), and I dreamed of it all night, and of the rushing leather band, and of the grinding of the ice in the river. Something made me keep my visit secret from Althea; an evil something, as I think it now.

The following day we had a lecture on light. It was one in a course in physics, or natural philosophy, as it was called in B—— College; just as they called Scotch psychology "Mental Philosophy," with capital letters; it was an archaic little place, and it was the first course that the German doctor had prevailed upon the college government to assign to him. The students sat at desks, ranged around the lecture platform, the floor of the hall being a concentric inclined plane; and Althea Hardy's desk was next to mine. Materialismus began with a brief sketch of the theory of sound; how it consisted in vibrations of the air, the coarsest medium of space, but could not dwell in ether; and how slow beats—blows of a hammer, for instance—had no more complex intellectual effect, but were mere consecutive noises; how the human organism ceased to detect these consecutive noises at about eight per second, until they reappeared at sixteen per second, the lowest tone which can be heard; and how, at something like thirty-two thousand per second these vibrations ceased to be heard, and were supposed unintelligible to humanity, being neither sound nor light—despite their rapid movement, dark and silent. But was all this energy wasted to mankind? Adverting one moment to the molecular, or rather mathematical, theory—first propounded by Democritus, re-established by Leibnitz, and never since denied—that the universe, both of mind and matter, body and soul, was made merely by innumerable, infinitesimal points of motion, endlessly gyrating among themselves—mere points, devoid of materiality, devoid also of soul, but each a centre of a certain force, which scientists entitle *gravitation,* philosophers deem *will,* and poets name *love*—he went on to Light. Light is a subtler emotion (he remarked here that he used the word *emotion* advisedly, as all emotions alike were, in substance, the subjective result of merely material motion). Light is a subtler emotion, dwelling in ether, but still nothing but a regular continuity of motion or molecular impact; to speak more plainly, successive beats or vibrations reappear intelligible to humanity as light, at something like 483,000,000,000 beats per second in the red ray. More exactly still, they appear first as *heat;* then as red, orange, yellow, all the colors of the spectrum, until they disappear again, through the violet ray, at something like 727,000,000,000 beats per second in the so-called chemical rays. "After that," he closed, "they are supposed unknown. The higher vibrations are supposed unintelligible to man, just as he fancies there is no more subtle medium than his (already hypothetical) ether. It is possible," said Materialismus, speaking in italics and looking at Althea, "*that these higher, almost infinitely rapid vibrations may be what are called the higher emotions or passions—like religion, love and hate—dwelling in a still more subtle, but yet material, medium, that poets and churches have picturesquely termed heart, conscience, soul.*" As he said this I too looked at Althea. I saw her bosom heaving; her lips were parted, and a faint rose was in her face. How womanly she was growing!

From that time I felt a certain fierceness against this German doctor. He had a way of patronizing me, of treating me as a man might treat some promising school-boy, while his manner to Althea was that of an equal—or a man of the world's to a favored lady. It was customary for the professors in B—— College to give little entertainments to their classes once in the winter; these usually took the form of tea-parties; but when it came to the doctor's turn, he gave a sleighing party to the neighboring city of A——, where we had an elaborate banquet at the principal hotel, with champagne to drink; and returned driving down the frozen river, the ice of which Dr. Mismus (for so we called him for short) had had tested for the occasion. The probable expense of this entertainment was discussed in the little town for many weeks after, and was by some estimated as high as two hundred dollars. The professor had hired, besides the large boat-sleigh, many single sleighs, in one of which he had returned, leading the way, and driving with Althea Hardy. It was then I determined to speak to her about her growing intimacy with this man.

I had to wait many weeks for an opportunity. Our winter sports at B—— used to end with a grand evening skating party on the Kennebec. Bonfires were built on the river, the safe mile or two above the falls was roped in with lines of Chinese lanterns, and a supper of hot oysters and coffee was provided at the big central fire. It was the fixed law of the place that the companion invited by any boy was to remain indisputably his for the evening. No second man would ever venture to join himself to a couple who were skating together on that night. I had asked Althea many weeks ahead to skate with me, and she had consented. The Doctor Materialismus knew this.

I, too, saw him nearly every day. He seemed to be fond of my company; of playing chess with me, or discussing metaphysics. Sometimes Althea was present at these arguments, in which I always took the idealistic side. But the little college had only armed me with Bain and Locke and Mill; and it may be imagined what a poor defence I could make with these against the German doctor, with his volumes of metaphysical realism and his knowledge of what Spinoza, Kant, Schopenhauer, and other defenders of us from the flesh could say on my side. Nevertheless, I sometimes appeared to have my victories. Althea was judge; and one day I well remember, when we were discussing the localization of emotion or of volition in the brain:

"Prove to me, if you may, even that every thought and hope and feeling of mankind is accompanied always by the same change in the same part of the cerebral tissue!" cried I. "Yet that physical change *is* not the soul-passion, but the effect of it upon the body; the mere trace in the brain of its passage, like the furrow of a ship upon the sea." And I looked at Althea, who smiled upon me.

"But if," said the doctor, "by the physical movement I produce the psychical passion? by the change of the brain-atoms *cause* the act of will? by a mere bit of glass-and-iron mechanism set *first* in motion, I make the prayer, or thought, or love, *follow*, in plain succession, to the machine's movement, on every soul that comes within its sphere—will you then say that the metaphor of ship and wake is a good one, when it is the wake that *precedes* the ship?"

"No," said I, smiling.

"Then come to my house to-night," said the doctor; "unless," he added with a sneer, "you are afraid to take such risks before your skating party." And then I saw Althea's lips grow bloodless, and my heart swelled within me.

"I will come," I muttered, without a smile.

"When?" said the professor.

"Now."

Althea suddenly ran between us. "You will not hurt him?" she said, appealingly to him. "Remember, oh, remember what he has before him!" And here Althea burst into a passion of weeping, and I looked in wild bewilderment from her to him.

"I vill go," said the doctor to me. "I vill leafe you to gonsole her." He spoke in his stronger German accent, and as he went out he beckoned me to the door. His sneer was now a leer, and he said:

"I vould kiss her there, if I vere you."

I slammed the door in his face, and when I turned back to Althea her passion of tears had not ceased, and her beautiful bright hair lay in masses over the poor, shabby desk. I did kiss her, on her soft face where the tears were. I did not dare to kiss her lips, though I think I could have done it before I had known this doctor. She checked her tears at once.

"Now I must go to the doctor's," I said. "Don't be afraid; he can do me or my soul no harm; and remember to-morrow night." I saw Althea's lips blanch again at this; but she looked at me with dry eyes, and I left her.

The winter evening was already dark, and as I went down the streets toward the river I heard the crushing of the ice over the falls. The old street where the doctor lived was quite deserted. Trade had been there in the old days, but now was nothing. Yet in the silence, coming along, I heard the whirr of steam, or, at least, the clanking of machinery and whirling wheels.

I toiled up the crazy staircase. The doctor was already in his room—in the same purple velvet he had worn before. On his study table was a smoking supper.

"I hope," he said, "you have not supped on the way?"

"I have not," I said. Our supper at our college table consisted of tea and cold meat and pie. The doctor's was of oysters, sweetbreads, and wine. After it he gave me an imported cigar, and I sat in his reclining-chair and listened to him. I remember that this chair reminded me, as I sat there, of a dentist's chair; and I good-naturedly wondered what operations he might perform on me—I helpless, passive with his tobacco and his wine.

"Now I am ready," said he. And he opened the door that led from his study into the old warehouse-room, and I saw him touch one of the steel levers opposite the rows of glass rods. "You see," he said, "my mechanism is a simple one. With all these rods of different lengths, and the almost infinite speed of revolution that I am able to gif them with the power that comes from the river applied through a chain of belted wheels, is a rosined leather tongue, like that of a music-box or the bow of a violin, touching each one; and so I get any number of beats per second that I will." (He always said *will,* this man, and never *wish.*)

"Now, listen," he whispered; and I saw him bend down another lever in the laboratory, and there came a grand bass note—a tone I have heard since only in 32-foot organ pipes. "Now, you see, it is Sound." And he placed his hand, as he spoke, upon a small crank or governor; and, as he turned it slowly, note by note the sound grew higher. In the other room I could see one immense wheel, revolving in an endless leather band, with the power that was furnished by the Kennebec, and as each sound rose clear, I saw the wheel turn faster.

Note by note the tones increased in pitch, clear and elemental. I listened, recumbent. There was a marvellous fascination in the strong production of those simple tones.

"You see I hafe no overtones," I heard the doctor say. "All is simple, because it is mechanism. It is the exact reproduction of the requisite mathematical number. I hafe many hundreds of rods of glass, and then the leather band can go so fast as I will, and the tongue acts upon them like the bow upon the violin."

I listened, I was still at peace; all this I could understand, though the notes came strangely clear. Undoubtedly, to get a definite finite number of beats per second was a mere question of mathematics. Empirically, we have always done it, with tuning-forks, organ-pipes, bells.

He was in the middle of the scale already; faster whirled that distant wheel, and the intense tone struck C in alt. I felt a yearning for some harmony; that terrible, simple, single tone was so elemental, so savage; it racked my nerves and strained them to unison, like the rosined bow drawn close against the violin-string itself. It grew intensely shrill; fearfully, piercingly shrill; shrill to the rending-point of the tympanum; and then came silence.

I looked. In the dusk of the adjoining warehouse the huge wheel was whirling more rapidly than ever.

The German professor gazed into my eyes, his own were bright with triumph, on his lips a curl of cynicism. "Now," he said, "you will have what you call emotions. But, first, I must bind you close."

I shrugged my shoulders amiably, smiling with what at the time I thought contempt, while he deftly took a soft white rope and bound me many times to his chair. But the rope was very strong, and I now saw that the frame-work of the chair was of iron. And even while he bound me, I started as if from a sleep, and became conscious of the dull whirring caused by the powerful machinery that abode within the house, and suddenly a great rage came over me.

I, fool, and this man! I swelled and strained at the soft white ropes that bound me, but in vain. . . . By God, I could have killed him then and there! . . . And he looked at me and grinned, twisting his face to fit his crooked soul. I strained at the ropes, and I think one of them slipped a bit, for his face blanched; and then I saw him go into the other room and press the last lever back a little, and it seemed to me the wheel revolved more slowly.

Then, in a moment, all was peace again, and it was as if I heard a low, sweet sound, only that there was no sound, but something like what you might dream the music of the spheres to be. He came to my chair again and unbound me.

My momentary passion had vanished. "Light your cigar," he said, "it has gone out." I did so. I had a strange, restful feeling, as of being at one with the world, a sense of peace, between the peace of death and that of sleep.

"This," he said, "is the pulse of the world; and it is Sleep. You remember, in the Nibelung-saga, when Erda, the Earth spirit, is invoked, unwillingly she appears, and then she says, *Lass mich schlafen*—let me sleep on—to Wotan, king of the gods? Some of the old myths are true enough, though not the Christian ones, most always. . . . This pulse of the earth seems to you dead silence, yet the beats are pulsing thousands a second faster than the highest sound. . . . For emotions are subtler things than sound, as you sentimental ones would say; you poets that talk of 'heart' and 'soul.' We men of science say it this way: That those bodily organs that answer to your myth of a soul are but more widely framed, more nicely textured, so as to respond to the impact of a greater number of movements in the second."

While he was speaking he had gone into the other room, and was bending the lever down once more; I flew at his throat. But even before I reached him my motive changed; seizing a Spanish knife that was on the table, I sought to plunge it in my breast. But, with a quick stroke of the elbow, as if he had been prepared for the attempt, he dashed the knife from my hand to the floor, and I sank in despair back into his arm-chair.

"Yes-s," said he, with a sort of hiss of content like a long-drawn sigh of relief. "Yes-s-s—I haf put my mechanik quickly through the Murder-motif without binding you again, after I had put it back to sleep."

"What do you mean?" I said, languidly. How could I ever hope to win Althea away from this man's wiles?

"When man's consciousness awakes from the sleep of the world, its first motive is Murder," said he; "you remember the Hebrew myth of Cain?" and he laughed silently. "Its next is Suicide; its third, Despair. This time I have put my mechanik quickly through the Murder movement, so your wish to kill me was just now but momentary."

There was an evil gleam in his eye as he said this.

"I leafe a dagger on the table, because if I left a pistol the subject would fire it, and that makes noise. Then at the motion of Suicide you tried to kill yourself: the suicide is one grade higher than the murderer. And now, you are in Despair."

He bent the lever further down and touched a small glass rod.

"And now, I will gife to you—I alone—all the emotions of which humanity is capable."

How much time followed, I know not; nor whether it was not all a dream, only that a dream can hardly be more vivid—as this was—than my life itself. First, a nightmare came of evil passions; after murder and suicide and despair came revenge, envy, hatred, greed of money, greed of power, lust. I say "came," for each one came on me with all the force the worst of men can feel. Had I been free, in some other place, I should inexorably have committed the crimes these evil passions breed, and there was always some pretext of a cause. Now it was revenge on Materialismus himself for his winning of Althea Hardy; now it was envy of his powers, or greed of his possessions; and then my roving eye fell on that strange picture of his I mentioned before; the face of the woman now seemed to be Althea's. In a glance all the poetry, all the sympathy of my mind or soul that I thought bound me to her had vanished, and in their place I only knew desire. The doctor's leer seemed to read my thoughts; he let the lever stay long at this speed, and then he put it back again to that strange rhythm of Sleep.

"So—I must rest you a little between times," he said. "Is my fine poet convinced?"

But I was silent, and he turned another wheel.

"All these are only evil passions," said I, "there may well be something physical in them."

"Poh—I can gife you just so well the others," he sneered. "I tell you why I do not gife you all at once——"

"You can produce lust," I answered, "but not love."

"Poh—it takes but a little greater speed. What you call love is but the multiple of lust and cosmic love, that is, gravitation."

I stared at the man.

"It is quite as I say. About two hundred thousand vibrations make in man's cerebrum what you call lust; about four billion per second, that is gravitation, make what the philosophers call will, the poets, cosmic love; this comes just after light, white light, which is the sum of all the lights. And their multiple again, of love and light, makes many sextillions, and that is love of God, what the priests name religion." . . . I think I grew faint, for he said, "You must hafe some refreshments, or you cannot bear it."

He broke some raw eggs in a glass, in some sherry, and placed it by my side, and I saw him bend the lever much farther.

"Perhaps," I spoke out, then, "you can create the emotion, or the mental existence—whatever you call it—of God himself." I spoke with scorn, for my mind was clearer than ever.

"I can—almost," he muttered. "Just now I have turned the rhythm to the thought millions, which lie above what you call evil passions, between them and what you call the good ones. It is all a mere question of degree. In the eye of science all are the same; morally, one is alike so good as the other. Only motion —that is life; and slower, slower, that is nearer death; and life is good, and death is evil."

"But I can have these thoughts without your machinery," said I.

"Yes," said he, "and I can cause them with it; that proves they are mechanical. Now, the rhythm is on the intellectual-process movement; hence you argue."

Millions of thoughts, fancies, inspirations, flashed through my brain as he left me to busy himself with other levers. How long this time lasted I again knew not; but it seemed that I passed through all the experience of human life. Then suddenly my thinking ceased, and I became conscious only of a bad odor by my side. This was followed in a moment by an intense scarlet light.

"Just so," he said, as if he had noted my expression; "it is the eggs in your glass, they altered when we passed through the chemical rays; they will now be rotten." And he took the glass and threw it out the window. "It was altered as we passed through the spectrum by no other process than the brain thinks."

He had darkened the room, but the light changed from red through orange, yellow, green, blue, violet; then, after a moment's darkness, it began again, more glorious than before. White, white it was now, most glorious; it flooded the old warehouse, and the shadows rolled from the dark places in my soul. And close on the light followed Hope again; hope of life, of myself, of the world, of Althea.

"Hope—it is the first of the motions you call virtuous," came his sibilant voice, but I heeded him not. For even as he spoke my soul was lifted unto Faith, and I knew that this man lied.

"I can do but one thing more," said he, "and that is—Love."

"I thought," said I, "you could make communion with the Deity."

"And so I could," he cried, angrily, "so I could; but I must first give my glass rod an infinite rotation; the number of vibrations in a second must be a number which is a multiple of *all* other numbers, however great; for that even my great fly-wheel must have an infinite speed. Ah, your 'loft with power' does not give me that. . . . But it would be only an idea if I could do that too, nothing but a rhythmic motion in your brain.". . .

Then my faith rose well above this idle chatter. But I kept silence; for again my soul had passed out of the ken of this German doctor. Althea I saw; Althea in the dark room before me; Althea, and I had communion with her soul. Then I knew indeed that I did love her.

The ecstasy of that moment knew no time; it may have been a minute or an hour, as we mortals measure it; it was but an eternity of bliss to me. . . . Then followed again faith and hope, and then I awoke and saw the room all radiant with the calm of that white light—the light that Dante saw so near to God.

But it changed again to violet, like the glacier's cave, blue like the heavens, yellow like the day; then faded through the scarlet into night.

Again I was in a sea of thoughts and phantasies; the inspiration of a Shakespeare, the fancy of a Mozart or a Titian, the study of a Newton, all in turn were mine. And then my evil dreams began. Through lust to greed of power, then to avarice, hatred, envy, and revenge, my soul was driven like a leaf before the autumn wind.

Then I rose and flew at his throat once more. "Thou liest!" I cried. "Heed not the rabble's cry—God lies NOT in a rotting egg!"

I remember no more.

When I regained consciousness it was a winter twilight, and the room was cold. I was alone in the doctor's study and the machinery in the house was stilled. . . . I went to the eastern window and saw that the twilight was not the twilight of the dawn. I must have slept all day. . . . As I turned back I saw a folded paper on the table, and read, in the doctor's hand:

"In six hours you have passed through all the thoughts, all the wills, and all the passions known to devils, men, or angels. You must now sleep deeply or you die. I have put the lever on the rhythm of the world, which is Sleep.

"In twelve hours I shall stop it, and you will wake.

"Then you had better go home and seek your finite sleep, or I have known men lose their mind."

I staggered out into the street, and sought my room. My head was still dizzy, my brain felt tired, and my soul was sere. I felt like an old man; and yet my heart was still half-drunk with sleep, and enamoured with it, entranced with that profound slumber of the world to which all consciousness comes as a sorrow.

The night was intensely cold; the stars were like blue fires;

a heavy ox-sledge went by me, creaking in the snow. It was a fine night for the river. I suddenly remembered that it must be the night for the skating party, and my engagement with Althea. And with her there came a memory of that love that I had felt for her, sublimated, as it had been, beyond all earthly love.

I hurried back to my room; and as I lit the lamp I saw a note addressed to me, in her handwriting, lying on my study table. I opened it; all it contained was in two phrases:

"Good-by; forgive me.

"ALTHEA."

I knew not what to think; but my heart worked quicker than my brain. It led me to Althea's house; the old lady with whom she lived told me that she had already started for the skating party. Already? I did not dare to ask with whom. It was a breach of custom that augured darkly, her not waiting for me, her escort.

On my way to the river I took the street by the house of Materialismus. They were not there. The old warehouse was dark in all its windows. I went in; the crazy wooden building was trembling with the Power; but all was dark and silent but the slow beating of the Power on the Murder pulse.

I snatched up the Spanish dagger where it still lay on the table, and rushed out of that devil's workshop and along the silent street to the river. Far up the stream I could already make out a rosy glow, the fires and lanterns of the skating party. I had no skates, but ran out upon the river in a straight line, just skirting the brink of the falls where the full flood maned itself and arched downward, steady, to its dissolution in the mist. I came to the place of pleasure, marked out by gay lines of paper lanterns; the people spoke to me, and some laughed, as I threaded my way through them; but I heeded not; they swerving and darting about me, like so many butterflies, I keeping to my line. By the time I had traversed the illuminated enclosure I had seen all who were in it. Althea was not among them.

I reached the farthest lantern, and looked out. The white river stretched broad away under the black sky, faintly mirroring large, solemn stars. It took a moment for my eyes, dazzled by the tawdry light, to get used to the quiet starlight; but then I fancied that I saw two figures, skating side by side, far up the river. They were well over to the eastern shore, skating up stream; a mile or more above them the road to A—— crossed the river, in a long covered bridge.

I knew that they were making for that road, where the doctor doubtless had a sleigh in waiting. By crossing diagonally, I could, perhaps, cut them off.

"Lend me your skates," I said to a friend who had come up and stood looking at me curiously. Before he well understood, I had torn them off his feet and fitted them to my own; and I remember that to save time I cut his ankle-strap off with the Spanish knife. A moment more and I was speeding up the silent river, with no light but the stars, and no guide but the two figures that were slowly creeping up in the shadow of the shore. I laughed aloud; I knew this German beau was no match for me in speed or strength. I did not throw the knife away, for I meant more silent and more certain punishment than a naked blow could give. The Murder motive still was in my brain.

I do not know when they first knew that I was coming. But I soon saw them hurrying, as if from fear; at least her strokes were feeble, and he seemed to be urging, or dragging her on. By the side of the river, hitched to the last post of the bridge, I could see a single horse and sleigh.

But I shouted with delight, for I was already almost even with them, and could easily dash across to the shore while they were landing. I kept to my straight line; I was now below the last pier of the bridge; and then I heard a laugh from him, answering my shout. Between me and the bank was a long open channel of rippling dark water, leading up and down, many miles, from beneath the last section of the bridge.

They had reached the shore, and he was dragging her, half reluctant, up the bank. In a minute, and he would have reached his horse.

I put the knife between my teeth and plunged in. In a few strokes of swimming I was across; but the ice was shelving on the other side, and brittle; and the strong stream had a tendency to drag me under. I got my elbows on the edge of ice, and it broke. Again I got my arms upon the shelving ice; it broke again.

I heard a wild cry from Althea—I cursed him—and I knew no more.

. . .

When I next knew life, it was spring; and I saw the lilac buds leafing by my window in the garden. I had been saved by the others—some of them had followed me up the river—unconscious, they told me, the dagger still clinched in my hand.

Althea I have never seen again. First I heard that she had married him; but then, after some years, came a rumor that she had not married him. Her father lost his fortune in a vain search for her, and died. After many years, she returned, alone. She lives, her beauty faded, in the old place.

Postscript

Paganism was the avowal of life; Christianity the sacrifice of it. So the world civilized has always separated at the two diverging roads, according as brain or blood has ruled their lives; the Turanian races, and after them the Latins, to assert life; the Semitic races, and after them the Teutons, to deny it. So the Church of Rome, as nearest in time to Paganism, has been nearer the avowal of life, has recognized, through all its inquisitions, human hearts; the Sects have sought to stifle them; the Puritans have posed to ignore them. Thus cruelty may be the crime of priests; hypocrisy has been the vice of preachers.

Hence my poor friend Tetherby, spinning his affections from his brain, tired with a mesh of head-wrought duties, died, or rather ceased to live, of a moral heart-failure. His heart was too good to be made out of brains alone; and his life was ended with the loss of that girl of his—what was her name, Myra, Marcia?—born, in the Northland, of a warmer blood, who fell a victim there, as the rose-tree does in too cold a climate, to the creeping things of earth.

MARVELOUS INVENTIONS

Almost all the inventions of the astonishingly inventive nineteenth century, as well as many of this century, were sketched in fiction before being put together in fact. But because their inventions have long since become actual, most of the stories of mechanical marvels have been superseded by their own success. Those aimed most at exciting the reader (such as "The Space Annihilator," which strives merely to present as a fantastic marvel a vaguely explained contraption we would call a radio) now only show the perils of playing on momentary wonder. Those trying to sketch technological inventions, no matter how damaged as fiction, do deserve something like the respect given to the actual inventions. J. D. Whelpley's "The Atoms of Chladni" shows how a story can achieve this kind of respect and still endure as fiction.

Because Whelpley, who helped Fitz-James O'Brien with the scientific aspects of "The Diamond Lens," made his own fictional speculation both imaginative and knowledgeable, he may have helped make it actual. Thomas Alva Edison, as a twelve-year-old newsboy selling *Harper's Monthly*, among other things, on the Grand Trunk Railroad, was almost undoubtedly hawking the issue that contained "The Atoms of Chladni," which describes in some detail the basis for several of his inventions.

But whether or not the technology of "The Atoms of Chladni" influenced Edison does not influence our engagement with it as fiction. "The Atoms of Chladni" endures, despite the century that has elapsed since its last printing, because it recognizes and dramatizes the very dangers inherent in its conception. Because it does not overvalue its mechanical marvel, it actually gains from the fact that the marvel has not only materialized but become, in a highly refined form, a commonplace. Interweavings of mystery, sex, society, and invention lure the reader into excitedly seeking to uncover the great discovery. The twentieth-century reader, who can see more starkly than the nineteenth-century reader the flaw in the machine and how it victimizes its creator, thereby becomes an even better victim of the fiction.

J. D. WHELPLEY
The Atoms of Chladni *

Gustav Mohler, the once celebrated inventor and mathematician, died last year (1858) in a private lunatic asylum. His wife, more accomplished than her husband, even in his best days, has also departed. The peace of God and the love of all went with her. To disclose the causes of Mohler's alienation from her, and of the insanity which overtook him soon after, will offend no man's pride, no woman's vanity. I wish, as a friend of Madam Mohler, to justify her. None who enjoyed her splendid hospitality or the delights of her conversation will be displeased with me for the attempt.

My first interview with Mohler was preconcerted by my friend P——, the *savant*. This was in the winter of 1854. We three met by appointment in a public library. My friend had been deceived by the serene enthusiasm of the inventor, and believed that he could communicate some valuable secrets. We sat at a round table in an alcove of the library inspecting plans and diagrams. For an hour the inventor explained, calculated; plunged into abysses of constructive dynamics; his voice sounded drearily, under the Gothic hollows of the room. The old folios of alchemy and philosophy, twin children of ignorance, that cumbered three sides of the alcove where we sat listening to this madman, seemed at last to nod and shake, in sympathy with his wild, interminably worded digressions. It was like the clown fighting with the hoop; intellect struggling in a vicious circle, maddened with its own exertion.

* *Harper's New Monthly Magazine*, 1859.

The enthusiast seemed to be between thirty and forty years of age; well formed, well dressed; a gentleman in manners. His voice and address were mild and insinuating, but the feeling he inspired most was compassion. His inventions were for the most part mere lunacies, violating every mechanical law. The *instinct* of common sense, a suspicion that he might be wrong, made him appear timid in his statements. He deferred to P——'s superior knowledge; asked him to point out the errors; smiled sadly when P—— intimated, with some asperity, his contempt for the whole matter.

I would willingly have talked to Mohler about himself, but his personal reserve repelled sympathy. He begged P—— to look farther into the invention (a new motive power); said that something might have escaped him in the calculations; but that, "as all these things were imparted to him by spiritual communication, he dared not abandon the research."

"Spirits," replied P——, with one of his cutting scientific laughs, "will not enable you to circumvent God; and it is He, the Maker of the universe, who condemns your invention. It would wreck the universe."

Mohler replied, meekly, that he should be grieved to think that his spirit-friends had deceived him. He then drew me aside, and with a gleaming look askance at P——, who remained yawning and fretting over the table, "He," said Mohler, "is a materialist; but in you I have confidence." He then alluded to another invention of his own, which, he said, had been perfected by evil spirits, and had ruined him.

The eyes of the lunatic dilated, and a visible tremor shook his frame, as he described the machine. "It was a means," he said, "to discover falsehood and treachery." The spirit of Chladni communicated that to him—Chladni, the Frenchman who discovered the dancing of the atoms. "It is the same," he said, "in the atoms of the brain; they vibrate in geometrical forms, which the soul reads."

P——, who had been watching us, alarmed at the maniacal excitement of Mohler, interrupted our conversation and hurried me away. Though the froth of madness had gathered upon his lips, the unfortunate inventor had still power enough over himself to show, in leave-taking, the urbanity of a gentleman.

As P—— and I left the library together, I expressed a wish

to learn something of the previous life of Gustav Mohler. P—— said I was over-curious in such matters; for his part, the history of a madman was, of all, least entertaining, and useful only to those intelligent but unhappy persons who have charge of asylums. Of Gustav Mohler he neither knew nor desired to know any thing farther, and regretted the hour wasted in his company; which had delayed an important analysis of earths in which he was about to engage that day, in company with Professor M. "I suppose," he added, with a half sneer, "you are seeking characters for a novel, and you fancy the history of this creature might furnish you a high-seasoned dish of the horrible."

And so we parted, in no very good humor with each other—I to my meditations, he to his earths.

Several months had passed, after this interview, before my accomplished and practical friend, the *savant,* saw fit to honor me with a visit. One cold, rainy night in November of the succeeding year I heard his firm, quick step in the hall. There was a knock, and the door of my room opened intrusively.

The *savant* stood in the door-way, his sharp nose peering under a glazed hat, and his form made shapeless by an ungainly waterproof cloak against the wind and rain of the night.

"Ah!" said he, "you are a fixture, I fear, by the fireside. But if you have courage to face this storm, I have a pleasure to propose."

"Come in; lay off your storm armor, and we will talk about your pleasure."

He complied in the hasty, discontented manner peculiar to him, threw his wet hat and cloak over a table covered with books and papers, and drew a chair.

"You will go with me," he said, authoritatively, "to Charles Montague's this evening."

"Forty-second Street—through a northeasterly storm! Be wise—I have ordered whisky and hot water, with lemons." I rang the bell.

Professor P—— had a weakness for punch, especially when I made it. He acquiesced, with a sigh.

"We can go late," said he. "There is to be a meeting of rare people. At least two entomologists, an antiquarian, and a collector of curiosities from Germany, who has a tourmalin which I must steal or buy; it is yellow, or rather gold-colored. Then there will be a woman there—a Mrs. Bertaldy, American; a wonder of science, whom you must see."

"P——, you are a fool. Scientific women are more odious to me than womanish men. The learning of a woman is only a desperate substitute for some lost attraction."

"Very true, perhaps; I will think about that: but Mrs. Bertaldy *is* a beautiful, not to say a fascinating woman; only thirty years of age—rich, independent, and a delightful conversationist."

"Hum! a widow?"

"Yes, at least I am so informed."

"A friend of the Montagues?"

"They vouch for her."

"And an American, you say?"

"Yes, with a foreign name—assumed, I suppose, to avoid some unpleasant recollections; scientific women, you know, have these things happen to them. Husband dead, and no children. Charles Montague swears that it is so; his wife protests it is so; and, of course, it must be so."

"Another glass, and I am with you. We will visit the Montagues, and talk with Mrs. Bertaldy; but if you oblige me to listen to any of your alchemists or virtuosi, I promise to insult them."

My first ten minutes' conversation with Mrs. Bertaldy was a disappointment. She was of the quiet school of manners, low-voiced, and without gesture or animation. Her features were regular, well formed, rather dark, with just the merest trace of sadness.

The difference between mediocrity in a woman and the *mean* of perfection is not instantly visible, unless to very fine observers. Mrs. Bertaldy made no impression at the first view, but I found myself returning often to speak with her. Her talk was neither apophthegm, argument, nor commentary; it was a kind of sympathetic music. She bore her part in the concert of good words in a subdued and tasteful manner, putting in a note of great power and sweetness here and there, when there was a rest or silence.

P—— was dissatisfied. Mrs. Bertaldy took no part in the noisy and tedious discussions of the *savans*. On our way home he pronounced her "a humbug—a false reputation." I, on the contrary, resolved to cultivate the acquaintance. It was agreeable. P—— sees no points but the salient, in men or things; he is merely a naturalist.

My new acquaintance was domiciled with the Montagues, and I soon became an expected visitor and friend of their guest. Not, I beg to have it understood, in the manner of a lover, or wife hunter, but simply of one seeking agreeable society. The fastidious Montague and his good lady were impenetrable about the "antecedents" of Mrs. Bertaldy; but they treated her with a confidence and respect which satisfied me that her previous history was known to them, and that their sentiments toward her were grounded in esteem. They seemed to be afraid of losing a word of hers, when she was conversing. Her knowledge was various and positive, but she spoke of things and persons as if each were a feeling more than an object. I was not long in discovering that a part of the charm of Mrs. Bertaldy's society lay in the graceful and kind attention with which she listened. She encouraged one to talk, and shaped and turned conversation with an easy power.

One morning in April, while we were enjoying the first warm air of spring, and the odor of flowers, in Montague's magnificent conservatory—the windows open to the south, and the caged birds cheering and whistling to each other amidst the orange-trees—I was describing a garden in the South; my language was apt and spontaneous. The lady listened with her delightful manner of pleased attention.

She was certainly a beautiful woman!

Her eyes dwelt upon mine, when, by I know not what association, the vision of the spirit-haunted enthusiast rose before me, and I was silent.

Mrs. Bertaldy became pale, and gazing on my face with an expression of terror, she exclaimed,

"You were thinking of him. How strange!"

"Yes," I said; "but do you know of *whom* I am thinking?"

"He is no longer living," she replied; "and we may now speak of him without wrong."

"Of Mohler, the enthusiast?"

"The same."

"How came you to know it was he I thought of?"

"You need not be surprised. We have been much together, and

though you have not named Mohler—he was my husband—you have made remarks and allusions which convinced me that you at least knew *him*, if not his history."

"True, I have spoken of his inventions, and often wished they were real and possible."

"And your allusions have made me shudder. Mohler was mad. You will think me mad, I am afraid, if I assure you that some of his inventions, the most wonderful of all, were perfected and applied before his reason left him."

"You were, then, the wife of this man?" I said, with a feeling of compassion.

"Yes. Our parents were foreign, though Gustav and I were born and educated in America."

"Will you tell me something of this marriage?" said I, touched with deep interest.

She sighed, but after a moment's meditation spoke with her usual manner.

"We were united by our parents. Mohler was in his twenty-first year; I but seventeen. We had no children; were rich, educated, luxurious. Mohler addicted himself to inventions, I to society. He faded into a recluse; I became a woman of the world. Our home was divided against itself. We occupied a double house in D—— Street. One half was reserved by Mohler for himself and his mechanics; the other half by me for my friends and visitors, whom he seldom saw. Within five years after our marriage I was left to my own guidance. Our parents died. Fearing the wasteful expenditure of Mohler on his strange inventions, they willed their property exclusively to me. Their fears for him were well-founded. On the anniversary of the seventh year of our marriage, at midnight, after a musical entertainment—I was then passionately fond of music—Mohler entered my chamber, which he had not visited for a year. He closed the door, locked it quietly, drew a chair to the bedside, facing me, and seated himself.

" 'Maria Bertaldy,' he said, after a silence which I took pains not to break, 'we are no longer man and wife.'

"I made no reply. My heart did not go out, as formerly, to meet him.

" 'My name is not yours,' he added.

" 'No? And why, Gustav?'

" 'My lawyer is about to furnish me with evidence which will make our continued union impossible.'

" 'Your lawyer!' I exclaimed, starting up, involuntarily. '*My* friend, Raymond Bonsall?'

" 'Your *friend,* Maria! Has he deceived me? Forgive me if I have wronged you. My soul is dark sometimes.'

"There was a manner so wretched and pleading with what he said, I could not forbear pity. His dress was soiled; his hair hung in elf locks; his eyes were bloodshot with glowering over furnace-fires. The poisonous fume of the crucible had driven the healthy tinge from his face, and given it the hue of parchment.

" 'It is many a long year,' said I, 'since you have looked at me with kindness.'

" 'I have deserved,' he answered, 'to lose your affection; but you should have taken better care of my honor and your own.'

" 'The guardianship of both seems to have been transferred to your lawyer.'

" 'I may believe, then, that you are indifferent in regard to that?'

" 'You may believe what you will. I have been long enough my own guardian to look to no one for advice or protection.'

" 'You are rich.'

" 'That is a consolation, truly. I am thus not without means of defense—more fortunate than most women.'

" 'And I have nothing but that of which you have been willing to deprive me.'

" 'Your accusations—more especially as you are the last person who is entitled to make them—I repel with contempt. For your loss of fortune, miserably expended in futilities, I am deeply grieved. If you are in need of money for your personal expenses, take freely of mine.'

" 'I am in debt.'

" 'How much?'

"He named a large sum. I rose, and going to the escritoir, wrote an order for the amount. He followed me. The tears were streaming from his eyes. Kneeling at my feet, he seized my hands and covered them with kisses.

"I had formerly entertained an affectionate regard for Gustav. We were at one time playmates, friends. Regret made me look kindly upon him.

"He caught eagerly at the indication.

" 'I will not rise, Maria,' he said, 'until you have forgiven the cruel accusation. So much goodness and generosity can not proceed from a faithless or dishonored wife.'

" 'You judge truly, my husband.'

"He rose from his knees, still holding my hands in both of his.

" 'You have saved me,' he said, 'by your liberality. Grant me still another favor: let the reconciliation be perfect.'

" 'Any thing for a better life; but only on one condition can you and I live happily, as at first.'

" 'And that is—?'

" 'That you change your occupation—give up these wild researches—spare your body and your soul, and live as other men do, in simplicity.'

" 'But,' said he, stammering, 'I have an invention of incalculable value. To give it up now would be to lose the labor of years.'

" 'And this other favor is—?'

" 'I must have means to continue my work.'

" 'I will not furnish you with the means of self-destruction.'

" 'Limit me. Your income is large; you will hardly miss what I require.'

" 'For how long?'

" 'One year. I shall then have perfected what will immortalize and enrich me. Pity me, Maria! We have no children. You have *your* pleasures and pursuits; I, only this; and this you deny me!' he exclaimed, with a slight bitterness, so artfully mingled with affection and repentance, my heart gave way. I consented.

"Gustav was not without personal beauty or manliness of character. He now studied again to please my tastes. We resumed our former relations. Though his days were devoted to labor, his evenings were given to me and my guests. His cheerfulness seemed to have returned. I was so happy in the change, I allowed him to draw from me large sums. My fortune was still ample; and I looked forward to the happy ending of the appointed year.

"You are doubtless surprised that I could so easily forgive his accusations. Satisfied that Raymond Bonsall, the lawyer, who had persecuted me, before the reconciliation, with unsolicited attentions, was the originator and cause of Mohler's suspicions, I had dismissed the subject from my thoughts. Indeed, my happiness expelled revengeful passions, even against Bonsall himself. As the friend of Gustav, I received him with courtesy, and he continued an accepted member of the refined and elegant society with which it was our good fortune to be surrounded.

"With surprising address Bonsall changed his plan. As before he had been secretly attentive, now he was openly and constantly devoted, but shunned me when alone.

"Bonsall's influence over Mohler became, at last, absolute and inscrutable. It did not satisfy me to hear them repeat, often and openly, that they were partners in the invention; that Bonsall had purchased an interest; and that they consulted together daily on its progress. Anxiety led me to observe them. Daily, at a certain hour in the afternoon, Bonsall entered the house and passed into the lower work-shop. There he would remain a while, and then retire. In the evening he appeared often in the drawing-room, and never failed to make himself agreeable to our friends.

"The instinct of a woman, correct in appreciating character and motives, fails always in sounding the complicated and strategic depth of masculine perfidy. I soon knew that Bonsall had become my enemy, and that his ultimate purpose was to avenge my repulses and defeat my reconciliation with Mohler; but the singularity and constancy of his behavior—attentive in public, and reserved and cautious when alone with me—together with the pains he used to create for himself relations more and more intimate with my husband, puzzled and confused me.

" 'Could it be,' thought I, 'that his public attentions, so embarrassing and yet so blameless; his watchfulness of my desires, when others could see them as well as he, are to impress a belief that his private relations are too intimate?'

"The suspicion gave me excessive uneasiness. I gradually broke the matter to Mohler; but he assured me I was mistaken; that Bonsall suffered remorse for the injury he had inflicted upon both of us; that our reconciliation alone consoled him; that Bonsall was his adviser in the invention, which already, at the eighth month of the stipulated period, had nearly reached perfection. His tenderness quieted my fears, and I too easily believed him.

"Soon after he proposed certain changes in the architecture and furniture of my apartments. His reasons seemed to me satisfactory and kind. I vacated the rooms for a month, leaving him to improve and alter. He wished to give me a surprise. The apartment was large, with a dressing-room and ante-chamber. These were refitted under Mohler's direction; after which, in company with a few friends, we visited the new rooms.

"The ceiling had been made slightly concave; in the centre was a large oval mirror. This mirror, so strangely placed overhead, excited general admiration. Bonsall was, or pretended to be, in raptures with it. I observed that the mirror, beautifully fair and polished, was not of glass, but of a metal resembling silver.

"From this brilliant centre-piece radiated panels exquisitely carved, with frescoes of graceful and simple design. The carpets, wall mirrors, fountain, statuettes, jewel and book-cases, tapestries, tinted and curtained windows, all were perfectly elegant, and fresh with living colors in harmonious combination.

"In the centre of the ceilings of the dressing-room and antechambers were smaller mirrors of the same metal. This new style of ornament, supported by adequate elegances, and a perfection of detail of which I had never before seen the parallel, occupied continual notice and remark. Some criticised and laughed, but the most admired; for the beauty of the effect was undeniable.

"I was surprised and delighted at the results of my husband's labors. That Mohler, a great inventor and mechanic, was also a master of design, I had always believed. With the genius of Benvenuto Cellini he united a philosophical intellect, and by long years of research in the metallurgic arts had acquired extraordinary tact. In the least details of the work of these rooms there was novelty and beauty, though, with the sole exception of the metal mirrors, I observed nothing absolutely new in material.

"Mohler did not fail to observe, and turn to his own advantage, my gratification and surprise. He at once sought and obtained leave from me to occupy a suit of apartments next above mine, in exchange for others on his side of the house, which, he said, were too dark and narrow for his purpose.

"I sent immediately for my housekeeper, ordered the change to be made, and the keys given to the master.

"By a tacit understanding we had never intruded upon each other. I had not penetrated the privacy of Mohler's work-rooms, where certain confidential artisans labored night and day; nor had he overstepped the limit on my side of the house. He breakfasted, and generally dined, in his atelier, superintending operations which required a constant oversight.

"For more than two months after the completion of my own apartments I was disturbed day and night by noises of repairs and changes going on above. Mohler assured me that this would not continue; that he had perfected and was erecting the delicate machinery of his invention.

"Want of curiosity is, I believe, a greater fault than the excess of it. I am naturally incurious. It did not irritate my fancy to remain in ignorance of secrets that did not seem to concern me. My husband and I lived together in a manner that was at least satisfactory. Our affection was only an agreeable friendship, such as many consider the happiest relation that can exist between husband and wife. Our too early and hasty marriage had kept us in ignorance of the joys and miseries dreamed of and realized only by mature and long-expectant passion.

"You will not suppose that life was therefore tedious or fruitless. My parents had given me a full and judicious education. I could speak and write several languages. Mature and difficult studies—philosophy, natural history, and even astronomy—established for me relations of amity with learned and accomplished men. I wrote verse and prose, attempted plays, observed and sympathized with political movements. In order to perfect myself in languages, I cultivated the admirable art of phonography, and would sometimes fix in writing the rapid and brilliant repartee of accomplished persons, who could forget my presence in the excitement of conversation. I learned to prefer the living to the written word. Literature for me was only a feeble reflection of reality; for I have never found in books that vivacity, that grace, that unfolding of the interior life, which makes social converse the culmination of all that is excellent and admirable.

"At the expiration of the year Mohler announced the completion of his grand work, which he had been seven years in perfecting. I thought he would have told me its purpose; but with a cold and embarrassed manner he presented me with a check upon his banker, just equal to the sum of all I had advanced to him during the year. His behavior was mortifying, and even alarming. I noticed a gradual change in the manners and conversation of Bonsall. He assumed airs of authority. Mohler gradually withdrew himself, and began to be reserved and serious; criticising my conduct, friends, principles, and tastes. More mysterious still was the gradual loss and defection of my most valued female acquaintances. My parlors were gradually deserted. Old friends dropped away. It was as though I had become suddenly poor, when, in fact, my wealth and magnificence of living had increased. Persons of good name no longer responded to or returned my invitations. I was alone with my wealth, dispossessed of its power and its enjoyments.

"I knew that Bonsall continued to visit the friends who had deserted me. He still frequented our house, was daily closeted with my husband, and treated me now with a careless indifference. Mohler, on the other hand, withdrew until he and I were completely separated. We no longer spoke to or even saw each other. My servants became insolent; I procured others, who, in their turn, insulted me. I grew careless of externals; lived retired, occupied with books and music. Through these I acquired fortitude to resist the contempt of the world. My knowledge increased. These sad months, interrupted by short visits to the country, produced no change in my social or marital relations, but gave me an inward strength and consolation which since then has served me like an arm of God whereon one may lean and sleep.

"While these changes were succeeding I enjoyed a source of consolation which I need only name and you will appreciate it; that was the correspondence of Charles Montague, then in Europe. He had been the friend and counselor of my parents, and continued his goodness to me after their death. I confided to him all my troubles, giving him each month a written narrative of events. He replied always in general terms, mentioning no names, and giving advice in such a form that it could be understood by no person but myself. This was a just precaution, for I had discovered a system of espionage which Bonsall and my husband maintained over me, a part of which was the inspection of private papers.

"Gradually all my valuable papers, receipts, copies of deeds, important correspondence with the agents who had charge of my large and increasing property, Montague's letters, my private journal, were abstracted. I made no complaint, trusted no person with my secrets.

"At the expiration of this year of estrangement and solitude, in the fall, Montague returned from Europe with his family, and fitted up this house. Mrs. M. I had not known until then. Neither of them had visited at my house, nor were they on terms of intimacy with any of my friends. Even Bonsall was a stranger to Montague, and Mohler had disliked and avoided him. Plain sense and honesty ran counter to his dreamy vanity.

"I was received by the Montagues with great kindness. I found the lady, as you have, intelligent and amiable, and the man himself become, from a mere guardian of my property, a warm and devoted friend. I consumed almost an entire day in narrating what had passed between myself, Bonsall, my husband, servants, and acquaintances.

"Montague made minutes, and compared the narrative with my correspondence.

" 'I am convinced,' he said, 'that there is a conspiracy; but whether your life and property, or merely a divorce, is the object, can not be determined without some action on your part. Find out the purpose of the changes that have been made in your apartments, and by all means visit and inspect those that are above you. You must do this for and by yourself. You are observing and not easily intimidated. You have a right to use any means that may be convenient—to pick locks, force open doors, seize and inspect papers, bribe servants, and in other ways defend yourself and obtain advantages over the enemy. Count no longer upon the good-will or affection of Mohler. He is resolved to sacrifice you and possess himself of your property, but is still at a loss for evidence.'

"With these words Montague concluded his advice. He then led me to a front window, and pointed to a dark figure in the shadow on the opposite side of the street.

" 'That person,' said Montague, 'is certainly a spy employed by Mohler and Bonsall. He arrived at the same moment with yourself, has passed the house many times, and now watches for your departure. He has an understanding with your coachman. I saw them conversing in the area about noon.'

"It was late, and I proposed to return home. Montague and his wife wished me to pass the night with them. 'But first,' said Charles, 'we will amuse ourselves a little with the spy.' He took pistols from a drawer, went out by the basement, and returned in a few moments to the study, where Mrs. M. and I were sitting, driving in the spy before him.

" 'Now, Sir,' said Charles, 'sit you down and tell your story.

Out with it. You are employed by Bonsall and Mohler to watch this lady.'

"The man grinned, nodded, and seated himself quietly near the door, much in the manner of a cat preparing to run.

" 'This person,' said Montague to us, 'is a volunteer detective, employed chiefly by weak-minded husbands and jealous wives. You can not insult him. He will voluntarily expose his person to any degree of violence short of maiming or murder. Kicks he pays no heed to. He passes in public for a sporting gentleman, and is, in fact and name, a Vampire. By-the-by, Mr. Crag,' said he, changing his tone, 'you may have forgotten me. You were employed, if I remember right, in the Parkins murder case, were you not?'

" 'Yes, Sir. You were counsel for defense.'

" 'Exactly. I think you followed me to my lodgings several times at night, and were shot through the leg for taking so much unnecessary trouble.'

" 'Yes.'

" 'Well, Mr. Crag, I caution you that the same, or a worse matter, will happen to you again, if you continue to watch persons entering my house. I may fire upon you.'

" 'The law will protect me.'

" 'Not at all. You watch my house; you are not a qualified policeman; you are consequently either a burglar or a conspirator. I can shoot you if I wish. You have admitted that Bonsall and Mohler employed you to watch this lady. Go to the table and write a full testimonial of the fact, or take a lodging in the Tombs to-night. Write dates, facts—all in full.'

"The Vampire did not evince any emotion, but refused to write. After some hesitation, however, he made a general confession of his motives in following and watching myself. It was to the effect that, on the 20th of October, of the year 185—, Raymond Bonsall, lawyer, of New York, and Gustav Mohler had sent for him to the house of said Mohler, and had there proposed to him to watch, follow, and dog the wife of Mohler, at all hours of the day and night, and to employ others to do the same, for the space of one month from that date; and to report all her actions, movements, speech, disguises, the names and occupations of all persons with whom she associated—in short, every particular of her conduct and life; for which they were to give the sum of twenty dollars a day, the half to Crag, and the rest to coachmen and assistants in his employ; that he had been occupied in this work ten days, and had each day given in a written account of his espionage. Crag rose to depart.

" 'You will see Bonsall and Mohler to-night,' said Montague, 'and report to them what has happened.'

" 'That,' said Crag, 'is impossible—they are out of town.'

" 'Good; then you can not. Please observe that I shall be in possession of Bonsall's papers within a month. If any of yours are found among them you will be terribly handled.'

" 'How?' said Crag, anxiously.

" 'I will have you up in the Parkins affair, and some other little matters—the burglary in D Street, for instance, 25th of June.'

"The Vampire's impassible countenance relaxed into a horrible smile. 'I see, Mr. Montague, that you are watching me. I will go; but let *her* look out. Bonsall has made up his mind; and he's got Swipes—a better man than I; and if they can't convict her of something they'll have her poisoned. Bonsall's a better man than you, Mr. Montague, and he's got the papers.'

" 'What papers?'

" 'Proofs against the lady. All kinds. A *will*, for instance.'

" 'A forgery?'

" 'In course; but you can't prove it.'

" 'How came you to know that?'

" 'Well, you know Bonsall wanted to get rid of Mohler and marry his widow, years ago. He was afraid to go the common way to work; so he encouraged him in working at his lunatic notions—some kind of machinery that no man ever heard of, thinking it would kill or craze him; but Mohler succeeded, and Bonsall had to lay a new plan. He furnished Mohler with the money to repay the loan he made from his wife. A German chemist Mohler has in his laboratory told me this. He can't speak English, but understands it, and I speak German. Well, Bonsall and Mohler have got a quantity of written evidence against Madam Mohler—a volume of it—all in writing—conversations of hers with some person who visits her room.'

"At this point of Crag's narrative Montague's innocent wife looked at me with a sorrowing and pitiful expression. I paid no heed to it.

" 'With your permission, Mr. Montague,' said I, 'let me continue the examination.'

"He acquiesced.

" 'Mr. Crag,' said I, 'do you believe that I conversed with any person in my room?'

" 'It's a common thing, marm, and it might be, for aught I know. Mohler believes it; but he is awfully perplexed to know who it was you were talking with. I believe Bonsall knew who it was, but he would not tell Mohler.'

" 'How came you to be so minutely informed?'

" 'Why, marm, you must know every profession has its ins and outs; it isn't enough to earn money, you must know how to get it when you have earned it; that is more than half. Now, when I am employed by any party to watch another I watches both; else I couldn't make it pay. I spend half my time watching Mohler and Bonsall, when they suppose I am after you. I thought there was small chance of a conviction, and I wanted to threaten Mohler and Bonsall for conspiracy, and make 'em pay a bonus at the end of the business, afore they gev up.'

" 'Well?'

" 'The German chemist, you must know, marm, agreed to divide with me, and will be ready with his evidence when he finds there is nothing more to be made out of Mohler, who agreed to give him a share in the invention, but was obliged to sell the chemist's share to Bonsall.'

" 'What is the invention?'

" 'I don't know—never could find out. These Germans are naterally mysterious about mechanical and chemical matters, though they'll tell any thing else.'

" 'What was the real purpose of Bonsall?'

" 'He hated you because you had slighted him. He has forged a will of old Bertaldy, your father. The chemist helped him to do that. This forged will leaves every thing to Mohler instead of yourself, and Mohler has mortgaged all in advance to Bonsall for funds to carry on the work. The chemist says that the invention is worth more than the telegraph; that Mohler is the greatest genius in the world or that ever lived; but, he says, a man without any feelings, marm, only bitter jealous—'

" 'Had Mohler a hand in the forging of the will?'

" 'No, that was Bonsall's work; but the other knew of it. He thought that the property should have been left to him to accomplish the "great and beneficial work;" so he called it, meaning the invention. You, madam, he said, spent money in frivolities; he, in doing good to the world.'

" 'Did he or Bonsall converse about my death?'

" 'No, marm; it is Mohler, I believe, who is to be made away with, if any one—not you; and then Bonsall would find a means to make you marry himself.'

" 'What means?' interposed Montague.

" 'Why, the common means, I suppose. He'd scare the lady into it. He'd have a pile of evidence against her to hurt her reputation, and women, you know, like the madam, are afraid of that. And there is the forged will in his possession, leaving all the property to Mohler, and Bonsall holding claims and notes covering the estate. In fact, he'd be sure to do it, Sir.'

"During the conversation I had written, in phonographic characters, all that had been said. Coming forward, I laid my note-book on the table. 'Mr. Crag,' I said, 'the testimony you have given is written here, word for word. I shall copy it in full, and I expect you to sign your name to it.'

" 'Not without pay, marm,' replied the Vampire, rising.

" 'You will remember,' said Montague, 'that these ladies are witnesses to your demand.'

" 'Black-mail, eh!' chuckled the Vampire. 'I never testify unless I am paid, and I never sign.'

" 'It is unnecessary,' said I, coming before Crag. 'You are one of three engaged in a double conspiracy against Mr. Mohler and myself for life, or money, or both.'

" 'I will dispense with the signature,' interposed Montague; 'but you must leave the city immediately, or suffer arrest for conspiracy.'

" 'It's a good job,' said the Vampire, reflectively, 'and I don't like to leave it. Can't you make an offer?—say fifty dollars on account, marm—and I'll keep dark for a month.'

" 'I'm afraid not.'

" 'In that case I can't go.'

"Montague looked at his wife; she pulled a bell-rope. The sight of Montague's pistol, which he cocked and held ready, kept the Vampire from moving, though he was near the door. A servant entered.

" 'John, go to Captain Melton, and tell him to send me a good officer.'

"Fifteen minutes of silence followed, during which time the Vampire neither moved nor spoke. The officer entered, recognized Crag, and took him away.

“The movement of our lives is a tide that floats us on toward an unknown destiny. This we call Providence. It is doubtless the will of God working in events and circumstances. It is rather like the motion of the great globe, moving silent and irresistible through the void of space. We struggle and fret with trifles, while Divinity wafts us onward. All is for the development of the soul; to strengthen, expand, and purify its powers. Grandeur will come hereafter; in this life there is only a nursing germ of goodness and power.

“These thoughts came first into my mind while I sat looking at the miserable face of the Vampire, waiting to be taken away like a rat in a cage. Anger, terror, revenge passed away like a cloud. I hated not Mohler, nor feared the wiles of the demoniacal Bonsall. Montague wished me to remain with him, using his house as an asylum. I thanked him, but declined the offer. He feared for my life. I knew too well the weakness of my enemies to entertain such fears.

“Montague imaged to himself, in the secret invention, some unheard-of infernal machine which would take life quietly. He believed that the metallic mirrors fixed in the ceilings of my apartments were a portion of the machinery. I promised that I would not sleep until the mystery of the mirrors had been explained.

“It was the third hour of the morning when I reached home, and entered, as usual, by the side-door of the garden. My servants were junketing in the kitchen. On Mohler's side of the house all was dark, closed, and silent. The conspirators were absent. I passed in unobserved, changed my dress, and went up stairs to the rooms above mine. The doors were locked. The door of the German chemist's room opposite stood ajar. A gas-jet, turned low, as the occupant had left it, guided me to a table. In a small side-drawer were several pass-keys of unusual shape. With one of these I succeeded in entering the machine-room, over my own. After closing the shutters and lighting the burners, I looked around me with a novel sensation of intense curiosity, not unmingled with fear.

“The apartment was of the full depth and width of the house; all the partitions having been removed, and the floors above supported by posts of wood. Over the centre of each room of my apartments, and consequently over each of the three metallic mirrors, stood a table about six feet square, of the usual height, solidly framed, and supporting pieces of machinery—a combination of clock-work, galvanic engines, wires coiled myriads of times around poised, pendent, or vibrating magnets; a microcosm of mechanical powers which it were impossible to describe. The three tables were connected by decuple systems of copper wires suspended from the ceiling by glass rods, and associated with a gang of batteries, sixty in number, arranged in double tiers along the side of the room, ten paces in length. From these came out a sickening fume of acid corrosion, the death and decay of metals. From these, it seemed to me, an electric power might be drawn equal to the lightning in destructive force.

"A shuddering horror seized and shook me as I gazed around upon this vast and gloomy apparatus, which some secret intimation told me had been accumulated and connected here to work for me either death or ruin; but the terror was momentary, and again I addressed myself with courage to the investigation.

"The floor of the apartment had been covered first with moss, and then with thick felt, which deadened the sound of footsteps. Around each of the tables, from their edges, depended threefold curtains of green baize. I raised one of these curtains, and the light penetrating beneath, revealed the upper surface of the metallic mirror, perfectly polished, of which the lower was a part of the ceiling of my rooms. Points of platina wire, as fine and pliable as spider-webs—perhaps a hundred in number—touched the mirror in a certain regular order, the surface upon which they rested being divided into the same number of mathematical figures, representing, as it seemed to me, the system of vibrations of the plate. The wires were connected above with the complicated magnetic machinery which rested on the table. The same arrangement appeared under each of the three tables.

"Equidistant from the tables, and nearly in the centre of the apartment, stood a wide desk, or writing-table, on which rested another piece of machinery, less complex than the others, but connected with all of them by a system of wires. This was evidently a telegraphic apparatus for the transmission of signals generated by the larger machinery. On the desk lay a record book, and a card marked with phonographic signs, for the use of the operator, corresponding with others upon the signal-wheel, and which were marked by a needle-point on a coil of paper, as in the ordinary telegraph.

"Facing the seat of the operator, on the table, stood a clock marking hours, minutes, and seconds.

"I seated myself at the desk, placed the record before me, and opened it at hazard. It was a journal of months, weeks, days, hours, minutes, and even seconds. There were three handwritings, giving the dates and moments of making entries. In these I recognized the alternate work of Mohler, Bonsall, and the German.

"Although the writings were phonographic, representing only the elementary sounds of the human voice, I read them easily.

"I had but just begun the perusal of the record when the touch of a cold hand upon my shoulder, like the fingers of a corpse, caused me to spring from my seat with a cry.

"It was Bonsall. He stepped forward as I rose. The short figure of this man, my persecutor, in his slouched hat and travelling cloak, with the eternal saturnine smile, and eyes twinkling savagely under black projecting brows, reminded me of all I had read of conspirators. His face, at that moment of horror, seemed to me like that of a vulture; the livid skin clung to the cheekbones, and the lines of the mouth were cruel and cold.

" 'I should not have returned here to-night,' he said, 'but for an accident. I was not so far distant but that a messenger could reach me with information of Crag's arrest by our friend Montague. He has, of course, betrayed every thing?'

" 'Yes,' I replied, reassured by the quiet manner of Bonsall, 'I am acquainted with the particulars of your conspiracy to destroy Mohler and myself.'

" 'Are you not afraid to confess the knowledge, alone with me in this solitary place?'

" 'Are you a murderer?'

" 'Alas! Madam, it is you who are the destroyer. I fear you now as one who controls my destiny, and can blast my good name and fortune with a word.'

"A long, deep sigh of relief escaped silently from me. I no longer feared Bonsall. He saw his advantage and hastened to improve it.

" 'Montague is my own and your husband's enemy. We employed a spy to observe him. The spy endeavored to extort money from your terrors. Lying is his vocation. Reasonable persons should not confide in the assertions of a Vampire. Cease to fear and believe him and he is powerless.'

" 'Mohler's first enemy,' I answered, 'is his own unnatural jealousy. You may, perhaps, claim a second place. But we need not speak of that at present.'

" 'Were not you tempted by an equal jealousy to penetrate the privacy of this apartment?'

" 'Beware, Sir, how you trespass upon my hospitality. Your presence in this house is merely tolerated. Retire. If you have any repentance or apology to submit, let it be in the light of day and in the presence of witnesses, *as heretofore*.'

"A flash of rage lighted up the noble but vulturine face. It was momentary. He assumed an attitude of polite humility, bowed low, and seemed willing to leave me, as I desired, but hesitated.

" 'Speak,' I said, quickly, 'if you have any thing to add: I wish to be alone.'

" 'Forget, if only for a moment,' said Bonsall, doubling his effort to appear humble and repentant—'forget your enmity, while I explain to you the uses of this mysterious apparatus. As a piece of mechanism it is the grandest achievement of modern science, and besides that,' he added, in a significant tone, 'you have an interest in the matter. It was made partly for you.'

"There was a cold, malicious impudence in the expression, 'It was partly for you,' that made me shrink; but I remembered my promise to the Montagues, and allowed the wily conspirator to engage my attention by a lucid and wonderfully condensed and simple explanation of the machinery. I had read and seen enough of chemistry and mechanics to comprehend all.

" 'It was you,' he said, 'who suggested the idea of the invention, though you were not conscious of it at the time. Five years ago, in the winter of the fifth year after your marriage, Mohler became intimately acquainted with me. The following summer he disclosed to me his suspicion of your fidelity. He knew that your affection for him had declined into a temperate and sisterly friendship, and he believed that you had given your heart to a man of more brilliancy and personal power than himself.'

" 'Whom did he suspect?'

" 'I am his counselor, and dare not violate confidence. His suspicions were soon after transferred to a person much more innocent.'

" 'Yourself?'

" 'Yes. I own that, at first, I was deeply impressed by your beauty and intelligence; but I soon learned that these were defended by your virtue against ordinary, or even extraordinary, temptations.'

" 'The "extraordinary" being the seductive manners and the wit of Mr. Bonsall.'

" 'The same, Madam,' replied the lawyer, coldly.

" 'Men of genius, Mr. Bonsall, are said to be the best judges of their own ability.'

" 'Even when it is a secret from the rest of the world. I admire the sarcasm; but let me proceed. You were reading aloud, to a circle of *savans,* a chapter from a French journal, reviving, with the vivacity and elegance peculiar to the scientific literature of France, the old discoveries of Chladni, who found that musical vibrations imparted to tablets of glass or metal caused particles of sand, or finer powders, which he strewed upon their surfaces, to assume a regular distribution, dancing and arranging themselves, like sentient beings, to the sound of music. The hand which held the pamphlet was a delicate, a beautiful hand, sparkling with diamonds, and blushing with the same intellectual enthusiasm which inspired a melodious voice that warbled, more than it uttered, the mellow periods of the author. The face, the form, the lips, the eyes, the fair rounded arm, and the grace of attitude—much more than the interest of what you read—inspired your auditors with admiration. Mohler alone suffered in that circle: jealousy devoured his heart. The admiring *savans* listened with delight while you spoke of the atoms of Chladni and of Epicurus, and led us, by a ravishing disquisition, from the cold, angular ideas of mechanics into the rich sunlight of poetry and philosophy. While the dancing atoms of Chladni became to me the cause of passionate admiration, they suggested to your jealous spouse a means, as he conceived, of proving your suspected infidelity, even in its least and slightest expressions.'

" 'Miserable man!' I exclaimed, with an expression of equal pity and scorn.

"Bonsall smiled furtively, and continued:

" 'Mohler found it necessary to have an adviser and a confidant. I became both. Yes, Madam, I confess it. An irresistible passion seized upon my heart. I burned to separate you, by all and any means, even the most criminal, from him, that I might induce you to become the wife of a man who could better appreciate you. You seemed to me a woman worthy of my highest ambition. I was ready to devote my existence to the hope of one day possessing you.

" 'Ah! beware, Madam, of despising me. You rejected my involuntary admiration. You made me, at last, an enemy; but,' he added, quietly, 'I am now repentant, and desire to become your friend.'

"Without waiting for my reply, Bonsall, throwing off his cloak, directed my attention first to a broad plate of thin metal suspended from the ceiling by threads of silk. Over this he strewed fine dust from a woolen bag, and then, as he drew a violin bow over its edge, I saw the dust gather and arrange itself in geometrical forms, consonant with the tone imparted.

" 'See,' said he, '*The* ATOMS *of Chladni.* They mark the tone; but the plate, as you well know, has become electrified by vibration. The mirrors of your ceiling are each a vibrating plate. From the upper surface of these rise wire conductors of the electric power generated by the vibration. This is faint and feeble at first, but, by passing through metallic threads coiled a thousand times round small magnets—each geometrical division of the plate corresponding with a magnet and with a radical sound of the human voice—it has power to connect and disconnect the keys of the batteries ten thousand times more powerful, giving motion to the wheels and pendulums, which, in their turn, move the needles of the register—with a slow or swift motion—piercing more or fewer points in this strip of paper, from which, by such wonderful means, has been read off and written every clearly articulated sound uttered in your apartments.'

"Not until that moment did the horrible reality flash through my heart, attended by a thrill of hatred and disgust as though given by the touch of a serpent. Hatred for Bonsall and withering scorn of my wretched husband took full possession of me.

"After a brief silence, during which I succeeded in mastering the violence of these emotions: 'This record, then,' I said, 'is the result of your labors?'

"'Yes,' he answered, with the old furtive smile playing about the cruel mouth; 'in that book your most secret and confidential conversations are recorded.'

"'Stolen property,' I said, taking up the book, 'goes back to the right owner.'

"'Ah!' said he, laughing, 'we have a duplicate, a copy to which you are welcome; but this one,' snatching the volume with a slight of hand, 'belongs to me.'

"'A gentleman!' I said, with I know not what sneering addition, for the littleness of the action inspired me with contempt.

"'A fine word, Madam, properly used—counterpart of the word "lady;" both significant of many virtues; and among those I class purity of mind and conduct. Look,' said he, placing and opening the volume before me. 'Read for yourself.'

"The day of the entry was Saturday of the week previous, one hour and five minutes past midnight. I read under this date the transcript of a conversation between two lovers, one of whom deplored the folly and jealousy of a silly husband; the other urged an elopement. Then followed signs of inarticulate sounds.

"Immediately after, dated at ten in the morning of the next day, was a conversation of mine with Marian, my dressing maid, concerning certain garments which she asked from me. I remembered the conversation.

"'There are ninety distinct entries of the record,' said Bonsall, closing the book, 'and of these, more than twenty are conversations between the same pair of affectionate lovers. All must have taken place in your room; and please observe, that whenever these interesting conversations have occurred you were at home and in your room.'

"'Either your machinery, or yourself, Mr. Bonsall, is a contemptible liar. I confess the ingenuity of the contrivance; but it seems to me that half a dozen perjured witnesses would have been a much less expensive and troublesome apparatus. Have you no better or more reasonable testimony than this? You are a lawyer; so am not I.'

"'It would be a profound gratification—yes, a happiness to me,' he answered, 'could you establish your innocence.'

"'I will do it here, and now. Put your machinery in order for its work. The ninety-first entry will explain the others.'

"The lawyer hesitated; but seeing no change of countenance or movement on my part, but only a certain resolute passivity, he proceeded—maintaining his *rôle* of disinterested friend—to adjust the telegraphic machinery and connect the galvanic apparatus in a continued chain. He may have been five minutes occupied in this manner, during which time a low murmur, like the frothing of the sea, rose from the three thousand couplets of electrified metals, eroded by the biting fluids of the troughs; then touching a heavy pendulum on each of the three tables, and communicating life to the apparatus by winding a powerful spring, he stood aside, and asked me what I would have him do next.

"Without replying, I raised the thick baize curtain which concealed the metal mirror under the larger of the tables, and, stooping down, uttered, slowly, a few distinct words. The clicking of the needle showed that they had been recorded, as I spoke, on the slip of paper at the telegraph desk.

" 'It appears to me,' said I, glancing at the scowling, troubled face of my enemy, 'that you do not at this moment enjoy so greatly the proof of my innocence, and—pardon me if I add—of your own villainy. Your villainous machine records words spoken in this room, above the mirror, as clearly as though they had been uttered below it, in my chamber. The enamored conversations that occupy so many pages of this volume, resembling a poor novel, have been composed by yourself; proving, Sir, the just equality of your literary talent and your virtue.'

"The dark eyes of Bonsall flashed malignant fires. Shuddering and shrugging with impotent rage, he began pacing with heavy strides, his hands clasped nervously behind him, back and forth the long room. Twice, as he passed me, he threw deadly glances. I wished to retire, but would not. There is something awfully attractive in the exhibition of destructive passions. My eyes followed the man, who at that moment contemplated every possibility of violence, with a fixed regard of terror and curiosity. I felt that we were acting a part, but the actors were sincere, and thought nothing of the possible scorn or applause that might follow the lifting of the curtain.

"At length utterance returned to him, and he gave vent to his accumulated rage in a curse. Raising his right arm, he cursed me as he passed before me, with the addition of such words as the man uses when he would destroy all possibility of reconciliation with the woman. The nervous arm, raised to enforce the language, in falling broke a link of the strong connecting-wire looped along from column to column. The surging murmurs of the batteries, the whirl of the magnets, and the click of the heavy pendulums, ceased on the instant. He stopped in his way.

" 'I see,' said he, 'that you, such as you are, have the advantage of me in self-command.'

"With a deep sigh he expelled the tumult from his breast.

" 'As easily,' he continued, 'as I can repair the slight injury my foolish rage has inflicted upon this thread of metal, so easily can I mend the mischief you have brought upon me by your discovery.'

"When Bonsall uttered this threat I lost all fear. Contempt made me laugh.

" 'There was a time,' he continued, 'when I loved you with a passion equal to my present hate.'

" 'Pray, Sir,' I said, 'may I inquire the cause of this heroical hatred?'

" 'Is it nothing to have suffered, year after year, the pangs of incurable love, until every thought, every action was absorbed in that one grief? If the passion soured into hate—'

" 'I gave you no invitation to indulge such folly.'

" 'True, you gave none. Becoming daily more beautiful, more lovely; as the days wore on, estranged more and more from your miserable husband—'

" 'Not a word of that, Sir! You were my accuser.'

" 'Yes, I own it. It was a crime—'

" 'Crime upon crime, Raymond. First, an unlawful passion; then treachery to a friend; then hatred of the object unlawfully loved; then futile conspiracy to defame, to rob. Do you call that *love*? Oh, fool!'

" 'It was not I who planned it; the wretch, Mohler, a mean, suspicious creature, cowardly, an intellect without a heart—it was he, Maria, who devised your ruin. He called on me to help him.'

" 'And you answered the call?'

"Bonsall was silent.

" 'There is no excuse. Your nature is evil. What you call love is an unholy passion that would sacrifice every thing to itself.'

" 'Would not the highest virtue do the same, Maria?'

" 'You are more subtle than I. Your subtlety of intellect has destroyed you.'

" 'Mixed motives. I loved you, nevertheless; ay, worshiped—that is the word; I love you still. Bid me die, and I will.'

" 'Love!'

" 'Yes, deep, absolute. It was your silence, your avoidance, aversion, that ruined me. Now I can speak freely with you, and I no longer hate.'

"In every woman's heart (surely in mine) there is a degree of compassion and forgiveness for those who suffer by the effects of love. It is God's will that it should be so; else all women would fly from men. Great as my abhorrence was—thoroughly as I despised the baseness of Raymond—an old secret preference, a long-suppressed feeling, crept up into my throat and choked me.

" 'Raymond,' I exclaimed, with an accent, I fear, not wholly harsh, 'you have chosen a base and crooked path to the favor of a woman who was once proud to call you friend. During the last two of seven tedious years you have not acted the part even of a friend—much less—'

" 'It was the accursed silence,' he exclaimed, eagerly. 'We should have been more honest.'

" '*We*, Raymond?'

" 'Yes, *we*. You loved me once.'

"I had gone too far to recede. My courage rose. Prudery would have been cruel and absurd. Could I, then, terminate this long career of crime by a simple explanation?

" 'A word more,' I said, 'before we end this conference—which, I hope, may save us both. Tell me for what purpose you conspired to deprive me of my fortune? That was the act, not of a despairing lover, but of an unprincipled sensualist. Why this complicated and cumbrous mass of conspiracy against me and mine?'

" 'Judge me as you will,' he answered. 'I have told you all. I would have restored all that I had taken from Mohler to you. I wished to load you with obligations. See, here are all the evidences.'

"He opened a drawer of the desk, drew forth a package of papers, and placed them in my hand. I accepted the gift. It was prudent to do so.

" 'Destroy these papers,' he continued, eagerly, 'and the work of infamy is undone.'

" 'I appreciate the motive, but how can I forget the crime?'

" 'By extending pardon to the criminal.'

"Oh! my friend, when the sun-rays of mercy spread over the soul their warm and tender light, are we to be blamed if we forget the strict laws of social propriety?

" 'Come near to me,' I said.

"He came and stood before me, with downcast eyes.

" 'If I will forget the past, will you forget it? Will you leave me now forever, and let silence cover all?'

" 'Death—death! I could not outlive the separation. Though it must come, while I live let me live near you!' he exclaimed, turning away, pale and convulsed.

" 'See,' he said, taking up one end of the broken wire, 'this poor mechanism is like your favor: while the wires are united—that is, your good-will, your pity—it gives life, power, hope; the strong currents of the soul flow on, and the man is powerful, useful, happy. Without this he is only a self-corroding machine. Pardon me,' he added, while a blush mantled his features, "if my long study of these magnetic laws has suggested an illustration that may seem mean and trivial to you; but the great laws work in souls as in Matter. Give me, then, your favor, or—'

"He touched, as he spoke, the other depending piece of the broken wire. A murmurous sound arose from the batteries. The pent-up, concentrated lightnings rushed from the wires through his frame, and he fell *dead* like one who has dropped suddenly asleep.

"I went to him, and regarded for a time, in silent awe, the upturned face of the dead. Ah! what a terrible anguish is compassion! It is the grief of God. Kneeling by the side of Raymond Bonsall, slain by a sudden, unlooked-for vengeance—the work, inadvertent, of his own hand—all the past fled away, and I thought only of the ages of remorse that, in another world, would punish the repentant but malformed, misguided soul. The tears were falling freely from my eyes as I knelt by the dead, when I heard behind me a step that I knew to be Mohler's.

"As I arose I saw the sordid figure of the German chemist creeping behind. When he saw me, and at a glance divined the nature of the accident that had befallen Bonsall, he shrank away and fled. As for Mohler, he could hardly clear his sense sufficiently to comprehend the calamity that had fallen upon himself. His jaw dropped; he fumbled with his hands. I felt no pity for him—why, I can not tell.

" 'Maria! What has happened to Bonsall? How did you get in here? Oh! I suppose you understand all now?'

" 'I do.'

" 'Bonsall is dead!' he murmured. 'Yes, I see the wires are broken. Three thousand pairs of plates—it would kill an ox! You say you understand the affair. Hum! You have read the evidence against you in the book?'

" 'Enough to know that Bonsall, who lies here dead, is the author of these infamous conversations attributed to me.'

" 'How—how?'

" 'Voices above the mirror are recorded as well as those spoken beneath.'

" 'I never once thought of that!'

" 'You? You, then, are not an accomplice?'

" 'No,' he said, hesitating, and placing his hand to his forehead, 'Indeed it troubles me much. Let us go to your room, Maria, and we will talk it over.'

"An insipid, futile smile played over his features. The suddenness of the discovery how he had been duped by Bonsall—the probable loss, in one moment, of wife, honor, friend, all the springs of a good life—smote through and through, and wounded to death the poor brain. I led him away like a child. But why did I feel no pity—none, ever?

"Mohler's lunacy, as you know, was permanent. To the last moment his brain worked upon inventions."

Two silver tears, moved gently from her large eyes by the remonstrance of a smile, coursed quietly down the cheeks of the beautiful narrator. Ah! soul full of great courage and compassion, it was with thee as with the king who did not change countenance when he saw his son led to execution, but wept grievously when a poor drunken bottle-companion went to his death.

It was a history known only to a few. I first have given it to the world. Under the names and dates I have assumed, a few only will recognize the real persons and events.

MEDICINE MEN

Medical science fiction bridges any gaps between the science fiction relating man to his machines and the science fiction penetrating into the psyche. The question "What is life?" may be the question asked by all fiction, but medical science fiction asks that question in very special ways, ways not only opened but made necessary by nineteenth-century medical research.

The century in which modern medicine was created, the century of Semmelweis, William T. G. Morton, Pasteur, Theodor Billroth, Lister, and Koch, was also the century in which medical men became main characters in fiction and wrote a good deal of science fiction themselves. It was the century of Drs. Frankenstein, Rappaccini, Chillingworth, Heidenhoff, and Moreau, and of Drs. Oliver Wendell Holmes and Silas Weir Mitchell (not to mention Dr. Arthur Conan Doyle). Although many other physicians wrote science fiction,* Holmes and Mitchell were distinct as important medical scientists who used fiction as a vehicle for speculation. In fact Holmes, as Dr. Clarence Obendorf points out in *The Psychiatric Novels of Dr. Oliver Wendell Holmes*, presented his brilliant psychiatric theories first as science fiction in *Elsie Venner* (1859) and *The Guardian Angel* (1867), then

* See John B. Hamilton, "Notes toward a Definition of Science Fiction," *Extrapolation*, 1962.

in the famous Phi Beta Kappa speech, "Mechanism in Thought and Morals" (1870), again in science fiction in *A Mortal Antipathy* (1884), and never in formal scientific papers. But I agree with Hamilton's evaluation of Silas Weir Mitchell as "by far the best fiction writer of all the physician novelists up to the twentieth century." Mitchell, like Holmes, was incredibly versatile and productive; in Hamilton's words:

> Silas Weir Mitchell . . . wrote six books of medical works, two of which are still standard basic treatises; over a hundred pioneering monographs on clinical neurology; and some studies on toxicology which are still consulted in medical schools. His literary work includes besides a translation of the Middle English poem "Pearl," fifteen novels, four children's books, and four volumes of short stories.

"Was He Dead?", the story included here, works the Frankenstein theme (it explicitly mentions Frankenstein and his monster) in ways that take advantage of Mitchell's knowledge of physiology and provide a significant form for speculation about it. The fiction to which it should be compared includes *Frankenstein* itself, "Rappaccini's Daughter," an anonymous story entitled "The Living Corpse" (*Putnam's*, 1853), Dr. Mary Jacobi's "A Martyr to Science" (*Putnam's*, 1869), Alvey Augustus Adee's "The Life Magnet" (*Putnam's*, 1870), William C. Morrow's "The Monster-Maker" (in *The Ape, The Idiot, and Other People*, 1897), and, most interestingly of all, Stephen Crane's "The Monster" (*Harper's Monthly*, 1898).

Crane's "The Monster" shares almost all the concerns of "Was He Dead?" and explores these concerns with much the same kind of action—a doctor brings back to life a man who is more or less dead and then has the responsibility of being in a sense his creator. "Was He Dead?" is clearly science fiction; is then "The Monster" science fiction? Although "The Monster" may not focus as precisely on the details of physiological process, neither does that fruitful patriarch of science fiction, *Frankenstein*. If "The Monster" is not science fiction, why not? A satisfactory answer to that question would reveal a great deal about the nature of science fiction and, for that matter, about all fiction. Perhaps one answer lies in the question Mitchell uses as his title, for "Was He Dead?" seeks to make possible travel from beyond the bourne.

SILAS WEIR MITCHELL, M.D.

Was He Dead? *

In the fickle glow of ruddy firelight the great egg of the dinornis swung solemnly through its long arc of motion. There are five eggs of the dinornis in the known world: four are in great museums, and the fifth belongs to my friend Purpel, and is one of the oddest of his many curiosities. The room I enter is spacious, and clad warmly with dark rows of books. Above them the walls are irregularly hidden by prints, pictures, and the poisoned weapons of savage tribes,—dark and sombre javelin and arrow,—with awful security of death about them, and none of the cold, quick gleam of honest steel. The light flashes on a great brass microscope with its sheltering glass, and half reveals in corners an endless confusion of the dexterous apparatus born of modern science. The glittering student-lamp on the central writing-table stands unlighted, deep in that comfortable confusion of letters, books, and papers, which is dear to certain men I know, and to them only is not confusion. Just above these a thread of steel wire held suspended the giant egg of the dinornis, which, as I have said, was now swinging in a vast round of motion, like a great white planet through the lights and shades of eternal space.

"Purpel," said I, "that egg cost you a hundred pounds. What demon of rashness possesses you to set it flying round the room?"

"Mercantile friend," replied the slight figure in the spacious arm-chair at the fireside, "it is a venture. If there be left in

* *Atlantic Monthly,* January 1870.

your dollar-driven soul any heirship of your great namesake, Sir Thomas, you will comprehend me. This egg is more dear to me than your biggest East-Indiaman, and yet I risk it, as you do the galleon, for what it fetches me out of the land of mystery. See the huge troubled wake it makes through my columns of pipe-breath." With this he blew forth a cloud such as went before the Israelites, and contentedly watched the swirl of the egg as it broke through the blue ribbons, dogged by its swift shadow on wall and bookcase.

"Sit down, Gresham," said my friend.

"Be so good, then, as to stop that infernal egg," said I. "Do you think I want ten pounds of lime on my head?"

"Bless you," returned Purpel, contentedly, "for a new idea. Perhaps it may be an *ovum infernale*. What proof have I that it was of dinornis hatch? A devil's egg! There's meat for thought, Mercator! However," he continued with a smile, "what is there we will not do for friendship?" And so saying he climbed on a chair, and, seizing the egg, checked its movement and left it hanging as by some witchcraft from its unseen thread.

"Have you seen Vance to-day? He was to be here at nine. I hope he won't fail us. My brain has been as fidgety as a geyser all day, and I want a little of his frosty, definite logic."

"I thought, doctor," said I, "that it was not always what you liked."

"What I liked!" said he, "I loathe it sometimes, just as I do my cold plunge of a morning in December; but, bless you, old man, it's a bitter good tonic for a fellow like me, with a Concord craze and a cross of French science. There he is. Speak of the devil!—How d' ye do, V.? There's your pipe on the jar yonder. Have a match?" And, so saying, he struck a lucifer, in whose yellow glare and splutter I noted the strong contrast of the two faces.

Purpel, short and slight, chiefly notable for a certain alertness of head-carriage, untamable brown locks, and a sombre sincerity of visage altogether American in type, mouth over-size and mobile, eyes large and wistful. Great admiration of this man has the shrewd, calm owner of the cool blue eyes which flash now in the gleam of matchlight through the slight eye-glass he wears. The face and head of my friend Vance are moulded, like his mind, in lines of proportioned and balanced beauty, with something architectural and severe about the forehead. Below are distinct features and watchful lips, like those of a judge accustomed to wait and sentence, only a tell-tale curve at the angles, a written record of many laughters, a wrinkle of mirth, says Purpel, who loves him and has for him that curious respect which genius, incapable of self-comprehension, has for talent, whose laws it can see and admire.

We are very old friends, and why I like them is easy to see; but why they return this feeling is less clear to me, who am merely a rather successful merchant, unlike them in all ways and in all pursuits. Perhaps a little of the flavor of their tastes has come to be mine by long companionship; or it may be that Purpel, who is sardonic at times, and talks charades, hovered about the truth when he said I represented in their talks the outside world of common opinion. "A sort of test-man," grins Vance; which troubles me little, knowing surely that they both love me well.

The three meerschaums slowly browning into the ripe autumn of their days were lighted, and we drew our chairs around the smouldering logs. I am afraid that Purpel's feet were on the mantel-ledge, at which I laughed for the hundredth time. "G.," said he,—for this was one of his ways, Vance being V.,—"don't you know it sends more blood to your head to feed the thinking-mill, and so accounts for the general superiority of the American race?"

"And Congressmen," added Vance.

"And tavern loafers," said I.

"Nonsense!" cried Purpel. "If the mill be of limited capacity, it were useless to run the Missouri over its water-wheel."

"One of your half-thoughts," returned Vance, "and nearly half believed."

"Not at all," said Purpel. "Does not everybody think best when lying down? More blood to the head, more thought and better."

"Well," I exclaimed, rashly, with a gleam of inspiration, "how about the circus fellows, doctor?"

"He's coming on," cried Vance, with a slap on the back. "Try it in your back counting-room an hour a day, and you will clean out Vanderbilt in a week."

"Now," said Purpel, irascibly, "here's the old story. You think along a railway track, V., and I wander about at my own will, like a boy in a wood. My chances of a find are the better of the two."

"You're like a boy in another way, old man," said the other. "You accumulate a wondrous lot of queer inutilities in those mental pockets of yours."

"Don't you know what my pet philosopher says?" returned Purpel. " 'Inutilities are stars whose light has not yet reached us.' Smoke the pipe of silence, V., if you have no better wisdom than that. To believe anything useless is only to confess that you are a hundred years too young."

"Come in," he exclaimed; for there was a knock at the door.

"A gentleman to see you, sir."

"Show him up," said Purpel. "What in the name of decency does any one but you two old heathen want with me at this hour!"

Presently the door opened, and a very ordinary-looking person entered the room. "Dr. Purpel?" said he, looking from one to the other.

"I am Dr. Purpel," said my friend; "what can I do for you? Take a seat. I beg pardon, but I did not catch your name."

"Thunderin' queer if you did," said the stranger, "when I never give it."

Vance touched my arm. "Too many for P., wasn't he?"

"Humph!" said Purpel, slightly nettled. "I suppose you can talk without a label. What is your errand?"

"Could I speak with you alone?" returned the stranger.

"I suppose so," said the doctor, lazily rising, and laying down his pipe. "I shall be back presently, V." And so saying he walked into a back room, followed by the visitor. The brief absence he had promised lengthened to an hour, when, as the clock struck twelve, he reappeared alone, and, hastily excusing himself, went out again. Vance and I presently ended our chat and went our ways homeward through the drifting snows of the January night.

Early next morning I received a request to meet Vance in the evening at our friend's rooms. We were still as constant companions as new ties and our varying roads through life would permit, so that any subject of strong interest to one was apt to call all of us together in council; and therefore it was I felt no surprise at a special appointment being thus made. I have already whispered to you that I represented to these men the gentler and better of the commonplaces of business existence. Purpel, I am told, is a fine specimen of what a man of genius becomes with the quickest blood of this century in his veins. Marvellously made to study with success the how, the why, and the wherefore of nature, he refuses to recognize a limit to philosophic thought, and delights to stand face to face with the hundred speechless sphinxes who frown upon us from those unknown lands which his favorite philosopher has described as

> "Filled with the quaintest surprises
> Of kaleidoscopic sunrises,
> Ghosts of the colors of earth,—
> Where the unseen has its birth."

Vance, a man of easy circumstances, represents a school of more regular and severe logic, but of less fertility, and for whom the sciences he loves are never so delightful as when he can chain their result within the iron lines of a set of equations. Purpel was at his old tricks again that evening, as we shook the snow from our boots, and, lighting the calumets, settled down into the easy comfort of the positions each liked the best. He was at his old tricks, I have said, for the great egg of the dinornis was swinging majestic in a vast curve, as if propelled at each flight through space by some unseen hand of power.

"I should get into the shadow of the charm it has for you, Purpel," said I, "if I watched it long."

"All motion is mystery," said he, musingly, "and all life is motion. What a stride it has. I suppose if it were big enough, and had a proportional initial impulse, some such world-egg might be set swinging through all eternity."

"Nothing is endless," said Vance. "Even the stars are shifting their courses. It would stop as they must. Motion is definite enough; it is only this wretched element of humanity which baffles us."

"Ay," said Purpel, "and for all we know it may be playing the mischief with the motor functions of the old globe herself. I don't suppose that we can have been digging and mining and tunnelling and carting the dirt from this place to that, without damaging the ballast of the poor old egg we live on. Human will may disturb the equilibrium so horribly some day, that we shall go tumbling through space with no more certainty than a lop-sided billiard-ball."

"May I be there to see!" said Vance, with a jolly laugh. "I think the dirt account will foot up even, during my time. Start something else, stupid;—you will take to Planchette next if you go on muddling your smoky old cerebrum much longer. How comes on the murder case?"

"It was about that I wanted to talk to you," said Purpel. "The anonymous gentleman who disturbed our talk last night is one of the detective force. He was sent to me by Fred Dysart, who is engaged for the nephew and niece. It seems that he wanted me to examine the wounds in the old woman's body. After making the proper inspection, I went over the premises with the curiosity one has in a case so utterly baffling. I cut off some of the blood-stains on the floor, but found nothing beyond what is usual."

"Is it always easy to detect blood-stains?" asked I.

"Usually," he replied, "it is. Always we can say whether or not the stain be blood, and whether it be that of a reptile, a bird, or a mammal, although we cannot be sure as to its being that of man or beast, the corpuscles of which differ only as to size. It has been made probable of late, however, that with very high microscopic powers even this may be attainable."

"I suppose," said Vance, "that some time or other we shall be able to swear to a man from some known peculiarity of his blood-globule. Missing I. S. may be known by his blood-globules, which belong to species *b*, variety 2."

"I doubt that," returned Purpel, not noticing the other's smile. "There does not seem to be anything less individual than the blood. It is the same in structure in youth and age. Individuality lies in the solids."

"So that," said Vance, "should the clown fool of Elizabeth have had his arteries run full of the blood of Shakespeare, it would not have helped him to jest the better."

"No, sir: nor if the case had been reversed, provided the blood were healthy, should we any the less have possessed Hamlet."

"How odd then," said I, "that popular phrase and thought should have selected the least individual portion of a man to express his qualities, or to indicate his descent and relationships.

You think," continued I, "that it would be absurd to try to rejuvenate an old man by filling his vessels with young blood."

"Perfectly so," said Purpel. "In fact, it has been tried over and over again. The blood of the young has been bought to fill the veins of age, and even ugliness, it is said, has sought a remedy by acquiring the blood which nourished rosy cheeks and rounded limbs."

"Who first tried it, Purpel?" asked Vance.

"No less a person than Christopher Wren is said to have proposed the use of transfusion, but it was first applied to a man about 1667 by one Daniel Magon, of Bonn. After this in numerous instances the blood of sheep or calves was thrown into the veins of men."

"And without injury?" asked Vance.

"Yes," added Purpel. "Nor could any change be perceived in the receiver of the blood from the animal. Not only is this as I state it, but it is still more strange that ammonia salts were employed to keep the blood fluid while using it. The persons who first invented transfusion also threw medicaments into the veins in disease, a method revived of late, but long disused. However, as usual, I am run away with by a doctor's hobby."

"I for one," cried Vance, "regret the failure. Think what delicious confusions of individualities must have resulted. How could the man of twenty, with silken beard and mustache, be expected to honor his bill for the wig he needed last week? The old beldame Nature sets us many queer sums, but she doesn't allow of her arrangements being so easily upset as they might be in such a case."

"It's a tempting subject, though," returned Purpel, "and perhaps we are not yet at the end of it."

"A tempting subject!" shouted Vance, in scorn. "Nonsense! you don't suppose I felt a molecule of me in earnest about it. A pretty nice subject for folks who believe that somewhere 'there is an eternal teapot.' You're getting worse all the time, and will want a full course of Emerson."

"Now, Vance," said Purpel, "that's a barred subject; and you know it, too. The kind of regard—"

"Gammon," said Vance, "I meant Emerson's Arithmetic, man. That's what you want,—definition of idea, numerical sharpness of thought, a course of mathematics."

"What!" returned Purpel, "do you fancy no one great who can not excel in algebra? Why, dear fellow, there are lines of research in which a mathematician could not excel, and for success in which a man must be almost as much poet as man of science. This is why imagination is so often highly developed in chemists and physiologists and certain physicists. What is it your philosopher says?—'Science is only Poetry sworn to truth on the altar of nature'; and this explains to us Haller and Davy and Goethe and Faraday, and is seen more or less in the marvellous gift of expression which we so frequently see illustrated in the writings of men of science. The first living naturalist in this country never yet has been able to comprehend how a symbol can come to express a number and be used as its representative. And as to the Emerson business, I don't believe you, V."

"Sir," said Vance, standing under the egg of the dinornis, "you are now talking the language of common humanity, for when a man says, 'I don't believe you,' he is simple, impressive, and unmistakable; but then it is so rare that a philosopher of your school ventures to be thus explicit. It is so easy to dress up a commonplace in new clothes, and foist off the old stupid as a bright and clever fellow."

"He's at my friends again, Gresham, and the best of the fun is, that he can't quote a line of the author he sneers at."

"Can't I?" retorted Vance, enchanted with Purpel's annoyance at this never-failing source of chaff. "Can't quote him? What's that he says about the Devil, P.?—O, where he calls him an 'animated Torrid Zone.' Now that was descriptive enough."

"Confound you, V.," broke in Purpel; "it was a humblebee he said that about."

"Then I don't see the connection of ideas," returned the other. "However, he has a neater way of saying one fibs than you have. It's neater, but bless us, P., isn't it—"

"Isn't it what?" cried Purpel. "What are you raging about?"

"Wait a little, and I'll tell you. There, fill my pipe for me, P., while I quote: 'If my brother repute my conscience with a lie (not of my telling), surely he has done me a good deed, for whether I lie is immaterial, so as that it causes another introspect. But, as concerns variety, there are two kinds of liars. This man lies to himself, and after is in earnest about it with the world. This other lies only to the world and is not self-deceived. Moreover, each century says to the last, You lie; so that to lie is only to prophesy.' Now, P., isn't that a more charitable mode of putting the case than just merely to say it isn't so? I wish I could give you page and line, but, as you see, my memory is good enough."

"Wretch," groaned Purpel, "your memory, indeed! You are too near this man to take in his dimensions.

> 'Men there be so broad and ample
> Other men are but a sample
> Of a corner of their being,
> Of a pin-space of their seeing.'

Let him answer you himself."

"I am satisfied," growled Vance. "Satiated, I may say. Let's get back to earth again. You were going to tell us about the murder, I believe."

"Yes, V. I feel really a great interest in the matter. I do not see how the nephew is to escape conviction."

"What are the circumstances?" I asked.

"The victim," replied Purpel, "was an old Quaker lady of slight means, who lived in a small three-story house off of Mill Street. On the day of the murder she drew a hundred dollars, which, as usual, she kept upon her person. The lower rooms were sub-let to others. She herself lived in a third-story back-room. The house is separated on the west by an alley from a blank wall of a warehouse. On the north there is a narrow area bounded by a tenement-house, about to be altered for some purpose, and at present without inhabitants above the first story. The old woman's rocking-chair was in its usual place, facing a table, and with its back to the north window. It had been pushed away from the table, and the body lay beside it on the floor. All of the blood, or nearly all, was in front of the chair, on the ceiling, walls, and table."

"Who gave the alarm?" asked I.

"No one," he answered, "until in the morning her niece found her on the floor with her throat cut. By the by, it must have been done early, because the girl left her at nine, and she usually read the paper a little later, and was in bed by ten. Now when found she lay alongside of her chair, dressed."

"But about the nephew?" said I.

"The nephew," continued Purpel, "is a man of forty or thereabouts. Like the rest of them, he seems to have led at some time an easier life, but is now a reporter in a small way, and is said to be engaged to the niece, his cousin. There is some evidence that he has plagued the old woman a good deal for money, and that he is one of your luckless people never actually starving, but never distinctly succeeding. He came to the house in the afternoon, stayed to tea, and remained with the old lady to read the paper to her after the niece left. The girl says he was alone with her only about a quarter of an hour, and she heard him shut the street door before she herself had finished undressing. When arrested he was found to have on his person fifty dollars in notes, one of which was identified by the clerk of the insurance company who paid the annuity. The most careful inspection detected no blood-stains upon any of his clothes, and he wore the same suit both days. Now, Vance, how does it strike you?"

"I have no decision to give," was his reply. "You have told me enough to hang him, and hanged I suppose he will be."

"There are numberless possibilities in his favor," said I.

"True," added Vance, "but at present it is the fashion to hang folks. What is his name?"

"Upton," said Purpel,—"Denis Upton."

"Good gracious!" exclaimed Vance. "Why, Gresham, you know that man. He was a small clerk in my uncle's employ. Don't you recall him,—a cleverish fellow, one of your massive youngsters, with huge, shaggy features and awkward ways. I am very sorry. I heard he had gone under the social ice a good while ago; but what a hideous ending! I must see him, P."

Somewhat awed by this unlooked-for revival of an old acquaintance, we suffered the talk to die out, and presently broke up and walked thoughtfully homeward.

I went next day with my friends, first to the house of Mrs. Gray, and then to visit Upton in jail. We accompanied the officer in charge through the various rooms, and Purpel and Vance carefully studied them in turn. In the room where the murder was done there were jets of dried blood on the walls, and a ghastly semi-fluid pool on the floor, but none behind the woman's chair, the back of which was towards the north window. Apparently the chair had been pushed away from the table, and she had advanced a step or two towards the door when the assault was made. There was no blood, however, on the door-handle or the north window.

Struck with the defective nature of the evidence, we left the house and made our visit to the prisoner, or rather Vance made his, for we waited in the keeper's rooms. By and by he returned, and as he had an engagement we agreed to meet at night and hear his account of the interview.

"I suppose it is our man, Vance?" said I.

"I am sorry to say it is," he replied, "and a more wretched being I have never seen. He told me a long story of endless ill luck and disappointments, through all of which this girl has clung to him tenaciously. He did not pretend to conceal from me that he had gambled and drunk at times, but his evil fortunes seem to have depended less on these vices than upon a certain want of practicality, if there be such a word."

"There is such a thing," said I.

"You wouldn't know him, Gresham. He is one of your colossally built men, with huge features, and nothing very nice about his face but his smile."

" 'Smile'!" said Purpel, "could the poor fellow smile?"

"So we are made," said Vance; "the moment rules us. I saw a fellow garroted in Havana, who killed a mosquito on his cheek a minute before they pinioned him."

"It seems ghastly," said I. "Is he greatly alarmed about himself?"

"No," returned Vance. "He comprehends his position, but I do really think he is so wretched with running the gauntlet of untiring ill luck, that he is in a manner indifferent, except as to this girl."

"And what of her?"

"Well, P., she is rather a character. I saw her at his request, and found a woman about thirty, with that hard, bony style of face which belongs to the acid type of Quaker. She must have had a rather dull sort of life, what with the old woman and the weary waiting for a future that never came. We had a pretty long talk, and at last she said, 'Does thee think him guilty?' I said, 'No.' And indeed, I do not. 'Does thee think it would clear him if another were to confess?' I said, 'Yes, certainly,' astonished, as you may suppose. Then she said, 'If thee wouldn't mind, I would like to be alone.' And so I came away."

A few days after this little talk, the woman was released, as no kind of suspicion appeared to cling to her; while about the man Upton the toils gathered closer and closer. As this story is only in a manner connected with ourselves and our talks, which, after all, are what I want to render, I hasten through the acts of this ugly drama. As Vance had foreseen, according to a present fashion Upton was convicted, and within a day or two his history and reputed crime were forgotten in the roar of the great city's tide of busy life, only to be recalled anew when the story of the gallows should be told to eager readers over comfortable breakfast-tables.

Amidst the general neglect, we three alone held to a sturdy belief in the innocence of the convicted man, who, like a hare sore beset by hounds, seemed to have cast himself down to await the coming death; altogether indifferent to its approach, so much worse did life seem to be than any death he could conceive of.

About a week before the day set for turning over this man's case to the judgment-seat of God, we met as of custom. It was a common habit with us, as it may be with other like circles, to sit a little time silent over the first freshly lighted pipes.

By and by the pleasant glamour of our Lady of the Leaf would come between us and the day's long labors and vexations; and, slaves no longer to custom or the world of men, we drifted away whithersoever the tides of thought or fancy might choose to carry us. It had been agreed that we should talk no longer of the tragedy which most men had already forgotten, and so it was that our chat turned on other matters.

"I saw to-day," said Vance, "that some one has been speculating upon the probable effect on the German mind of the use of tobacco; but I suspect that before long there will be no nation sufficiently smokeless for comparison."

"Possibly, not," said I. "It is said that the Indian, the primary smoker, has never used it to that excess which other races have done."

"He lives out of doors," said Purpel, "and the pipe has no bane for the dweller in tent or wigwam."

"I can vouch for that," returned Vance; "but, how curious it is that we alone should chew, and that the German soldier, who chewed inveterately during the Thirty Years' War, should have utterly abandoned the vice."

"I never knew of the facts," said Purpel; "but all honor to the Dutchman. As to tobacco, it is utterly vain to oppose it;

nor do I for one believe that it is hurtful when moderately used by men of matured development. I might, I don't say I would, give up this old meerschaum for a wife; but I think I should like to be as certain of the woman's power to soothe and charm as I am of my pipe's, before I ventured on the exchange. I suppose it does hurt some folks' cerebral organs, but it seems to me somehow very strange that this or that drug should have the power to interfere with the machinery of a thing as spiritual as thought. It is really impossible, reason as we may, for us to dissociate the higher mental qualities from some relationship with a sphere of activities beyond those which we can study."

"And yet," said Vance, "we have, scientifically speaking, every evidence to relate thought in all its forms to material changes in brain tissue. Given certain conditions which insure the integrity of nerve-matter,—and we think, remember, imagine. Take any one of these away, and we do these things ill or not at all."

"To me," said Purpel, "the strangest part of the problem lies in the fact that, whereas the forms of mental activity are so distinct, we have no notable differentiation in the tissues of the various parts of the brain set apart for their production."

"Nor," said Vance, "is there any apparent distinction in texture between the average brain and that of La Place or Newton."

"Difference of bulk or weight there probably is," added Purpel; "but nothing that accounts for the vast separation in the character of the products of the contrasted brains we are talking of."

"Of course, it bewilders *me,*" said I, humbly. "If you see a very strong man, one exceptional in his way, he seems always to possess a vast quantity of muscle; now, the amount of increase of brain-tissue needed to make the difference between commonplace and genius seems to be so small as to fill me with astonishment."

"But, G.," said Purpel, "do not you think it quite impossible to compare the two forms of result? The muscle is only one element in the making of a perfect human machine for the evolution of physical force such as motion. The nerves stand for something here, and the nerve-centres also; for in spite of the popular notion that a muscular man alone is strong, it really seems as though amount of muscle-mass might be but the least important element in the case, and nerve-force the greatest."

"How so?" said I.

"Because," said Purpel, "you may see the slightly-built insane man exhibiting the power of an athlete."

"Considering, then," said Vance, "the whole nervo-muscular apparatus for causing motion, we see it attain its maximum of power in the insane or convulsed—"

"It is so said," broke in Purpel, "but whether truly or not, I doubt a little. An insane man is so indifferent to the pains which often come of utterly reckless exertion, that it is hard to compare the vigor thus exhibited with that of health. If I understood you aright, you were going on to point out that the mental organs possess no power to produce, when diseased, the highest mental result."

"Not unless genius be truly madness,—for the 'great wit' of the couplet means that, I presume," said I.

"I do not believe much in their near alliance!" exclaimed Purpel. "And I fully agree with the great Frenchman, who said of this theory that, were it so, genius would more often be inherited."

"And is it not?" said Vance.

"No," replied Purpel. "Talents are often matter of descent; and as a rule, two clever people are more apt to leave able descendants than two fools; but genius, so far as I can remember, is very rarely inherited."

"No doubt, you are correct," said Vance; "and, in fact, there is a curious and self-born difficulty in the continuity of any great faculties in a line of descent."

"How?" said I.

"Thus," returned Vance. "It has been clearly shown that the descendants of great men are few in number; and this depends upon a law of the human economy, by virtue of which the overuse of the intellectual powers lessens the activity of the generative faculties, and thus, because a man is a hero, or statesman, or poet, he is likely to leave fewer descendants; and for a similar reason these run a greater risk of being imperfect creatures than the babies of the next mechanic."

"The children of the brain slay the children of the body," said Purpel.

"A rather bold mode of statement," replied Vance, "but, to return a little,—when I think it over, it does seem to me that the diseased brain may often turn out the larger amount of product; but then the quality is poor, while the muscle, brain, and system give you in the crazed—if the public be correct—not only amount of force, but swiftness of motion, and unequalled endurance of exertion. In other words, the best is evolved only when a morbid element is thrown in. What say you to that, P.?"

"I still doubt the facts," cried Purpel.

"Ah, ha!" said I, "you and V. seem to have exchanged parts to-night. How is it, V.?"

"Which accounts for his talking so well," said Purpel; "but, to return again."

"Is there such a thing possible as stimulating the mental organs with electricity?"

"No," said Purpel. "Some few of the central organs of motion and sensation may be galvanized in animals so as to give response. But many nerve-centres, those included, to which we assign the parentage of mental states, make no sign when irritated in this manner."

Said Vance: "You cannot reach them in life, I mean in man."

"No," returned Purpel; "but we can reach them in living animals."

"Where? alas!" was the answer. "You have a practical impossibility of reply, either owing to the injury done, or because the animal is defective in its power to express mental states."

"Why not try it on man?" said I.

"Would you be pleased to volunteer?" retorted Vance, with a laugh.

"You can find a man to do anything conceivable," I continued; "but for this especial business you must look farther."

"Well," said Vance, "to return on our tracks. If, as Purpel told us last week, the organs of special sense record only in their own language the prick of a pin or an electric shock—"

"Stop," said I; "what do you mean?"

"Only this," said Purpel, taking up the thread of talk, "that if you hurt the globe of the eye so as to press on the optic nerve, you will feel it as a flash of light only. So in the mouth, an electric discharge is felt as a taste, and a like conclusion is probable as to hearing."

"I see," said I; "and now, Vance, as I interrupted you, what were you about to say?"

"I was thinking," said he, "that in like manner irritating or electrizing the nerves which must run from one mental organ to another might call out the special function of the part, whether as thought, memory, fancy, or what not. However, I presume one would get about as orderly replies as when disease does act on these nerve-wires, or as when a thunder-storm meddles with the telegraph-lines."

"Humph!" returned Purpel; "you had best not get beyond your last, old friend, and your last is a little ahead of most of your notions."

"Well," said I, with one of those queer flashes of inspiration that come to a dull fellow who lives enough among his intellectual betters to rub off on him, now and then, a little of their phosphorus,—"well," said I, "of course, Purpel, such an experiment tried on a living man would produce endless confusion of mind and all kind of interferences; but suppose you could keep alive only the intellectual organs, and could contrive to stimulate them one at a time."

I never can tell whether Vance is in earnest or in jest, unless he takes out his pencil and a card and begins, Let $a + b =$ etc., and let q be etc. This time his soul on a sudden revolted at the wildness of the talk into which we had wandered.

"Ho, ho!" said he, "who started all this nonsense?" And then he went off into a furious tirade against the feebleness with which men talked, and urged the need for mathematical training and the like.

Meanwhile, Purpel had passed into one of his thoughtfullest of moods, and was slowly navigating about the room around chairs and tables. At last he exclaimed: "Yes, yes, it must be that even thought and imaginations have a material basis without which we should know them not. Even Paul could conceive of no resurrection that did not include the body. If I can take a severed hand and keep it alive two or three days, and it responds to a blow by muscular motion, and sweats, and *is* alive, why not be able some day to keep alive the brain-organs separately, and get replies from them, which, even if disordered, would tell us what they do, what their work is?"

"Do you mean," said I, "that it is in any way possible after a part is dead to restore it to life?"

"That depends," he returned, "upon what you call alive. A great savant secured the hand of a man guillotined at 8 A.M.

After fourteen hours it was cold and stiff. He then threw into its arteries blood taken from his own arm. Presently the fluid began to flow from the veins. The supply was kept up in this manner, and the returning blood was aerated by agitation. In a few minutes the member flushed, and then began to assume the hue of life. The stiffness of death departed, and the muscles contracted when struck or when galvanized. As long as he sustained the supply of blood,—and he did this for six hours,—so long did the separated part exhibit all the phenomena of life. Was it dead before? We cannot say that it was not alive afterwards."

"It appears, then," said Vance, "that life is what one of your biologists called it, an assemblage of conditions—of more or less interdependent conditions."

"A partial statement of the case," continued Purpel, "for there is more in life than so vague a definition covers."

"But," said I, "can you in like manner revive the brain?"

"I was about to say so," said he. "The same experimenter repeated his process on dogs apparently dead from various causes, and by letting out the blood from the veins of the neck so as to relieve the over-distended heart, and then throwing blood into the arteries of the head, he succeeded in restoring certain of his animals to life. As the blood entered, the visage altered, the features moved, the eyes opened, and the pupils changed their size under varying amounts of light. Of course the brain acted, but how completely we cannot say."

"And," said Vance, "has this been tried on man?"

"No," replied Purpel, "not under precisely the same conditions; but there is no reason why it should not succeed as well with him as with the dog. In but few, I presume, would recovery occur, but in some, at least, it might do so."

"What a hideous thought," said Vance, "to bring a man back to life only to die anew. There are some folks for whom I would prefer not to assume such a responsibility."

"Yet," said Purpel, "we assume it for every dying man we preserve alive. The doctor's instinct is to save life. The after-consequences lie not with him."

"If I were the vitalized victim," said Vance, "I should look upon you very much as Frankenstein's monster did upon his maker. You would have to provide me with board and lodging to the uttermost limit of my secondary existence; and as to what expensive tastes I might bring back with me from the nether world, who can say?"

"I would risk it," said Purpel, smiling. "Who's there?" he added; for at this moment his servant opened the door in haste, exclaiming: "Here's a woman, sir, would come up all I could do!" "Who,—what?" said Purpel, as a figure swept past the man into the room, and stood facing the light, a strange and unpleasant intruder.

"Good gracious!" said Vance. "Miss Gray, what on earth brought you here at this hour?" It was the niece of the murdered woman.

The figure before us threw back a worn tweed cloak, and stood erect, in a faded silk dress fitting closely her gaunt frame. She held a Quaker bonnet in her hand, and her face and hair were wet with the sleet of the storm without. A stern, set face, with the features drawn into lines of pain and care, a weary look about the mouth, and the eyes of one hunted down by a sorrow too awful for mortality to bear.

"Can nothing be done?" said the woman. "Must he die?"

So startling was this appearance, that for a moment all of us were alike confounded. Then Purpel said kindly, "Sit down by the fire, Miss Gray"; and presently he had taken her bonnet and cloak and seated her close to the blazing logs, which I quickly piled on the fire.

For a moment the warmth seemed to capture her physical sense of comfort, and she bent over, holding both hands to the blaze. Then, on a sudden, she turned to Vance, and exclaimed, with a quick look of curious cunning: "I don't want thee to tell, but—I did it. I want thee to go with me to—to—somebody, and let me tell them the way it was done; but don't tell him. He'd say it wasn't so. Thee won't tell him, will thee?"

"Of course not," said Vance; "but, Miss Gray, no one thinks you did it."

"But they'll believe me. They'll believe me," she cried. "Come, we have no time to lose. Where's the bonnet? Let me go."

"What shall we do, Purpel?" said I.

He made me no answer, but as she rose he faced her, and, placing a hand on each of her shoulders, said, firmly: "We none of us think he did it, my poor woman. We are sure he did not. We have done and are doing all we can to save him. Will not this content you, without your taking a lie upon your own soul? You are half crazed,—and no wonder; but you know that you did not do this thing. Still no one has a right to stop you, and I myself will go with you to the district-attorney, and secure you a hearing, although as to his believing you I have the gravest doubts."

"Yes," she cried, "who else could have done it? I believe I did it. I can see myself doing it. I mean I did it. Isn't thee ashamed to be near me? Come!" Purpel made us a sign to remain, and was leaving the room, when she turned suddenly. "And if," she exclaimed, "O, gracious God! if, if they will not—believe me, and—they kill him, surely—surely, he must come back and see me, and say, 'Little woman?'—Perhaps thee doesn't know that's what he calls me. Sometimes 'little woman,' and sometimes 'little thee and thou.' What was I saying? He will say, 'The dead lie not, being so near to God, and I am white of this sin.' "

"This is horrible," cried Vance. "For God's sake, take her away. Stay, I will get a hack from the corner." And so saying, he left the room, followed by Purpel and Miss Gray, who paused a moment on the threshold to say to me, "Thee does not think him guilty?"

"Who,—I?" I returned; "no indeed."

"Well," she added, "don't thee mind me. I ask everybody that." And then impatiently turning to Purpel, she added, "Why does thee wait? Thee will get into trouble should thee try to keep me."

I was too excited for sleep, and therefore piled up the logs anew, and, lighting a pipe, occupied myself with such thoughts as chose to be my guests until my two friends came back, having restored the poor half-crazed girl to the kindly custody of a lady of her own sect, from whose home she had escaped that evening. It were needless to add that, although Miss Gray told a story of the murder cunningly consistent, it broke down under the slightest inspection, and she finally owned to the authorities her complete innocence of all share in the murder. From this time, however, she continued to invent similar but varying accounts, until at last her mind gave way totally, and she was sent to an asylum for the insane.

To return to ourselves. Purpel and Vance, after telling me

what they had done upon leaving me, silently sat for a time, until at last Purpel broke out abruptly in this wise:—

"If a man should return from the dead, surely he would be believed, and why should he not be made to speak? Vance, do you think there would be wrong done to any if—if—it were possible so far to resuscitate a dead man as to get from him a confession of guilt or innocence?"

"What," said I, "as your *savant* revived his dogs?"

"Why not?" returned Purpel.

"Well, of all the wild schemes!" cried Vance.

"Wild or not," said Purpel, "it is possible, and especially after death from asphyxia."

"But what would the law say, Purpel," said I, "in case you revived the man permanently?"

"We need not do that," he replied.

"Need not," said Vance. "Why, man, to let him die after revival would be murder."

"Queer dilemma," said I. "The law kills a man; you bring him to life again, ask a question or two, and let him depart. Suit for malpractice by surviving relatives."

"The law has had its way with him, hanged him, and pronounced him dead," said Purpel; "will it go back on its verdict and say he was not dead? I would take that risk, and in this case without a fear."

"And I also," added Vance; "but the thing is absurd. Why talk about it at all! Let us go, it is near daybreak." And so the talk ended.

For the next week Purpel was unusually silent, and we saw little of him until the day after that which hastened poor Denis Upton out of the world. He died, like many a man, asserting his freedom from guilt; but experience had too distinctly taught the worthlessness of this test of innocence, and few pitied his fate or doubted the justice of his punishment.

As usual, we met at Purpel's rooms quite late at night, and found him in a singularly restless mood, walking about and muttering half-aloud, while his great dinornis-egg swung to and fro above him, apparently as restless as its owner.

"Another chance gone," he said. "Another; and life so short, so very short."

"What are you maundering about, P.?" said Vance.

"Only a little disappointment," returned the other.

"Pass your hat round," said Vance, "and we will drop in our little sympathies. What's all that stuff in the corner, P.?" he asked, pointing to a pile of tubing, battery-cells, and brass implements.

"Well," replied Purpel, "you may laugh if you like,—but I meant to have made the effort to resuscitate the poor wretch they hanged yesterday. It might have succeeded partially or completely, but at the least I should have tried, and even entire failure would have taught me something."

Vance tapped his forehead, looking at me. "Quite gone," said he; "the wreck of a fine mind, Gresham."

But Purpel was too deeply interested for jesting, and replied, rather fiercely for him: "Have your joke, if it pleases you to be merry over such a theme as yesterday's. I, for one—"

"Purpel, Purpel," said Vance, interrupting him, "nobody thinks of jesting about that. I was only smiling at your woful visage. That woman's face haunts me like a ghost. Was it her words which brought you to think of this strange experiment?"

"Those, and my own ideas on the scientific aspect of the subject," said Purpel; "but, no matter; poor Upton's friends interposed at the last minute, and denied me the chance of a trial."

"If the opportunity should recur," said Vance, "let me see the experiment."

"I shall be very glad to do so," returned Purpel. "To-day I the more sorrowfully regret my failure in this present instance, because I have learned that which more than ever makes me certain that an innocent man was murdered yesterday,—a man as guiltless of blood as you or I, Vance."

"Indeed," said I, "what has occurred?"

"I will tell you," he said. "Do you remember the relation of Mrs. Gray's house to those nearest it?"

"Perfectly," said I.

"It was separated by an alley from a blank wall on the west, and by a space of eight or ten feet from a small house on the north," said Vance.

"Exactly," continued Purpel; "and in this house were windows a little above the level of those belonging to Mrs. Gray's residence. When the police examined the premises they found the window of the room opposite to Mrs. Gray's with the shutters barred. Her own dwelling had no outside shutters. On the lower story lived a cobbler, who was distinctly shown to have been elsewhere at the time of the murder."

"I remember the man," said I. "He exhibited the utmost nervousness during his cross-examination. You do not think him guilty, Purpel?"

"Certainly not," said the latter. "The other tenants had been ordered out by the landlord, so that he might make a change in the house, which with the next two was to be altered into a carpenter's-shop. They had already begun to repair the roof, and the two upper stories were piled full of lumber for the purpose of serving as scaffolding on the roof, which was to be raised several feet."

"But what kept the cobbler there?" said I.

"He had still three months to stay before his lease was out," said Vance. "I remember the question in court, and his reply. Go on, P."

"I myself," continued Purpel, "have never before inspected his premises; but this morning, under an impulse which I can scarcely explain, I set out quite early and found the cobbler at work. I explained to him that I had felt some curiosity about the Gray murder, and asked him to go with me over the house. At first he was crusty enough, but a little money and a bland word or two made him willing. I went directly to the room opposite to Mrs. Gray's. It was pitch-dark, and I felt an oppressive consciousness that I was about to learn something strange and terrible connected with the woman's fate. The cobbler opened the window, and the chill of what I might call expectant horror passed away with the light of day. The cobbler assured me that, owing to various causes, among others the failure of the owner, the lumber on the floor had remained unused. The window-sash was easily raised or lowered; the space between that and the opposite window was nine feet ten inches, as I learned by measurement. I next proceeded to examine the window-ledge and sash, but found nothing. Then I turned over the boards lying nearest to the wall, but still in vain; the cobbler assuring me repeatedly that 'them detectives had been and done just the same.' At last, however, I raised a board which lay flat against the wall, partly below the window; and on it, near to one end, I found four small spots not over a line wide, and further along a larger one,—dark brown, nearly black spots. What were they? A hundred years ago no man on God's earth could have told: in an hour or two I should know. Do you wonder I was excited?"

"Wonder," said I,—"it is terrible; I am almost sorry you found them. What next, Purpel?"

"I thought," said he, "that my quest was at an end. You shall hear how strangely I was mistaken. I turned to the cobbler, without pointing out the spots, and asked him to bring me up some sharp tool. In a minute or two he returned with his cobbler's-knife, and with this I readily shaved away the chips now on yonder table, which were the only portions of the plank thus stained. As I was about to hand him the knife, a chill went through me, with one of those singular mental presentiments such as sometimes foreshadow the idea about to appear to you in full distinctness of conception. The knife was perfectly new. 'This tool is very sharp, I see,' said I; 'it must have been recently bought.'

" 'Well,' said he, snappishly, 'what then,—suppose it was? I ain't got no more time to waste. Give me my knife, and let me shut up the place.' Without heeding him, I continued, 'When did you buy that knife?' "

"Think I should have postponed that question," said Vance, "until we were down stairs."

"Don't stop him," cried I. "What next, Purpel?"

"The man said, of course, he didn't see as it was any of my business. I replied, that it was easy to get an answer in other ways, upon which he surlily closed the window, muttering to himself while I went slowly down stairs. Once in his shop, I turned on him quite abruptly and repeated my question, upon which he ordered me to put down the knife and clear out. Then I made a rash venture. Said I, 'You bought that knife not very long after the murder. Where is the old knife?' You should have seen the man;—he looked at me a moment quite cowed, and then exclaimed:—

" 'You don't mean to say you think I done it. I swear I didn't. I don't know nothin' about them knives, except just that I missed my old knife the day that 'ere murder was done; I missed it, sir, and I kind a knowed them as done it must have stole my knife, so I went and buyed a new one, and was afeared to say more about it.'

" 'Great heavens!' said I, 'you have hanged an innocent man, you coward! Afraid! what were you afraid of?'

" 'Don't be hard on me, sir,' he said. 'I am a poor man, and if I'd a told about this, don't you think I'd a laid in jail for witness; and who was to look after my wife and little uns?'

" 'Is this possible?' said I. 'You fool, your wife and babies would have been well enough cared for; and now—Why did I not think of all this a week ago?'

" 'You won't speak of it,' said the man, 'you won't tell nobody.'

" 'Tell!' said I, 'come along with me, instantly.' He pleaded very hard, but I was altogether remorseless; and in half an hour he had made his confession to the district-attorney. There, Vance, you have my story."

We drew long breaths, Vance and I, and a vision of the gallows went through my brain, filling me with a horror too deep for speech.

At last, Vance said, "And is it blood, Purpel?"

"Beyond a doubt," answered the latter, "and as surely the blood of Mrs. Gray."

Here he crossed the room, and, returning, showed us the chips he had cut away, each with its drop of dark brownish red.

"But," said I, after a pause, "this might have been blood from the finger of one of the workmen."

"Might have been, but is not," returned Purpel.

"And the cobbler," added Vance,—"is he free from suspicion?"

"You forget," said I, "that he proved an alibi without flaw."

"Moreover," continued Purpel, "I noticed that the cobbler is left-handed, which in a trade like his must be a very awkward defect. Now, if you will remember one of our former talks, you will recall that I considered the murder to have been done by a man who, standing behind the woman, suddenly placed a hand on her mouth and with the other inflicted a single wound in the neck. That wound was made with the right hand, being deepest on the left side of her neck. The men,—I suspect there were two, —gained access to the empty rooms of the house I visited to-day. At night they opened the window and put a plank across, quietly. The old woman, who was, as you have heard, quite deaf, is first startled by the cold air from the opened window. She rises suddenly, and is seized from behind. Perhaps she struggles, resisting the effort to rob her. Perhaps the murder may have been prearranged. It matters not now. There is resistance, a sharp knife drawn athwart the throat, and the robbery is effected. One confederate is probably somewhat bloody, the other less so or not at all. The latter shuts the window behind them, withdraws the plank, and bars the shutters of the cobbler's house, through which they escape, unnoticed."

"If," said Vance, "your view be correct, they premeditated only plunder at first, but in passing through the cobbler's workroom they probably seized the knife as a weapon which might prove useful."

"I suspect it was as you state it, Purpel," said I. "The persons who did this deed must have been thorough adepts in crime, or they would have been incapable either of planning such a scheme or of carrying it out so calmly as to leave only these very slight traces. The little blood you found probably dropped on the plank as they crawled over it."

"There might have been more," returned Purpel; "and had I made this examination earlier, I should possibly have found further traces, since it is scarcely conceivable that a red-handed murderer should have failed to put a wet hand somewhere, in such a way as to leave a mark."

"And what better for it all is poor Upton?" said Vance. "We shall find few, I think, so credulous as to believe the tale we have heard to-night."

And so it proved; for although every effort was made to set the matter in a clear light before the public, it was generally regarded as only a barefaced attempt on the part of Upton's friends to save his memory from just reproach.

Months went by, and we had ceased at length to talk of the horrible tragedy which for a little while had disturbed the still waters of our quiet lives. One evening, late in the next winter, both Vance and myself received from Purpel a hasty note, stating that he meant next day to attempt the experiment which he had failed to try in the former instance. When we met in the evening, he explained to us that he had made such arrangements as would enable him to secure the body of a criminal who was to be hanged on the following morning. The man in question was a friendless wretch, who had been guilty of every known crime, and who was at last to suffer for one of the most cold-blooded murders on the records of the courts. His body was to be delivered to Purpel as soon as possible after the execution. Our friend, for obvious reasons, desired to have no other assistance than our own, and he now proceeded to instruct us carefully as to the means he intended to use, so that no time should be lost during the necessary operations.

On the following day, a little after noon, we assembled in the laboratory back of Purpel's house, where he was accustomed to carry on such of his researches as involved the use of animals. It was a bare whitewashed room, scantily furnished, and rather too dark. We lit the gas-lights, however, above the central table, and with a certain awe awaited the coming of the body. Thanks to Purpel's purse, we had not long to rest in suspense. In about an hour after the execution, a covered wagon was driven into the stable at the side of the lot, and the two men in charge deposited the corpse on the table, and drove away, with a good round fee as their reward.

Purpel hastily withdrew the sheet in which the man was wrapped, and exposed a powerful frame clad in a red shirt and worn black clothes. The face was mottled red and white, marked with many scars, and of utterly wolfish ferocity.

"The body is warm," said Purpel; "and now, as to the heart," he added. "I cannot hear it beat, but possibly the auricles may still be moving faintly."

As speedily as possible arrangements were made, by opening a vein in the neck, so as to relieve the heart, and allow of the outflow of blood. Then a simple pump capable of sucking up blood from a basin of that fluid and of forcing it into the brain was fitted by double tubes to the two great arteries which supply the brain. Vance was then taught how to move the chest-walls by elevating the arms and alternately compressing the breast, so as to make artificial breathing.

"It is very clever," said Vance, coolly, "but it won't work, P."

"Well," said the latter, "if I get a partial success it will suffice. I have no desire to restore a scoundrel like this to the world again." So saying, the experiment began, while profound silence was kept by one and all of us.

At last said Purpel, "Look!" The mottled tints of the visage were slowly fading away. The eyes lost their glaze, the lips grew red, slight twitches crossed the face here and there. At last the giant's chest heaved once slowly, as of itself, then paused, and stirred again.

I looked at Purpel: he was deadly pale.

Said Vance, huskily: "Stop, Purpel, stop!—he will live. I will not go on."

"A moment," urged Purpel, "only a moment."

"Look!" said I; for the eyes rolled to and fro, and I even thought they seemed to follow my movements.

Suddenly said Vance, "Who spoke? What was that?" A hoarse murmur startled us all.

"He spoke," said I. "It spoke."

"Impossible!" said Purpel. "Raise his head a little. Lift the plank."

"Hush!" I cried.

A whisper broke from the lips of the wretch before us. "The plank," he said,—"only an old woman,—the plank."

We looked at one another, each whiter than his fellow.

"I will not stand this," screamed Vance. "You hear—you hear, —Mrs. Gray;—this man did it. He—he killed her,—killed Mrs. Gray."

"Gray," said the living dead man, "gray hair, yes."

"Purpel," said I, sternly, "this is enough. You must stop."

"Nay, I will stop," exclaimed Vance; and with an uncontrollable impulse he overturned the vase of blood on the floor.

"It is well," said Purpel. "Hush, V. What is that he says? See, the color changes. Ah! he said, 'Mother, mother!' "

"No more, and enough!" cried Vance. "Have we sinned in this thing? Let us go."

INTO THE PSYCHE

Perhaps the most widely exciting science of the nineteenth century and almost certainly the most influential on fiction was psychology. The century which began with Mesmer and ended with Freud began in America with Charles Brockden Brown and ended with Henry James.

Because the aims of psychological science and of almost all fiction overlap, it is extremely difficult to separate the science fiction which explores human psychology from any fiction which aims at psychological revelation. But even if psychological science fiction is limited only to stories about hypnotic states, extrasensory perception, teleportation, identity transfers, and extraordinary psychological experiments, still the nineteenth century stands as its first great age.

While mesmerism was building the bases of modern psychology, the mesmerist was becoming a conventional figure not only in science fiction but in realistic fiction as well. In the 'forties mesmerism was displayed on the lecture platform, in the drawing room, and in fiction as different as William Gilmore Simms's comic "Mesmerides in a Stage Coach; or, Passes en Passant" (*Godey's*, 1845), Poe's "Mesmeric Revelation," "A Tale of the Ragged Mountains," and "The Facts in the Case of M. Valdemar," and James Kirk Paulding's effort to restore sanity, "The

New Science; or, The Village Bewitched" (*Graham's*, 1846). In the 'fifties, Hawthorne was using mesmerism as a central symbol of inhuman domination in *The House of the Seven Gables* (1851) and *The Blithedale Romance* (1852). By the 'seventies and 'eighties, James in "Professor Fargo" (*Galaxy*, 1874) and Howells in *The Undiscovered Country* (1880) were using mesmerism as a symbol of profound human sordidness. By the time Claggart confronts Billy Budd in Melville's last fiction (1891), his "mesmeristic" glances have the symbolic weight of hundreds of fictional mesmerists behind them.

Unlike mesmerism, an observable phenomenon which could be handled in realistic fiction, extrasensory perception and identity transfers had to be either bases of science fictions or incursions of science-fictional elements into other fiction. Poe ("A Tale of the Ragged Mountains"), Bellamy ("To Whom This May Come" and "At Pinney's Ranch"), Bierce ("John Bartine's Watch," "The Death of Halpin Frayser," "A Psychological Shipwreck," *et al.*), and, in the first decade of this century, Howells ("A Case of Metaphantasmia" and "Though One Rose from the Dead") all wrote finished short pieces of science fiction based on extrasensory perception and identity transfers, and most of James's psychological ghost stories have close, often intricate, relations with these phenomena.

Whether the psychological ghost story and the plain ghost story—and both were conventional modes of nineteenth-century fiction—should be categorized as science fiction is debatable. But insofar as one calls science what the pre-eminent American psychologist William James was doing in his work with the Society for Psychical Research, one must call science fiction what his brother Henry was doing in "The Turn of the Screw," "The Jolly Corner," "The Ghostly Rental," and "Sir Dominick Ferrand," to name a few. And behind all of James's ghostly tales lie the conventions and expectations of all the psychological science fiction from late eighteenth-century gothicism on.

The psychological science fiction of the nineteenth century, culminating in James, forms a distinguished body of writing. Unlike the science fiction about space travel, marvelous inventions, and biological experimentation, psychological science fiction attains timelessness with ease; or at least so it appears to us, who are no closer to extraordinary psychic phenomena than the nineteenth century.

THOMAS WENTWORTH HIGGINSON AND HIS DREAMER

Thomas Wentworth Higginson (1823-1911), remembered for his early recognition and encouragement of Emily Dickinson's poetry, wrote a number of biographical, historical, and critical studies, an obscure novel and volume of poems, some sketches, and one extraordinary story—"The Monarch of Dreams."

There could be no more striking comparison with "The Monarch of Dreams" than the hallucinatory sequence in Hermann Hesse's *Steppenwolf*. Just like Higginson's Ayrault, Hesse's Steppenwolf loses himself in the magic mirror world of his own ego. Yet because Hesse's work is fantasy, Higginson's science fiction, each creates different kinds of connections between the prismatic prison of the ego and the world of everyday external life. That is, Hesse makes all the mechanism and processes of the revelation as fantastic as what it reveals, leaving them beyond any realistic explanation, whereas Higginson's focus is largely on the mechanism and processes themselves and their proximity to everyday occurrences. The trapped ego in *Steppenwolf* is lured by fantastic devices into its interior world of fantasy; in "The Monarch of Dreams" the ego traps itself as it deliberately, almost routinely, moves into its interior world of fantasy in order to conduct a scientific experiment.

Disinterested science does not move Ayrault into this world, but Ayrault is for that reason no less a scientist. At a time when the reading populace of the western world was excitedly consuming the most bizarre and perhaps truly earthshaking psychological researches, Higginson presented as a kind of archetypal psychological explorer a new variant of Hawthorne's scientist—still isolated, obsessed, and overreaching—but now manipulating no one or thing but himself. The plight in Hawthorne which most nearly resembles Ayrault's is that of Ethan Brand, who, after a lifetime of obsessive psycho-moral research, is imaged forth in a dog chasing his own tail. Ayrault's science comes as a tantalizing lure from his mind and leads him into the closed circle of the mind.

"The Monarch of Dreams" is a fine story, but certainly not a perfect one. The reader may wish that Ayrault's sister were not the sentimental creation that she is; he may wish that Higginson had simply omitted the last sentence, or, better yet, omitted from it the pronoun "his." But if he reflects on the fact that Higginson himself during the Civil War, as the extremely dedicated and far-seeing colonel of the first regiment of Negro soldiers, had done more than shoot people, the reader may see that the story does not end by offering mere warfare as a meaningful alternative to perfectly cellular existence. He would then have only to regret that Higginson had not in "The Monarch of Dreams" dramatized the external world as clearly as the internal—and as its magnified projection.

THOMAS WENTWORTH HIGGINSON

The Monarch of Dreams *

φάσμα δόξει δόμων ἀνάσσειν.

Aeschylus, Agamemnon, 391.

He who forsakes the railways and goes wandering through the hill-country of New England must adopt one rule as invariable. When he comes to a fork in the road, and is told that both ways lead to the desired point, he must simply ask which road is the better; and, on its being pointed out, must at once take the other. The explanation is easy. The passers-by will always recommend the new road, which keeps to the valley and avoids the hills; but the old road, now deserted by the general public, ascends the steeper grades, and thus offers the more desirable views.

Turning to the old road, you soon feel that both houses and men are, in a manner, stranded. They see very little of the world, and are under no stimulus to keep themselves in repair. You are wholly beyond the dreary sway of French roofs; and the caricatures of good Queen Anne's day are far from you. If any farm-house on the hill-road was really built within the reign of that much-abused potentate, it is probably a solid, square mansion of brick, three stories high, blackened with time, and frowning rather gloomily from some hilltop,—as essentially a part of the past as an Irish round tower or a Scotch border fortress. A branching elm-tree or two may droop above it. It is partly screened from the road by a lilac hedge, and by what seems an unnecessarily large wood-pile. A low stone wall surrounds the ample barns and sheds, made of unpainted wood, and now gray with age; and near these is a neglected garden, where phlox and

* Separate publication, 1886.

pinks and tiger-lilies are intersected with irregular hedges of tree-box. The house looks upon gorgeous sunsets and distant mountain ranges, and lakes surrounded by pine and chestnut woods. Against a lurid sky, or in a brooding fog, it is as impressive in the landscape as a feudal castle; and like that, it is almost deserted: human life has slipped away from it into the manufacturing village, swarming with French Canadians, in the valley below.

It was in such a house that Francis Ayrault had finally taken up his abode, leaving behind him the old family homestead in a Rhode Island seaside town. A series of domestic cares and watchings had almost broken him down: nothing debilitates a man of strong nature like the too prolonged and exclusive exercise of the habit of sympathy. At last, when the very spot where he was born had been chosen as a site for a new railway station, there seemed nothing more to retain him. He needed utter rest and change; and there was no one left on earth whom he profoundly loved, except a little sunbeam of a sister, the child of his father's second marriage. This little five-year-old girl, of whom he was sole guardian, had been christened by the quaint name of Hart, after an ancestor, Hart Ayrault, whose moss-covered tombstone the child had often explored with her little fingers, to trace the vanishing letters of her own name.

The two had arrived one morning from the nearest railway station to take possession of the old brick farmhouse. Ayrault had spent the day in unpacking and in consultations with Cyrus Gerry,—the farmer from whom he had bought the place, and who was still to conduct all outdoor operations. The child, for her part, had compelled her old nurse to follow her through every corner of the buildings. They were at last seated at an early supper, during which little Hart was too much absorbed in the novelty of wild red raspberries to notice, even in the most casual way, her brother's worn and exhausted look.

"Brother Frank," she incidentally remarked, as she began upon her second saucerful of berries, "I love you!"

"Thank you, darling," was his mechanical reply to the customary ebullition. She was silent for a time, absorbed in her pleasing pursuit, and then continued more specifically, "Brother Frank, you are the kindest person in the whole world! I am so glad we came here! May we stay here all winter? It must be lovely in the winter; and in the barn there is a little sled with only one runner gone. Brother Frank, I love you so much, I don't know what I shall do! I love you a thousand pounds, and fifteen, and eleven and a half, and more than tongue can tell besides! And there are three gray kittens,—only one of them is almost all white,—and Susan says I may bring them for you to see in the morning."

Half an hour later, the brilliant eyes were closed in slumber; the vigorous limbs lay in perfect repose; and the child slept that night in the little room beside her brother's, on the same bed that she had occupied ever since she had been left motherless. But her brother lay awake, absorbed in a project too fantastic to be talked about, yet which had really done more than anything else to bring him to that lonely house.

There has belonged to Rhode Islanders, ever since the days of Roger Williams, a certain taste for the ideal side of existence. It is the only State in the American Union where chief justices habitually write poetry, and prosperous manufacturers print essays on the Freedom of the Will. Perhaps, moreover, Francis Ayrault held something of these tendencies from a Huguenot ancestry, crossed with a strain of Quaker blood. At any rate it was there, and asserted itself at this crisis of his life. Being in a manner detached from almost all ties, he resolved to use his opportunity in a direction yet almost unexplored by man. His earthly joys being prostrate, he had resolved to make a mighty effort at self-concentration, and to render himself what no human being had ever yet been,—the ruler of his own dreams.

Coming from a race of day-dreamers, Ayrault had inherited an unusual faculty of dreaming also by night; and, like all persons having an especial gift, he perhaps overestimated its importance. He easily convinced himself that no exertion of the intellect during wakeful hours can for an instant be compared with that we employ in dreams. The finest brain-structures of Shakespeare or Dante, he reasoned, are yet but such stuff as dreams are made of; and the stupidest rustic, the most untrained mind, will sometimes have, could they be but written out, visions that surpass those of these masters. From the dog that hunts in dreams, up to Coleridge dreaming "Kubla Khan" and interrupted by the man on business from Porlock, every sentient, or even half-sentient, being reaches its height of imaginative action in dreams. In these alone, Ayrault reasoned, do we grasp something beyond ourselves: every other function is self-limited, but who can set a limit to his visions? Of all forms of the Inner Light, they afford the very inmost; in these is fulfilled the early maxim of Friends,—that a man never rises so high as when he knows not where he is going. On awaking, indeed, we cannot even tell where we have just been. Probably the very utmost wealth of our remembered dreams is but a shred and fragment of those whose memory we cannot grasp.

But Ayrault had been vexed, like all others, by the utter incongruity of successive dreams. This sublime navigation still waited, like that of balloon voyages, for a rudder. Dreams, he reasoned, plainly try to connect themselves. We all have the frequent experience of half-recognizing new situations or even whole trains of ideas. We have seen this view before; reached this point; struck in some way the exquisite chord of memory. When half-aroused, or sometimes even long after clear consciousness, we seem to draw a half-drowned image of association from the deep waters of the mind; then another, then another, until dreaming seems inseparably entangled with waking. Again, over nightly dreams we have at least a certain amount of negative control, sufficient to bring them to an end. Ayrault had long since discovered and proved to himself the fact, insisted upon by Currie and by Macnish, that a nightmare can be banished by compelling one's self to remember that it is unreal. Again and again, during sleep, had he cast himself from towers, dropped from balloons, fallen into the sea,—and all unscathed. This way of ending an unpleasant dream was but a negative power indeed; but it was a substantial one: it implied the existence of some completer authority. If we can stop motion, we can surely originate it. He had already searched the books, therefore, for recorded instances of more positive control.

There was opium of course; but he was one of those on whom opium has little exciting influence, and so far as it had any, it only made his visions more incoherent. Haschish was in this respect still worse. It was not to be thought of, that one should resort, for the sake of dreams, to raw meat, like Dryden and Fuseli; or to other indigestible food, like Mrs. Radcliffe. The experiments of Giron de Buzareingues promised a little more; for he actually obtained recurrent dreams. He used to sleep with his knees uncovered on cool nights, and fancied during his sleep that he was riding in a stage-coach, where the lower extremities are apt to grow cold. Again, by wearing a nightcap over the front part of his head only, he seemed, when asleep, to be uncovering before a religious procession, and feeling chilly in the nape of the neck; this same result being obtained on several different occasions. It was recorded of some one else, that, by letting his feet hang over the bedside, he repeatedly imagined himself tottering on the brink of a precipice. Even these crude and superficial experiments had a value, Ayrault thought. If coarse physical processes could affect the mind's action, could not the will by some more powerful levers control the silent reveries of the night?

He derived some encouragement, too, from such instances as that recorded of Alderman Clay of Newark, England, during the siege of that town by Cromwell. He dreamed on three successive nights that his house had taken fire. Because of this supposed warning, he removed his family from the dwelling; and, when it was afterwards really burned by Cromwell's troops, left a bequest of a hundred pounds to supply penny loaves to the town poor, in acknowledgment of his marvellous escape. It is true that the three dreams were apparently mere repetitions of one another, and in no way continuous; it is true that they were not the result of any conscious will. So much the better: they were produced by the continuous working of some powerful mental influence; and this again was the result of external conditions. The experiment could not be reproduced. One could not be always dreaming under pressure of a cannonade by Cromwell, any more than Charles Lamb's Chinese people could be always burning down their houses in order to taste the flavor of roast pig. But the point was, that if dreams could be made to recur by accidental circumstances, the same thing might perhaps be effected by conscious thought.

Now that he was in a position for free experiment, he hoped to accomplish something more substantial than any casual or vague results; and he therefore so arranged his methods as to avoid interruption. Instead of exciting himself by day, he adopted a course of strict moderation; took his food regularly with the little girl, amused by her prattle; began systematic exercise on horseback and on foot; avoided society and the newspapers; and went to bed at an early hour, locking himself into a wing of the large farmhouse, the little Hart sleeping in a room within his. Once retired, he did not permit himself to be called on any pretext. Hart always slept profoundly; and with her first call of waking in the morning, he rang the bell for old Susan, who took the child away. It would have left him more free, of course, to intrust her altogether to the nurse's charge, but to this he could not bring himself. She was his one sacred trust, and not even his beloved projects could wholly displace her.

The thought had occurred to him, long since, at what point to apply his efforts for the control of his dreams. He had been quite fascinated, some time before, by a large photograph in a shop window, of the well-known fortress known as Mont Saint Michel, in Normandy. Its steepness, its airy height, its winding and returning stairways, its overhanging towers and machicolations, had struck him as appealing powerfully to that sense of the vertical which is, for some reason or other, so peculiarly strong in dreams. We are rarely haunted by visions of plains; often of mountains. The sensation of uplifting or downlooking is one of our commonest nightly experiences. It seemed to Ayrault that by going to sleep with the vivid mental image in his brain of a sharp and superb altitude like that of Mont Saint Michel, he could avail himself of this magic, whatever it was, that lay in the vertical line. Casting himself off into the vast sphere of dreams, with the thread of his fancy attached to this fine image, he might risk what would next come to him; as a spider anchors his web and then floats away on it. In the silence of the first night at the farmhouse,—a stillness broken only by the answering cadence of two whip-poor-wills in the neighboring pinewood,—Ayrault pondered long over the beautiful details of the photograph, and then went to sleep.

That night he was held, with the greatest vividness and mastery, in the grasp of a dream such as he had never before experienced. He found himself on the side of a green hill, so precipitous that he could only keep his position by lying at full length, clinging to the short, soft grass, and imbedding his feet in the turf. There were clouds about him: he could see but a short distance in any direction, nor was any sign of a human being within sight. He was absolutely alone upon the dizzy slope, where he hardly dared to look up or down, and where it took all his concentration of effort to keep a position at all. Yet there was a kind of friendliness in the warm earth; a comfort and fragrance in the crushed herbage. The vision seemed to continue indefinitely; but at last he waked and it was clear day. He rose with a bewildered feeling, and went to little Hart's room. The child lay asleep, her round face tangled in her brown curls, and one plump, tanned arm stretched over her eyes. She waked at his step, and broke out into her customary sweet asseveration, "Brother Frank, I love you!"

Dismissing the child, he pondered on his first experiment. It had succeeded, surely, in so far as he had given something like a direction to his nightly thought. He could not doubt that it was the picture of Mont Saint Michel which had transported him to the steep hillside. That day he spent in the most restless anxiety to see if the dream would come again. Writing down all that he could remember of the previous night's vision, he studied again the photograph that had so touched his fancy, and then he closed his eyes. Again he found himself—at some time between night and morning—on the high hillside, with the clouds around him. But this time the vapors lifted, and he could see that the hill stretched for an immeasurable distance on each side, always at the same steep slope. Everywhere it was covered with human beings,—men, women, and children,—all trying to pursue various semblances of occupation; but all clinging to the short grass. Sometimes he thought—but this was not positive—that he saw one of them lose his hold and glide downwards. For this he cared strangely little; but he waked feverish, excited, trembling. At last his effort had succeeded: he had, by an effort of will, formed a connection between two dreams.

He came down to breakfast exhilarated and eager. What triumph of mind, what ranges of imagination equalled those now opening before him! As an outlet for his delight, he gave up the day to little Hart, always ready to monopolize. With her he visited the cows in the barn, the heifers in the pasture; heard their names, their traits, and—with much vagueness of arithmetic—their ages. She explained to him that Brindle was cross, and Mabel roguish; and that she had put her arm around little Pet's neck. Animals are to children something almost as near as human beings, because they have those attributes of humanity which children chiefly prize,—instinct and affection. Then Hart had the horses to exhibit, the pigs, a few sheep, and a whole poultry-yard of chickens. She was already initiated into the art and mystery of looking for hen's eggs, and indeed already trotted about after Cyrus Gerry, a little acolyte at the altar of farming. "She likes to play at it," said Cyrus, "same as my boys do: but just call it work, and—there! I don't blame 'em. The fact is," he added apologetically, "neither me nor my boys like to be kep' always at the same dull roundelay o' choppin' wood and doin' chores."

It was quite true that Cyrus Gerry and his boys, like many a New England farm household, had certain tastes and aptitudes that sadly interfered with their outdoor work. One son played the organ in the neighboring city, another was teaching himself the violin, and the third filled the barn with half-finished models of machinery. Cyrus himself read over and over again, in the winter evenings, his one favorite book,—a translation of Lamartine's "History of the Girondists,"—pronounced habitually Guyrondists; and he found in its pages a pithy illustration for every event that could befall his chosen hero, Humanity. Most of his warnings were taken from the career of Robespierre, and his high and heroic examples from Vergniaud; while these characters lost nothing in vigor by being habitually quoted as "Robyspierry," and "Virginnyord."

In the service of his little sister, Ayrault explored that day many an old barn and shed; while she took thrilling leaps from the haymow or sat with the three gray kittens in her lap. Together they decked the parlors with gay masses of mountain laurel, or with the first-found red lilies, or with white water-lilies, from the pond. To the child, life was full of incident on that lonely farm. One day it was a young woodchuck caught in a trap, and destined to be petted; another day, the fearful assassination of a whole brood of young chickens by a culprit owl; the next, a startling downfall of a whole nest of swallows in the chimney. On this particular day she chattered steadily, and Ayrault enjoyed it. But that night he lost utterly the new-found control of his dream, and waked in irritation with himself and the world.

He spent the next day alone. It cost Hart a few tears to lose her new-found playmate, but a tame pigeon consoled her. That night Ayrault pondered long over his memoranda of previous dreaming, and over the photograph with which he had begun the spell, and was rewarded by a renewal of his visions; but this time wavering and uncertain. Sometimes he was again on the bare hillside, clutching at the soft grass; then the scene shifted to some castle, whose high battlements he was climbing; then he found himself among the Alps, treading some narrow path between rock and glacier, with the tinkling herd of young goats crowding round him for comradeship and impeding his progress; again, he was following the steep course of some dried brook among the Scottish Highlands, or pausing to count the deserted hearthstones of a vanished people. Always at short intervals he reverted to the grassy hill; it seemed the foundation of his visions, the rest were like dreams within dreams. At last a heavier sleep came on, featureless and purposeless, till he waked unrefreshed.

On the following night he grasped his dream once more. Again he found himself on the precipitous slope, this time looking off through clear air upon that line of detached mountain peaks, Wachusett, Monadnock, Mossilauke, which make the southern outposts of New England hills. In the valley lay pellucid lakes, set in summer beauty,—while he clung to his perilous hold. Presently there came a change; the mountain sank away softly beneath him, and the grassy slope remained a plain. The men and women, his former companions, had risen from their reclining postures and were variously busy; some of them even looked at him, but there was nothing said. Great spaces of time appeared to pass: suns rose and set. Sometimes one of the crowd would throw down his implements of labor, turn his face to the westward, walk swiftly away, and disappear. Yet some one else would take his place, so that the throng never perceptibly diminished. Ayrault began to feel rather unimportant in all this gathering, and the sensation was not agreeable.

On the succeeding night the hillside vanished, never to recur; but the vast plain remained, and the people. Over the wide landscape the sunbeams shed passing smiles of light, now here, now there. Where these shone for a moment, faces looked joyous, and Ayrault found, with surprise, that he could control the distribution of light and shade. This pleased him; it lifted him into conscious importance. There was, however, a singular want of all human relation in the tie between himself and all these people. He felt as if he had called them into being, which indeed he had; and could annihilate them at pleasure, which perhaps could not be so easily done. Meanwhile, there was a certain hardness in his state of mind toward them; indeed, why should a dreamer feel patience or charity or mercy toward those who exist but in his mind? Ayrault at any rate felt none; the sole thing which disturbed him was that they sometimes grew a little dim, as if they might vanish and leave him unaccompanied. When this happened, he drew with conscious volition a gleam of light over them, and thereby refreshed their life. They enhanced his weight in the universe: he would no more have parted with them than a Highland chief with his clansmen.

For several nights after this he did not dream. Little Hart became ill and his mind was preoccupied. He had to send for physicians, to give medicine, to be up with the child at night. The interruption vexed him; and he was also pained to find that there seemed to be a slight barrier between himself and her. Yet he was rigorously faithful to his duties as nurse; he even liked to hold her hand, to soothe her pain, to watch her sweet, patient face. Like Coleridge in misanthropic mood, he saw, not felt, how beautiful she was. Then, with the rapidity of childish convalescence, she grew well again; and he found with joy that he could resume the thread of his dream-life.

Again he was on his boundless plain, with his circle of silent allies around him. Suddenly they all vanished, and there rose before him, as if built out of the atmosphere, a vast building, which he entered. It included all structures in one,—legislative halls where men were assembled by hundreds, waiting for him; libraries, where all the books belonged to him, and whole alcoves were filled with his own publications; galleries of art, where he had painted many of the pictures, and selected the rest. Doors and corridors led to private apartments; lines of obsequious servants stood for him to pass. There seemed no other proprietor, no guests; all was for him; all flattered his individual greatness. Suddenly it occurred to him that he was painfully alone. Then he began to pass eagerly from hall to hall, seeking an equal companion, but in vain. Wherever he went, there was a trace of some one just vanished,—a book laid down, a curtain still waving. Once he fairly came, he thought, upon the object of his pursuit; all retreat was cut off, and he found himself face to face with a mirror that reflected back to him only his own features. They had never looked to him less attractive.

Ayrault's control of his visions became plainly more complete with practice, at least as to their early stages. He could lie down to sleep with almost a perfect certainty that he should begin where he left off. Beyond this, alas! he was powerless. Night after night he was in the same palace, but always differently occupied, and always pursuing, with unabated energy, some new vocation. Sometimes the books were at his command, and he grappled with whole alcoves; sometimes he ruled a listening senate in the halls of legislation; but the peculiarity was that there were always menials and subordinates about him, never an equal. One night, in looking over these obsequious crowds, he made a startling discovery. They either had originally, or were acquiring, a strange resemblance to one another, and to some person whom he had somewhere seen. All the next day, in his waking hours, this thought haunted him. The next night it flashed upon him that the person whom they all so closely resembled, with a likeness that now amounted to absolute identity, was himself.

From the moment of this discovery, these figures multiplied; they assumed a mocking, taunting, defiant aspect. The thought was almost more than he could bear, that there was around him a whole world of innumerable and uncontrollable beings, every one of whom was Francis Ayrault. As if this were not sufficient, they all began visibly to duplicate themselves before his eyes. The confusion was terrific. Figures divided themselves into twins, laughing at each other, jeering, running races, measuring heights, actually playing leap-frog with one another. Worst of all, each one of these had as much apparent claim to his personality as he himself possessed. He could no more retain his individual hold upon his consciousness than the infusorial animalcule in a drop of water can know to which of its subdivided parts the original individuality attaches. It became insufferable, and by a mighty effort he waked.

The next day, after breakfast, old Susan sought an interview with Ayrault, and taxed him roundly with neglect of little Hart's condition. Since her former illness she never had been quite the same; she was growing pale and thin. As her brother no longer played with her, she only moped about with her kitten, and talked to herself. It touched Ayrault's heart. He took pains to be with the child that day, carried her for a long drive, and went to see her guinea-hen's eggs. That night he kept her up later than usual, instead of hurrying her off as had become his wont; he really found himself shrinking from the dream-world he had with such effort created. The most timid and shy person can hardly hesitate more about venturing among a crowd of strangers than Francis Ayrault recoiled, that evening, from the thought of this mob of intrusive persons, every one of whom reflected his own image. Gladly would he have undone the past, and swept them all away forever. But the shrinking was all on one side. The moment he sank to sleep, they all crowded upon him, laughing, frolicking, claiming detestable intimacy. No one among strangers ever longed for a friendly face, as he, among these intolerable duplicates, longed for the sight of a stranger. It was worse yet when the images grew smaller and smaller, until they had shrunk to a pin's length. He found himself trying with all his strength of will to keep them at their ampler size, with only the effect that they presently became no larger than the heads of pins. Yet his own individuality was still so distributed among them that it could not be distinguished from them; but he found himself merged in this crowd of little creatures an eighth of an inch long.

As the days went on old Susan kept repeating her warnings about Hart, and finally proposed to take her into her own room. "She does not get sound sleep, sir; she complains of her dreams." "Of what dreams?" said Ayrault. "Oh, about you, sir," was the reply, "she sees you very often, and a great many people who look just like you." Ayrault sank back in his chair terrified. Was it not enough that his own life was hopelessly haunted by a turbulent kingdom of his own creating? but must the malign influence extend also to this innocent child? He watched Hart the next morning at breakfast—she looked pale and had circles under her eyes, and glanced at him timidly; her eager endearments were all gone. A terrible temptation crossed Ayrault's mind for a moment, to employ this unspoiled nature in the perilous path of experiments on which he had entered. It vanished from him as soon as it had presented itself. He would tread his course alone, and send the child away, rather than risk any transmitted peril for her young life. It may be that her dreams had only an accidental resemblance to his; at any rate she was sent away on a visit, and they were soon forgotten.

After the child had gone, a feeling of deep sadness fell on Ayrault. By night he was tangled in the meshes of a dream-life that had become a nightmare; by day there was now nothing to arouse him. The child's insatiable affection, her ardent ebullitions, were absent. Cyrus Gerry's watchful and speculative mind grew suspicious and critical.

"I shouldn't wonder," he said to his wife, "if there was gettin' to be altogether too much dreamin'. There was Robyspierry, he was what you might call a dreamer. But that Virginnyord he was much nigher my idee of an American citizen."

"Got somethin' on his mind, think likely?" said the slow and placid Mrs. Gerry, who seldom had much upon hers.

"Dunno as I know," responded Cyrus. "But there, what if he has? As I look at it, humanity, a-ploddin' over this planet, meets with consid'able many left-handed things. And the best way I know of is to summons up courage and put right through 'em."

Cyrus's conceptions of humanity might, however, rise to such touches of Wandering-Jew comprehensiveness as this, and yet not reach Ayrault, who went his way lonelier than ever.

Having long since fallen out of the way of action, or at best grown satisfied to imagine enterprises and leave others to execute them, he now, more than ever, drifted on from day to day. There had been a strike at the neighboring manufacturing village, and there was to be a public meeting, at which he was besought, as a person not identified with either party, to be present, and throw his influence for peace. It touched him, and he meant to attend. He even thought of a few things, which, if said, might do good; then forgot the day of the meeting, and rode ten miles in another direction. Again, when at the little post-office one day, he was asked by the postmaster to translate several letters in the French language, addressed to that official, and coming from an unknown village in Canada. They proved to contain anxious inquiries as to the whereabouts of a pretty young French girl, whom Ayrault had occasionally met driving about in what seemed doubtful company. His sympathy was thoroughly aroused by the anxiety of the poor parents, from whom the letters came. He answered them himself, promising to interfere in behalf of the girl; delayed, day by day, to fulfil the promise; and when he at last looked for her she was not to be found. Yet, while his power of efficient action waned, his dream-power increased. His little people were busier about him than ever, though he controlled them less and less. He was Gulliver bound and fettered by Lilliputians.

But a more stirring appeal was on its way to him. The storm

of the civil war began to roll among the hills; regiments were recruited, camps were formed. The excitement reached the benumbed energies of Ayrault. Never, indeed, had he felt such a thrill. The old Huguenot pulse beat strongly within him. For days, and even nights, these thoughts possessed his mind, and his dreams utterly vanished. Then there was a lull in the excitement; recruiting stopped, and his nightly habit of confusing visions set in again with dreary monotony. Then there was a fresh call for troops. An old friend of Ayrault's came to a neighboring village, and held a noon-day meeting in one of the churches to recruit a company. Ayrault listened with absorbed interest to the rousing appeal, and, when recruits were called for, was the first to rise. It turned out that the matter could not be at once consummated, as the proper papers were not there. Other young men from the neighborhood followed Ayrault's example, and it was arranged that they should all go to the city for regular enlistment the next day. All that afternoon was spent in preparations, and in talking with other eager volunteers, who seemed to look to Ayrault as their head. It was understood, they told him, that he would probably be an officer in the company. He felt himself a changed being; he was as if floating in air, and ready to swim off to some new planet. What had he now to do with that pale dreamer who had nourished his absurd imaginings until he had barely escaped being controlled by them? When they crossed his mind it was only to make him thank God for his escape. He flung wide the windows of his chamber. He hated the very sight of the scene where his proud vision had been fulfilled, and he had been Monarch of Dreams. No matter: he was now free, and the spell was broken. Life, action, duty, honor, a redeemed nation, lay before him; all entanglements were cut away.

That evening there went a summons through the little village that opened the door of every house. A young man galloped out from the city, waking the echoes of the hills with his somewhat untutored bugle-notes, as he dashed along. Riding from house to house of those who had pledged themselves, he told the news. There had been a great defeat; reinforcements had been summoned instantly; and the half-organized regiment, undrilled, unarmed, not even uniformed, was ordered to proceed that night to the front, and replace in the forts round Washington other levies that were a shade less raw. Every man desiring to enlist must come instantly; yet, as before daybreak the regiment would pass by special train on the railway that led through the village, those in that vicinity might join it at the station, and have still a few hours at home. They were hurried hours for Ayrault, and toward midnight he threw himself on his bed for a moment's repose, having left strict orders for his awakening. He gave not one thought to his world of visions; had he done so, it would have only been to rejoice that he had eluded them forever.

Let a man at any moment attempt his best, and his life will still be at least half made up of the accumulated results of past action. Never had Ayrault seemed so absolutely safe from the gathered crowd of his own delusions: never had they come upon him with a power so terrific. Again he was in those stately halls which his imagination had so laboriously built up: again the mob of unreal beings came around him, each more himself than he was. Ayrault was beset, encircled, overwhelmed; he was in a manner lost in the crowd of himself. If any confused thought of his projected army life entered his dream, it utterly subordinated itself; or merely helped to emphasize the vastness and strengthen the sway of that phantom army to which he had given himself, and of which he was already the pledged recruit.

In the midst of this tumultuous dreaming, came confused sounds from without. There was the rolling of railway wheels, the scream of locomotive engines, the beating of drums, the cheers of men, the report and glare of fireworks. Mingled with all, there came the repeated sound of knocking at his own door, which he had locked, from mere force of habit, ere he lay down. The sounds seemed only to rouse into new tumult the figures of his dream. These suddenly began to increase steadily in size, even as they had before diminished; and the waxing was more fearful than the waning. From being Gulliver among the Lilliputians, Ayraut was Gulliver in Brobdingnag. Each image of himself, before diminutive, became colossal: they blocked his path; he actually could not find himself, could not tell which was he that should arouse himself, in their vast and endless self-multiplication. He became vaguely conscious, amidst the bewilderment, that the shouts in the village were subsiding, the illuminations growing dark; and the train with its young soldiers was again in motion, throbbing and resounding among the hills, and bearing the lost opportunity of his life away—away—away.

AMBROSE BIERCE AND SCIENCE FICTION

Ambrose Bierce's science fiction, rendering its subject in explicit and simple surface drama rather than obscure and complex buried symbolism, often comes close to pure speculation. The title of the volume in which Bierce eventually collected his best science fiction informs the reader what his response to each story should be: *Can Such Things Be?*

The first edition (1893) of *Can Such Things Be?* contains, in addition to the two brief pieces reprinted in the present volume, such tales as "The Death of Halpin Frayser," in which the sexual love of a mother and son destroys him when she psychically directs a man to kill him while he dreams that she is killing him; "The Realm of the Unreal," in which a hypnotist is able to trap people into a realm "dominated by whatever delusions and hallucinations" he suggests; various stories of various kinds of ghosts; and "John Bartine's Watch" (see page 378). When Bierce prepared *Can Such Things Be?* for the 1909 Collected Works, he added a number of stories previously unpublished or uncollected. These include such interesting pieces as "A Diagnosis of Death," in which the old gothic device of a being stepping out of his portrait comes with a "scientific" explanation; "A Tough Tussle," in which the dead man destroys the living; "A Resumed Identity" (see page 378); and his two famous works of science fiction, "The Damned Thing" and "Moxon's Master." *

When one submits "Moxon's Master" to that simple question "Can Such Things Be?" some surprising things begin to emerge from its simple, explicit surface. First of all, the question itself quickly becomes the central question of cybernetics: Can a machine "think"? Then the story can be seen, as Edna Kenton pointed out in "Ambrose Bierce and 'Moxon's Master'" (*The Bookman*, 1925), as "the master story that keys all the others" in Bierce's entire corpus.

"Moxon's Master" begins with the first-person narrator phrasing two questions: " 'Are you serious?—do you really believe that a machine thinks?' " Moxon, inventor of the chess-playing robot that in the end will strangle him in response to his triumphant cry of " 'Checkmate!' ", replies like this:

> "What is a 'machine'? The word has been variously defined. Here is one definition from a popular dictionary: 'Any instrument or organization by which power is applied and made effective, or a desired effect produced.' Well, then, is not a man a machine? And you will admit that he thinks—or thinks he thinks."

Miss Kenton turns the key this way:

> Read "Moxon's Master," and then, in its light, reread "The Man and the Snake," "A Horseman in the Sky," "An Occurrence at Owl Creek Bridge," even "The Boarded Window." . . . you will have the . . . delight of seeing Harker Braynton's intentions and fears in presence of the Snake, his master; Carter Druse's "performance of an involuntary act" before the horseman in the sky; Peyton Farquehar on Owl Creek Bridge in

* The various histories of science fiction have mistakenly attributed both these works to the 1893 edition of *Can Such Things Be?* "The Damned Thing" was first published sometime before 1896 in *Town Topics* and then collected in the 1898 edition of *In the Midst of Life;* neither of the standard Bierce bibliographies lists any publication prior to 1909 for "Moxon's Master."

> the veritable act of "running down"; Murlock, in "The Boarded Window," rushing too swiftly upon his fear and then retreating from it, only to meet the ultimate horror.
>
> For always, in the multiplied works, there is a "key" story that unlocks the others. . . . If man is a machine set in motion by fear, and Bierce saw him so, he must write about him so. And in the seventy tales of "In the Midst of Life" and "Can Such Things Be?" he most surely does.

If to Bierce man is a machine governed by unconscious forces, then his fiction, to be true to his vision, cannot stop with man. This is why it tends toward pure speculation about the forces which may, existing beyond human ken, govern man.

Such a fiction does not satisfy the dominant critical criteria of Bierce's time or our own, and this, together with a lack of a solid tradition of this kind of fiction, may help explain Bierce's problems in writing it and our problems in coming to terms with it—unless we approach it from the direction of modern speculative science fiction. Given the assumption which was to find expression in "Moxon's Master," Bierce was driven to explore into the areas of "The Damned Thing" (inconceivable other forms of life) and the two pieces collected in this volume, "A Psychological Shipwreck" (inconceivable psychic dimensions) and "Mysterious Disappearances" (inconceivable physical dimensions). Like all early explorers, Bierce was more a map-maker than a map-user.

AMBROSE BIERCE

A Psychological Shipwreck *

In the summer of 1874 I was in Liverpool, whither I had gone on business for the mercantile house of Bronson & Jarrett, New York. I am William Jarrett; my partner was Zenas Bronson. The firm failed last year, and unable to endure the fall from affluence to poverty he died.

Having finished my business, and feeling the lassitude and exhaustion incident to its dispatch, I felt that a protracted sea voyage would be both agreeable and beneficial, so instead of embarking for my return on one of the many fine passenger steamers I booked for New York on the sailing vessel *Morrow*, upon which I had shipped a large and valuable invoice of the goods I had bought. The *Morrow* was an English ship with, of course, but little accommodation for passengers, of whom there were only myself, a young woman and her servant, who was a middle-aged negress. I thought it singular that a traveling English girl should be so attended, but she afterward explained to me that the woman had been left with her family by a man and his wife from South Carolina, both of whom had died on the same day at the house of the young lady's father in Devonshire—a circumstance in itself sufficiently uncommon to remain rather distinctly in my memory, even had it not afterward transpired in conversation with the young lady that the name of the man was William Jarrett, the same as my own. I knew that a

* *Can Such Things Be?*, 1893, 1909.

branch of my family had settled in South Carolina, but of them and their history I was ignorant.

The *Morrow* sailed from the mouth of the Mersey on the 15th of June and for several weeks we had fair breezes and unclouded skies. The skipper, an admirable seaman but nothing more, favored us with very little of his society, except at his table; and the young woman, Miss Janette Harford, and I became very well acquainted. We were, in truth, nearly always together, and being of an introspective turn of mind I often endeavored to analyze and define the novel feeling with which she inspired me—a secret, subtle, but powerful attraction which constantly impelled me to seek her; but the attempt was hopeless. I could only be sure that at least it was not love. Having assured myself of this and being certain that she was quite as whole-hearted, I ventured one evening (I remember it was on the 3d of July) as we sat on deck to ask her, laughingly, if she could assist me to resolve my psychological doubt.

For a moment she was silent, with averted face, and I began to fear I had been extremely rude and indelicate; then she fixed her eyes gravely on my own. In an instant my mind was dominated by as strange a fancy as ever entered human consciousness. It seemed as if she were looking at me, not *with*, but *through*, those eyes—from an immeasurable distance behind them—and that a number of other persons, men, women and children, upon whose faces I caught strangely familiar evanescent expressions, clustered about her, struggling with gentle eagerness to look at me through the same orbs. Ship, ocean, sky—all had vanished. I was conscious of nothing but the figures in this extraordinary and fantastic scene. Then all at once darkness fell upon me, and anon from out of it, as to one who grows accustomed by degrees to a dimmer light, my former surroundings of deck and mast and cordage slowly resolved themselves. Miss Harford had closed her eyes and was leaning back in her chair, apparently asleep, the book she had been reading open in her lap. Impelled by surely I cannot say what motive, I glanced at the top of the page; it was a copy of that rare and curious work, "Denneker's Meditations," and the lady's index finger rested on this passage:

"To sundry it is given to be drawn away, and to be apart from the body for a season; for, as concerning rills which would flow across each other the weaker is borne along by the stronger, so there be certain of kin whose paths intersecting, their souls do bear company, the while their bodies go fore-appointed ways, unknowing."

Miss Harford arose, shuddering; the sun had sunk below the horizon, but it was not cold. There was not a breath of wind; there were no clouds in the sky, yet not a star was visible. A hurried tramping sounded on the deck; the captain, summoned from below, joined the first officer, who stood looking at the barometer. "Good God!" I heard him exclaim.

An hour later the form of Janette Harford, invisible in the darkness and spray, was torn from my grasp by the cruel vortex of the sinking ship, and I fainted in the cordage of the floating mast to which I had lashed myself.

It was by lamplight that I awoke. I lay in a berth amid the familiar surroundings of the stateroom of a steamer. On a couch opposite sat a man, half undressed for bed, reading a book. I recognized the face of my friend Gordon Doyle, whom I had met in Liverpool on the day of my embarkation, when he was himself about to sail on the steamer *City of Prague*, on which he had urged me to accompany him.

After some moments I now spoke his name. He simply said, "Well," and turned a leaf in his book without removing his eyes from the page.

"Doyle," I repeated, "did they save *her*?"

He now deigned to look at me and smiled as if amused. He evidently thought me but half awake.

"Her? Whom do you mean?"

"Janette Harford."

His amusement turned to amazement; he stared at me fixedly, saying nothing.

"You will tell me after a while," I continued; "I suppose you will tell me after a while."

A moment later I asked: "What ship is this?"

Doyle stared again. "The steamer *City of Prague*, bound from Liverpool to New York, three weeks out with a broken shaft. Principal passenger, Mr. Gordon Doyle; ditto lunatic, Mr. William Jarrett. These two distinguished travelers embarked together, but they are about to part, it being the resolute intention of the former to pitch the latter overboard."

I sat bolt upright. "Do you mean to say that I have been for three weeks a passenger on this steamer?"

"Yes, pretty nearly; this is the 3d of July."

"Have I been ill?"

"Right as a trivet all the time, and punctual at your meals."

"My God! Doyle, there is some mystery here; do have the goodness to be serious. Was I not rescued from the wreck of the ship *Morrow?*"

Doyle changed color, and approaching me, laid his fingers on my wrist. A moment later, "What do you know of Janette Harford?" he asked very calmly.

"First tell me what *you* know of her?"

Mr. Doyle gazed at me for some moments as if thinking what to do, then seating himself again on the couch, said:

"Why should I not? I am engaged to marry Janette Harford, whom I met a year ago in London. Her family, one of the wealthiest in Devonshire, cut up rough about it, and we eloped—are eloping rather, for on the day that you and I walked to the landing stage to go aboard this steamer she and her faithful servant, a negress, passed us, driving to the ship *Morrow*. She would not consent to go in the same vessel with me, and it had been deemed best that she take a sailing vessel in order to avoid observation and lessen the risk of detection. I am now alarmed lest this cursed breaking of our machinery may detain us so long that the *Morrow* will get to New York before us, and the poor girl will not know where to go."

I lay still in my berth—so still I hardly breathed. But the subject was evidently not displeasing to Doyle, and after a short pause he resumed:

"By the way, she is only an adopted daughter of the Harfords. Her mother was killed at their place by being thrown from a horse while hunting, and her father, mad with grief, made away with himself the same day. No one ever claimed the child, and after a reasonable time they adopted her. She has grown up in the belief that she is their daughter."

"Doyle, what book are you reading?"

"Oh, it's called 'Denneker's Meditations.' It's a rum lot, Janette gave it to me; she happened to have two copies. Want to see it?"

He tossed me the volume, which opened as it fell. On one of the exposed pages was a marked passage:

"To sundry it is given to be drawn away, and to be apart from the body for a season; for, as concerning rills which would flow across each other the weaker is borne along by the stronger, so there be certain of kin whose paths intersecting, their souls do bear company, the while their bodies go fore-appointed ways, unknowing."

"She had—she has—a singular taste in reading," I managed to say, mastering my agitation.

"Yes. And now perhaps you will have the kindness to explain how you knew her name and that of the ship she sailed in."

"You talked of her in your sleep," I said.

A week later we were towed into the port of New York. But the *Morrow* was never heard from.

EDWARD BELLAMY AND SCIENCE FICTION

. . . in Edward Bellamy we were rich in a romantic imagination surpassed only by Hawthorne's.

William Dean Howells, Introduction to *The Blindman's World and Other Stories*

Edward Bellamy was certainly the most influential science fiction writer of the nineteenth century. The impact of *Looking Backward, 2000-1887* (1888), that classic story of time travel, on American politics and economics and on all subsequent utopianism is a subject of unending investigation. *Looking Backward* predicted that all the trusts would develop into a public monolith which would make not only possible but inevitable an economy and government of reason, and a society of love. Immediately hundreds of clubs sprang up all over America to implement Bellamy's socio-economic system (known as Nationalism); wrathful dystopian responses arose to meet the challenge of this utopian vision; the Nationalist Party was formed; and the main lines of twentieth-century economic ideological conflict were clearly drawn.

We can see the kinds of responses produced by *Looking Backward* simply by looking at the contents of one number of one magazine, the June 1890 issue of the *Overland Monthly*, a number devoted to nothing but Bellamy and his effects:

BERNARD MOSES, Social Transformation
GERALDINE MEYRICK, The Ethics of Nationalism
EDWARD BERWICK, Farming in the Year 2000, A.D.

H. PEEBLES, The Theories of Bellamy Compared with the Utopias of the Past
HARRY CADMAN, The Future of Industrialism
JOHN HENRY BARNABAS, A Hero of the Twentieth Century
FRANCIS E. SHELDON, If It Were Come [poem]
KURD LASSWITZ, Pictures Out of the Future
ANON., Herbert Spencer's Utopia
H. ELTON SMITH, The Last Sinner
M. W. SHINN, A Fifth Shall Close the Drama of the Day [poem]
JOHN S. HITTELL, Looking Backward in Peru
CHARLES S. GREENE, A Combine [poem]
PAULINE CARSTEN CURTIS, In the Year '26
F. I. VASSAULT, Nationalism in California
ANON., Corporations, Trusts, Capital and Labor, I

This one number contains no fewer than four original future-scene science fictions, a future-scene poem, two reviews of utopian fiction, and an extract from one of Kurd Lasswitz's science fictions (a footnote points out that Lasswitz had been publishing what is now called extrapolation since 1871).

Each of the four original science fictions assumes the accuracy of Bellamy's predictions, and then proceeds. "Farming in the Year 2000, A.D." is actually contrived to fit as an insert into *Looking Backward;* it elaborates on a detail of Bellamy's vision much in the manner of the present-day Soviet utopists who elaborate on their communally shared notion of utopia. A *science* fiction, it describes how farming, benefiting from new electric equipment, organic fertilizers made from "the refuse of cities," and nitrogenous fertilizers obtained "from that omnipresent and inexhaustible nitrogen mine, the atmosphere," fits into the glorious world of *Looking Backward.* "A Hero of the Twentieth Century," which describes the effete love affair between a girl who yearns for the romance she finds in nineteenth-century novels and a boy who is appalled by her demand that he be a hero, and "In the Year '26," which describes the sad fate of

Juliana West (the only child of Julian West, the time traveler of *Looking Backward*) in the twenty-first century, are rather mild anti-utopian protests against Bellamy's ecstatic proclamations. "The Last Sinner" is a much more violent reaction, which looks surprisingly like the most conventional kind of twentieth-century dystopia: an individualist rebels against the state's rule of reason, asserting his ego-centered values in ways strikingly similar to those of the ego-worshipping hero of Ayn Rand's *Anthem* (which "The Last Sinner" almost matches in fanatical revulsion against humanism). The author of this piece, like many other contemporaries, reacted to Bellamy's predictions not with an indifferent dismissal but an alarmed concurrence.

As this number of the *Overland Monthly* suggests, *Looking Backward* occasioned as significant a reaction in utopian, dystopian, and science fiction as it did in the world of politics, economics, and society. Literally hundreds of books assailed and supported, sympathetically imitated or jeeringly aped Bellamy's fictional methods and arguments. And Twain's *A Connecticut Yankee in King Arthur's Court,* which sends its time traveler in the opposite direction, appeared, one should note, the year after *Looking Backward.*

One innovation of *Looking Backward* is its original use of the dream device. Nineteenth-century future-scene utopian writing used dream as a conventional means of voyaging into the perfect future world. Time travelers in works from Louis Sebastian Mercier's *L'An deux mille quatre cent quarante. Reve s'il fût jamais* (1770) through Mary Griffith's *Three Hundred Years Hence* (1836) to Julian Hawthorne's "June, 1993" (1893) are usually all dreamers who wake back in the "real" world of their own century. Bellamy's time traveler falls asleep, wakes in the future, then falls asleep and wakes back in the nineteenth century. At this point both he and the reader believe that he has waked from a utopian dream. But as it turns out, his reawakening in the past was the dream, and he really is in the perfect future world—in which the nineteenth century exists only as a nightmare from which history has brought escape.

This device of *Looking Backward* recalls the obscure fact that Bellamy wrote some other extremely interesting science fiction, science fiction which, focusing intensely on the nature of fiction, might make one read *Looking Backward* in a different light. Among many things, one learns from this science fiction what Bellamy himself, in such later works as "Woman in the Year 2000" (1891), "Christmas in the Year 2000" (1895), and *Equality* (1897) was not to keep clearly in mind—that science fiction as speculation, like all speculation, is tentative as well as suggestive.

In *Dr. Heidenhoff's Process* (1880) electric charges are used to blot out psychologically disturbing traumatic memories. In this early work, the dream device may seem to be used in the conventional way—the marvelous scientific process is all a dream. But the reader must then ask himself how his experience, empathically awakening from a fictional character's dream, differs from the experience of the dreamer. Madeline Brand's true lover dreams that Dr. Heidenhoff's process destroys Madeline's memory that she had been seduced by another and that, restored to innocence, she blissfully weds him. He awakens to find the dream a fiction, the reality Madeline's suicide.

The two stories reprinted in this volume should be read with reference to each other, with reference to *Looking Backward*, and with reference to the place Bellamy assigned them in his collection of short fiction entitled *The Blindman's World and Other Stories* (1898). *The Blindman's World* begins with the title story and ends with "To Whom This May Come." That is, it begins with a story which explores what life might be like if we could see the future and ends with a story which explores what life might be like if we could see into each other's minds. Life in the two hypothetical worlds is in all essential respects the same and is beatifically different from life in the actual world.

This may suggest that Bellamy in these two stories is arguing for the desirability of neither prevision nor telepathy but rather for changing views of the world as it is and might be. Then when one notices that life in these two worlds is in all essential respects much like life in the year 2000 in *Looking Backward*, one must ask about that work whether the same kind of speculation is not going on, and whether it does not warn against taking *Looking Backward* quite so much as prediction and prescription. Economic institutions in the world of the novel provide exactly what prevision and telepathy provide in the two short stories—a contrafactual basis upon which to build a perfect world.

When one turns to the short stories sandwiched between "The Blindman's World" and "To Whom This May Come" in *The Blindman's World and Other Stories*, something even more curious occurs. The story about the sense of the future and the story about the most intimate kind of human communication frame an assortment of short fictions, which, like all fictions, involve the problems of human time and communication. Framed in this way, these other stories open up new dimensions of fiction.

In "The Old Folks' Party" a group of young men and women in 1875 decide to assume the roles they think they will be playing fifty years hence (there are hints that Bellamy is thinking in terms of a variation on Hawthorne's "Dr. Heidegger's Experiment"). At their next weekly meeting they will become what they call "ghosts of the future." Their insights into the problems of exchanging identity and traveling through time, even before they do so, are quite penetrating:

> ". . . there are half a dozen of each one of us, or a dozen if you please, one in fact for each epoch of life, and each slightly or almost wholly different from the others. Each one of these epochs is foreign and inconceivable to the others, as ourselves at seventy now are to us. It's as hard to suppose ourselves old as to imagine swapping identities with another. And when we get

> old it will be just as hard to realize that we were ever young. So that the different periods of life are to all intents and purposes different persons. . . ."

The next week, at the party, the "old folks" find that they have to create the entire world in which they have their being, the world of 1925. They become, in other words, science fictionists. So here is a fiction in which the characters themselves are both creators of a future world and creatures within their own creation. They become so possessed by their fiction, so deluded by their prevision, so entrapped in their interrelations as "old folks," that they have to wrench themselves back into their youth; it is as though "waking from a nightmare."

Like "The Old Folks' Party," "Lost" is an investigation of the problems of identity in time. A beautiful girl, lost to the protagonist, reappears years later as an entirely different creature—a "broadly molded, comfortable-looking matron." Appalled, he wonders, "What had the woman to do with" the girl he has been seeking:

> She was not this woman, nor was she dead in any conceivable natural way so that her girlish spirit might have remained eternally fixed. She was nothing. She was nowhere.

The insights are similar to those in some of the earliest American short stories, "Rip Van Winkle," William Austin's "Peter Rugg, the Missing Man," and Hawthorne's "Wakefield." But here these insights reflect back and forth upon the beatific speculations of "The Blindman's World" and "To Whom This May Come."

"At Pinney's Ranch" and "With the Eyes Shut" weave the strands of extraordinary kinds of movement in time and between identities into still other patterns. In "At Pinney's Ranch" a man, "separated from his family" (because he is suspected of a murder) "almost as hopelessly as if he were dead," assumes a new name and a new life. When he learns that he is free to return he also learns that his wife, thinking him dead, has promised to marry another man. To stop the wedding, he tries to communicate with her by mental telepathy and apparently succeeds. This message in the blind prepares the way for "To Whom This May Come," the final vision of telepathic communication. "With the Eyes Shut" is a dream journey into a world which has virtually replaced all writing with phonographic contrivances. It is a world of talking books, letters, newspapers, clocks, and trains—in short, another kind of blindman's world. And like most of Bellamy's purely speculative worlds, it is an ecstatically delightful world for its inhabitants and fictional visitors.

Bellamy's mind and fiction were truly speculative, making each "What if?"—whether about prevision, telepathy, phonography, or economics—generate a new world. Each speculative gambit begins by making one change in the actual world, and then demonstrates, with perfect logic, that the world thus generated—or, more aptly, regenerated—might be a perfect one.

EDWARD BELLAMY

To Whom This May Come *

It is now about a year since I took passage at Calcultta in the ship Adelaide for New York. We had baffling weather till New Amsterdam Island was sighted, where we took a new point of departure. Three days later, a terrible gale struck us. Four days we flew before it, whither, no one knew, for neither sun, moon, nor stars were at any time visible, and we could take no observation. Toward midnight of the fourth day, the glare of lightning revealed the Adelaide in a hopeless position, close in upon a low-lying shore, and driving straight toward it. All around and astern far out to sea was such a maze of rocks and shoals that it was a miracle we had come so far. Presently the ship struck, and almost instantly went to pieces, so great was the violence of the sea. I gave myself up for lost, and was indeed already past the worst of drowning, when I was recalled to consciousness by being thrown with a tremendous shock upon the beach. I had just strength enough to drag myself above the reach of the waves, and then I fell down and knew no more.

When I awoke, the storm was over. The sun, already halfway up the sky, had dried my clothing, and renewed the vigor of my bruised and aching limbs. On sea or shore I saw no vestige of my ship or my companions, of whom I appeared the sole survivor. I was not, however, alone. A group of persons, apparently the inhabitants of the country, stood near, observing me with looks of friendliness which at once freed me from apprehension as to

* *Harper's*, 1888.

my treatment at their hands. They were a white and handsome people, evidently of a high order of civilization, though I recognized in them the traits of no race with which I was familiar.

Seeing that it was evidently their idea of etiquette to leave it to strangers to open conversation, I addressed them in English, but failed to elicit any response beyond deprecating smiles. I then accosted them successively in the French, German, Italian, Spanish, Dutch, and Portuguese tongues, but with no better results. I began to be very much puzzled as to what could possibly be the nationality of a white and evidently civilized race to which no one of the tongues of the great seafaring nations was intelligible. The oddest thing of all was the unbroken silence with which they contemplated my efforts to open communication with them. It was as if they were agreed not to give me a clue to their language by even a whisper; for while they regarded one another with looks of smiling intelligence, they did not once open their lips. But if this behavior suggested that they were amusing themselves at my expense, that presumption was negatived by the unmistakable friendliness and sympathy which their whole bearing expressed.

A most extraordinary conjecture occurred to me. Could it be that these strange people were dumb? Such a freak of nature as an entire race thus afflicted had never indeed been heard of, but who could say what wonders the unexplored vasts of the great Southern Ocean might thus far have hid from human ken? Now, among the scraps of useless information which lumbered my mind was an acquaintance with the deaf-and-dumb alphabet, and forthwith I began to spell out with my fingers some of the phrases I had already uttered to so little effect. My resort to the sign language overcame the last remnant of gravity in the already profusely smiling group. The small boys now rolled on the ground in convulsions of mirth, while the grave and reverend seniors, who had hitherto kept them in check, were fain momentarily to avert their faces, and I could see their bodies shaking with laughter. The greatest clown in the world never received a more flattering tribute to his powers to amuse than had been called forth by mine to make myself understood. Naturally, however, I was not flattered, but on the contrary entirely discomfited. Angry I could not well be, for the deprecating manner in which all, excepting of course the boys, yielded to their perception of the ridiculous, and the distress they showed at their failure in self-control, made me seem the aggressor. It was as if they were very sorry for me, and ready to put themselves wholly at my service, if I would only refrain from reducing them to a state of disability by being so exquisitely absurd. Certainly this evidently amiable race had a very embarrassing way of receiving strangers.

Just at this moment, when my bewilderment was fast verging on exasperation, relief came. The circle opened, and a little elderly man, who had evidently come in haste, confronted me, and, bowing very politely, addressed me in English. His voice was the most pitiable abortion of a voice I had ever heard. While having all the defects in articulation of a child's who is just beginning to talk, it was not even a child's in strength of tone, being in fact a mere alternation of squeaks and whispers inaudible a rod away. With some difficulty I was, however, able to follow him pretty nearly.

"As the official interpreter," he said, "I extend you a cordial welcome to these islands. I was sent for as soon as you were discovered, but being at some distance, I was unable to arrive until this moment. I regret this, as my presence would have saved you embarrassment. My countrymen desire me to intercede with you to pardon the wholly involuntary and uncontrollable mirth provoked by your attempts to communicate with them. You see, they understood you perfectly well, but could not answer you."

"Merciful heavens!" I exclaimed, horrified to find my surmise correct; "can it be that they are all thus afflicted? Is it possible that you are the only man among them who has the power of speech?"

Again it appeared that, quite unintentionally, I had said something excruciatingly funny; for at my speech there arose a sound of gentle laughter from the group, now augmented to quite an assemblage, which drowned the plashing of the waves on the beach at our feet. Even the interpreter smiled.

"Do they think it so amusing to be dumb?" I asked.

"They find it very amusing," replied the interpreter, "that their inability to speak should be regarded by any one as an affliction; for it is by the voluntary disuse of the organs of articulation that they have lost the power of speech, and, as a consequence, the ability even to understand speech."

"But," said I, somewhat puzzled by this statement, "didn't

you just tell me that they understood me, though they could not reply, and are they not laughing now at what I just said?"

"It is you they understood, not your words," answered the interpreter. "Our speech now is gibberish to them, as unintelligible in itself as the growling of animals; but they know what we are saying, because they know our thoughts. You must know that these are the islands of the mind-readers."

Such were the circumstances of my introduction to this extraordinary people. The official interpreter being charged by virtue of his office with the first entertainment of shipwrecked members of the talking nations, I became his guest, and passed a number of days under his roof before going out to any considerable extent among the people. My first impression had been the somewhat oppressive one that the power to read the thoughts of others could be possessed only by beings of a superior order to man. It was the first effort of the interpreter to disabuse me of this notion. It appeared from his account that the experience of the mind-readers was a case simply of a slight acceleration, from special causes, of the course of universal human evolution, which in time was destined to lead to the disuse of speech and the substitution of direct mental vision on the part of all races. This rapid evolution of these islanders was accounted for by their peculiar origin and circumstances.

Some three centuries before Christ, one of the Parthian kings of Persia, of the dynasty of the Arsacidæ, undertook a persecution of the soothsayers and magicians in his realms. These people were credited with supernatural powers by popular prejudice, but in fact were merely persons of special gifts in the way of hypnotizing, mind-reading, thought transference, and such arts, which they exercised for their own gain.

Too much in awe of the soothsayers to do them outright violence, the king resolved to banish them, and to this end put them, with their families, on ships and sent them to Ceylon. When, however, the fleet was in the neighborhood of that island, a great storm scattered it, and one of the ships, after being driven for many days before the tempest, was wrecked upon one of an archipelago of uninhabited islands far to the south, where the survivors settled. Naturally, the posterity of the parents possessed of such peculiar gifts had developed extraordinary psychical powers.

Having set before them the end of evolving a new and advanced order of humanity, they had aided the development of these powers by a rigid system of stirpiculture. The result was that, after a few centuries, mind-reading became so general that language fell into disuse as a means of communicating ideas. For many generations the power of speech still remained voluntary, but gradually the vocal organs had become atrophied, and for several hundred years the power of articulation had been wholly lost. Infants for a few months after birth did, indeed, still emit inarticulate cries, but at an age when in less advanced races these cries began to be articulate, the children of the mind-readers developed the power of direct vision, and ceased to attempt to use the voice.

The fact that the existence of the mind-readers had never been found out by the rest of the world was explained by two considerations. In the first place, the group of islands was small, and occupied a corner of the Indian Ocean quite out of the ordinary track of ships. In the second place, the approach to the islands was rendered so desperately perilous by terrible currents, and the maze of outlying rocks and shoals, that it was next to impossible for any ship to touch their shores save as a wreck. No ship at least had ever done so in the two thousand years since the mind-readers' own arrival, and the Adelaide had made the one hundred and twenty-third such wreck.

Apart from motives of humanity, the mind-readers made strenuous efforts to rescue shipwrecked persons, for from them alone, through the interpreters, could they obtain information of the outside world. Little enough this proved when, as often happened, the sole survivor of the shipwreck was some ignorant sailor, who had no news to communicate beyond the latest varieties of forecastle blasphemy. My hosts gratefully assured me that, as a person of some little education, they considered me a veritable godsend. No less a task was mine than to relate to them the history of the world for the past two centuries, and often did I wish, for their sakes, that I had made a more exact study of it.

It is solely for the purpose of communicating with shipwrecked strangers of the talking nations that the office of the interpreters exists. When, as from time to time happens, a child is born with some powers of articulation, he is set apart, and trained to talk in the interpreters' college. Of course the partial atrophy of the vocal organs, from which even the best interpreters suffer, renders many of the sounds of language impossible for them. None, for instance, can pronounce *v, f,* or *s;* and as to the sound represented by *th,* it is five generations since the last interpreter lived who could utter it. But for the occasional intermarriage of shipwrecked strangers with the islanders, it is probable that the supply of interpreters would have long ere this quite failed.

I imagine that the very unpleasant sensations which followed the realization that I was among people who, while inscrutable to me, knew my every thought, were very much what any one would have experienced in the same case. They were very comparable to the panic which accidental nudity causes a person among races whose custom it is to conceal the figure with drapery. I wanted to run away and hide myself. If I analyzed my feeling, it did not seem to arise so much from the consciousness of any particularly heinous secrets, as from the knowledge of a swarm of fatuous, ill-natured, and unseemly thoughts and half thoughts concerning those around me, and concerning myself, which it was insufferable that any person should peruse in however benevolent a spirit. But while my chagrin and distress on this account were at first intense, they were also very short-lived, for almost immediately I discovered that the very knowledge that my mind was overlooked by others operated to check thoughts that might be painful to them, and that, too, without more effort of the will than a kindly person exerts to check the utterance of disagreeable remarks. As a very few lessons in the elements of courtesy cures a decent person of inconsiderate speaking, so a brief experience among the mind-readers went far in my case to check inconsiderate thinking. It must not be supposed, however, that courtesy among the mind-readers prevents them from thinking pointedly and freely concerning one another upon serious occasions, any more than the finest courtesy among the talking races restrains them from speaking to one another with entire plainness when it is desirable to do so. Indeed, among the mind-readers, politeness never can extend to the point of insincerity, as among talking nations, seeing that it is always one another's real and inmost thought that they read. I may fitly mention here, though it was not till later that I fully understood why it must necessarily be so, that one need feel far less chagrin at the complete revelation of his weaknesses to a mind-reader than at the slightest betrayal of them to one of another race. For the very reason that the mind-reader reads all your thoughts, particular thoughts are judged with reference to the general tenor of thought. Your characteristic and habitual frame of mind is what he takes account of. No one need fear being misjudged by a mind-reader on account of sentiments or emotions which are not representative of the real character or general attitude. Justice may, indeed, be said to be a necessary consequence of mind-reading.

As regards the interpreter himself, the instinct of courtesy was not long needed to check wanton or offensive thoughts. In all my life before, I had been very slow to form friendships, but before I had been three days in the company of this stranger of a strange race, I had become enthusiastically devoted to him. It was impossible not to be. The peculiar joy of friendship is the sense of being understood by our friend as we are not by others, and yet of being loved in spite of the understanding. Now here was one whose every word testified to a knowledge of my secret thoughts and motives which the oldest and nearest of my former friends had never, and could never, have approximated. Had such a knowledge bred in him contempt of me, I should neither have blamed him nor been at all surprised. Judge, then, whether the cordial friendliness which he showed was likely to leave me indifferent.

Imagine my incredulity when he informed me that our friendship was not based upon more than ordinary mutual suitability of temperaments. The faculty of mind-reading, he explained, brought minds so close together, and so heightened sympathy, that the lowest order of friendship between mind-readers implied a mutual delight such as only rare friends enjoyed among other races. He assured me that later on, when I came to know others of his race, I should find, by the far greater intensity of sympathy and affection I should conceive for some of them, how true this saying was.

It may be inquired how, on beginning to mingle with the mind-readers in general, I managed to communicate with them, seeing that, while they could read my thoughts, they could not, like the interpreter, respond to them by speech. I must here explain that, while these people have no use for a spoken language, a written language is needful for purposes of record. They consequently all know how to write. Do they, then, write Persian? Luckily for me, no. It appears that, for a long period after mind-reading was fully developed, not only was spoken language disused, but also written, no records whatever having been kept during this period. The delight of the people in the newly found power of direct mind-to-mind vision, whereby pictures of the total mental state were communicated, instead of the imperfect descriptions of single thoughts which words at best could give, induced an invincible distaste for the laborious impotence of language.

When, however, the first intellectual intoxication had, after several generations, somewhat sobered down, it was recognized that records of the past were desirable, and that the despised medium of words was needful to preserve it. Persian had meanwhile been wholly forgotten. In order to avoid the prodigious task of inventing a complete new language, the institution of the interpreters was now set up, with the idea of acquiring through them a knowledge of some of the languages of the outside world from the mariners wrecked on the islands.

Owing to the fact that most of the castaway ships were English, a better knowledge of that tongue was acquired than of any other, and it was adopted as the written language of the people. As a rule, my acquaintances wrote slowly and laboriously, and yet the fact that they knew exactly what was in my mind rendered their responses so apt that, in my conversations with the slowest speller of them all, the interchange of thought was as rapid and incomparably more accurate and satisfactory than the fastest talkers attain to.

It was but a very short time after I had begun to extend my acquaintance among the mind-readers before I discovered how truly the interpreter had told me that I should find others to whom, on account of greater natural congeniality, I should become more strongly attached than I had been to him. This was in no wise, however, because I loved him less, but them more. I would fain write particularly of some of these beloved friends, comrades of my heart, from whom I first learned the undreamed-of possibilities of human friendship, and how ravishing the satisfactions of sympathy may be. Who, among those who may read this, has not known that sense of a gulf fixed between soul and soul which mocks love! Who has not felt that loneliness which oppresses the heart that loves it best! Think no longer that this gulf is eternally fixed, or is any necessity of human nature. It has no existence for the race of our fellow-men which I describe, and by that fact we may be assured that eventually it will be bridged also for us. Like the touch of shoulder to shoulder, like the clasping of hands, is the contact of their minds and their sensation of sympathy.

I say that I would fain speak more particularly of some of my friends, but waning strength forbids, and moreover, now that I think of it, another consideration would render any comparison of their characters rather confusing than instructive to a reader. This is the fact that, in common with the rest of the mind-readers, they had no names. Every one had, indeed, an arbitrary sign for his designation in records, but it has no sound value. A register of these names is kept, so they can at any time be ascertained, but it is very common to meet persons who have forgotten titles which are used solely for biographical and official purposes. For social intercourse names are of course superfluous, for these people accost one another merely by a mental act of attention, and refer to third persons by transferring their mental pictures,—something as dumb persons might by means of photographs. Something so, I say, for in the pictures of one another's personalities which the mind-readers conceive, the physical aspect, as might be expected with people who directly contemplate each other's minds and hearts, is a subordinate element.

I have already told how my first qualms of morbid self-consciousness at knowing that my mind was an open book to all around me disappeared as I learned that the very completeness of the disclosure of my thoughts and motives was a guarantee that I would be judged with a fairness and a sympathy such as even self-judgment cannot pretend to, affected as that is by so many subtle reactions. The assurance of being so judged by every one might well seem an inestimable privilege to one accustomed to a world in which not even the tenderest love is any pledge of comprehension, and yet I soon discovered that open-mindedness had a still greater profit than this. How shall I describe the delightful exhilaration of moral health and cleanness, the breezy oxygenated mental condition, which resulted from the consciousness that I had absolutely nothing concealed! Truly I may say that I enjoyed myself. I think surely that no one needs to have had my marvelous experience to sympathize with this portion of it. Are we not all ready to agree that this having a curtained chamber where we may go to grovel, out of the sight of our fellows, troubled only by a vague apprehension that God may look over the top, is the most demoralizing incident in the human condition? It is the existence within the soul of this secure refuge of lies which has always been the despair of the saint and the exultation of the knave. It is the foul cellar which taints the whole house above, be it never so fine.

What stronger testimony could there be to the instinctive consciousness that concealment is debauching, and openness our only cure, than the world-old conviction of the virtue of confession for the soul, and that the uttermost exposing of one's worst and foulest is the first step toward moral health? The wickedest man, if he could but somehow attain to writhe himself inside out as to his soul, so that its full sickness could be seen, would feel ready for a new life. Nevertheless, owing to the utter impotence of the words to convey mental conditions in their totality, or to give other than mere distortions of them, confession is, we must needs admit, but a mockery of that longing for self-revelation to which it testifies. But think what health and soundness there must be for souls among a people who see in every face a conscience which, unlike their own, they cannot sophisticate, who confess one another with a glance, and shrive with a smile! Ah, friends, let me now predict, though ages may elapse before the slow event shall justify me, that in no way will the mutual vision of minds, when at last it shall be perfected, so enhance the blessedness of mankind as by rending the veil of self, and leaving no spot of darkness in the mind for lies to hide in. Then shall the soul no longer be a coal smoking among ashes, but a star in a crystal sphere.

From what I have said of the delights which friendship among the mind-readers derives from the perfection of the mental rapport, it may be imagined how intoxicating must be the experience when one of the friends is a woman, and the subtle attractions and correspondences of sex touch with passion the intellectual sympathy. With my first venturing into society I had begun, to their extreme amusement, to fall in love with the women right and left. In the perfect frankness which is the condition of all intercourse among this people, these adorable women told me that what I felt was only friendship, which was a very good thing, but wholly different from love, as I should well know if I were beloved. It was difficult to believe that the melting emotions which I had experienced in their company were the result merely of the friendly and kindly attitude of their minds toward mine; but when I found that I was affected in the same way by every gracious woman I met, I had to make up my mind that they must be right about it, and that I should have to adapt myself to a world in which, friendship being a passion, love must needs be nothing less than rapture.

The homely proverb, "Every Jack has his Gill," may, I suppose, be taken to mean that for all men there are certain women expressly suited by mental and moral as well as by physical constitution. It is a thought painful, rather than cheering, that this may be the truth, so altogether do the chances preponderate against the ability of these elect ones to recognize each other even if they meet, seeing that speech is so inadequate and so misleading a medium of self-revelation. But among the mind-readers, the search for one's ideal mate is a quest reasonably sure of being crowned with success, and no one dreams of wedding unless it be; for so to do, they consider, would be to throw away the choicest blessing of life, and not alone to wrong themselves and their unfound mates, but likewise those whom they themselves and those undiscovered mates might wed. Therefore, passionate pilgrims, they go from isle to isle till they find each other, and, as the population of the islands is but small, the pilgrimage is not often long.

When I met her first we were in company, and I was struck by the sudden stir and the looks of touched and smiling interest with which all around turned and regarded us, the women with moistened eyes. They had read her thought when she saw me, but this I did not know, neither what was the custom in these matters, till afterward. But I knew, from the moment she first fixed her eyes on me, and I felt her mind brooding upon mine, how truly I had been told by those other women that the feeling with which they had inspired me was not love.

With people who become acquainted at a glance, and old friends in an hour, wooing is naturally not a long process. Indeed, it may be said that between lovers among mind-readers there is no wooing, but merely recognition. The day after we met, she became mine.

Perhaps I cannot better illustrate how subordinate the merely physical element is in the impression which mind-readers form of their friends than by mentioning an incident that occurred some months after our union. This was my discovery, wholly by accident, that my love, in whose society I had almost constantly been, had not the least idea what was the color of my eyes, or whether my hair and complexion were light or dark. Of course, as soon as I asked her the question, she read the answer in my mind, but she admitted that she had previously had no distinct impression on those points. On the other hand, if in the blackest midnight I should come to her, she would not need to ask who the comer was. It is by the mind, not the eye, that these people know one another. It is really only in their relations to soulless and inanimate things that they need eyes at all.

It must not be supposed that their disregard of one another's bodily aspect grows out of any ascetic sentiment. It is merely a necessary consequence of their power of directly apprehending mind, that whenever mind is closely associated with matter the latter is comparatively neglected on account of the greater interest of the former, suffering as lesser things always do when placed in immediate contrast with greater. Art is with them confined to the inanimate, the human form having, for the reason mentioned, ceased to inspire the artist. It will be naturally and quite correctly inferred that among such a race physical beauty is not the important factor in human fortune and felicity that it elsewhere is. The absolute openness of their minds and hearts to one another makes their happiness far more dependent on the moral and mental qualities of their companions than upon their physical. A genial temperament, a wide-grasping, godlike intellect, a poet soul, are incomparably more fascinating to them than the most dazzling combination conceivable of mere bodily graces.

A woman of mind and heart has no more need of beauty to win love in these islands than a beauty elsewhere of mind or heart. I should mention here, perhaps, that this race, which makes so little account of physical beauty, is itself a singularly handsome one. This is owing doubtless in part to the absolute compatibility of temperaments in all the marriages, and partly also to the reaction upon the body of a state of ideal mental and moral health and placidity.

Not being myself a mind-reader, the fact that my love was rarely beautiful in form and face had doubtless no little part in attracting my devotion. This, of course, she knew, as she knew all my thoughts, and, knowing my limitations, tolerated and forgave the element of sensuousness in my passion. But if it must have seemed to her so little worthy in comparison with the high spiritual communion which her race know as love, to me it became, by virtue of her almost superhuman relation to me, an ecstasy more ravishing surely than any lover of my race tasted before. The ache at the heart of the intensest love is the impotence of words to make it perfectly understood to its object. But my passion was without this pang, for my heart was absolutely open to her I loved. Lovers may imagine, but I cannot describe, the ecstatic thrill of communion into which this consciousness transformed every tender emotion. As I considered what mutual love must be where both parties are mind-readers, I realized the high communion which my sweet companion had sacrificed for me. She might indeed comprehend her lover and his love for her, but the higher satisfaction of knowing that she was comprehended by him and her love understood, she had foregone. For that I should ever attain the power of mind-reading was out of the question, the faculty never having been developed in a single lifetime.

Why my inability should move my dear companion to such depths of pity I was not able fully to understand until I learned that mind-reading is chiefly held desirable, not for the knowledge of others which it gives its possessors, but for the self-knowledge which is its reflex effect. Of all they see in the minds of others, that which concerns them most is the reflection of themselves, the photographs of their own characters. The most obvious consequence of the self-knowledge thus forced upon them is to render them alike incapable of self-conceit or self-depreciation. Every one must needs always think of himself as he is, being no more able to do otherwise than is a man in a hall of mirrors to cherish delusions as to his personal appearance.

But self-knowledge means to the mind-readers much more than this,—nothing less, indeed, than a shifting of the sense of identity. When a man sees himself in a mirror, he is compelled to distinguish between the bodily self he sees and his real self, which is within and unseen. When in turn the mind-reader comes to see the mental and moral self reflected in other minds as in mirrors, the same thing happens. He is compelled to distinguish between this mental and moral self which has been made objective to him, and can be contemplated by him as impartially as if it were another's, from the inner ego which still remains subjective, unseen, and indefinable. In this inner ego the mind-readers recognize the essential identity and being, the noumenal self, the core of the soul, and the true hiding of its eternal life, to which the mind as well as the body is but the garment of a day.

The effect of such a philosophy as this—which, indeed, with the mind-readers is rather an instinctive consciousness than a philosophy—must obviously be to impart a sense of wonderful superiority to the vicissitudes of this earthly state, and a singular serenity in the midst of the haps and mishaps which threaten or befall the personality. They did indeed appear to me, as I never dreamed men could attain to be, lords of themselves.

It was because I might not hope to attain this enfranchisement from the false ego of the apparent self, without which life seemed to her race scarcely worth living, that my love so pitied me.

But I must hasten on, leaving a thousand things unsaid, to relate the lamentable catastrophe to which it is owing that, instead of being still a resident of those blessed islands, in the full enjoyment of that intimate and ravishing companionship which by contrast would forever dim the pleasures of all other human society, I recall the bright picture as a memory under other skies.

Among a people who are compelled by the very constitution of their minds to put themselves in the places of others, the sympathy which is the inevitable consequence of perfect comprehension renders envy, hatred, and uncharitableness impossible. But of course there are people less genially constituted than others, and these are necessarily the objects of a certain distaste on the part of associates. Now, owing to the unhindered impact of minds upon one another, the anguish of persons so regarded, despite the tenderest consideration of those about them, is so great that they beg the grace of exile, that, being out of the way, people may think less frequently upon them. There are numerous small islets, scarcely more than rocks, lying to the north of the archipelago, and on these the unfortunates are permitted to live. Only one lives on each islet, as they cannot endure each other even as well as the more happily constituted can endure them. From time to time supplies of food are taken to them, and of course, any time they wish to take the risk, they are permitted to return to society.

Now, as I have said, the fact which, even more than their out-of-the-way location, makes the islands of the mind-readers unapproachable, is the violence with which the great antarctic current, owing probably to some configuration of the ocean bed, together with the innumerable rocks and shoals, flows through and about the archipelago.

Ships making the islands from the southward are caught by this current and drawn among the rocks, to their almost certain destruction; while, owing to the violence with which the current sets to the north, it is not possible to approach at all from that direction, or at least it has never been accomplished. Indeed, so powerful are the currents that even the boats which cross the narrow straits between the main islands and the islets of the unfortunate, to carry the latter their supplies, are ferried over by cables, not trusting to oar or sail.

The brother of my love had charge of one of the boats engaged in this transportation, and, being desirous of visiting the islets, I accepted an invitation to accompany him on one of his trips. I know nothing of how the accident happened, but in the fiercest part of the current of one of the straits we parted from the cable and were swept out to sea. There was no question of stemming the boiling current, our utmost endeavors barely sufficing to avoid being dashed to pieces on the rocks. From the first, there was no hope of our winning back to the land, and so swiftly did we drift that by noon—the accident having befallen in the morning—the islands, which are low-lying, had sunk beneath the southwestern horizon.

Among these mind-readers, distance is not an insuperable obstacle to the transfer of thought. My companion was in communication with our friends, and from time to time conveyed to me messages of anguish from my dear love; for, being well aware of the nature of the currents and the unapproachableness of the islands, those we had left behind, as well as we ourselves, knew well we should see each other's faces no more. For five days we continued to drift to the northwest, in no danger of starvation, owing to our lading of provisions, but constrained to unintermitting watch and ward by the roughness of the weather. On the fifth day my companion died from exposure and exhaustion. He died very quietly,—indeed, with great appearance of relief. The life of the mind-readers while yet they are in the body is so largely spiritual that the idea of an existence wholly so, which seems vague and chill to us, suggests to them a state only slightly more refined than they already know on earth.

After that I suppose I must have fallen into an unconscious state, from which I roused to find myself on an American ship bound for New York, surrounded by people whose only means of communicating with one another is to keep up while together a constant clatter of hissing, guttural, and explosive noises, eked out by all manner of facial contortions and bodily gestures. I frequently find myself staring open-mouthed at those who address me, too much struck by their grotesque appearance to bethink myself of replying.

I find that I shall not live out the voyage, and I do not care to. From my experience of the people on the ship, I can judge how I should fare on land amid the stunning Babel of a nation of talkers. And my friends,—God bless them! how lonely I should feel in their very presence! Nay, what satisfaction or consolation, what but bitter mockery, could I ever more find in such human sympathy and companionship as suffice others and once sufficed me,—I who have seen and known what I have seen and known! Ah, yes, doubtless it is far better I should die; but the knowledge of the things that I have seen I feel should not perish with me. For hope's sake, men should not miss the glimpse of the higher, sun-bathed reaches of the upward path they plod. So thinking, I have written out some account of my wonderful experience, though briefer far, by reason of my weakness, than fits the greatness of the matter. The captain seems an honest, well-meaning man, and to him I shall confide the narrative, charging him, on touching shore, to see it safely in the hands of some one who will bring it to the world's ear.

NOTE.—The extent of my own connection with the foregoing document is sufficiently indicated by the author himself in the final paragraph.—E. B.

SPACE TRAVEL

In September 1835 the New York *Sun* began serial publication of the "Great Astronomical Discoveries Lately Made by Sir John Herschel, L.L., D.F.R.S., &c., at the Cape of Good Hope." These discoveries, presented as reprints from "The Supplement to the Edinburgh Journal of Science," described in detail the operations of a gigantic new telescope and what had been seen through it on the surface of the moon—many animals similar to those on earth, bison with organic sunshades, blue unicorns, and an elegant civilization of bat-winged humanoids.

When what was later to become known as Richard Adams Locke's "The Moon Hoax" hit the streets, this is what happened (as described in the standard account, prefaced to the 1852 bound edition):

> By the afternoon of the day on which the introductory portion of it only had appeared, not a copy of the paper could be procured at any price, notwithstanding a very large extra edition had been provided, in anticipation of an unusual demand. This was increased from day to day, until the utmost capacity of the steam cylinder-press failed to afford an adequate supply. The office was besieged by thousands of applicants, from dawn till midnight, during the entire week the publication occupied. . . . The almost universal impres-

> sion and expression of the multitude was that of confident wonder and insatiable credence. . . .
>
> A party of professors from one of our most eminent colleges [Yale] were among the number of inquirers. . . .
>
> It was soon very generally denounced as "a hoax" by the public press, but not until nearly every press in the country had become its captivated victim.

After victimizing this country, "The Moon Hoax" took Europe, where popular excitement if anything was wilder and where belief in Locke's version of life on the moon is said to have persisted in outlying areas for two or three generations. As for the *Sun*, it owed its survival to this fantasy of the moon.

"The Moon Hoax" has this in common with the actual explorations of space, which have now been going on for a decade: extreme vulnerability to time. Of what interest now are the details of life on Locke's fantastic moon and the details of yesterday's space flight? Today's actualities—mundane, lunar, and astral—whelm alike the fantasies and actualities of all past space explorations which have no connections outside time, releasing them only as the flotsam of history.

The science fiction of space travel, even more than science fiction which focuses on biological and psychological processes, cannot rely on the distances and dimensions which seem to give it its imaginative power. Literature of voyages to the moon and beyond has an ancient tradition, which has been well studied in several recent books, but who can read with interest many of these flights into space? For most of them demonstrate what a short space it is that the human imagination can usually fly. The two stories of the nineteenth century closest to our present flights into space are Edward Everett Hale's "The Brick Moon" (1869) and its sequel "Life in the Brick Moon" (1870), which, as Moskowitz proclaims, "stand as the *first* stories anywhere ever to mention an artificial earth satellite," evidence that Hale "was the first human being to conceive of an artificial earth satellite and to put his thoughts on paper." This may be very interesting, but I defy anybody to find the two stories very interesting.

Instead of thinking in terms of yesterday an orbit of the earth, today a vision of the moon, tomorrow a visit to the planets, and after that the universe, it is far more far-reaching to think of space travel in terms of the physical dimensions available to it and the fictional dimensions it may open into. The selections here categorized under space travel include a voyage out (to another planet), a voyage in (into a drop of water), and the possibilities of voyages for which we have no accurate prepositions (of? other dimensions). These selections span the range of fictional dimensions as well as physical dimensions; that is, they include space travel as a means of conducting social extrapolation and comparison, psychological investigation, and physical speculation.

EDWARD BELLAMY
The Blindman's World *

The narrative to which this note is introductory was found among the papers of the late Professor S. Erastus Larrabee, and, as an acquaintance of the gentleman to whom they were bequeathed, I was requested to prepare it for publication. This turned out a very easy task, for the document proved of so extraordinary a character that, if published at all, it should obviously be without change. It appears that the professor did really, at one time in his life, have an attack of vertigo, or something of the sort, under circumstances similar to those described by him, and to that extent his narrative may be founded on fact. How soon it shifts from that foundation, or whether it does at all, the reader must conclude for himself. It appears certain that the professor never related to any one, while living, the stranger features of the experience here narrated, but this might have been merely from fear that his standing as a man of science would be thereby injured.

THE PROFESSOR'S NARRATIVE

At the time of the experience of which I am about to write, I was professor of astronomy and higher mathematics at Abercrombie College. Most astronomers have a specialty, and mine was the study of the planet Mars, our nearest neighbor but one in the Sun's little family. When no important celestial phenom-

* *Atlantic Monthly*, 1886.

ena in other quarters demanded attention, it was on the ruddy disc of Mars that my telescope was oftenest focused. I was never weary of tracing the outlines of its continents and seas, its capes and islands, its bays and straits, its lakes and mountains. With intense interest I watched from week to week of the Martial winter the advance of the polar ice-cap toward the equator, and its corresponding retreat in the summer; testifying across the gulf of space as plainly as written words to the existence on that orb of a climate like our own. A specialty is always in danger of becoming an infatuation, and my interest in Mars, at the time of which I write, had grown to be more than strictly scientific. The impression of the nearness of this planet, heightened by the wonderful distinctness of its geography as seen through a powerful telescope, appeals strongly to the imagination of the astronomer. On fine evenings I used to spend hours, not so much critically observing as brooding over its radiant surface, till I could almost persuade myself that I saw the breakers dashing on the bold shore of Kepler Land, and heard the muffled thunder of avalanches descending the snow-clad mountains of Mitchell. No earthly landscape had the charm to hold my gaze of that far-off planet, whose oceans, to the unpracticed eye, seem but darker, and its continents lighter, spots and bands.

Astronomers have agreed in declaring that Mars is undoubtedly habitable by beings like ourselves, but, as may be supposed, I was not in a mood to be satisfied with considering it merely habitable. I allowed no sort of question that it was inhabited. What manner of beings these inhabitants might be I found a fascinating speculation. The variety of types appearing in mankind even on this small Earth makes it most presumptuous to assume that the denizens of different planets may not be characterized by diversities far profounder. Wherein such diversities, coupled with a general resemblance to man, might consist, whether in mere physical differences or in different mental laws, in the lack of certain of the great passional motors of men or the possession of quite others, were weird themes of never-failing attractions for my mind. The El Dorado visions with which the virgin mystery of the New World inspired the early Spanish explorers were tame and prosaic compared with the speculations which it was perfectly legitimate to indulge, when the problem was the conditions of life on another planet.

It was the time of the year when Mars is most favorably situated for observation, and, anxious not to lose an hour of the precious season, I had spent the greater part of several successive nights in the observatory. I believed that I had made some original observations as to the trend of the coast of Kepler Land between Lagrange Peninsula and Christie Bay, and it was to this spot that my observations were particularly directed.

On the fourth night other work detained me from the observing-chair till after midnight. When I had adjusted the instrument and took my first look at Mars, I remember being unable to restrain a cry of admiration. The planet was fairly dazzling. It seemed nearer and larger than I had ever seen it before, and its peculiar ruddiness more striking. In thirty years of observations, I recall, in fact, no occasion when the absence of exhalations in our atmosphere has coincided with such cloudlessness in that of Mars as on that night. I could plainly make out the white masses of vapor at the opposite edges of the lighted disc, which are the mists of its dawn and evening. The snowy mass of Mount Hall over against Kepler Land stood out with wonderful clearness, and I could unmistakably detect the blue tint of the ocean of De La Rue, which washes its base,—a feat of vision often, indeed, accomplished by star-gazers, though I had never done it to my complete satisfaction before.

I was impressed with the idea that if I ever made an original discovery in regard to Mars, it would be on that evening, and I believed that I should do it. I trembled with mingled exultation and anxiety, and was obliged to pause to recover my self-control. Finally, I placed my eye to the eye-piece, and directed my gaze upon the portion of the planet in which I was especially interested. My attention soon became fixed and absorbed much beyond my wont, when observing, and that itself implied no ordinary degree of abstraction. To all mental intents and purposes I was on Mars. Every faculty, every susceptibility of sense and intellect, seemed gradually to pass into the eye, and become concentrated in the act of gazing. Every atom of nerve and will power combined in the strain to see a little, and yet a little, and yet a little, clearer, farther, deeper.

The next thing I knew I was on the bed that stood in a corner of the observing-room, half raised on an elbow, and gazing intently at the door. It was broad daylight. Half a dozen men, including several of the professors and a doctor from the village, were around me. Some were trying to make me lie down, others were asking me what I wanted, while the doctor was urging me to drink some whiskey. Mechanically repelling their offices, I pointed to the door and ejaculated, "President Byxbee—coming," giving expression to the one idea which my dazed mind at that moment contained. And sure enough, even as I spoke the door opened, and the venerable head of the college, somewhat blown with climbing the steep stairway, stood on the threshold. With a sensation of prodigious relief, I fell back on my pillow.

It appeared that I had swooned while in the observing-chair, the night before, and had been found by the janitor in the morning, my head fallen forward on the telescope, as if still observing, but my body cold, rigid, pulseless, and apparently dead.

In a couple of days I was all right again, and should soon have forgotten the episode but for a very interesting conjecture which had suggested itself in connection with it. This was nothing less than that, while I lay in that swoon, I was in a conscious state outside and independent of the body, and in that state received impressions and exercised perceptive powers. For this extraordinary theory I had no other evidence than the fact of my knowledge in the moment of awaking that President Byxbee was coming up the stairs. But slight as this clue was, it seemed to me unmistakable in its significance. That knowledge was certainly in my mind on the instant of arousing from the swoon. It certainly could not have been there before I fell into the swoon. I must therefore have gained it in the mean time; that is to say, I must have been in a conscious, percipient state while my body was insensible.

If such had been the case, I reasoned that it was altogether unlikely that the trivial impression as to President Byxbee had been the only one which I had received in that state. It was far more probable that it had remained over in my mind, on waking from the swoon, merely because it was the latest of a series of impressions received while outside the body. That these impressions were of a kind most strange and startling, seeing that they were those of a disembodied soul exercising faculties more spiritual than those of the body, I could not doubt. The desire to know what they had been grew upon me, till it became a longing which left me no repose. It seemed intolerable that I should have secrets from myself, that my soul should withhold its experiences from my intellect. I would gladly have consented that the acquisitions of half my waking lifetime should be blotted out, if so be in exchange I might be shown the record of what I had seen and known during those hours of which my waking memory showed no trace. None the less for the conviction of its hopelessness, but rather all the more, as the perversity of our human nature will have it, the longing for this forbidden lore grew on me, till the hunger of Eve in the Garden was mine.

Constantly brooding over a desire that I felt to be vain, tantalized by the possession of a clue which only mocked me, my physical condition became at length affected. My health was disturbed and my rest at night was broken. A habit of walking in my sleep, from which I had not suffered since childhood, recurred, and caused me frequent inconvenience. Such had been, in general, my condition for some time, when I awoke one morning with the strangely weary sensation by which my body usually betrayed the secret of the impositions put upon it in sleep, of which otherwise I should often have suspected nothing. In going into the study connected with my chamber, I found a number of freshly written sheets on the desk. Astonished that any one should have been in my rooms while I slept, I was astounded, on looking more closely, to observe that the handwriting was my own. How much more than astounded I was on reading the matter that had been set down, the reader may judge if he shall peruse it. For these written sheets apparently contained the longed-for but despaired-of record of those hours when I was absent from the body. They were the lost chapter of my life; or rather, not lost at all, for it had been no part of my waking life, but a stolen chapter,—stolen from that sleep-memory on whose mysterious tablets may well be inscribed tales as much more marvelous than this as this is stranger than most stories.

It will be remembered that my last recollection before awaking in my bed, on the morning after the swoon, was of contemplating the coast of Kepler Land with an unusual concentration of attention. As well as I can judge,—and that is no better than any one else,—it is with the moment that my bodily powers succumbed and I became unconscious that the narrative which I found on my desk begins.

THE DOCUMENT FOUND ON MY DESK

Even had I not come as straight and swift as the beam of light that made my path, a glance about would have told me to what part of the universe I had fared. No earthly landscape could have been more familiar. I stood on the high coast of Kepler Land where it trends southward. A brisk westerly wind was blowing and the waves of the ocean of De La Rue were thundering at my feet, while the broad blue waters of Christie Bay stretched away to the southwest. Against the northern horizon, rising out of the ocean like a summer thunder-head, for which at first I mistook it, towered the far-distant, snowy summit of Mount Hall.

Even had the configuration of land and sea been less familiar, I should none the less have known that I stood on the planet whose ruddy hue is at once the admiration and puzzle of astronomers. Its explanation I now recognized in the tint of the atmosphere, a coloring comparable to the haze of Indian summer, except that its hue was a faint rose instead of purple. Like the Indian summer haze, it was impalpable, and without impeding the view bathed all objects near and far in a glamour not to be described. As the gaze turned upward, however, the deep blue of space so far overcame the roseate tint that one might fancy he were still on Earth.

As I looked about me I saw many men, women, and children. They were in no respect dissimilar, so far as I could see, to the men, women, and children of the Earth, save for something almost childlike in the untroubled serenity of their faces, unfurrowed as they were by any trace of care, of fear, or of anxiety. This extraordinary youthfulness of aspect made it difficult, indeed, save by careful scrutiny, to distinguish the young from the middle-aged, maturity from advanced years. Time seemed to have no tooth on Mars.

I was gazing about me, admiring this crimson-lighted world, and these people who appeared to hold happiness by a tenure so much firmer than men's, when I heard the words, "You are welcome," and, turning, saw that I had been accosted by a man with the stature and bearing of middle age, though his countenance, like the other faces which I had noted, wonderfully combined the strength of a man's with the serenity of a child's. I thanked him, and said,—

"You do not seem surprised to see me, though I certainly am to find myself here."

"Assuredly not," he answered. "I knew, of course, that I was to meet you to-day. And not only that, but I may say I am already in a sense acquainted with you, through a mutual friend, Professor Edgerly. He was here last month, and I met him at that time. We talked of you and your interest in our planet. I told him I expected you."

"Edgerly!" I exclaimed. "It is strange that he has said nothing of this to me. I meet him every day."

But I was reminded that it was in a dream that Edgerly, like myself, had visited Mars, and on awaking had recalled nothing of his experience, just as I should recall nothing of mine. When will man learn to interrogate the dream soul of the marvels it sees in its wanderings? Then he will no longer need to improve his telescopes to find out the secrets of the universe.

"Do your people visit the Earth in the same manner?" I asked my companion.

"Certainly," he replied; "but there we find no one able to recognize us and converse with us as I am conversing with you, although myself in the waking state. You, as yet, lack the knowledge we possess of the spiritual side of the human nature which we share with you."

"That knowledge must have enabled you to learn much more of the Earth than we know of you," I said.

"Indeed it has," he replied. "From visitors such as you, of whom we entertain a concourse constantly, we have acquired familiarity with your civilization, your history, your manners, and even your literature and languages. Have you not noticed that I am talking with you in English, which is certainly not a tongue indigenous to this planet?"

"Among so many wonders I scarcely observed that," I answered.

"For ages," pursued my companion, "we have been waiting for you to improve your telescopes so as to approximate the power of ours, after which communication between the planets would be easily established. The progress which you make is, however, so slow that we expect to wait ages yet."

"Indeed, I fear you will have to," I replied. "Our opticians already talk of having reached the limits of their art."

"Do not imagine that I spoke in any spirit of petulance," my companion resumed. "The slowness of your progress is not so remarkable to us as that you make any at all, burdened as you are by a disability so crushing that if we were in your place I fear we should sit down in utter despair."

"To what disability do you refer?" I asked. "You seem to be men like us."

"And so we are," was the reply, "save in one particular, but there the difference is tremendous. Endowed otherwise like us, you are destitute of the faculty of foresight, without which we should think our other faculties well-nigh valueless."

"Foresight!" I repeated. "Certainly you cannot mean that it is given you to know the future?"

"It is given not only to us," was the answer, "but, so far as we know, to all other intelligent beings of the universe except yourselves. Our positive knowledge extends only to our system of moons and planets and some of the nearer foreign systems, and it is conceivable that the remoter parts of the universe may harbor other blind races like your own; but it certainly seems unlikely that so strange and lamentable a spectacle should be duplicated. One such illustration of the extraordinary deprivations under which a rational existence may still be possible ought to suffice for the universe."

"But no one can know the future except by inspiration of God," I said.

"All our faculties are by inspiration of God," was the reply, "but there is surely nothing in foresight to cause it to be so regarded more than any other. Think a moment of the physical analogy of the case. Your eyes are placed in the front of your heads. You would deem it an odd mistake if they were placed behind. That would appear to you an arrangement calculated to defeat their purpose. Does it not seem equally rational that the mental vision should range forward, as it does with us, illuminating the path one is to take, rather than backward, as with you, revealing only the course you have already trodden, and therefore have no more concern with? But it is no doubt a merciful provision of Providence that renders you unable to realize the grotesqueness of your predicament, as it appears to us."

"But the future is eternal!" I exclaimed. "How can a finite mind grasp it?"

"Our foreknowledge implies only human faculties," was the reply. "It is limited to our individual careers on this planet. Each of us foresees the course of his own life, but not that of other lives, except so far as they are involved with his."

"That such a power as you describe could be combined with merely human faculties is more than our philosophers have ever dared to dream," I said. "And yet who shall say, after all, that it is not in mercy that God has denied it to us? If it is a happiness, as it must be, to foresee one's happiness, it must be most depressing to foresee one's sorrows, failures, yes, and even one's death. For if you foresee your lives to the end, you must anticipate the hour and manner of your death,—is it not so?"

"Most assuredly," was the reply. "Living would be a very precarious business, were we uninformed of its limit. Your ignorance of the time of your death impresses us as one of the saddest features of your condition."

"And by us," I answered, "it is held to be one of the most merciful."

"Foreknowledge of your death would not, indeed, prevent your dying once," continued my companion, "but it would deliver you from the thousand deaths you suffer through uncertainty whether you can safely count on the passing day. It is not the death you die, but these many deaths you do not die, which shadow your existence. Poor blindfolded creatures that you are, cringing at every step in apprehension of the stroke that perhaps is not to fall till old age, never raising a cup to your lips with the knowledge that you will live to quaff it, never sure that you will meet again the friend you part with for an hour, from whose hearts no happiness suffices to banish the chill of an ever-present dread, what idea can you form of the Godlike security with which we enjoy our lives and the lives of those we love! You have a saying on earth, 'To-morrow belongs to God;' but here to-morrow belongs to us, even as to-day. To you, for some inscrutable purpose, He sees fit to dole out life moment by moment, with no assurance that each is not to be the last. To us He gives a lifetime at once, fifty, sixty, seventy years,—a divine gift indeed. A life such as yours would, I fear, seem of little value to us; for such a life, however long, is but a moment long, since that is all you can count on."

"And yet," I answered, "though knowledge of the duration of your lives may give you an enviable feeling of confidence while the end is far off, is that not more than offset by the daily growing weight with which the expectation of the end, as it draws near, must press upon your minds?"

"On the contrary," was the response, "death, never an object of fear, as it draws nearer becomes more and more a matter of indifference to the moribund. It is because you live in the past that death is grievous to you. All your knowledge, all your affections, all your interests, are rooted in the past, and on that account, as life lengthens, it strengthens its hold on you, and memory becomes a more precious possession. We, on the contrary, despise the past, and never dwell upon it. Memory with us, far from being the morbid and monstrous growth it is with you, is scarcely more than a rudimentary faculty. We live wholly in the future and the present. What with foretaste and actual taste, our experiences, whether pleasant or painful, are exhausted of interest by the time they are past. The accumulated treasures of memory, which you relinquish so painfully in death, we count no loss at all. Our minds being fed wholly from the future, we think and feel only as we anticipate; and so, as the dying man's future contracts, there is less and less about which he can occupy his thoughts. His interest in life diminishes as the ideas which it suggests grow fewer, till at the last death finds him with his mind a *tabula rasa,* as with you at birth. In a word, his concern with life is reduced to a vanishing point before he is called on to give it up. In dying he leaves nothing behind."

"And the after-death," I asked,—"is there no fear of that?"

"Surely," was the reply, "it is not necessary for me to say that a fear which affects only the more ignorant on Earth is not known at all to us, and would be counted blasphemous. Moreover, as I have said, our foresight is limited to our lives on this planet. Any speculation beyond them would be purely conjectural, and our minds are repelled by the slightest taint of uncertainty. To us the conjectural and the unthinkable may be called almost the same."

"But even if you do not fear death for itself," I said, "you have hearts to break. Is there no pain when the ties of love are sundered?"

"Love and death are not foes on our planet," was the reply. "There are no tears by the bedsides of our dying. The same beneficent law which makes it so easy for us to give up life forbids us to mourn the friends we leave, or them to mourn us. With you, it is the intercourse you have had with friends that is the source of your tenderness for them. With us, it is the anticipation of the intercourse we shall enjoy which is the foundation of fondness. As our friends vanish from our future with the approach of their death, the effect on our thoughts and affections is as it would be with you if you forgot them by lapse of time. As our dying friends grow more and more indifferent to us, we, by operation of the same law of our nature, become indifferent to them, till at the last we are scarcely more than kindly and sympathetic watchers about the beds of those who regard us equally without keen emotions. So at last God gently unwinds instead of breaking the bands that bind our hearts together, and makes death as painless to the surviving as to the dying. Relations meant to produce our happiness are not the means also of torturing us, as with you. Love means joy, and that alone, to us, instead of blessing our lives for a while only to desolate them later on, compelling us to pay with a distinct and separate pang for every thrill of tenderness, exacting a tear for every smile."

"There are other partings than those of death. Are these, too, without sorrow for you?" I asked.

"Assuredly," was the reply. "Can you not see that so it must needs be with beings freed by foresight from the disease of memory? All the sorrow of parting, as of dying, comes with you from the backward vision which precludes you from beholding your happiness till it is past. Suppose your life destined to be blessed by a happy friendship. If you could know it beforehand, it would be a joyous expectation, brightening the intervening years and cheering you as you traversed desolate periods. But no; not till you meet the one who is to be your friend do you know of him. Nor do you guess even then what he is to be to you, that you may embrace him at first sight. Your meeting is cold and indifferent. It is long before the fire is fairly kindled between you, and then it is already time for parting. Now, indeed, the fire burns well, but henceforth it must consume your heart. Not till they are dead or gone do you fully realize how dear your friends were and how sweet was their companionship. But we—we see our friends afar off coming to meet us, smiling already in our eyes, years before our ways meet. We greet them at first meeting, not coldly, not uncertainly, but with exultant kisses, in an ecstasy of joy. They enter at once into the full possession of hearts long warmed and lighted for them. We meet with that delirium of tenderness with which you part. And when to us at last the time of parting comes, it only means that we are to contribute to each other's happiness no longer. We are not doomed, like you, in parting, to take away with us the delight we brought our friends, leaving the ache of bereavement in its place, so that their last state is worse than their first. Parting here is like meeting with you, calm and unimpassioned. The joys of anticipation and possession are the only food of love with us, and therefore Love always wears a smiling face. With you he feeds on dead joys, past happiness, which are likewise the sustenance of sorrow. No wonder love and sorrow are so much alike on Earth. It is a common saying among us that, were it not for the spectacle of the Earth, the rest of the worlds would be unable to appreciate the goodness of God to them; and who can say that this is not the reason the piteous sight is set before us?"

"You have told me marvelous things," I said, after I had reflected. "It is, indeed, but reasonable that such a race as yours should look down with wondering pity on the Earth. And yet, before I grant so much, I want to ask you one question. There is known in our world a certain sweet madness, under the influence of which we forget all that is untoward in our lot, and would not change it for a god's. So far is this sweet madness regarded by men as a compensation, and more than a compensation, for all their miseries that if you know not love as we know it, if this loss be the price you have paid for your divine foresight, we think ourselves more favored of God than you. Confess that love, with its reserves, its surprises, its mysteries, its revelations, is necessarily incompatible with a foresight which weighs and measures every experience in advance."

"Of love's surprises we certainly know nothing," was the reply. "It is believed by our philosophers that the slightest surprise would kill beings of our constitution like lightning; though of course this is merely theory, for it is only by the study of Earthly conditions that we are able to form an idea of what surprise is like. Your power to endure the constant buffetings of the unexpected is a matter of supreme amazement to us; nor, according to our ideas, is there any difference between what you call pleasant and painful surprises. You see, then, that we cannot envy you these surprises of love which you find so sweet, for to us they would be fatal. For the rest, there is no form of happiness which foresight is so well calculated to enhance as that of love. Let me explain to you how this befalls. As the growing boy begins to be sensible of the charms of woman, he finds himself, as I dare say it is with you, preferring some type of face and form to others. He dreams oftenest of fair hair, or may be of dark, of blue eyes or brown. As the years go on, his fancy, brooding over what seems to it the best and loveliest of every type, is constantly adding to this dream-face, this shadowy form, traits and lineaments, hues and contours, till at last the picture is complete, and he becomes aware that on his heart thus subtly has been depicted the likeness of the maiden destined for his arms.

"It may be years before he is to see her, but now begins with him one of the sweetest offices of love, one to you unknown. Youth on Earth is a stormy period of passion, chafing in restraint or rioting in excess. But the very passion whose awaking makes this time so critical with you is here a reforming and educating influence, to whose gentle and potent sway we gladly confide our children. The temptations which lead your young men astray have no hold on a youth of our happy planet. He hoards the treasures of his heart for its coming mistress. Of her alone he thinks, and to her all his vows are made. The thought of license would be treason to his sovereign lady, whose right to all the revenues of his being he joyfully owns. To rob her, to abate her high prerogatives, would be to impoverish, to insult, himself; for she is to be his, and her honor, her glory, are his own. Through all this time that he dreams of her by night and day, the exquisite reward of his devotion is the knowledge that she is aware of him as he of her, and that in the inmost shrine of a maiden heart his image is set up to receive the incense of a tenderness that needs not to restrain itself through fear of possible cross or separation.

"In due time their converging lives come together. The lovers meet, gaze a moment into each other's eyes, then throw themselves each on the other's breast. The maiden has all the charms that ever stirred the blood of an Earthly lover, but there is another glamour over her which the eyes of Earthly lovers are shut to,—the glamour of the future. In the blushing girl her lover sees the fond and faithful wife, in the blithe maiden the patient, pain-consecrated mother. On the virgin's breast he beholds his children. He is prescient, even as his lips take the first-fruits of hers, of the future years during which she is to be his companion, his ever-present solace, his chief portion of God's goodness. We have read some of your romances describing love as you know it on Earth, and I must confess, my friend, we find them very dull.

"I hope," he added, as I did not at once speak, "that I shall not offend you by saying we find them also objectionable. Your literature possesses in general an interest for us in the picture it presents of the curiously inverted life which the lack of foresight compels you to lead. It is a study especially prized for the development of the imagination, on account of the difficulty of conceiving conditions so opposed to those of intelligent beings in general. But our women do not read your romances. The notion that a man or woman should ever conceive the idea of marrying a person other than the one whose husband or wife he or she is destined to be is profoundly shocking to our habits of thought. No doubt you will say that such instances are rare among you, but if your novels are faithful pictures of your life, they are at least not unknown. That these situations are inevitable under the conditions of earthly life we are well aware, and judge you accordingly; but it is needless that the minds of our maidens should be pained by the knowledge that there anywhere exists a world where such travesties upon the sacredness of marriage are possible.

"There is, however, another reason why we discourage the use of your books by our young people, and that is the profound effect of sadness, to a race accustomed to view all things in the morning glow of the future, of a literature written in the past tense and relating exclusively to things that are ended."

"And how do you write of things that are past except in the past tense?" I asked.

"We write of the past when it is still the future, and of course in the future tense," was the reply. "If our historians were to wait till after the events to describe them, not alone would nobody care to read about things already done, but the histories themselves would probably be inaccurate; for memory, as I have said, is a very slightly developed faculty with us, and quite too indistinct to be trustworthy. Should the Earth ever establish communication with us, you will find our histories of interest; for our planet, being smaller, cooled and was peopled ages before yours, and our astronomical records contain minute accounts of the Earth from the time it was a fluid mass. Your geologists and biologists may yet find a mine of information here."

In the course of our further conversation it came out that, as a consequence of foresight, some of the commonest emotions of human nature are unknown on Mars. They for whom the future has no mystery can, of course, know neither hope nor fear. Moreover, every one being assured what he shall attain to and what not, there can be no such thing as rivalship, or emulation, or any sort of competition in any respect; and therefore all the brood of heart-burnings and hatreds, engendered on Earth by the strife of man with man, is unknown to the people of Mars, save from the study of our planet. When I asked if there were not, after all, a lack of spontaneity, of sense of freedom, in leading lives fixed in all details beforehand, I was reminded that there was no difference in that respect between the lives of the people of Earth and of Mars, both alike being according to God's will in every particular. We knew that will only after the event, they before,—that was all. For the rest, God moved them through their wills as He did us, so that they had no more sense of compulsion in what they did than we on Earth have in carrying out an anticipated line of action, in cases where our anticipations chance to be correct. Of the absorbing interest which the study of the plan of their future lives possessed for the people of Mars, my companion spoke eloquently. It was, he said, like the fascination to a mathematician of a most elaborate and exquisite demonstration, a perfect algebraical equation, with the glowing realities of life in place of figures and symbols.

When I asked if it never occurred to them to wish their futures different, he replied that such a question could only have been asked by one from the Earth. No one could have foresight, or clearly believe that God had it, without realizing that the future is as incapable of being changed as the past. And not only this, but to foresee events was to foresee their logical necessity so clearly that to desire them different was as impossible as seriously to wish that two and two made five instead of four. No person could ever thoughtfully wish anything different, for so closely are all things, the small with the great, woven together by God that to draw out the smallest thread would unravel creation through all eternity.

While we had talked the afternoon had waned, and the sun had sunk below the horizon, the roseate atmosphere of the planet imparting a splendor to the cloud coloring, and a glory to the land and sea scape, never paralleled by an earthly sunset. Already the familiar constellations appearing in the sky reminded me how near, after all, I was to the Earth, for with the unassisted eye I could not detect the slightest variation in their position. Nevertheless, there was one wholly novel feature in the heavens, for many of the host of asteroids which circle in the zone between Mars and Jupiter were vividly visible to the naked eye. But the spectacle that chiefly held my gaze was the Earth, swimming low on the verge of the horizon. Its disc, twice as large as that of any star or planet as seen from the Earth, flashed with a brilliancy like that of Venus.

"It is, indeed, a lovely sight," said my companion, "although to me always a melancholy one, from the contrast suggested between the radiance of the orb and the benighted condition of its inhabitants. We call it 'The Blindman's World.' " As he spoke he turned toward a curious structure which stood near us, though I had not before particularly observed it.

"What is that?" I asked.

"It is one of our telescopes," he replied. "I am going to let you take a look, if you choose, at your home, and test for yourself the powers of which I have boasted;" and having adjusted the instrument to his satisfaction, he showed me where to apply my eye to what answered to the eye-piece.

I could not repress an exclamation of amazement, for truly he had exaggerated nothing. The little college town which was my home lay spread out before me, seemingly almost as near as when I looked down upon it from my observatory windows. It was early morning, and the village was waking up. The milkmen were going their rounds, and workmen, with their dinner-pails, where hurrying along the streets. The early train was just leaving the railroad station. I could see the puffs from the smoke-stack, and the jets from the cylinders. It was strange not to hear the hissing of the steam, so near I seemed. There were the college buildings on the hill, the long rows of windows flashing back the level sunbeams. I could tell the time by the college clock. It struck me that there was an unusual bustle around the buildings, considering the earliness of the hour. A crowd of men stood about the door of the observatory, and many others were hurrying across the campus in that direction. Among them I recognized President Byxbee, accompanied by the college janitor. As I gazed they reached the observatory, and, passing through the group about the door, entered the building. The president was evidently going up to my quarters. At this it flashed over me quite suddenly that all this bustle was on my account. I recalled how it was that I came to be on Mars, and in what condition I had left affairs in the observatory. It was high time I were back there to look after myself.

Here abruptly ended the extraordinary document which I found that morning on my desk. That it is the authentic record of the conditions of life in another world which it purports to be I do not expect the reader to believe. He will no doubt explain it as another of the curious freaks of somnambulism set down in the books. Probably it was merely that, possibly it was something more. I do not pretend to decide the question. I have told all the facts of the case, and have no better means for forming an opinion than the reader. Nor do I know, even if I fully believed it the true account it seems to be, that it would have affected my imagination much more strongly than it has. That story of another world has, in a word, put me out of joint with ours. The readiness with which my mind has adapted itself to the Martial point of view concerning the Earth has been a singular experience. The lack of foresight among the human faculties, a lack I had scarcely thought of before, now impresses me, ever more deeply, as a fact out of harmony with the rest of our nature, belying its promise,—a moral mutilation, a deprivation arbitrary and unaccountable. The spectacle of a race doomed to walk backward, beholding only what has gone by, assured only of what is past and dead, comes over me from time to time with a sadly fantastical effect which I cannot describe. I dream of a world where love always wears a smile, where the partings are as tearless as our meetings, and death is king no more. I have a fancy, which I like to cherish, that the people of that happy sphere, fancied though it may be, represent the ideal and normal type of our race, as perhaps it once was, as perhaps it may yet be again.

FITZ-JAMES O'BRIEN AND SCIENCE FICTION

Fitz-James O'Brien was a profligate, prodigal, dashing, versifying Irishman who came to New York in 1852, became one of the leading Bohemians of ante-bellum Gotham, and died in 1862 from an inadequately treated minor wound inflicted in an audaciously heroic duel with a Confederate officer. A minor, time-serving magazinist, O'Brien would long ago have been forgotten if he had not written a handful of brilliantly original short stories. These stories range from wildly fantastic expressionistic surrealism—such as "From Hand to Mouth," in which the narrator sits in the Hotel de Coup d'œil surrounded by countless disembodied but functioning eyes, ears, mouths, and hands—through realistic fantasy—such as "The Wondersmith," in which a band of gypsies manufactures an army of toy soldiers, equips them with poisoned weapons, gives them souls, and almost succeeds in having them kill all the Christian children at Christmas, and "The Lost Room," in which the narrator has his room literally taken away by a pair of apparently fiendish, orgiastically carousing couples—to science fiction—such as "How I Overcame My Gravity," "What Was It? A Mystery," and "The Diamond Lens." O'Brien's significance as a writer lies in this science fiction.

"How I Overcame My Gravity," published in *Harper's*

Monthly two years after O'Brien's death, is an interesting but rather slight tale undercut by the use of dream to explain away its action, if that is what really happens. The mad-inventor narrator, who believes he has already solved "the problem of aerial locomotion" by enunciating his "grand principle of progression by means of atmospheric inclined planes," now tells of his first meeting with the toy gyroscope, which he describes, in great detail, as a wondrous and strange invention. He immediately sets about to construct a gyroscopic vehicle, which, launched by a catapulting mechanism, will carry him vast distances by suborbital flight. A group of friends watch him launch his extremely rapidly spinning gyroscopic capsule (the setup for his inner-space travel strikingly resembles the initial setup for the time travel in Wells's *The Time Machine*). After launching, the narrator realizes that he had not made the capsule strong enough to withstand the centrifugal forces he is employing, the capsule disintegrates at apogee, and he awakes to find himself clutching his wife's silver tea-urn. The story has two interesting aspects. First, it contains a detailed, reasonably accurate, and significant technological speculation; the principle of gyroscopic stability at extremely high speeds is of course the basis for modern inertial guidance systems in both airplanes and rockets. Secondly, and more significantly for science fiction if not for science, the dream device may possibly be much more functional than it would at first appear, for if the technological adventure is a dream, there is no way of determining when the dream began. That is, because the beginning of the dream cannot be distinguished from the rest of the narrator's life, one is not at all sure that at the end he has awakened into a less dream-like reality. This is not then the kind of dream device which makes the science fiction a mere dream (as in Mary Griffith's *Three Hundred Years Hence* or Edward Page Mitchell's "The Tachypomp"); it is more like those fictional dreams which suggest that anything may be a dream (as in Hawthorne's "Young Goodman Brown,"

Poe's *Narrative of Arthur Gordon Pym,* and Twain's *The Great Dark.*

"What Was It? A Mystery" (*Harper's Monthly,* 1859) is the prototype for the science fiction of the inexplainable alien being who can be cataloged neither as ghost, freak, nor visitor from another planet or dimension. The essential characteristic of this kind of being is that he represents a mystery, violating at least one of our habitual ways of perceiving phenomena. This particular being cannot be seen, and O'Brien provides only a pure speculation to account for him:

> "Here is a solid body which we touch, but which we cannot see. The fact is so unusual that it strikes us with terror. Is there no parallel, though, for such a phenomenon? Take a piece of pure glass. It is tangible and transparent. A certain chemical coarseness is all that prevents its being so entirely transparent as to be totally invisible. It is not *theoretically impossible,* mind you, to make a glass which shall not reflect a single ray of light,—a glass so pure and homogeneous in its atoms that the rays from the sun will pass through it as they do through the air, refracted but not reflected. We do not see the air, and yet we feel it."

The possible influence of "What Was It?" on de Maupassant's "The Horla" (1887) and its almost certain influence on Bierce's "The Damned Thing" (ante 1896) and H. P. Lovecraft's "The Color Out of Space" (1927) is not as significant as the common direction to which all these tales point, toward open-ended, rather than closed, speculation.

"The Diamond Lens," published in the *Atlantic* the year before, is far and away O'Brien's most original, most influential, and best work. In this story O'Brien opened up to fiction all of the dimensions of the microscopic worlds. The microscope may have suggested the Lilliputians of *Gulliver's Travels,* but they are certainly not microscopic beings. Perhaps before "The Diamond Lens" there were fictional plunges into the microscopic worlds, but they have not as yet come to light. "Microcosmus," a slightly earlier work by O'Brien's friend William North, has long since been lost. When "The Diamond Lens" appeared, O'Brien was accused of having stolen it from "Microcosmus"; his denial, printed in the New York *Evening Post*, January 20, 1858, seems convincing— and is interesting for other reasons:

> In the composition of "The Diamond Lens" I derived considerable aid from Doctor J. D. Whelpley of this city, himself an accomplished writer and practical microscopist. To him I am indebted for some valuable suggestions connected with the scientific mechanism of the plot, and he was a witness of the gradual development of the story under my hands.

This statement suggests the extent to which O'Brien was concerned with the scientific veracity of his story, and it also points to the existence of an early team approach to the writing of science fiction, something which has recently become common. And J. D. Whelpley's "The Atoms of Chladni" appeared just two years after "The Diamond Lens."

Scientific veracity in "The Diamond Lens" comes from O'Brien's skillful use of the history and principles of microscopes. In fact, a diamond lens had actually been used for microscopic investigations, as described in 1827 in *The Quarterly Journal of Science* and *The Franklin Journal*. Of course O'Brien could hardly be expected to give a scientific explanation for Animula. This would have to wait for the settlers who were to come behind "The Diamond Lens"—such as Theodore Sturgeon's "Microcosmic God" (1941), in which the scientist breeds and develops an advanced society of humanoid microbes, and James Blish's *The Seedling Stars* (1957), in which manipulated human genes produce a microscopic race of men (some of whom discover an Animula-like figure of their own size). Before genetic manipulation came along, the followers of "The Diamond Lens" tried all kinds of fantastic ways to break through into the microscopic worlds, from Twain's *The Great Dark* (discussed on pp. 375-8), which uses dream to make the microscopic world become the real world, to Henry Hasse's "He Who Shrank" (1936), which uses an unexplained chemical to propel the ever-shrinking protagonist through microscopic worlds within worlds within worlds without end.

Much praised, much imitated, "The Diamond Lens" has yet to be explicated. Perhaps the best place to begin is in the fantasy of childhood:

> I had a little husband, no bigger than my thumb;
> I put him in a pint-pot, and there I bid him drum.
> I gave him some garters, to garter up his hose,
> And a little pocket handkerchief to wipe his pretty nose.
>
> Mother Goose

Or, as Humbert Humbert puts it in *Lolita*, "What I had madly possessed was not she, but my own creation, another fanciful Lolita." O'Brien's real importance lies not just in opening up to fiction the microscopic dimensions of existence but in opening up to fiction the psychological dimensions of what we can perceive in the microscopic dimensions.

The hallucinatory nature of the objective world was certainly a common subject of fiction before "The Diamond Lens," but O'Brien may have been the first to dramatize what happens when the scientific vision becomes more and more microscopically precise until it approaches perfection. On one hand then lies the Scylla of the psyche, unconsciously projecting one's own image into objects. On the other hand lies the Charybdis of the self, ultimately finding one's own image in objects, as described in Sir Arthur Eddington's summary of modern physics:

> ... we have found that where science has progressed the farthest, the mind has but regained from nature that which the mind has put into nature.

> We have found a strange foot-print on the shores of the unknown. We have devised profound theories, one after another, to account for its origin. At last, we have succeeded in reconstructing the creature that made the foot-print. And Lo! it is our own.
>
> *Space, Time and Gravitation* (1959 ed.)

The question, as O'Brien so brilliantly perceived, is how to keep the infinitude of external dimensions from absorbing or being absorbed by the infinitude of internal dimensions. Or, as the narrator of "The Diamond Lens" puts it in his opening sentence: "From a very early period of my life the entire bent of my inclinations had been towards microscopic investigations." The conventional interpretation of the story has it as the drama of a man who falls in love with the beautiful girl he finds living in a droplet of water. This interpretation overlooks the most significant dimensions of this microscopic discovery, for O'Brien is dealing as much with the world of the mind as with the world on the slide. What the narrator sees as he peers into the minute hole in his diamond lens and perceives a refracted image of beauty is the heart of all ambiguities inherent in the relations between the subjective and objective worlds.

The narrator, one immediately learns, typifies the isolated, asexual, introverted, dehumanized, peeper-in at life, toying with objects in a narcissistic frenzy. He is much like Owen Warland of "The Artist of the Beautiful," who " 'would turn the sun out of its orbit and derange the whole course of time, if . . . his ingenuity could grasp anything bigger than a child's toy,' " and who finds a real woman too gross. He is also much like Aylmer, who is revolted by the most beautiful woman in the world because he is fatally fascinated with an image of ideal femininity projected from his own mind. After falling in love with his microscopic image of feminine perfection, the narrator of "The Diamond Lens" sees in the *danseuse* reputed to be "the most beautiful and graceful woman in the world" nothing but "muscular limbs," "thick ankles," "cavernous eyes," "crudely painted cheeks," and "gross, discordant movements." "With an exclamation of disgust that drew every eye" upon him, he flees in the middle of her *pas-de-fascination* to return "home to feast my eyes once more on the lovely form of my sylph."

O'Brien uses two myths to define the relation between the narrator and his Animula, and, by so doing, redefines these myths in terms of his science fiction. The first is the myth of Eden. Before the appearance of Animula in his microscopic world, the narrator is a willfully isolated kind of Adam: "I was like one who, having discovered the ancient Eden still existing in all its primitive glory, should resolve to enjoy it in solitude. . . ." But as Eve was made out of Adam, so the narrator begins the process:

> Like all active microscopists, I gave my imagination full play. Indeed, it is a common complaint against many such, that they supply the defects of their instruments with the creations of their brains. I imagined depths beyond depths in Nature. . . .

Finally, after letting himself become possessed by a pair of fiends, a fiendish vision, and a fiendish suggestion, he finds a mate in his Eden:

> It was a female human shape. When I say "human," I mean it possessed the outlines of humanity,—but there the analogy ends. Its adorable beauty lifted it illimitable heights beyond the loveliest daughter of Adam.

The loveliest daughter of Adam did not come from the normal procreative process; the first female human shape was a piece of himself.

The Eden myth describes the cleavage of man into man and woman. The other myth O'Brien employs dramatizes the reverse, the joining of a woman and a man into one being—the archetypal hermaphrodite. O'Brien is quite explicit about relating Animula to Salmacis, the narrator to Hermaphroditus: "She lay at full length in the transparent medium, in which she supported herself with ease, and gambolled with the enchanting grace that the nymph Salmacis might have exhibited when she sought to conquer the modest Hermaphroditus." The source of this myth is Ovid's *Metamorphoses*, Book IV, lines 285-389, which is well worth examining in relation to "The Diamond Lens," for it provides much of the basic structure of the story and displays in a naked form many of its central concerns.

The myth is the explanation of why the waters of a particular fountain make men weak, feeble, and effeminate. Hermaphroditus leaves his native home to seek out unknown places. He comes upon a lovely pool inhabited by a beautiful nymph who burns with desire for him. She lures him into the pool by hiding from his sight, then strips, swims to him, and wraps her naked body around his. He struggles to escape, but she implores the gods never to let them be separated; then:

> Their mingled bodies become a single form,
> As the grafted twig and bark join themselves,
> Growing together into maturity.
> So they, embraced, their limbs entwined, become
> Not two, but a double form, not a girl
> Nor a boy, but neither and yet either.

The notion that this myth was a variant of the creation of Eve from Adam dates back at least to 1632, to George Sandys's commentary in his translation of the *Metamorphoses*. Sandys also pointed out the resemblance of both stories to Plato's myth that man was first created hermaphroditic, then split into male and female, and ever since has yearned to return to the original unity. By the time of "The Diamond Lens," some mythographers were explaining all these myths in terms of a primeval belief in a hermaphroditic god who created the universe out of itself. Under

"Hermaphroditus," Charles Anthon's *Classical Dictionary*, a standard mid-nineteenth-century reference work, summarizes the leading authorities on the myth:

> The doctrine of androgynous divinities lies at the very foundation of the earliest pagan worship. The union of the two sexes was regarded by the earliest priesthoods as a symbol of the generation of the universe. . . . [they taught that] before the creation, the productive power existed alone in the immensity of space. When the process of creation commenced, this power divided itself into two portions, and discharged the functions of an active and a passive being, a male and a female. . . . the priests changed their ordinary vestments, and assumed those of the other sex in the ceremonies instituted in honour of these gods, for the purpose of expressing their double nature.

The narrator, absorbed into his "newly discovered world," does not know "how long this worship of my strange divinity went on." Whether or not O'Brien is dealing with the alleged sources of the Hermaphroditus-Salmacis myth, the dimensions of "The Diamond Lens" are not only microscopic and psychological but mythic as well.

"The Diamond Lens" ends by subsuming both myths to which it refers—Adam and Eve, Hermaphroditus and Salmacis—and possibly their common mythic sources, under the fantasies of the primitive time of individual life. The narrator, exposed to his vision and exposed by it, reverts first to childhood ("I sobbed myself to sleep like a child"), then to infancy ("I determined to make some effort to wean myself"), and finally to virtual pre-existence:

> When I awoke out of a trance of many hours, I found myself lying amid the wreck of my instrument, myself as shattered in mind and body as it. I crawled feebly to my bed, from which I did not rise for months.

FITZ-JAMES O'BRIEN
The Diamond Lens *

I

THE BENDING OF THE TWIG

From a very early period of my life the entire bent of my inclinations had been towards microscopic investigations. When I was not more than ten years old, a distant relative of our family, hoping to astonish my inexperience, constructed a simple microscope for me, by drilling in a disk of copper a small hole, in which a drop of pure water was sustained by capillary attraction. This very primitive apparatus, magnifying some fifty diameters, presented, it is true, only indistinct and imperfect forms, but still sufficiently wonderful to work up my imagination to a preternatural state of excitement.

Seeing me so interested in this rude instrument, my cousin explained to me all that he knew about the principles of the microscope, related to me a few of the wonders which had been accomplished through its agency, and ended by promising to send me one regularly constructed, immediately on his return to the city. I counted the days, the hours, the minutes, that intervened between that promise and his departure.

Meantime I was not idle. Every transparent substance that bore the remotest resemblance to a lens I eagerly seized upon, and employed in vain attempts to realize that instrument, the theory of whose construction I as yet only vaguely comprehended. All panes of glass containing those oblate spheroidal knots familiarly known as "bull's eyes" were ruthlessly destroyed, in the hope of obtaining lenses of marvellous power. I even went

* *Atlantic Monthly*, 1858.

so far as to extract the crystalline humor from the eyes of fishes and animals, and endeavored to press it into the microscopic service. I plead guilty to having stolen the glasses from my Aunt Agatha's spectacles, with a dim idea of grinding them into lenses of wondrous magnifying properties,—in which attempt it is scarcely necessary to say that I totally failed.

At last the promised instrument came. It was of that order known as Field's simple microscope, and had cost perhaps about fifteen dollars. As far as educational purposes went, a better apparatus could not have been selected. Accompanying it was a small treatise on the microscope,—its history, uses, and discoveries. I comprehended then for the first time the "Arabian Nights Entertainments." The dull veil of ordinary existence that hung across the world seemed suddenly to roll away, and to lay bare a land of enchantments. I felt towards my companions as the seer might feel towards the ordinary masses of men. I held conversations with Nature in a tongue which they could not understand. I was in daily communication with living wonders, such as they never imagined in their wildest visions. I penetrated beyond the external portal of things, and roamed through the sanctuaries. Where they beheld only a drop of rain slowly rolling down the window-glass, I saw a universe of beings animated with all the passions common to physical life, and convulsing their minute sphere with struggles as fierce and protracted as those of men. In the common spots of mould, which my mother, good housekeeper that she was, fiercely scooped away from her jam pots, there abode for me, under the name of mildew, enchanted gardens, filled with dells and avenues of the densest foliage and most astonishing verdure, while from the fantastic boughs of these microscopic forests hung strange fruits glittering with green, and silver, and gold.

It was no scientific thirst that at this time filled my mind. It was the pure enjoyment of a poet to whom a world of wonders has been disclosed. I talked of my solitary pleasures to none. Alone with my microscope, I dimmed my sight, day after day and night after night, poring over the marvels which it unfolded to me. I was like one who, having discovered the ancient Eden still existing in all its primitive glory, should resolve to enjoy it in solitude, and never betray to mortal the secret of its locality.

The rod of my life was bent at this moment. I destined myself to be a microscopist.

Of course, like every novice, I fancied myself a discoverer. I was ignorant at the time of the thousands of acute intellects engaged in the same pursuit as myself, and with the advantage of instruments a thousand times more powerful than mine. The names of Leeuwenhoek, Williamson, Spencer, Ehrenberg, Schultz, Dujardin, Schact, and Schleiden were then entirely unknown to me, or if known, I was ignorant of their patient and wonderful researches. In every fresh specimen of cryptogamia which I placed beneath my instrument I believed that I discovered wonders of which the world was as yet ignorant. I remember well the thrill of delight and admiration that shot through me the first time that I discovered the common wheel animalcule (*Rotifera vulgaris*) expanding and contracting its flexible spokes, and seemingly rotating through the water. Alas! as I grew older, and obtained some works treating of my favorite study, I found that I was only on the threshold of a science to the investigation of which some of the greatest men of the age were devoting their lives and intellects.

As I grew up, my parents, who saw but little likelihood of anything practical resulting from the examination of bits of moss and drops of water through a brass tube and a piece of glass, were anxious that I should choose a profession. It was their desire that I should enter the counting-house of my uncle, Ethan Blake, a prosperous merchant, who carried on business in New York. This suggestion I decisively combated. I had no taste for trade; I should only make a failure; in short, I refused to become a merchant.

But it was necessary for me to select some pursuit. My parents were staid New England people, who insisted on the necessity of labor; and therefore, although, thanks to the bequest of my poor Aunt Agatha, I should, on coming of age, inherit a small fortune sufficient to place me above want, it was decided that, instead of waiting for this, I should act the nobler part, and employ the intervening years in rendering myself independent.

After much cogitation I complied with the wishes of my family, and selected a profession. I determined to study medicine at the New York Academy. This disposition of my future suited me. A removal from my relatives would enable me to dispose of my time as I pleased without fear of detection. As long as I paid my Academy fees, I might shirk attending the lectures if I chose; and, as I never had the remotest intention of standing an examination, there was no danger of my being "plucked." Besides, a metropolis was the place for me. There I could obtain excellent instruments, the newest publications, intimacy with men of pursuits kindred with my own,—in short, all things necessary to insure a profitable devotion of my life to my beloved science. I had an abundance of money, few desires that were not bounded by my illuminating mirror on one side and my object-glass on the other; what, therefore, was to prevent my becoming an illustrious investigator of the veiled worlds? It was with the most buoyant hopes that I left my New England home and established myself in New York.

II

THE LONGING OF A MAN OF SCIENCE

My first step, of course, was to find suitable apartments. These I obtained, after a couple of days' search, in Fourth Avenue; a very pretty second-floor unfurnished, containing sitting-room, bedroom, and a smaller apartment which I intended to fit up as a laboratory. I furnished my lodgings simply, but rather elegantly, and then devoted all my energies to the adornment of the temple of my worship. I visited Pike, the celebrated optician, and passed in review his splendid collection of microscopes,—Field's Compound, Hingham's, Spencer's, Nachet's Binocular (that founded on the principles of the stereoscope), and at length fixed upon that form known as Spencer's Trunnion Microscope, as combining the greatest number of improvements with an almost perfect freedom from tremor. Along with this I purchased every possible accessory,—draw-tubes, micrometers, a *camera-lucida*, lever-stage, achromatic condensers, white cloud illuminators, prisms, parabolic condensers, polarizing apparatus, forceps, aquatic boxes, fishing-tubes, with a host of other articles, all of which would have been useful in the hands of an experienced microscopist, but, as I afterwards discovered, were not of the slightest present value to me. It takes years of practice to know how to use a complicated microscope. The optician looked suspiciously at me as I made these wholesale purchases. He evidently was uncertain whether to set me down as some scientific celebrity or a madman.

I think he inclined to the latter belief. I suppose I was mad. Every great genius is mad upon the subject in which he is greatest. The unsuccessful madman is disgraced and called a lunatic.

Mad or not, I set myself to work with a zeal which few scientific students have ever equalled. I had everything to learn relative to the delicate study upon which I had embarked,—a study involving the most earnest patience, the most rigid analytic powers, the steadiest hand, the most untiring eye, the most refined and subtile manipulation.

For a long time half my apparatus lay inactively on the shelves of my laboratory, which was now most amply furnished with every possible contrivance for facilitating my investigations. The fact was that I did not know how to use some of my scientific accessories,—never having been taught microscopics,—and those whose use I understood theoretically were of little avail, until by practice I could attain the necessary delicacy of handling. Still, such was the fury of my ambition, such the untiring perseverance of my experiments, that, difficult of credit as it may be, in the course of one year I became theoretically and practically an accomplished microscopist.

During this period of my labors, in which I submitted specimens of every substance that came under my observation to the action of my lenses, I became a discoverer,—in a small way, it is true, for I was very young, but still a discoverer. It was I who destroyed Ehrenberg's theory that the *Volvox globator* was an animal, and proved that his "monads" with stomachs and eyes were merely phases of the formation of a vegetable cell, and were, when they reached their mature state, incapable of the act of conjugation, or any true generative act, without which no organism rising to any stage of life higher than vegetable can be said to be complete. It was I who resolved the singular problem of rotation in the cells and hairs of plants into ciliary attraction, in spite of the assertions of Mr. Wenham and others, that my explanation was the result of an optical illusion.

But notwithstanding these discoveries, laboriously and painfully made as they were, I felt horribly dissatisfied. At every step I found myself stopped by the imperfections of my instruments. Like all active microscopists, I gave my imagination full play. Indeed, it is a common complaint against many such, that they supply the defects of their instruments with the creations of their brains. I imagined depths beyond depths in Nature which the limited power of my lenses prohibited me from exploring. I lay awake at night constructing imaginary microscopes of immeasurable power, with which I seemed to pierce through all the envelopes of matter down to its original atom. How I cursed those imperfect mediums which necessity through ignorance compelled me to use! How I longed to discover the secret of some perfect lens, whose magnifying power should be limited only by the resolvability of the object, and which at the same time should be free from spherical and chromatic aberrations, in short from all the obstacles over which the poor microscopist finds himself continually stumbling! I felt convinced that the simple microscope, composed of a single lens of such vast yet perfect power was possible of construction. To attempt to bring the compound microscope up to such a pitch would have been commencing at the wrong end; this latter being simply a partially successful endeavor to remedy those very defects of the simple instrument, which, if conquered, would leave nothing to be desired.

It was in this mood of mind that I became a constructive microscopist. After another year passed in this new pursuit, experimenting on every imaginable substance,—glass, gems, flints, crystals, artificial crystals formed of the alloy of various vitreous materials,—in short, having constructed as many varieties of lenses as Argus had eyes, I found myself precisely where I started, with nothing gained save an extensive knowledge of glass-making. I was almost dead with despair. My parents were surprised at my apparent want of progress in my medical studies, (I had not attended one lecture since my arrival in the city,) and the expenses of my mad pursuit had been so great as to embarrass me very seriously.

I was in this frame of mind one day, experimenting in my laboratory on a small diamond,—that stone, from its great refracting power, having always occupied my attention more than any other,—when a young Frenchman, who lived on the floor above me, and who was in the habit of occasionally visiting me, entered the room.

I think that Jules Simon was a Jew. He had many traits of the Hebrew character: a love of jewelry, of dress, and of good living. There was something mysterious about him. He always had something to sell, and yet went into excellent society. When I say sell, I should perhaps have said peddle; for his operations were generally confined to the disposal of single articles,—a picture, for instance, or a rare carving in ivory, or a pair of duelling-pistols, or the dress of a Mexican *caballero*. When I was first furnishing my rooms, he paid me a visit, which ended in my purchasing an antique silver lamp, which he assured me was a Cellini,—it was handsome enough even for that,—and some other knickknacks for my sitting-room. Why Simon should pursue this petty trade I never could imagine. He apparently had plenty of money, and had the *entrée* of the best houses in the city,—taking care, however, I suppose, to drive no bargains within the enchanted circle of the Upper Ten. I came at length to the conclusion that this peddling was but a mask to cover some greater object, and even went so far as to believe my young acquaintance to be implicated in the slave-trade. That, however, was none of my affair.

On the present occasion, Simon entered my room in a state of considerable excitement.

"*Ah! mon ami!*" he cried, before I could even offer him the ordinary salutation, "it has occurred to me to be the witness of the most astonishing things in the world. I promenade myself to the house of Madame——How does the little animal—*le renard*—name himself in the Latin?"

"Vulpes," I answered.

"Ah! yes,—Vulpes. I promenade myself to the house of Madame Vulpes."

"The spirit medium?"

"Yes, the great medium. Great Heavens! what a woman! I write on a slip of paper many of questions concerning affairs the most secret,—affairs that conceal themselves in the abysses of my heart the most profound; and behold! by example! what occurs? This devil of a woman makes me replies the most truthful to all of them. She talks to me of things that I do not love to talk of to myself. What am I to think? I am fixed to the earth!"

"Am I to understand you, M. Simon, that this Mrs. Vulpes replied to questions secretly written by you, which questions related to events known only to yourself?"

"Ah! more than that, more than that," he answered, with an air of some alarm. "She related to me things— But," he added, after a pause, and suddenly changing his manner, "why occupy ourselves with these follies? It was all the biology, without doubt. It goes without saying that it has not my credence.—But why are we here, *mon ami*? It has occurred to me to discover the most beautiful thing as you can imagine,—a vase with green lizards on it, composed by the great Bernard Palissy. It is in my apartment; let us mount. I go to show it to you."

I followed Simon mechanically; but my thoughts were far from Palissy and his enamelled ware, although I, like him, was seeking in the dark after a great discovery. This casual mention of the spiritualist, Madame Vulpes, set me on a new track. What if this spiritualism should be really a great fact? What if, through communication with subtiler organisms than my own, I could reach at a single bound the goal, which perhaps a life of agonizing mental toil would never enable me to attain?

While purchasing the Palissy vase from my friend Simon, I was mentally arranging a visit to Madame Vulpes.

III

THE SPIRIT OF LEEUWENHOEK

Two evenings after this, thanks to an arrangement by letter and the promise of an ample fee, I found Madame Vulpes awaiting me at her residence alone. She was a coarse-featured woman, with a keen and rather cruel dark eye, and an exceedingly sensual expression about her mouth and under jaw. She received me in perfect silence, in an apartment on the ground floor, very sparely furnished. In the centre of the room, close to where Mrs. Vulpes sat, there was a common round mahogany table. If I had come for the purpose of sweeping her chimney, the woman could not have looked more indifferent to my appearance. There was no attempt to inspire the visitor with any awe. Everything bore a simple and practical aspect. This intercourse with the spiritual world was evidently as familiar an occupation with Mrs. Vulpes as eating her dinner or riding in an omnibus.

"You come for a communication, Mr. Linley?" said the medium, in a dry, business-like tone of voice.

"By appointment,—yes."

"What sort of communication do you want?—a written one?"

"Yes,—I wish for a written one."

"From any particular spirit?"

"Yes."

"Have you ever known this spirit on this earth?"

"Never. He died long before I was born. I wish merely to obtain from him some information which he ought to be able to give better than any other."

"Will you seat yourself at the table, Mr. Linley," said the medium, "and place your hands upon it?"

I obeyed,—Mrs. Vulpes being seated opposite me, with her hands also on the table. We remained thus for about a minute and a half, when a violent succession of raps came on the table, on the back of my chair, on the floor immediately under my feet, and even on the windowpanes. Mrs. Vulpes smiled composedly.

"They are very strong to-night," she remarked. "You are fortunate." She then continued, "Will the spirits communicate with this gentleman?"

Vigorous affirmative.

"Will the particular spirit he desires to speak with communicate?"

A very confused rapping followed this question.

"I know what they mean," said Mrs. Vulpes, addressing herself to me; "they wish you to write down the name of the particular spirit that you desire to converse with. Is that so?" she added, speaking to her invisible guests.

That it was so was evident from the numerous affirmatory responses. While this was going on, I tore a slip from my pocketbook, and scribbled a name, under the table.

"Will this spirit communicate in writing with this gentleman?" asked the medium once more.

After a moment's pause, her hand seemed to be seized with a violent tremor, shaking so forcibly that the table vibrated. She said that a spirit had seized her hand and would write. I handed her some sheets of paper that were on the table, and a pencil. The latter she held loosely in her hand, which presently began to move over the paper with a singular and seemingly involuntary motion. After a few moments had elapsed, she handed me the paper, on which I found written, in a large, uncultivated hand, the words, "He is not here, but has been sent for." A pause of a minute or so now ensued, during which Mrs. Vulpes remained perfectly silent, but the raps continued at regular intervals. When the short period I mention had elapsed, the hand of the medium was again seized with its convulsive tremor, and she wrote, under this strange influence, a few words on the paper, which she handed to me. They were as follows:—

"I am here. Question me.

"LEEUWENHOEK."

I was astounded. The name was identical with that I had written beneath the table, and carefully kept concealed. Neither was it at all probable that an uncultivated woman like Mrs. Vulpes should know even the name of the great father of microscopics. It may have been biology; but this theory was soon doomed to be destroyed. I wrote on my slip—still concealing it from Mrs. Vulpes—a series of questions, which, to avoid tediousness, I shall place with the responses, in the order in which they occurred.

I.—Can the microscope be brought to perfection?

SPIRIT.—Yes.

I.—Am I destined to accomplish this great task?

SPIRIT.—You are.

I.—I wish to know how to proceed to attain this end. For the love which you bear to science, help me!

SPIRIT.—A diamond of one hundred and forty carats, submitted to electro-magnetic currents for a long period, will experience a rearrangement of its atoms *inter se,* and from that stone you will form the universal lens.

I.—Will great discoveries result from the use of such a lens?

SPIRIT.—So great that all that has gone before is as nothing.

I.—But the refractive power of the diamond is so immense, that the image will be formed within the lens. How is that difficulty to be surmounted?

SPIRIT.—Pierce the lens through its axis, and the difficulty is obviated. The image will be formed in the pierced space, which will itself serve as a tube to look through. Now I am called. Good night.

I cannot at all describe the effect that these extraordinary communications had upon me. I felt completely bewildered. No biological theory could account for the *discovery* of the lens. The medium might, by means of biological *rapport* with my mind, have gone so far as to read my questions, and reply to them coherently. But biology could not enable her to discover that magnetic currents would so alter the crystals of the diamond as to remedy its previous defects, and admit of its being polished into a perfect lens. Some such theory may have passed through my head, it is true; but if so, I had forgotten it. In my excited condition of mind there was no course left but to become a convert, and it was in a state of the most painful nervous exaltation that I left the medium's house that evening. She accompanied me to the door, hoping that I was satisfied. The raps followed us as we went through the hall, sounding on the balusters, the flooring, and even the lintels of the door. I hastily expressed my satisfaction, and escaped hurriedly into the cool night air. I walked home with but one thought possessing me,—how to obtain a diamond of the immense size required. My entire means multiplied a hundred times over would have been inadequate to its purchase. Besides, such stones are rare, and become historical. I could find such only in the regalia of Eastern or European monarchs.

IV

THE EYE OF MORNING

There was a light in Simon's room as I entered my house. A vague impulse urged me to visit him. As I opened the door of his sitting-room unannounced, he was bending, with his back toward me, over a carcel lamp, apparently engaged in minutely examining some object which he held in his hands. As I entered, he started suddenly, thrust his hand into his breast pocket, and turned to me with a face crimson with confusion.

"What!" I cried, "poring over the miniature of some fair lady? Well, don't blush so much; I won't ask to see it."

Simon laughed awkwardly enough, but made none of the negative protestations usual on such occasions. He asked me to take a seat.

"Simon," said I, "I have just come from Madame Vulpes."

This time Simon turned as white as a sheet, and seemed stupefied, as if a sudden electric shock had smitten him. He babbled some incoherent words, and went hastily to a small closet where he usually kept his liquors. Although astonished at his emotion,

I was too preoccupied with my own idea to pay much attention to anything else.

"You say truly when you call Madame Vulpes a devil of a woman," I continued. "Simon, she told me wonderful things to-night, or rather was the means of telling me wonderful things. Ah! if I could only get a diamond that weighed one hundred and forty carats!"

Scarcely had the sigh with which I uttered this desire died upon my lips, when Simon, with the aspect of a wild beast, glared at me savagely, and, rushing to the mantelpiece, where some foreign weapons hung on the wall, caught up a Malay creese, and brandished it furiously before him.

"No!" he cried in French, into which he always broke when excited. "No! you shall not have it! You are perfidious! You have consulted with that demon, and desire my treasure! But I will die first! Me! I am brave! You cannot make me fear!"

All this, uttered in a loud voice trembling with excitement, astounded me. I saw at a glance that I had accidentally trodden upon the edges of Simon's secret, whatever it was. It was necessary to reassure him.

"My dear Simon," I said, "I am entirely at a loss to know what you mean. I went to Madame Vulpes to consult with her on a scientific problem, to the solution of which I discovered that a diamond of the size I just mentioned was necessary. You were never alluded to during the evening, nor, so far as I was concerned, even thought of. What can be the meaning of this outburst? If you happen to have a set of valuable diamonds in your possession, you need fear nothing from me. The diamond which I require you could not possess; or, if you did possess it, you would not be living here."

Something in my tone must have completely reassured him; for his expression immediately changed to a sort of constrained merriment, combined, however, with a certain suspicious attention to my movements. He laughed, and said that I must bear with him; that he was at certain moments subject to a species of vertigo, which betrayed itself in incoherent speeches, and that the attacks passed off as rapidly as they came. He put his weapon aside while making this explanation, and endeavored, with some success, to assume a more cheerful air.

All this did not impose on me in the least. I was too much

accustomed to analytical labors to be baffled by so flimsy a veil. I determined to probe the mystery to the bottom.

"Simon," I said, gayly, "let us forget all this over a bottle of Burgundy. I have a case of Lausseure's *Clos Vougeot* down-stairs, fragrant with the odors and ruddy with the sunlight of the Côte d'Or. Let us have up a couple of bottles. What say you?"

"With all my heart," answered Simon, smilingly.

I produced the wine and we seated ourselves to drink. It was of a famous vintage, that of 1848, a year when war and wine throve together,—and its pure but powerful juice seemed to impart renewed vitality to the system. By the time we had half finished the second bottle, Simon's head, which I knew was a weak one, had begun to yield, while I remained calm as ever, only that every draught seemed to send a flush of vigor through my limbs. Simon's utterance became more and more indistinct. He took to singing French *chansons* of a not very moral tendency. I rose suddenly from the table just at the conclusion of one of those incoherent verses, and, fixing my eyes on him with a quiet smile, said: "Simon, I have deceived you. I learned your secret this evening. You may as well be frank with me. Mrs. Vulpes, or rather one of her spirits, told me all."

He started with horror. His intoxication seemed for the moment to fade away, and he made a movement towards the weapon that he had a short time before laid down. I stopped him with my hand.

"Monster!" he cried, passionately, "I am ruined! What shall I do? You shall never have it! I swear by my mother!"

"I don't want it," I said; "rest secure, but be frank with me. Tell me all about it."

The drunkenness began to return. He protested with maudlin earnestness that I was entirely mistaken,—that I was intoxicated; then asked me to swear eternal secrecy, and promised to disclose the mystery to me. I pledged myself, of course, to all. With an uneasy look in his eyes, and hands unsteady with drink and nervousness, he drew a small case from his breast and opened it. Heavens! How the mild lamp-light was shivered into a thousand prismatic arrows, as it fell upon a vast rose-diamond that glittered in the case! I was no judge of diamonds, but I saw at a glance that this was a gem of rare size and purity. I looked at Simon with wonder, and—must I confess it?—with envy. How could he have obtained this treasure? In reply to my questions, I could just gather from his drunken statements (of which, I fancy, half the incoherence was affected) that he had been superintending a gang of slaves engaged in diamond-washing in Brazil; that he had seen one of them secrete a diamond, but, instead of informing his employers, had quietly watched the negro until he saw him bury his treasure; that he had dug it up and fled with it, but that as yet he was afraid to attempt to dispose of it publicly,—so valuable a gem being almost certain to attract too much attention to its owner's antecedents,—and he had not been able to discover any of those obscure channels by which such matters are conveyed away safely. He added, that, in accordance with the oriental practice, he had named his diamond by the fanciful title of "The Eye of Morning."

While Simon was relating this to me, I regarded the great diamond attentively. Never had I beheld anything so beautiful. All the glories of light, ever imagined or described, seemed to pulsate in its crystalline chambers. Its weight, as I learned from Simon, was exactly one hundred and forty carats. Here was an amazing coincidence. The hand of Destiny seemed in it. On the very evening when the spirit of Leeuwenhoek communicates to me the great secret of the microscope, the priceless means which he directs me to employ start up within my easy reach! I determined, with the most perfect deliberation, to possess myself of Simon's diamond.

I sat opposite to him while he nodded over his glass, and calmly revolved the whole affair. I did not for an instant contemplate so foolish an act as a common theft, which would of course be discovered, or at least necessitate flight and concealment, all of which must interfere with my scientific plans. There was but one step to be taken,—to kill Simon. After all, what was the life of a little peddling Jew, in comparison with the interests of science? Human beings are taken every day from the condemned prisons to be experimented on by surgeons. This man, Simon, was by his own confession a criminal, a robber, and I believed on my soul a murderer. He deserved death quite as much as any felon condemned by the laws; why should I not, like government, contrive that his punishment should contribute to the progress of human knowledge?

The means for accomplishing everything I desired lay within

my reach. There stood upon the mantel-piece a bottle half full of French laudanum. Simon was so occupied with his diamond, which I had just restored to him, that it was an affair of no difficulty to drug his glass. In a quarter of an hour he was in a profound sleep.

I now opened his waistcoat, took the diamond from the inner pocket in which he had placed it, and removed him to the bed, on which I laid him so that his feet hung down over the edge. I had possessed myself of the Malay creese, which I held in my right hand, while with the other I discovered as accurately as I could by pulsation the exact locality of the heart. It was essential that all the aspects of his death should lead to the surmise of self-murder. I calculated the exact angle at which it was probable that the weapon, if levelled by Simon's own hand, would enter his breast; then with one powerful blow I thrust it up to the hilt in the very spot which I desired to penetrate. A convulsive thrill ran through Simon's limbs. I heard a smothered sound issue from his throat, precisely like the bursting of a large air-bubble, sent up by a diver, when it reaches the surface of the water; he turned half round on his side, and, as if to assist my plans more effectually, his right hand, moved by some mere spasmodic impulse, clasped the handle of the creese, which it remained holding with extraordinary muscular tenacity. Beyond this there was no apparent struggle. The laudanum, I presume, paralyzed the usual nervous action. He must have died instantaneously.

There was yet something to be done. To make it certain that all suspicion of the act should be diverted from any inhabitant of the house to Simon himself, it was necessary that the door should be found in the morning *locked on the inside*. How to do this, and afterwards escape myself? Not by the window; that was a physical impossibility. Besides, I was determined that the windows *also* should be found bolted. The solution was simple enough. I descended softly to my own room for a peculiar instrument which I had used for holding small slippery substances, such as minute spheres of glass, etc. This instrument was nothing more than a long slender hand-vice, with a very powerful grip, and a considerable leverage, which last was accidentally owing to the shape of the handle. Nothing was simpler than, when the key was in the lock, to seize the end of its stem in this vice, through the keyhole, from the outside, and so lock the door. Previously, however, to doing this, I burned a number of papers on Simon's hearth. Suicides almost always burn papers before they destroy themselves. I also emptied some more laudanum into Simon's glass,—having first removed from it all traces of wine,—cleaned the other wine-glass, and brought the bottles away with me. If traces of two persons drinking had been found in the room, the question naturally would have arisen, Who was the second? Besides, the wine-bottles might have been identified as belonging to me. The laudanum I poured out to account for its presence in his stomach, in case of a *post-mortem* examination. The theory naturally would be, that he first intended to poison himself, but, after swallowing a little of the drug, was either disgusted with its taste, or changed his mind from other motives, and chose the dagger. These arrangements made, I walked out, leaving the gas burning, locked the door with my vice, and went to bed.

Simon's death was not discovered until nearly three in the afternoon. The servant, astonished at seeing the gas burning,—the light streaming on the dark landing from under the door,—peeped through the keyhole and saw Simon on the bed. She gave the alarm. The door was burst open, and the neighborhood was in a fever of excitement.

Every one in the house was arrested, myself included. There was an inquest; but no clew to his death beyond that of suicide could be obtained. Curiously enough, he had made several speeches to his friends the preceding week, that seemed to point to self-destruction. One gentleman swore that Simon had said in his presence that "he was tired of life." His landlord affirmed that Simon, when paying him his last month's rent, remarked that "he would not pay him rent much longer." All the other evidence corresponded,—the door locked inside, the position of the corpse, the burnt papers. As I anticipated, no one knew of the possession of the diamond by Simon, so that no motive was suggested for his murder. The jury, after a prolonged examination, brought in the usual verdict, and the neighborhood once more settled down into its accustomed quiet.

V
ANIMULA

The three months succeeding Simon's catastrophe I devoted night and day to my diamond lens. I had constructed a vast galvanic battery, composed of nearly two thousand pairs of plates,—a higher power I dared not use, lest the diamond should be calcined. By means of this enormous engine I was enabled to send a powerful current of electricity continually through my great diamond, which it seemed to me gained in lustre every day. At the expiration of a month I commenced the grinding and polishing of the lens, a work of intense toil and exquisite delicacy. The great density of the stone, and the care required to be taken with the curvatures of the surfaces of the lens, rendered the labor the severest and most harassing that I had yet undergone.

At last the eventful moment came; the lens was completed. I stood trembling on the threshold of new worlds. I had the realization of Alexander's famous wish before me. The lens lay on the table, ready to be placed upon its platform. My hand fairly shook as I enveloped a drop of water with a thin coating of oil of turpentine, preparatory to its examination,—a process necessary in order to prevent the rapid evaporation of the water. I now placed the drop on a thin slip of glass under the lens, and throwing upon it, by the combined aid of a prism and a mirror, a powerful stream of light, I approached my eye to the minute hole drilled through the axis of the lens. For an instant I saw nothing save what seemed to be an illuminated chaos, a vast luminous abyss. A pure white light, cloudless and serene, and seemingly limitless as space itself, was my first impression. Gently, and with the greatest care, I depressed the lens a few hair's-breadths. The wondrous illumination still continued, but as the lens approached the object a scene of indescribable beauty was unfolded to my view.

I seemed to gaze upon a vast space, the limits of which extended far beyond my vision. An atmosphere of magical luminousness permeated the entire field of view. I was amazed to see no trace of animalculous life. Not a living thing, apparently, inhabited that dazzling expanse. I comprehended instantly that, by the wondrous power of my lens, I had penetrated beyond the grosser particles of aqueous matter, beyond the realms of infusoria and protozoa, down to the original gaseous globule, into whose luminous interior I was gazing, as into an almost boundless dome filled with a supernatural radiance.

It was, however, no brilliant void into which I looked. On every side I beheld beautiful inorganic forms, of unknown texture, and colored with the most enchanting hues. These forms presented the appearance of what might be called, for want of a more specific definition, foliated clouds of the highest rarity; that is, they undulated and broke into vegetable formations, and were tinged with splendors compared with which the gilding of our autumn woodlands is as dross compared with gold. Far away into the illimitable distance stretched long avenues of these gaseous forests, dimly transparent, and painted with prismatic hues of unimaginable brilliancy. The pendent branches waved along the fluid glades until every vista seemed to break through half-lucent ranks of many-colored drooping silken pennons. What seemed to be either fruits or flowers, pied with a thousand hues, lustrous and ever varying, bubbled from the crowns of this fairy foliage. No hills, no lakes, no rivers, no forms animate or inanimate, were to be seen, save those vast auroral copses that floated serenely in the luminous stillness, with leaves and fruits and flowers gleaming with unknown fires, unrealizable by mere imagination.

How strange, I thought, that this sphere should be thus condemned to solitude! I had hoped, at least, to discover some new form of animal life,—perhaps of a lower class than any with which we are at present acquainted,—but still, some living organism. I found my newly discovered world, if I may so speak, a beautiful chromatic desert.

While I was speculating on the singular arrangements of the internal economy of Nature, with which she so frequently splinters into atoms our most compact theories, I thought I beheld a form moving slowly through the glades of one of the prismatic forests. I looked more attentively, and found that I was not mistaken. Words cannot depict the anxiety with which I awaited the nearer approach of this mysterious object. Was it merely some inanimate substance, held in suspense in the attenuated atmosphere of the globule? or was it an animal endowed with vitality and motion? It approached, flitting behind the gauzy, colored veils of cloud-foliage, for seconds dimly revealed, then vanishing. At last the violet pennons that trailed nearest to me vibrated; they were gently pushed aside, and the Form floated out into the broad light.

It was a female human shape. When I say "human," I mean it possessed the outlines of humanity,—but there the analogy ends. Its adorable beauty lifted it illimitable heights beyond the loveliest daughter of Adam.

I cannot, I dare not, attempt to inventory the charms of this divine revelation of perfect beauty. Those eyes of mystic violet, dewy and serene, evade my words. Her long, lustrous hair following her glorious head in a golden wake, like the track sown in heaven by a falling star, seems to quench my most burning phrases with its splendors. If all the bees of Hybla nestled upon my lips, they would still sing but hoarsely the wondrous harmonies of outline that enclosed her form.

She swept out from between the rainbow-curtains of the cloud-trees into the broad sea of light that lay beyond. Her motions were those of some graceful Naiad, cleaving, by a mere effort of her will, the clear, unruffled waters that fill the chambers of the sea. She floated forth with the serene grace of a frail bubble ascending through the still atmosphere of a June day. The perfect roundness of her limbs formed suave and enchanting curves. It was like listening to the most spiritual symphony of Beethoven the divine, to watch the harmonious flow of lines. This, indeed, was a pleasure cheaply purchased at any price. What cared I, if I had waded to the portal of this wonder through another's blood? I would have given my own to enjoy one such moment of intoxication and delight.

Breathless with gazing on this lovely wonder, and forgetful for an instant of everything save her presence, I withdrew my eye from the microscope eagerly,—alas! As my gaze fell on the thin slide that lay beneath my instrument, the bright light from mirror and from prism sparkled on a colorless drop of water! There, in that tiny bead of dew, this beautiful being was forever imprisoned. The planet Neptune was not more distant from me than she. I hastened once more to apply my eye to the microscope.

Animula (let me now call her by that dear name which I subsequently bestowed on her) had changed her position. She had again approached the wondrous forest, and was gazing earnestly upwards. Presently one of the trees—as I must call them —unfolded a long ciliary process, with which it seized one of the gleaming fruits that glittered on its summit, and, sweeping slowly down, held it within reach of Animula. The sylph took it in her delicate hand and began to eat. My attention was so entirely absorbed by her, that I could not apply myself to the task of determining whether this singular plant was or was not instinct with volition.

I watched her, as she made her repast, with the most profound attention. The suppleness of her motions sent a thrill of delight through my frame; my heart beat madly as she turned her beautiful eyes in the direction of the spot in which I stood. What would I not have given to have had the power to precipitate myself into that luminous ocean, and float with her through those groves of purple and gold! While I was thus breathlessly following her every movement, she suddenly started, seemed to listen for a moment, and then cleaving the brilliant ether in which she was floating, like a flash of light, pierced through the opaline forest, and disappeared.

Instantly a series of the most singular sensations attacked me. It seemed as if I had suddenly gone blind. The luminous sphere was still before me, but my daylight had vanished. What caused this sudden disappearance? Had she a lover or a husband? Yes, that was the solution! Some signal from a happy fellow-being had vibrated through the avenues of the forest, and she had obeyed the summons.

The agony of my sensations, as I arrived at this conclusion, startled me. I tried to reject the conviction that my reason forced upon me. I battled against the fatal conclusion,—but in vain. It was so. I had no escape from it. I loved an animalcule!

It is true that, thanks to the marvellous power of my microscope, she appeared of human proportions. Instead of presenting the revolting aspect of the coarser creatures, that live and struggle and die, in the more easily resolvable portions of the water-drop, she was fair and delicate and of surpassing beauty. But of what account was all that? Every time that my eye was withdrawn from the instrument, it fell on a miserable drop of water, within which, I must be content to know, dwelt all that could make my life lovely.

Could she but see me once! Could I for one moment pierce

the mystical walls that so inexorably rose to separate us, and whisper all that filled my soul, I might consent to be satisfied for the rest of my life with the knowledge of her remote sympathy. It would be something to have established even the faintest personal link to bind us together,—to know that at times, when roaming through those enchanted glades, she might think of the wonderful stranger, who had broken the monotony of her life with his presence, and left a gentle memory in her heart!

But it could not be. No invention of which human intellect was capable could break down the barriers that Nature had erected. I might feast my soul upon her wondrous beauty, yet she must always remain ignorant of the adoring eyes that day and night gazed upon her, and, even when closed, beheld her in dreams. With a bitter cry of anguish I fled from the room, and, flinging myself on my bed, sobbed myself to sleep like a child.

VI

THE SPILLING OF THE CUP

I arose the next morning almost at daybreak, and rushed to my microscope. I trembled as I sought the luminous world in miniature that contained my all. Animula was there. I had left the gas-lamp, surrounded by its moderators, burning, when I went to bed the night before. I found the sylph bathing, as it were, with an expression of pleasure animating her features, in the brilliant light which surrounded her. She tossed her lustrous golden hair over her shoulders with innocent coquetry. She lay at full length in the transparent medium, in which she supported herself with ease, and gambolled with the enchanting grace that the nymph Salmacis might have exhibited when she sought to conquer the modest Hermaphroditus. I tried an experiment to satisfy myself if her powers of reflection were developed. I lessened the lamp-light considerably. By the dim light that remained, I could see an expression of pain flit across her face. She looked upward suddenly, and her brows contracted. I flooded the stage of the microscope again with a full stream of light, and her whole expression changed. She sprang forward like some substance deprived of all weight. Her eyes sparkled and her lips moved. Ah! if science had only the means of conducting and reduplicating sounds, as it does the rays of light, what carols of happiness would then have entranced my ears! what jubilant hymns to Adonaïs would have thrilled the illumined air!

I now comprehended how it was that the Count de Gabalis peopled his mystic world with sylphs,—beautiful beings whose breath of life was lambent fire, and who sported forever in regions of purest ether and purest light. The Rosicrucian had anticipated the wonder that I had practically realized.

How long this worship of my strange divinity went on thus I scarcely know. I lost all note of time. All day from early dawn, and far into the night, I was to be found peering through that wonderful lens. I saw no one, went nowhere, and scarce allowed myself sufficient time for my meals. My whole life was absorbed in contemplation as rapt as that of any of the Romish saints. Every hour that I gazed upon the divine form strengthened my passion,—a passion that was always overshadowed by the maddening conviction, that, although I could gaze on her at will, she never, never could behold me!

At length, I grew so pale and emaciated, from want of rest, and continual brooding over my insane love and its cruel conditions, that I determined to make some effort to wean myself from it. "Come," I said, "this is at best but a fantasy. Your imagination has bestowed on Animula charms which in reality she does not possess. Seclusion from female society has produced this morbid condition of mind. Compare her with the beautiful women of your own world, and this false enchantment will vanish."

I looked over the newspapers by chance. There I beheld the advertisement of a celebrated *danseuse* who appeared nightly at Niblo's. The Signorina Caradolce had the reputation of being the most beautiful as well as the most graceful woman in the world. I instantly dressed and went to the theatre.

The curtain drew up. The usual semicircle of fairies in white muslin were standing on the right toe around the enamelled flower-bank, of green canvas, on which the belated prince was sleeping. Suddenly a flute is heard. The fairies start. The trees open, the fairies all stand on the left toe, and the queen enters. It was the Signorina. She bounded forward amid thunders of applause, and, lighting on one foot, remained poised in air. Heavens! was this the great enchantress that had drawn monarchs at her chariot-wheels? Those heavy muscular limbs, those thick ankles, those cavernous eyes, that stereotyped smile, those crudely painted cheeks! Where were the vermeil blooms, the liquid expressive eyes, the harmonious limbs of Animula?

The Signorina danced. What gross, discordant movements! The play of her limbs was all false and artificial. Her bounds were painful athletic efforts; her poses were angular and distressed the eye. I could bear it no longer; with an exclamation of disgust that drew every eye upon me, I rose from my seat in the very middle of the Signorina's *pas-de-fascination,* and abruptly quitted the house.

I hastened home to feast my eyes once more on the lovely form of my sylph. I felt that henceforth to combat this passion would be impossible. I applied my eye to the lens. Animula was there,—but what could have happened? Some terrible change seemed to have taken place during my absence. Some secret grief seemed to cloud the lovely features of her I gazed upon. Her face had grown thin and haggard; her limbs trailed heavily; the wondrous lustre of her golden hair had faded. She was ill!—ill, and I could not assist her! I believe at that moment I would have gladly forfeited all claims to my human birthright, if I could only have been dwarfed to the size of an animalcule, and permitted to console her from whom fate had forever divided me.

I racked my brain for the solution of this mystery. What was it that afflicted the sylph? She seemed to suffer intense pain. Her features contracted, and she even writhed, as if with some internal agony. The wondrous forests appeared also to have lost half their beauty. Their hues were dim and in some places faded away altogether. I watched Animula for hours with a breaking heart, and she seemed absolutely to wither away under my very eye. Suddenly I remembered that I had not looked at the water-drop for several days. In fact, I hated to see it; for it reminded me of the natural barrier between Animula and myself. I hurriedly looked down on the stage of the microscope. The slide was still there,—but, great heavens! the water-drop had vanished! The awful truth burst upon me; it had evaporated, until it had become so minute as to be invisible to the naked eye; I had been gazing on its last atom, the one that contained Animula,—and she was dying!

I rushed again to the front of the lens, and looked through.

Alas! the last agony had seized her. The rainbow-hued forests had all melted away, and Animula lay struggling feebly in what seemed to be a spot of dim light. Ah! the sight was horrible: the limbs once so round and lovely shrivelling up into nothings; the eyes—those eyes that shone like heaven—being quenched into black dust; the lustrous golden hair now lank and discolored. The last throe came. I beheld that final struggle of the blackening form—and I fainted.

When I awoke out of a trance of many hours, I found myself lying amid the wreck of my instrument, myself as shattered in mind and body as it. I crawled feebly to my bed, from which I did not rise for months.

They say now that I am mad; but they are mistaken. I am poor, for I have neither the heart nor the will to work; all my money is spent, and I live on charity. Young men's associations that love a joke invite me to lecture on Optics before them, for which they pay me, and laugh at me while I lecture. "Linley, the mad microscopist," is the name I go by. I suppose that I talk incoherently while I lecture. Who could talk sense when his brain is haunted by such ghastly memories, while ever and anon among the shapes of death I behold the radiant form of my lost Animula!

DIMENSIONAL SPECULATION AS SCIENCE FICTION

When science fiction moves far enough toward pure physical speculation it meets the most speculative kind of science, and the two become indistinguishable. One can see this clearly in the literature about new physical dimensions. The reader is invited to ask himself how he would (if he would) distinguish among Bierce's "Mysterious Disappearances," which appeared as fiction, and the accompanying two brief speculations on new dimensions, which appeared as science. And when he has made his distinctions, let him then test them against Edward Abbott Abbott's *Flatland* (1884; now available in a paper reissue), narrated by "A Square" who is forced into a third dimension and into contemplation of many other dimensions.

By 1894, literature—both scientific and science fictional—about "the fourth dimension" had become so familiar that Kipling published in *Cosmopolitan* a story entitled "An Error in the Fourth Dimension" which turns out, after playing upon the reader's expectations, to be not about four physical dimensions at all. Perhaps it was only after familiarity had made possible this kind of contempt, that a truly non-speculative science fiction about new dimensions was possible. So one finds Mary E. Wilkins Freeman writing in 1903 "The Hall Bedroom," a splendid tale, but a tale which uses new physical dimensions only to create new psychological dimensions. The journal of a lodger in the hall bedroom is presented in a framing narrative by "a highly respectable woman." Each night the lodger has delicious experiences with a different one of his senses in a world of another dimension. The seductiveness of this other world reminds one of "The Monarch of Dreams" and Conrad Aiken's "Silent Snow, Secret Snow." After his journal ends, his mysterious disappearance and its aftermath are described by the plain-minded landlady:

> They found another room, a long narrow one, the length of the hall bedroom, but narrower, hardly more than a closet. There was no window, nor door, all there was in it was a sheet of paper covered with figures, as if somebody had been doing sums. They made a lot of talk about those figures, and they tried to make out that the fifth dimension, whatever that is, was proved, but they said afterward they didn't prove anything.

This story displays by contrast how close to pure speculation Bierce's "Mysterious Disappearances" really is. One might consider this as a very tentative means to arrange some kind of spectrum: When a fiction moves away from a question of what might be toward a question of the emotional consequences of what might be, it moves from speculation to dramatization.

(ANON.)

Four-Dimensional Space *

Possibly the question, What is the fourth dimension? may admit of an indefinite number of answers. I prefer, therefore, in proposing to consider Time as a fourth dimension of our existence, to speak of it as *a* fourth dimension rather than *the* fourth dimension. Since this fourth dimension cannot be introduced into space, as commonly understood, we require a new kind of space for its existence, which we may call time-space. There is then no difficulty in conceiving the analogues in this new kind of space, of the things in ordinary space which are known as lines, areas, and solids. A straight line, by moving in any direction not in its own length, generates an area; if this area moves in any direction not in its own plane it generates a solid; but if this solid moves in any direction, it still generates a solid, and nothing more. The reason of this is that we have not supposed it to move in the fourth dimension. If the straight line moves in its own direction, it describes only a straight line; if the area moves in its own plane, it describes only an area; in each case, motion in the dimensions in which the thing exists, gives us only a thing of the same dimensions; and, in order to get a thing of higher dimensions, we must have motion in a new dimension. But, as the idea of motion is only applicable in space of three dimensions, we must replace it by another which is applicable in our fourth dimension of time. Such an idea is that of successive existence. We must, therefore, conceive that there is a new three-

* From *Nature,* 1885.

dimensional space for each successive instant of time; and, by picturing to ourselves the aggregate formed by the successive positions in time-space of a given solid during a given time, we shall get the idea of a four-dimensional solid, which may be called a sur-solid. It will assist us to get a clearer idea, if we consider a solid which is in a constant state of change, both of magnitude and position; and an example of a solid which satisfies this condition sufficiently well, is afforded by the body of each of us. Let any man picture to himself the aggregate of his own bodily forms from birth to the present time, and he will have a clear idea of a sur-solid in time-space.

Let us now consider the sur-solid formed by the movement, or rather, the successive existence, of a cube in time-space. We are to conceive of the cube, and the whole of the three-dimensional space in which it is situated, as floating away in time-space for a given time; the cube will then have an initial and a final position, and these will be the end boundaries of the sur-solid. It will therefore have sixteen points, namely, the eight points belonging to the initial cube, and the eight belonging to the final cube. The successive positions (in time-space) of each of the eight points of the cube, will form what may be called a time-line; and adding to these the twenty-four edges of the initial and final cubes, we see that the sur-solid has thirty-two lines. The successive positions (in time-space) of each of the twelve edges of the cube, will form what may be called a time area; and, adding these to the twelve faces of the initial and final cubes, we see that the sur-solid has twenty-four areas. Lastly, the successive positions (in time-space) of each of the six faces of the cube, will form what may be called a time-solid; and, adding these to the initial and final cubes, we see that the sur-solid is bounded by eight solids. These results agree with the statements in your article. But it is not permissible to speak of the sur-solid as resting in "spacc," we must rather say that the section of it by any time is a cube resting (or moving) in "space."

AMBROSE BIERCE
Mysterious Disappearances *

The Difficulty of Crossing a Field

One morning in July, 1854, a planter named Williamson, living six miles from Selma, Alabama, was sitting with his wife and a child on the veranda of his dwelling. Immediately in front of the house was a lawn, perhaps fifty yards in extent between the house and public road, or, as it was called, the "pike." Beyond this road lay a close-cropped pasture of some ten acres, level and without a tree, rock, or any natural or artificial object on its surface. At the time there was not even a domestic animal in the field. In another field, beyond the pasture, a dozen slaves were at work under an overseer.

Throwing away the stump of a cigar, the planter rose, saying: "I forgot to tell Andrew about those horses." Andrew was the overseer.

Williamson strolled leisurely down the gravel walk, plucking a flower as he went, passed across the road and into the pasture, pausing a moment as he closed the gate leading into it, to greet a passing neighbor, Armour Wren, who lived on an adjoining plantation. Mr. Wren was in an open carriage with his son James, a lad of thirteen. When he had driven some two hundred yards from the point of meeting, Mr. Wren said to his son: "I forgot to tell Mr. Williamson about those horses."

Mr. Wren had sold to Mr. Williamson some horses, which were to have been sent for that day, but for some reason not now remembered it would be inconvenient to deliver them until the

* *Can Such Things Be?*, 1893, 1909.

morrow. The coachman was directed to drive back, and as the vehicle turned Williamson was seen by all three, walking leisurely across the pasture. At that moment one of the coach horses stumbled and came near falling. It had no more than fairly recovered itself when James Wren cried: "Why, father, what has become of Mr. Williamson?"

It is not the purpose of this narrative to answer that question.

Mr. Wren's strange account of the matter, given under oath in the course of legal proceedings relating to the Williamson estate, here follows:

"My son's exclamation caused me to look toward the spot where I had seen the deceased [*sic*] an instant before, but he was not there, nor was he anywhere visible. I cannot say that at the moment I was greatly startled, or realized the gravity of the occurrence, though I thought it singular. My son, however, was greatly astonished and kept repeating his question in different forms until we arrived at the gate. My black boy Sam was similarly affected, even in a greater degree, but I reckon more by my son's manner than by anything he had himself observed. [This sentence in the testimony was stricken out.] As we got out of the carriage at the gate of the field, and while Sam was hanging [*sic*] the team to the fence, Mrs. Williamson, with her child in her arms and followed by several servants, came running down the walk in great excitement, crying: 'He is gone, he is gone! O God! what an awful thing!' and many other such exclamations, which I do not distinctly recollect. I got from them the impression that they related to something more than the mere disappearance of her husband, even if that had occurred before her eyes. Her manner was wild, but not more so, I think, than was natural under the circumstances. I have no reason to think she had at that time lost her mind. I have never since seen nor heard of Mr. Williamson."

This testimony, as might have been expected, was corroborated in almost every particular by the only other eye-witness (if that is a proper term)—the lad James. Mrs. Williamson had lost her reason and the servants were, of course, not competent to testify. The boy James Wren had declared at first that he *saw* the disappearance, but there is nothing of this in his testimony given in court. None of the field hands working in the field to which Williamson was going had seen him at all, and the most rigorous search of the entire plantation and adjoining country failed to supply a clew. The most monstrous and grotesque fictions, originating with the blacks, were current in that part of the State for many years, and probably are to this day; but what has been here related is all that is certainly known of the matter. The courts decided that Williamson was dead, and his estate was distributed according to law.

An Unfinished Race

James Burne Worson was a shoemaker who lived in Leamington, Warwickshire, England. He had a little shop in one of the by-ways leading off the road to Warwick. In his humble sphere he was esteemed an honest man, although like many of his class in English towns he was somewhat addicted to drink. When in liquor he would make foolish wagers. On one of these too frequent occasions he was boasting of his prowess as a pedestrian and athlete, and the outcome was a match against nature. For a stake of one sovereign he undertook to run all the way to Coventry and back, a distance of something more than forty miles. This was on the 3d day of September in 1873. He set out at once, the man with whom he had made the bet—whose name is not remembered—accompanied by Barham Wise, a linen draper, and Hamerson Burns, a photographer, I think, following in a light cart or wagon.

For several miles Worson went on very well, at an easy gait, without apparent fatigue, for he had really great powers of endurance and was not sufficiently intoxicated to enfeeble them. The three men in the wagon kept a short distance in the rear, giving him occasional friendly "chaff" or encouragement, as the spirit moved them. Suddenly—in the very middle of the roadway, not a dozen yards from them, and with their eyes full upon him—the man seemed to stumble, pitched headlong forward, uttered a terrible cry and vanished! He did not fall to the earth —he vanished before touching it. No trace of him was ever discovered.

After remaining at and about the spot for some time, with aimless irresolution, the three men returned to Leamington, told their astonishing story and were afterward taken into custody. But they were of good standing, had always been considered truthful, were sober at the time of the occurrence, and nothing ever transpired to discredit their sworn account of their extraordinary adventure, concerning the truth of which, nevertheless, public opinion was divided, throughout the United Kingdom. If they had something to conceal, their choice of means is certainly one of the most amazing ever made by sane human beings.

Charles Ashmore's Trail

The family of Christian Ashmore consisted of his wife, his mother, two grown daughters, and a son of sixteen years. They lived in Troy, New York, were well-to-do, respectable persons, and had many friends, some of whom, reading these lines, will doubtless learn for the first time the extraordinary fate of the young man. From Troy the Ashmores moved in 1871 or 1872 to Richmond, Indiana, and a year or two later to the vicinity of Quincy, Illinois, where Mr. Ashmore bought a farm and lived on it. At some little distance from the farmhouse was a spring with a constant flow of clear, cold water, whence the family derived its supply for domestic use at all seasons.

On the evening of the 9th of November in 1878, at about nine o'clock, young Charles Ashmore left the family circle about the hearth, took a tin bucket and started toward the spring. As he did not return, the family became uneasy, and going to the door by which he had left the house, his father called without receiving an answer. He then lighted a lantern and with the eldest daughter, Martha, who insisted on accompanying him, went in search. A light snow had fallen, obliterating the path, but making the young man's trail conspicuous; each footprint was plainly defined. After going a little more than half-way—perhaps seventy-five yards—the father, who was in advance, halted, and elevating his lantern stood peering intently into the darkness ahead.

"What is the matter, father?" the girl asked.

This was the matter: the trail of the young man had abruptly ended, and all beyond was smooth, unbroken snow. The last footprints were as conspicuous as any in the line; the very nail-marks were distinctly visible. Mr. Ashmore looked upward, shading his eyes with his hat held between them and the lantern. The stars were shining; there was not a cloud in the sky; he was denied the explanation which had suggested itself, doubtful as it would have been—a new snowfall with a limit so plainly defined. Taking a wide circuit round the ultimate tracks, so as to leave them undisturbed for further examination, the man proceeded to the spring, the girl following, weak and terrified. Neither had spoken a word of what both had observed. The spring was covered with ice, hours old.

Returning to the house they noted the appearance of the snow on both sides of the trail its entire length. No tracks led away from it.

The morning light showed nothing more. Smooth, spotless, unbroken, the shallow snow lay everywhere.

Four days later the grief-stricken mother herself went to the spring for water. She came back and related that in passing the spot where the footprints had ended she had heard the voice of her son and had been eagerly calling to him, wandering about the place, as she had fancied the voice to be now in one direction, now in another, until she was exhausted with fatigue and emotion. Questioned as to what the voice had said, she was unable to tell, yet averred that the words were perfectly distinct. In a moment the entire family was at the place, but nothing was heard, and the voice was believed to be an hallucination caused by the mother's great anxiety and her disordered nerves. But for months afterward, at irregular intervals of a few days, the voice was heard by the several members of the family, and by others. All declared it unmistakably the voice of Charles Ashmore; all agreed that it seemed to come from a great distance, faintly, yet with entire distinctness of articulation; yet none could determine its direction, nor repeat its words. The intervals of silence grew longer and longer, the voice fainter and farther, and by midsummer it was heard no more.

If anybody knows the fate of Charles Ashmore it is probably his mother. She is dead.

SCIENCE TO THE FRONT

In connection with this subject of "mysterious disappearance" —of which every memory is stored with abundant example— it is pertinent to note the belief of Dr. Hern, of Leipsic; not by way of explanation, unless the reader may choose to take it so, but because of its intrinsic interest as a singular speculation. This distinguished scientist has expounded his views in a book entitled "Verschwinden und Seine Theorie," which has attracted some attention, "particularly," says one writer, "among the followers of Hegel, and mathematicians who hold to the actual existence of a so-called non-Euclidean space—that is to say, of space which has more dimensions than length, breadth, and thickness—space in which it would be possible to tie a knot in an endless cord and to turn a rubber ball inside out without 'a solution of its continuity,' or in other words, without breaking or cracking it."

Dr. Hern believes that in the visible world there are void places—*vacua*, and something more—holes, as it were, through which animate and inanimate objects may fall into the invisible world and be seen and heard no more. The theory is something like this: Space is pervaded by luminiferous ether, which is a material thing—as much a substance as air or water, though almost infinitely more attenuated. All force, all forms of energy must be propagated in this; every process must take place in it which takes place at all. But let us suppose that cavities exist in this otherwise universal medium, as caverns exist in the earth, or cells in a Swiss cheese. In such a cavity there would be absolutely nothing. It would be such a vacuum as cannot be artificially produced; for if we pump the air from a receiver there remains the luminiferous ether. Through one of these cavities light could not pass, for there would be nothing to bear it. Sound could not come from it; nothing could be felt in it. It would not have a single one of the conditions necessary to the action of any of our senses. In such a void, in short, nothing whatever could occur. Now, in the words of the writer before quoted— the learned doctor himself nowhere puts it so concisely: "A man inclosed in such a closet could neither see nor be seen; neither hear nor be heard; neither feel nor be felt; neither live nor die, for both life and death are processes which can take place only where there is force, and in empty space no force could exist." Are these the awful conditions (some will ask) under which the friends of the lost are to think of them as existing, and doomed forever to exist?

Baldly and imperfectly as here stated, Dr. Hern's theory, in so far as it professes to be an adequate explanation of "mysterious disappearances," is open to many obvious objections; to fewer as he states it himself in the "spacious volubility" of his book. But even as expounded by its author it does not explain, and in truth is incompatible with some incidents of, the occurrences related in these memoranda: for example, the sound of Charles Ashmore's voice. It is not my duty to indue facts and theories with affinity.

A. B.

ARTHUR E. BOSTWICK

From "Four-Dimensional Space" *

If a man were limited to two dimensions instead of three—if, for instance, he lived on a sheet of paper as a picture does—he would know of nothing outside the sheet. A race of men might live in every one of a pile of a million sheets of paper, and it would be physically impossible that they should ever communicate or even be aware of the possibility of each other's existence, though the distance separating any two would be less than the thousandth of an inch. So, three-dimensional universes may be packed closely together in four-dimensional space, and we may be surrounded —almost touched—by myriads of beings like ourselves, of whose existence we are unconscious and into whose sphere we cannot come.

* *New Science Review*, 1896.

TIME TRAVEL

When one says time travel what one really means is an extraordinary dislocation of someone's consciousness in time. Every day we all travel in time in a number of ways. We travel as the sun rises and sets, the hands of the clock turn, our bodies age, and the world changes, in memory, in anticipation, in the loss of consciousness of measured time (as sometimes happens in sleep, daydreaming, abstract contemplation, intense emotional states, entertainment), and in all restorations of the consciousness of measured time. Time travel fiction simply asks us to exaggerate some part of our everyday time travel.

We may do this by observing and thus sharing someone else's extraordinary movement of consciousness in time. This is the case in the time travel fiction which employs mesmerism, drugs, a blow on the head, freezing, or any exceptionally long sleep ("Rip Van Winkle," *Looking Backward,* Wells's *When the Sleeper Wakes, A Connecticut Yankee in King Arthur's Court,* Mayakovsky's *The Bedbug*), a dream (see pp. 278-9), a machine or distortion of space (Wells's *The Time Machine,* "Missing One's Coach: An Anachronism" [see p. 376], Heinlein's "By His Bootstraps," much recent time travel fiction), immortality (the Struldbruggs in *Gulliver's Travels,* Virginia Woolf's *Orlando,* Clarissa in Gore Vidal's *Messiah*), racial, ancestral, or exchanged memory ("A Tale of the Ragged Mountains," London's *Before Adam*, perhaps James's *The Sense of the Past*), extraordinary anticipation (Bellamy's "The Old Folks' Party"), and so on. The other mode of time travel makes the reader himself the time traveler, shifting him, as soon as he recognizes the scene, into an unfamiliar time. All fiction which takes place entirely in a future scene is this kind of time travel. All fiction which takes place in prehistory is conventionally considered this kind of time travel, though historical fiction, for some reason or other, is not. (The supposed differences between historical and prehistorical fiction might well be worth contemplation, perhaps together with the notion that prehistory is reconstructed by scientists, history by historians.)

Four of the five time travel stories in this book represent the second mode because almost all nineteenth-century time travel short stories in the first mode are radically flawed. They either end with an embarrassed confession that it's all been a dream, or use physical devices without considering their paradoxes (focus on the paradoxes of time travel, as in Bradbury's "A Sound of Thunder," William Tenn's "Me, Myself, and I," and many of Damon Knight's time travel stories, is one of the most interesting developments in modern science fiction), or move a traveler wildly in time without exploring the consequences of this movement on his mind (most works which dramatized what this might really do to the time traveler almost unavoidably became full-length—*Looking Backward*, *A Connecticut Yankee*, *The Sense of the Past*).

The most remarkable thing about the time travel literature of the nineteenth century is that it now, in the twentieth century, represents in itself a kind of time travel for us. To move into past visions of the future or past is to shift our own consciousness in time in extraordinary ways.

BEYOND THE PAST

The nineteenth century began with battles raging about the age of the earth itself. By the middle of the century geological time had largely overwhelmed Biblical time and the main battleground between organized Christianity and science on the prehistorical front had shifted to man himself. With the extension of past time far beyond history and the extension of man's identity until it became a blur in the primeval world, a new field opened for science fiction. By the end of the nineteenth century, the fiction laid in remote prehistory and dealing with beings who were or were not quite men was fast on its way to becoming a tradition. In these anthropological romances mankind, as Leo Henkin has put it in *Darwinism in the English Novel, 1860-1910* (1940), "is usually pictured at some dramatic point in the history of the race, about to turn aside from ape-stock and enter upon his heritage as *Homo sapiens;* or on the verge of making a discovery fundamental to his survival and to his ultimate civilization."

"Christmas 200,000 B.C.," by Stanley Waterloo, whose popular full-length anthropological romance *The Story of Ab: A Tale of the Time of the Cave Men* (1897) had gone into three editions before Wells's "A Story of the Stone Age" (1899) appeared, exemplifies the fiction of prehistory without displaying most of the faults which make so much of it unreadable. Waterloo, that is, does not have one caveman make discoveries which probably occupied the entire race for thousands of years, nor does he have a caveman and cave-girl who behave (and this is all too common) like a Victorian stage hero and stage heroine among stage villains, nor does he try to generate hundreds of pages out of a single gimmick. Though slight, "Christmas 200,000 B.C." is memorable. One only wishes that Waterloo had not seen the survival of yellow hair as the emblem of mental evolution.

STANLEY WATERLOO

Christmas 200,000 B.C. *

It was Christmas in the year 200,000 B.C. It is true that it was not called Christmas then—our ancestors at that date were not much given to the celebration of religious festivals—but, taking the Gregorian calendar and counting backward just 200,000 plus 1887 years this particular day would be located. There was no formal celebration, but, nevertheless, a good deal was going on in the neighborhood of the home of Fangs. Names were not common at the time mentioned, but the more advanced of the cave-dwellers had them. Man had so far advanced that only traces of his ape origin remained, and he had begun to have a language. It was a queer "clucking" sort of language, something like that of the Bushmen, the low type of man yet to be found in Africa, and it was not very useful in the expression of ideas, but then primitive man didn't have many ideas to express. Names, so far as used, were at this time derived merely from some personal quality or peculiarity. Fangs was so called because of his huge teeth. His mate was called She Fox; his daughter, not Nellie, nor Jennie, nor Mamie—young ladies did not affect the "ie" then—but Red Lips. She was, for the age, remarkably pretty and refined. She could cast eyes which told a story at a suitor, and there were several kinds of snake she would not eat. She was a merry, energetic girl, and was the most useful member of the family in tree-climbing. She was an only child and rather petted. Her

* Internal references establish 1887 as date of composition and, presumably, of publication, but I have been unable to find a printing earlier than its inclusion in Waterloo's *The Wolf's Long Howl,* 1899.

father or mother rarely knocked her down with a very heavy club when angry, and after her fourteenth year rarely assaulted her at all. So far as She Fox was concerned, this kindness largely resulted from discretion, the daughter having in the last encounter so belabored the mother that she was laid up for a week. The father abstained chiefly because the daughter had become useful. Red Lips was now eighteen.

Fangs was a cave-dweller. His home was sumptuously furnished. The floor of the cave was strewn with dry grass, something that in most other caves was lacking. Fangs was a prominent citizen. He was one of the strongest men in the valley. He had killed Red Beard, another prominent citizen, in a little dispute over priority of right to possession of a dead mastodon discovered in a swamp, and had for years been the terror of every cave man in the region who possessed anything worth taking.

On this particular morning, which would have been Christmas morning had it not come too early in the world's history, Fangs left the cave after eating the whole of a water-fowl he had killed with a stone the night before and some half dozen field mice which his wife had brought in. She Fox and Red Lips had for breakfast only the bones of the duck and some roots dug in the forest. Fangs carried with him a huge club, and in a rough pouch made of the skin of some small wild animal a collection of stones of convenient size for throwing. This was before man had invented the bow or even the crude stone ax. He came back in a surly mood because he had found nothing and killed nothing, but he brought a companion with him. This companion, whom he had met in the woods, was known as Wolf, because his countenance reminded one of a wolf. He could hardly be called a gentleman, even as times and terms went then. He was evidently not of an old family, for he possessed something more than a rudimentary tail, and, had his face looked less like that of a wolf, it would have been that of a baboon. He was hairy, and his speech of rough gutturals was imperfect. He could pronounce but few words. He was, however, very strong, and Fangs rather liked him.

What Fangs did when he came in was to propose a matrimonial alliance. That is, he grasped his daughter by the arm and led her up to Wolf, and then pointing to an abandoned cave in the hillside not far distant, pushed them toward it. They did not have marriage ceremonies 200,000 B.C. Wolf, who had evidently been informed of Fangs's desire and who was himself in favor of the alliance, seized the girl and began dragging her off to the new home and the honeymoon. She resisted, and shrieked, and clawed like a wild-cat. Her mother, She Fox, came running out, club in hand, but was promptly knocked down by Fangs, who then dragged her into the cave again. Meanwhile the bridegroom was hauling the bride away through furze and bushes at a rapid rate. Red Lips had ceased to struggle, and was thinking. Her thoughts were not very well defined nor clear, but one thing she knew well—she did not want to live in a cave with Wolf. She had a fancy that she would prefer to live instead with Yellow Hair, a young cave man who had not yet selected a mate, and who was remarkably fleet of foot. They were now very near the cave, and she knew that unless she exerted herself housekeeping would begin within a very few moments. Wolf was strong, but slow of movement. Red Lips was only less swift than Yellow Hair. An idea occurred to her. She bent her head and buried her strong teeth deep in the wrist of the man who was half-carrying, half-dragging her through the underwood.

With a howl which justified his name, Wolf for an instant released his hold. That instant allowed the girl's escape. She leaped away like a deer and darted into the forest. Yelling with pain and rage, Wolf pursued her. She gained on him steadily as she ran, but there was a light snow upon the ground, and she could be followed by the trail which her pursuer took up doggedly and determinedly. He knew that he could tire her out and catch her in time. He solaced himself for her temporary escape by thinking, as he ran, how fiercely he would beat his bride before starting for the cave again, and as he thought his teeth showed like those of a dog of to-day.

The chase lasted for hours, and Red Lips had gained perhaps a mile upon her pursuer when her strength began to flag. The pace was telling upon her. She had run many miles. She was almost hopeless of escape when she emerged into a little glade, where sat a man gnawing contentedly at a raw rabbit. He leaped to his feet as the girl appeared, but a moment later recognized her and smiled. The man was Yellow Hair. He reached out part of the rabbit he was devouring, and Red Lips, whose breakfast

had, as already mentioned, been a light one, tore at it and consumed it in a moment. Then she told of what had happened.

"We will kill Wolf, and you shall live with me," said Yellow Hair.

Red Lips assented eagerly, and the two consulted together. Near them was a hill, one side of which was a precipice. At the base of the precipice ran a path. The result of the consultation was that Yellow Hair left the girl, and making a swift circuit, came upon the precipice from the farther side, and crouched low upon its summit. The girl ran along the path at the bottom of the declivity for some distance, then, entering a defile which crossed it at right angles, herself made a turn, climbed the hill and joined Yellow Hair. From where they were lying they could see the glade they had just left.

Wolf entered the glade, and noted where the footsteps of the girl and those of a man came together. For a moment or two he appeared troubled and suspicious; then his face cleared. He saw that the tracks had diverged again. He had recognized the man's tracks as those of Yellow Hair.

"Yellow Hair is afraid of my strong arm," he thought. "He dare not stay with Red Lips. I shall catch her soon and beat her and take her with me."

The two crouching upon the precipice watched his every movement. They had rolled to the edge of the declivity a rock as huge as they could control, and now together held it poised over the pathway. Wolf came hurrying along, his head bent down like that of a hound on the scent of game. He reached a spot just beneath the two, and then with a sudden united effort they shoved over the rock. It thundered down upon the unfortunate Wolf with an accuracy which spoke well for the eyes and hands of the lovers. The man was crushed horribly. The two above scrambled down, laughing, and Yellow Hair took from the dead Wolf a necklace of claws and fastened it proudly upon his own person.

"Now we will go to my cave," said he.

"No," said Red Lips; "my father will look for Wolf to-morrow, and will find him. Then he will come and kill us. We must go and kill him tonight."

"Yes," said Yellow Hair.

Hand in hand the two started for the cave of Fangs. The side hill in which it was situated was very steep, and the lovers thought they could duplicate the affair with Wolf. "We must cripple him, anyway," said Yellow Hair, "for I am not strong enough to fight him alone. His club is heavy."

They reached the vicinity of the cave and crept above it. Having, with great difficulty, secured a rock in position to be rolled down, they waited for Fangs to appear. He came out about dusk, and stretched out his arms lazily, when the two above released the rock. It rolled down swiftly and with great force, but there was no such sheer drop afforded as when Wolf was killed, and Fangs heard the stone coming and almost eluded it. It caught one of his legs, as he tried to leap aside, and broke it. Fangs fell to the ground.

With a yell of triumph Yellow Hair bounded to where the crippled man lay and began pounding him upon the head with his club. Fangs had a very thick head. He struggled vigorously, and succeeded in catching Yellow Hair by the wrist. Then he drew the younger man to him and began to throttle him. The case of Yellow Hair was desperate. Fangs's great strength was too much for him. His stifled yells told of his agony.

It was at this juncture that Red Lips demonstrated her quality as a girl of decision and of action. A sharp fragment of slate, several pounds in weight, lay at her feet. She seized it and bounded forward to where the struggle was going on. The back of Fangs's head was fairly exposed. The girl brought down the sharp stone upon it just where the head and spinal column joined, and the crashing thud told of the force of the blow. Delivered with such strength upon such a spot there could be but one result. The man could not have been killed more quickly. Yellow Hair released himself from the dead giant's embrace and rose to his feet. Then, after a short breathing time, to make assurance sure, he picked up his club and battered the head of Fangs until there could be no chance of his resuscitation. The performance was unnecessary, but neither Yellow Hair nor Red Lips was aware of the fact. Their knowledge of anatomy was limited. Neither knew the effect of such a blow delivered properly at the base of the brain.

Yellow Hair finally ceased his exercise and rested on his club. "Shall we go to my cave now?" said he.

"Why should we?" said Red Lips. "Let us take this cave. There is dry grass on the floor."

They entered the cave. She Fox, who had witnessed what had occurred, sat in one corner, and looked up doubtfully as they entered. "I am tired," said Yellow Hair, and he laid himself down and went to sleep.

She Fox looked at her daughter. "I killed three hedgehogs to-day," she whispered.

The new mistress of the cave looked at her kindly. "Go out and dig some roots," she said, "and come back with them, and then with them and the hedgehogs we will have a feast."

She Fox went out and returned in an hour with roots and nuts. Red Lips awakened Yellow Hair, and all three fed ravenously and merrily. It was a great occasion in the cave of the late Fangs. There was no such Christmas feast, at the same time a wedding feast, in any other cave in all the region. And the sequel to the events of the day was as happy as the day itself. Yellow Hair and Red Lips somehow avoided being killed, and grew old together, and left a numerous progeny.

MARK TWAIN
AND SCIENCE FICTION

Because of Mark Twain's long interest in geology, astronomy, the marvelous aspects of biology, and speculative psychic research, much of his fiction reflects awarenesses of geological time, astronomical distances, microscopic dimensions, and extraordinary psychic possibilities. Still it may come as a shock to think of Twain as a writer of science fiction. Yet what is probably his second-best full-length work is not only a piece of science fiction, but a classic piece (and one that is, as we shall see, a good deal more completely science fiction than has ever been recognized). And in addition to *A Connecticut Yankee in King Arthur's Court* and the piece reprinted here, "From the 'London Times' of 1904," Twain's science fiction includes such varied experiments as "The Curious Republic of Gondour" (1875), an extrapolated utopia in which votes are proportioned according to money and education; *The Comedy of Those Extraordinary Twins* (1894), which explores in broadly comic terms the problems of a pair of heads who share a body (derived from the actual Tocci twins); *Tom Sawyer Abroad* (1894), which describes the semi-circumnavigation of the world in a balloon (Twain had, according to A. B. Paine, begun working on this idea in 1868 but gave it up because of Verne's *Five Weeks in a Balloon*); *Extracts from Captain Stormfield's Visit to Heaven*

(1909), which looks at the idea of a physical heaven in terms of spatial and temporal dimensions; and *The Great Dark,* which deserves special attention.

Even in its unfinished state, *The Great Dark* (finally available in the long-suppressed *Letters from the Earth*) is a minor masterpiece which hints of a potential to have become Twain's finest creation. Together with Hawthorne's incomplete romances, Poe's incomplete *Narrative of Arthur Gordon Pym,* and James's incomplete *The Sense of the Past,* it lies, like a skeleton, as a marker of the frontiers of nineteenth-century American science fiction.

Twain's ambition was nothing less than to express the relations between dream and what we call waking reality as the reversible relations between a nightmare microcosm of infinitely expanded time, in which the most incredible horrors become humdrum, and a waking cosmos of infinitely compressed time, terrifying because of what its humdrum activities hide. Briefly, this is the action: a pleasant bourgeois chap peers through the microscope he has just bought for his daughter into a drop of water and is astounded by the monsters he sees; he falls asleep and dreams that he and his family are on a ship which has been sailing for an incredibly long time within the drop of water; he learns that only he, no other member of his family or the crew, looks upon this microscopic existence as a dream; eventually, like the others, he accepts the other life as the dream; after many years of sailing amidst huge protozoan monsters and the most overwhelming of tragic and grotesque adventures, he returns to the other world; even though he has been "asleep" for barely a minute, his experiences in the microscopic world have been so long and so large that he now believes he is dreaming and that he will reawaken into the terrible watery world; that is, he once again is the only being who thinks of his present existence as dream. This brief description of the narrative and of Twain's outlined conclusion does not even hint of the extraordinary effects that Twain achieves by using his peculiar mode of realistic narration to chronicle life in the most fantastic and eerie of worlds. Scenes in which the narrator's wife matter-of-factly recalls the time when her parents died because of "the Great White Glare" (the light from the microscope's mirror) and in which the narrator's children insist that horses are dream animals, gigantic protozoa the only real animals—scenes like these do not so much suggest Kafka, and Poe's *Narrative of Arthur Gordon Pym,* as suggest what Twain might have written if he could have brought *The Great Dark* to completion.

Twain's only complete major work of science fiction, *A Connecticut Yankee in King Arthur's Court* (1889), has a lot more to do with the dimensions and concerns and methods of *The Great Dark* than might be supposed. The usual interpretation of *A Connecticut Yankee* sees it as a fantasy in which time travel is merely a device to get an ingenious nineteenth-century American into sixth-century England. But Hank Morgan's voyage into time and his return exactly parallel the voyage into microscopic space and the return of the narrator of *The Great Dark.* Morgan makes his initial trip by apparently (I shall return to this point) fantastic means, while his return trip is quite in an established convention of nineteenth-century science fiction—he sleeps for thirteen centuries. When he returns, his consciousness has been twice dislocated, just like that of the dimensional traveler in *The Great Dark.* Again one question is, Which is the dream?

Twain here combines two kinds of time travel, travel by a contemporary into past time and travel by a man from the past into contemporary time. To see the issues and possibilities set up by this double movement in time, one should compare *A Connecticut Yankee* with such works as the anonymous "Missing One's Coach: An Anachronism" (*Edinburgh Review,* 1838), in which a nineteenth-century man, encountering a "fault in the strata of time," meets the Venerable Bede (note the connections with Bede's treatise on the calculation of time, *De Ratione Temporum*) in the eighth century; *Looking Backward*, which appeared the year before and in which the time traveler sleeps his way into the future, dreams that he has awakened back in the present, and then reawakens in the future; and James's unfinished *The Sense of the Past*, in which alter egos from 1820 and *circa* 1910 switch places in time.

A Connecticut Yankee is concerned with a good deal more than the results of time travel; it is also concerned, in a wildly speculative but serious way, with the possibility of identity transference in time. This too was a conventional mode of nineteenth-century science fiction and had a lot to do with one of Twain's interests, and with one of the prime interests of nineteenth-century science fiction, the transference of thoughts in space.

In his 1891 essay called "Mental Telegraphy" (and also in the 1895 essay, "Mental Telegraphy Again"), Twain speculates freely about the possibilities latent in thought transference:

> This age seems to have exhausted invention nearly; still, it has one important contract on its hands yet—the invention of the *phrenophone;* that is to say, a method whereby the communicating of mind with mind may be brought under command and reduced to certainty and system. The telegraph and the telephone are going to become too slow and wordy for our needs. We must have the *thought* itself shot into our minds from a distance; then, if we need to put it into words, we can do that tedious work at our leisure. Doubtless the something which conveys our thoughts through the air from brain to brain is a finer and subtler form of electricity, and all we need do is to find out how to capture it and how to force it to do its work, as we have had to do in the case of the electric currents. Before the day of telegraphs neither one of these marvels would have seemed any easier to achieve than the other.

At the end of this essay, Twain makes the connection between these possibilities and one of the central questions of both *The Great Dark* and *A Connecticut Yankee in King Arthur's Court:*

> Now, how are you to tell when you are awake? What are you to go by? People bite their fingers to find out. Why, you can do that in a dream.

The possibility of unwittingly living a dream leads directly to one of the possibilities of identity transference in time. This possibility is the subject of Bierce's "John Bartine's Watch: A Story by a Physician," in which the title character dies when, because he loses his grip on time, his long-dead great-grandfather takes over his identity, "A Resumed Identity," in which awakening into life after a long suspension is fatal, and "A Psychological Shipwreck," included here; Jack London's *Before Adam,* an anthropological romance in which the narrator presents his dreams of prehistory as the memories of a remote ancestor called up by a dissociation of identity in time; William Dean Howells's "A Case of Metaphantasmia," in which someone's dream (none knows whose) becomes everybody's temporary reality; Richard Rice's "The White Sleep of Auber Hurn," in which the title character disappears from our space-time world when an alternative space-time world, which some might call a dream world, plucks him bodily beyond perception; and, of course, Poe's "A Tale of the Ragged Mountains" and James's *The Sense of the Past.* The possibility attains a sublimated form in Jung's notion of the collective unconscious.

"From the 'London Times' of 1904" offers a striking comparison to the wild speculation of *The Great Dark* and *A Connecticut Yankee.* Here Twain concocts nothing like his "phrenophone" but extrapolates in a cautious, conservative way from the technology of 1898 to the possibilities of the very near future, 1904. The concern is still, however, transference of thought and image through time and space. The means are now entirely credible;

that is, they are recognizably physical and technological rather than apparently psychical and speculative.

Curiously, "From the 'London Times' of 1904" is one of the few science fictions of the nineteenth century which predicts an invention earlier rather than later than it was to come. (To appreciate Twain's matter-of-fact account of the telelectroscope, one should compare it to all those nineteenth-century science fictions which present modern commonplaces as extravagant fantasy.) "From the 'London Times' of 1904" represents the other side of Twain's speculative science fiction, a side which reflects what is practical, limited, almost actual, while hinting of the other side, which reflects upon the state called dream.

MARK TWAIN
From the "London Times" of 1904 *

I
Correspondence of the "London Times"

CHICAGO, APRIL 1, 1904

I resume by cable-telephone where I left off yesterday. For many hours, now, this vast city—along with the rest of the globe, of course—has talked of nothing but the extraordinary episode mentioned in my last report. In accordance with your instructions, I will now trace the romance from its beginnings down to the culmination of yesterday—or to-day; call it which you like. By an odd chance, I was a personal actor in a part of this drama myself. The opening scene plays in Vienna. Date, one o'clock in the morning, March 31, 1898. I had spent the evening at a social entertainment. About midnight I went away, in company with the military attachés of the British, Italian, and American embassies, to finish with a late smoke. This function had been appointed to take place in the house of Lieutenant Hillyer, the third attaché mentioned in the above list. When we arrived there we found several visitors in the room: young Szczepanik; [1] Mr. K., his financial backer; Mr. W., the latter's secretary; and Lieutenant Clayton of the United States army. War was at that time threatening between Spain and our country, and Lieutenant Clayton had been sent to Europe on military business. I was well acquainted with young Szczepanik and his two friends, and I knew Mr. Clayton slightly. I had met him at West Point years before, when he was a cadet. It was when General Merritt was

[1] Pronounced (approximately) Ze*pan*nik. [M.T.]

* *The Century Magazine*, 1898.

superintendent. He had the reputation of being an able officer, and also of being quick-tempered and plain-spoken.

This smoking-party had been gathered together partly for business. This business was to consider the availability of the telelectroscope for military service. It sounds oddly enough now, but it is nevertheless true that at that time the invention was not taken seriously by any one except its inventor. Even his financial supporter regarded it merely as a curious and interesting toy. Indeed, he was so convinced of this that he had actually postponed its use by the general world to the end of the dying century by granting a two years' exclusive lease of it to a syndicate, whose intent was to exploit it at the Paris World's Fair.

When we entered the smoking-room we found Lieutenant Clayton and Szczepanik engaged in a warm talk over the telelectroscope in the German tongue. Clayton was saying:

"Well, you know *my* opinion of it, anyway!" and he brought his fist down with emphasis upon the table.

"And I do not value it," retorted the young inventor, with provoking calmness of tone and manner.

Clayton turned to Mr. K., and said:

"*I* cannot see why you are wasting money on this toy. In my opinion, the day will never come when it will do a farthing's worth of real service for any human being."

"That may be; yes, that may be; still, I have put the money in it, and am content. I think, myself, that it is only a toy; but Szczepanik claims more for it, and I know him well enough to believe that he can see farther than I can—either with his telelectroscope or without it."

The soft answer did not cool Clayton down; it seemed only to irritate him the more; and he repeated and emphasized his conviction that the invention would never do any man a farthing's worth of real service. He even made it a "brass" farthing, this time. Then he laid an English farthing on the table, and added:

"Take that, Mr. K., and put it away; and if ever the telelectroscope does any man an actual service,—mind, a *real* service,—please mail it to me as a reminder, and I will take back what I have been saying. Will you?"

"I will"; and Mr. K. put the coin in his pocket.

Mr. Clayton now turned toward Szczepanik, and began with

a taunt—a taunt which did not reach a finish; Szczepanik interrupted it with a hardy retort, and followed this with a blow. There was a brisk fight for a moment or two; then the attachés separated the men.

The scene now changes to Chicago. Time, the autumn of 1901. As soon as the Paris contract released the telelectroscope, it was delivered to public use, and was soon connected with the telephonic systems of the whole world. The improved "limitless-distance" telephone was presently introduced, and the daily doings of the globe made visible to everybody, and audibly discussable, too, by witnesses separated by any number of leagues.

By and by Szczepanik arrived in Chicago. Clayton (now captain) was serving in that military department at the time. The two men resumed the Viennese quarrel of 1898. On three different occasions they quarreled, and were separated by witnesses. Then came an interval of two months, during which time Szczepanik was not seen by any of his friends, and it was at first supposed that he had gone off on a sight-seeing tour and would soon be heard from. But no; no word came from him. Then it was supposed that he had returned to Europe. Still, time drifted on, and he was not heard from. Nobody was troubled, for he was like most inventors and other kinds of poets, and went and came in a capricious way, and often without notice.

Now comes the tragedy. On the 29th of December, in a dark and unused compartment of the cellar under Captain Clayton's house, a corpse was discovered by one of Clayton's maid-servants. It was easily identified as Szczepanik's. The man had died by violence. Clayton was arrested, indicted, and brought to trial, charged with this murder. The evidence against him was perfect in every detail, and absolutely unassailable. Clayton admitted this himself. He said that a reasonable man could not examine this testimony with a dispassionate mind and not be convinced by it; yet the man would be in error, nevertheless. Clayton swore that he did not commit the murder, and that he had had nothing to do with it.

As your readers will remember, he was condemned to death. He had numerous and powerful friends, and they worked hard to save him, for none of them doubted the truth of his assertion. I did what little I could to help, for I had long since become a close friend of his, and thought I knew that it was not in his character to inveigle an enemy into a corner and assassinate him. During 1902 and 1903 he was several times reprieved by the governor; he was reprieved once more in the beginning of the present year, and the execution-day postponed to March 31.

The governor's situation has been embarrassing, from the day of the condemnation, because of the fact that Clayton's wife is the governor's niece. The marriage took place in 1899, when Clayton was thirty-four and the girl twenty-three, and has been a happy one. There is one child, a little girl three years old. Pity for the poor mother and child kept the mouths of grumblers closed at first; but this could not last forever,—for in America politics has a hand in everything,—and by and by the governor's political opponents began to call attention to his delay in allowing the law to take its course. These hints have grown more and more frequent of late, and more and more pronounced. As a natural result, his own party grew nervous. Its leaders began to visit Springfield and hold long private conferences with him. He was now between two fires. On the one hand, his niece was imploring him to pardon her husband; on the other were the leaders, insisting that he stand to his plain duty as chief magistrate of the State, and place no further bar to Clayton's execution. Duty won in the struggle, and the governor gave his word that he would not again respite the condemned man. This was two weeks ago. Mrs. Clayton now said:

"Now that you have given your word, my last hope is gone, for I know you will never go back from it. But you have done the best you could for John, and I have no reproaches for you. You love him, and you love me, and we both know that if you could honorably save him, you would do it. I will go to him now, and be what help I can to him, and get what comfort I may out of the few days that are left to us before the night comes which will have no end for me in life. You will be with me that day? You will not let me bear it alone?"

"I will take you to him myself, poor child, and I will be near you to the last."

By the governor's command, Clayton was now allowed every indulgence he might ask for which could interest his mind and soften the hardships of his imprisonment. His wife and child spent the days with him; I was his companion by night. He was removed from the narrow cell which he had occupied during such a dreary stretch of time, and given the chief warden's roomy and comfortable quarters. His mind was always busy with the catastrophe of his life, and with the slaughtered inventor, and he now took the fancy that he would like to have the telelectroscope and divert his mind with it. He had his wish. The connection was made with the international telephone-station, and day by day, and night by night, he called up one corner of the globe after another, and looked upon its life, and studied its strange sights, and spoke with its people, and realized that by grace of this marvelous instrument he was almost as free as the birds of the air, although a prisoner under locks and bars. He seldom spoke, and I never interrupted him when he was absorbed in this amusement. I sat in his parlor and read and smoked, and the nights were very quiet and reposefully sociable, and I found them pleasant. Now and then I would hear him say, "Give me Yedo"; next, "Give me Hong-Kong"; next, "Give me Melbourne." And I smoked on, and read in comfort, while he wandered about the remote under-world, where the sun was shining in the sky, and the people were at their daily work. Sometimes the talk that came from those far regions through the microphone attachment interested me, and I listened.

Yesterday—I keep calling it yesterday, which is quite natural, for certain reasons—the instrument remained unused, and that, also, was natural, for it was the eve of the execution-day. It was spent in tears and lamentations and farewells. The governor and the wife and child remained until a quarter past eleven at night, and the scenes I witnessed were pitiful to see. The execution was to take place at four in the morning. A little after eleven a sound of hammering broke out upon the still night, and there was a glare of light, and the child cried out, "What is that, papa?" and ran to the window before she could be stopped, and clapped her small hands, and said: "Oh, come and see, mama—such a pretty thing they are making!" The mother knew—and fainted. It was the gallows!

She was carried away to her lodging, poor woman, and Clayton and I were alone—alone, and thinking, brooding, dreaming. We might have been statues, we sat so motionless and still. It was a wild night, for winter was come again for a moment, after the habit of this region in the early spring. The sky was starless and black, and a strong wind was blowing from the lake. The silence in the room was so deep that all outside sounds seemed exaggerated by contrast with it. These sounds were fitting ones; they harmonized with the situation and the conditions: the boom and thunder of sudden storm-gusts among the roofs and chimneys, then the dying down into moanings and wailings about the eaves and angles; now and then a gnashing and lashing rush of sleet along the window-panes; and always the muffled and uncanny hammering of the gallows-builders in the courtyard. After an age of this, another sound—far off, and coming smothered and faint through the riot of the tempest—a bell tolling twelve! Another age, and it tolled again. By and by, again. A dreary, long interval after this, then the spectral sound floated to us once more—one, two, three; and this time we caught our breath: sixty minutes of life left!

Clayton rose, and stood by the window, and looked up into the black sky, and listened to the thrashing sleet and the piping wind; then he said: "That a dying man's last of earth should be—this!" After a little he said: "I must see the sun again—the sun!" and the next moment he was feverishly calling: "China! Give me China—Peking!"

I was strangely stirred, and said to myself: "To think that it is a mere human being who does this unimaginable miracle—turns winter into summer, night into day, storm into calm, gives the freedom of the great globe to a prisoner in his cell, and the sun in his naked splendor to a man dying in Egyptian darkness!"

I was listening.

"What light! what brilliancy! what radiance! . . . This is Peking?"

"Yes."

"The time?"

"Mid-afternoon."

"What is the great crowd for, and in such gorgeous costumes? What masses and masses of rich color and barbaric magnificence! And how they flash and glow and burn in the flooding sunlight! What *is* the occasion of it all?"

"The coronation of our new emperor—the Czar."

"But I thought that that was to take place yesterday."

"This *is* yesterday—to you."

"Certainly it is. But my mind is confused, these days; there are reasons for it. . . . Is this the beginning of the procession?"

"Oh, no; it began to move an hour ago."

"Is there much more of it still to come?"

"Two hours of it. Why do you sigh?"

"Because I should like to see it all."

"And why can't you?"

"I have to go—presently."

"You have an engagement?"

After a pause, softly: "Yes." After another pause: "Who are these in the splendid pavilion?"

"The imperial family, and visiting royalties from here and there and yonder in the earth."

"And who are those in the adjoining pavilions to the right and left?"

"Ambassadors and their families and suites to the right; unofficial foreigners to the left."

"If you will be so good, I—"

Boom! That distant bell again, tolling the half-hour faintly through the tempest of wind and sleet. The door opened, and the governor and the mother and child entered—the woman in widow's weeds! She fell upon her husband's breast in a passion of sobs, and I—I could not stay; I could not bear it. I went into the bedchamber, and closed the door. I sat there waiting—waiting—waiting, and listening to the rattling sashes and the blustering of the storm. After what seemed a long, long time, I heard a rustle and movement in the parlor, and knew that the clergyman and the sheriff and the guard were come. There was some low-voiced talking; then a hush; then a prayer, with a sound of sobbing; presently, footfalls—the departure for the gallows; then the child's happy voice: "Don't cry *now*, mama, when we've got papa again, and taking him home."

The door closed; they were gone. I was ashamed: I was the only friend of the dying man that had no spirit, no courage. I stepped into the room, and said I would be a man and would follow. But we are made as we are made, and we cannot help it. I did not go.

I fidgeted about the room nervously, and presently went to the window, and softly raised it,—drawn by that dread fascination which the terrible and the awful exert,—and looked down upon the courtyard. By the garish light of the electric lamps I saw the little group of privileged witnesses, the wife crying on her uncle's breast, the condemned man standing on the scaffold with the halter around his neck, his arms strapped to his body, the black cap on his head, the sheriff at his side with his hand on the drop, the clergyman in front of him with bare head and his book in his hand.

"I am the resurrection and the life—"

I turned away. I could not listen; I could not look. I did not know whither to go or what to do. Mechanically, and without knowing it, I put my eye to that strange instrument, and there was Peking and the Czar's procession! The next moment I was leaning out of the window, gasping, suffocating, trying to speak, but dumb from the very imminence of the necessity of speaking. The preacher could speak, but I, who had such need of words—

"And may God have mercy upon your soul. Amen."

The sheriff drew down the black cap, and laid his hand upon the lever. I got my voice.

"Stop, for God's sake! The man is innocent. Come here and see Szczepanik face to face!"

Hardly three minutes later the governor had my place at the window, and was saying:

"Strike off his bonds and set him free!"

Three minutes later all were in the parlor again. The reader will imagine the scene; I have no need to describe it. It was a sort of mad orgy of joy.

A messenger carried word to Szczepanik in the pavilion, and one could see the distressed amazement dawn in his face as he listened to the tale. Then he came to his end of the line, and talked with Clayton and the governor and the others; and the wife poured out her gratitude upon him for saving her husband's life, and in her deep thankfulness she kissed him at twelve thousand miles' range.

The telelectrophonoscopes of the globe were put to service now, and for many hours the kings and queens of many realms (with here and there a reporter) talked with Szczepanik, and praised him; and the few scientific societies which had not already made him an honorary member conferred that grace upon him.

How had he come to disappear from among us? It was easily explained. He had not grown used to being a world-famous person, and had been forced to break away from the lionizing that was robbing him of all privacy and repose. So he grew a beard, put on colored glasses, disguised himself a little in other ways, then took a fictitious name, and went off to wander about the earth in peace.

Such is the tale of the drama which began with an inconsequential quarrel in Vienna in the spring of 1898, and came near ending as a tragedy in the spring of 1904. MARK TWAIN.

II

Correspondence of the "London Times"

CHICAGO, APRIL 5, 1904

To-day, by a clipper of the Electric Line, and the latter's Electric Railway connections, arrived an envelop from Vienna, for Captain Clayton, containing an English farthing. The receiver of it was a good deal moved. He called up Vienna, and stood face to face with Mr. K., and said:

"I do not need to say anything; you can see it all in my face. My wife has the farthing. Do not be afraid—she will not throw it away." M. T.

III

Correspondence of the "London Times"

CHICAGO, APRIL 23, 1904

Now that the after developments of the Clayton case have run their course and reached a finish, I will sum them up. Clayton's romantic escape from a shameful death steeped all this region in an enchantment of wonder and joy—during the proverbial nine days. Then the sobering process followed, and men began to take thought, and to say: "But *a man was killed*, and Clayton killed him." Others replied: "That is true: we have been overlooking that important detail; we have been led away by excitement."

The feeling soon became general that Clayton ought to be tried again. Measures were taken accordingly, and the proper representations conveyed to Washington; for in America, under the new paragraph added to the Constitution in 1899, second trials are not State affairs, but national, and must be tried by the most august body in the land—the Supreme Court of the United States. The justices were therefore summoned to sit in Chicago. The session was held day before yesterday, and was opened with the usual impressive formalities, the nine judges appearing in their black robes, and the new chief justice (Lemaitre) presiding. In opening the case, the chief justice said:

"It is my opinion that this matter is quite simple. The prisoner at the bar was charged with murdering the man Szczepanik; he was tried for murdering the man Szczepanik; he was fairly tried, and justly condemned and sentenced to death for murdering the man Szczepanik. It turns out that the man Szczepanik was not murdered at all. By the decision of the French courts in the Dreyfus matter, it is established beyond cavil or question that the decisions of courts are permanent and cannot be revised. We are obliged to respect and adopt this precedent. It is upon precedents that the enduring edifice of jurisprudence is reared. The prisoner at the bar has been fairly and righteously condemned to death for the murder of the man Szczepanik, and, in my opinion, there is but one course to pursue in the matter: he must be hanged."

Mr. Justice Crawford said:

"But, your Excellency, he was pardoned on the scaffold for that."

"The pardon is not valid, and cannot stand, because he was pardoned for killing a man whom he had not killed. A man cannot be pardoned for a crime which he has not committed; it would be an absurdity."

"But, your Excellency, he did kill a man."

"That is an extraneous detail; we have nothing to do with it. The court cannot take up this crime until the prisoner has expiated the other one."

Mr. Justice Halleck said:

"If we order his execution, your Excellency, we shall bring about a miscarriage of justice; for the governor will pardon him again."

"He will not have the power. He cannot pardon a man for a crime which he has not committed. As I observed before, it would be an absurdity."

After a consultation, Mr. Justice Wadsworth said:

"Several of us have arrived at the conclusion, your Excellency, that it would be an error to hang the prisoner for killing Szczepanik, but only for killing the other man, since it is proven that he did not kill Szczepanik."

"On the contrary, it is proven that he *did* kill Szczepanik. By the French precedent, it is plain that we must abide by the finding of the court."

"But Szczepanik is still alive."

"So is Dreyfus."

In the end it was found impossible to ignore or get around the French precedent. There could be but one result: Clayton was delivered over to the executioner. It made an immense excitement; the State rose as one man and clamored for Clayton's pardon and retrial. The governor issued the pardon, but the Supreme Court was in duty bound to annul it, and did so, and poor Clayton was hanged yesterday. The city is draped in black, and, indeed, the like may be said of the State. All America is vocal with scorn of "French justice," and of the malignant little soldiers who invented it and inflicted it upon the other Christian lands.

M. T.

THE PERFECT FUTURE

Today, the heyday of anti-utopia, when Zamiatin's *We*, *Brave New World*, *1984*, Albert Guerard's *Night Journey*, Gore Vidal's *Messiah*, Bradbury's *Fahrenheit 451*, John MacDonald's "Spectator Sport," and Pohl and Kornbluth's *The Space Merchants* represent virtually orthodox Western literary views of the future, the orthodox nineteenth-century American view of the future may seem quaint and naïve. But the nineteenth-century American view of the future as eutopia, the good place, is by no means entirely out of date. Surviving in present-day political rhetoric and in the hopes of great masses of people, this view of the future still moves the present, even in the West.

In the East this view has not only survived but triumphed. Hundreds of almost routine nineteenth-century American eutopias of the future would conform perfectly to the official Sino-Soviet view of the future. And this view dominates almost all of Soviet science fiction as well as a good deal of Chinese and Soviet domestic and foreign policy. (Chinese science fiction is unavailable to us, but one would certainly guess that it has the same basic vision as Soviet science fiction.) Works such as Victor Saparin's "The Trial of Tantalus," Valentina Zhuravleva's "The Astronaut," the Strugatskys' "Six Matches," and Ivan Yefremov's *Andromeda* see essentially the same future, though often quite differently achieved, as all those nineteenth-century American works which now seem so quaint and naïve. "Immortality must be love immortal," the last words of "In the Year Ten Thousand," could be the ending of many Soviet science fictions, but of indeed few contemporary American science fictions. Perhaps, ironically enough, that great Russian creation, Dostoevski's underground man, enunciates most lucidly the dominant Western view of both twentieth-century Sino-Soviet and nineteenth-century American eutopianism:

> Then the utopian palace of crystal will be erected; then . . . well, then, those will be the days of bliss.
>
> Of course, you can't guarantee (it's me speaking now) that it won't be deadly boring (for what will there be to do when everything is predetermined by timetables?) But, on the other hand, everything will be planned very reasonably.
>
> But then, one might do anything out of boredom. Golden pins are stuck into people out of boredom. But that's nothing. What's really bad (this is me speaking again) is that the golden pins will be welcomed then. The trouble with man is that he's stupid. Phenomenally stupid. That is, even if he's not really stupid, he's so ungrateful that another creature as ungrateful cannot be found. I, for one, wouldn't be the least surprised if, in that future age of reason, there suddenly appeared a gentleman with an ungrateful, or shall we say, retrogressive smirk, who, arms akimbo, would say:
>
> "What do you say, folks, let's send all this reason to hell, just to get all these logarithm tables out from under our feet and go back to our own stupid ways."
>
> That isn't so annoying in itself; what's bad is that this gentleman would be sure to find followers. That's the way man is made.*

Of course the dominant nineteenth-century American view of the future was not a unanimous view. Reacting against it,

* Translated by Andrew R. MacAndrew (New York: Signet Classic, 1961).

anti-utopianism attained its basic modern form, the dystopia, in which the dream of the good place turns out to be a nightmare. Hawthorne's *The Blithedale Romance,* which appeared five years after the demise of Brook Farm, four years after the abortive revolutions of 1848, and four years also after *The Communist Manifesto,* marks an important turning point, standing as perhaps the last great statement of the classical anti-utopian position: utopia can't work. After this develops that characteristically modern anti-utopian position: utopia may work all too well.

WILLIAM HARBEN

In the Year Ten Thousand *

A.D. 10,000. An old man, more than six hundred years of age, was walking with a boy through a great museum. The people who were moving around them had beautiful forms, and faces which were indescribably refined and spiritual.

"Father," said the boy, "you promised to tell me to-day about the Dark Ages. I like to hear how men lived and thought long ago."

"It is no easy task to make you understand the past," was the reply. "It is hard to realize that man could have been so ignorant as he was eight thousand years ago, but come with me; I will show you something."

He led the boy to a cabinet containing a few time-worn books bound in solid gold.

"You have never seen a book," he said, taking out a large volume and carefully placing it on a silk cushion on a table. "There are only a few in the leading museums of the world. Time was when there were as many books on earth as inhabitants."

"I cannot understand," said the boy with a look of perplexity on his intellectual face. "I cannot see what people could have wanted with them; they are not attractive; they seem to be useless."

The old man smiled. "When I was your age, the subject was too deep for me; but as I grew older and made a close study of the history of the past, the use of books gradually became plain

* *The Arena,* 1892.

to me. We know that in the year 2000 they were read by the best minds. To make you understand this, I shall first have to explain that eight thousand years ago human beings communicated their thoughts to one another by making sounds with their tongues, and not by mind-reading, as you and I do. To understand me, you have simply to read my thoughts as well as your education will permit; but primitive man knew nothing about thought-intercourse, so he invented speech. Humanity then was divided up in various races, and each race had a separate language. As certain sounds conveyed definite ideas, so did signs and letters; and later, to facilitate the exchange of thought, writing and printing were invented. This book was printed."

The boy leaned forward and examined the pages closely; his young brow clouded. "I cannot understand," he said, "it seems so useless."

The old man put his delicate fingers on the page. "A line of these words may have conveyed a valuable thought to a reader long ago," he said, reflectively. "In fact, this book purports to be a history of the world up to the year 2000. Here are some pictures," he continued, turning the worn leaves carefully. "This is George Washington; this a pope of a church called the Roman Catholic; this is a man named Gladstone, who was a great political leader in England. Pictures then, as you see, were very crude. We have preserved some of the oil paintings made in those days. Art was in its cradle. In producing a painting of an object, the early artists mixed colored paints and spread them according to taste on stretched canvas or on the walls or windows of buildings. You know that our artists simply throw light and darkness into space in the necessary variations, and the effect is all that could be desired in the way of imitating nature. See that landscape in the alcove before you. The foliage of the trees, the grass, the flowers, the stretch of water, have every apparance of life because the light which produces them is alive."

The boy looked at the scene admiringly for a few minutes, then bent again over the book. Presently he recoiled from the pictures, a strange look of disgust struggling in his tender features.

"These men have awful faces," he said. "They are so unlike people living now. The man you call a pope looks like an animal. They all have huge mouths and frightfully heavy jaws. Surely men could not have looked like that."

"Yes," the old man replied, gently. "There is no doubt that human beings then bore a nearer resemblance to the lower animals than we now do. In the sculpture and portraits of all ages we can trace a gradual refinement in the appearances of men. The features of the human race to-day are more ideal. Thought has always given form and expression to faces. In those dark days the thoughts of men were not refined. Human beings died of starvation and lack of attention in cities where there were people so wealthy that they could not use their fortunes. And they were so nearly related to the lower animals that they believed in war. George Washington was for several centuries reverenced by millions of people as a great and good man; and yet under his leadership thousands of human beings lost their lives in battle."

The boy's susceptible face turned white.

"Do you mean that he encouraged men to kill one another?" he asked, bending more closely over the book.

"Yes, but we cannot blame him; he thought he was right. Millions of his countrymen applauded him. A greater warrior than he was a man named Napoleon Bonaparte. Washington fought under the belief that he was doing his country a service in defending it against enemies, but everything in history goes to prove that Bonaparte waged war to gratify a personal ambition to distinguish himself as a hero. Wild animals of the lowest orders were courageous, and would fight one another till they died; and yet the most refined of the human race, eight or nine thousand years ago, prided themselves on the same ferocity of nature. Women, the gentlest half of humanity, honored men more for bold achievements in shedding blood than for any other quality. But murder was not only committed in wars; men in private life killed one another; fathers and mothers were now and then so depraved as to put their own children to death; and the highest tribunals of the world executed murderers without dreaming that it was wrong, erroneously believing that to kill was the only way to prevent killing."

"Did no one in those days realize that it was horrible?" asked the youth.

"Yes," answered the father, "as far back as ten thousand years ago there was an humble man, it is said, who was called Jesus Christ. He went from place to place, telling every one he met that the world would be better if men would love one another as themselves."

"What kind of man was he?" asked the boy, with kindling eyes.

"He was a spiritual genius," was the earnest reply, "and the greatest that has ever lived."

"Did he prevent them from killing one another?" asked the youth, with a tender upward glance.

"No, for he himself was killed by men who were too barbarous to understand him. But long after his death his words were remembered. People were not civilized enough to put his teachings into practice, but they were able to see that he was right."

"After he was killed, did the people not do as he had told them?" asked the youth, after a pause of several minutes.

"It seems not," was the reply. "They said no human being could live as he had directed. And when he had been dead for several centuries, people began to say that he was the Son of God who had come to earth to show men how to live. Some even believed that he was God himself."

"Did they believe that he was a person like ourselves?"

The old man reflected for a few minutes, then, looking into the boy's eager face, he answered: "That subject will be hard for you to understand. I will try to make it plain. To the unformed minds of early humanity there could be nothing without a personal creator. As man could build a house with his own hands, and was superior to his work, so he argued that some unknown being, greater than all visible things, had made the universe. They called that being by different names according to the language they spoke. In English the word used was 'God.' "

"They believed that somebody had made the universe!" said the boy, "how very strange!"

"No, not somebody as you comprehend it," replied the father gently, "but some vague, infinite being who punished the evil and rewarded the good. Men could form no idea of a creator that did not in some way resemble themselves; and as they could subdue their enemies through fear and by the infliction of pain, so did they believe that God would punish those who did not please him. Some people long ago believed that God's punishment was inflicted after death for eternity. The numerous beliefs about the personality and laws of the creator caused more bloodshed in the gloomy days of the past than anything else. Religion was the foundation of many of the most horrible wars. People committed thousands of crimes in the name of the God of the universe. Men and women were burned alive because they would not believe certain creeds, and yet they adhered to convictions equally as preposterous; but you will learn all these things later in life. That picture before you was the last queen of England, called Victoria."

"I hoped that the women would not have such repulsive features as the men," said the boy, looking critically at the picture, "but this face makes me shudder. Why do they all look so coarse and brutal?"

"People living when this queen reigned had the most degrading habit that ever blackened the history of mankind."

"What was that?" asked the youth.

"The consumption of flesh. They believed that animals, fowls, and fish were created to be eaten."

"Is it possible?" The boy shuddered convulsively, and turned away from the book. "I understand now why their faces repel me so. I do not like to think that we have descended from such people."

"They knew no better," said the father. "As they gradually became more refined they learned to burn the meat over flames and to cook it in heated vessels to change its appearance. The places where animals were killed and sold were withdrawn to retired places. Mankind was slowly turning from the habit, but they did not know it. As early as 2050 learned men, calling themselves vegetarians, proved conclusively that the consumption of such food was cruel and barbarous, and that it retarded refinement and mental growth. However, it was not till about 2300 that the vegetarian movement became of marked importance. The most highly educated classes in all lands adopted vegetarianism, and only the uneducated continued to kill and eat animals. The vegetarians tried for years to enact laws prohibiting the consumption of flesh, but opposition was very strong. In America in 2320 a colony was formed consisting of about three hundred thousand vegetarians. They purchased large tracts of land in what was known as the Indian Territory, and there made their homes, determined to prove by example the efficacy of their tenets. Within the first year the colony had doubled its number: people joined it from all parts of the globe. In the year 4000 it was a country of its own, and was the wonder of the world. The brightest minds were born there. The greatest discoveries and inventions were made by its inhabitants. In 4030 Gillette discovered the process of manufacturing crystal. Up to that time people had built their houses of natural stone, inflammable wood, and metals; but the new material, being fireproof and beautiful in its various colors, was used for all building purposes. In 4050 Holloway found the submerged succession of mountain chains across the Atlantic Ocean, and intended to construct a bridge on their summits; but the vast improvement in air ships rendered his plans impracticable.

"In 4051 John Saunders discovered and put into practice thought-telegraphy. This discovery was the signal for the introduction in schools and colleges of the science of mind-reading, and by the year 5000 so great had been the progress in that branch of knowledge that words were spoken only among the lowest of the uneducated. In no age of the world's history has there been such an important discovery. It civilized the world. Its early promoters did not dream of the vast good mind-reading would accomplish. Slowly it killed evil. Societies for the prevention of evil thought were organized in all lands. Children were born pure of mind and grew up in purity. Crime was choked out of existence. If a man had an evil thought, it was read in his heart, and he was not allowed to keep it. Men at first shunned evil for fear of detection, and then grew to love purity.

"In the year 6021 all countries of the world, having then a common language, and being drawn together in brotherly love by constant exchange of thought, agreed to call themselves a union without ruler or rulers. It was the greatest event in the history of the world. Certain sensitive mind students in Germany, who had for years been trying to communicate with other planets through the channel of thought, declared that, owing to the terrestrial unanimity of purpose in that direction, they had received mental impressions from other worlds, and that thorough interplanetary intercourse was a future possibility.

"Important inventions were made as the mind of humanity grew more elevated. Thornton discovered the plan to heat the earth's surface from its internal fire, and this discovery made journeys to the wonderful ice-bound countries situated at the North and the South Poles easy of accomplishment. At the North Pole, in the extensive concave lands, was found a peculiar race of men. Their sun was the great perpetually boiling lake of lava which bubbled from the centre of the earth in the bottom of their bowl-shaped world. And a strange religion was theirs! They believed that the earth was a monster on whose hide they had to live for a mortal lifetime, and that to the good was given the power after death to walk over the icy waste to their god, whose starry eyes they could see twinkling in space, and that the evil were condemned to feed the fire in the stomach of the monster as long as it lived. They told beautiful stories about the creation of their world, and held that if they lived too near the hot, dazzling mouth of evil, they would become blinded to the soft, forgiving eyes of the god of space. Hence they suffered the extreme cold of the lands near the frozen seas, believing that the physical ordeal prepared them for the icy journey to immortal rest after death. But there were those who hungered after the balmy atmosphere and the wonderful fruits and flowers that grew in the lowlands, and they lived there in indolence and so-called sin."

The old man and his son left the museum and walked into a wonderful park. Flowers of the most beautiful kinds and of sweetest fragrance grew on all sides. They came to a tall tower, four thousand feet in height, built of manufactured crystal. Something, like a great white bird, a thousand feet long, flew across the sky and settled down on the tower's summit.

"This was one of the most wonderful inventions of the Seventieth century," said the old man. "The early inhabitants of the earth could not have dreamed that it would be possible to go around it in twenty-four hours. In fact, there was a time when they were not able to go around it at all. Scientists were astonished when a man called Malburn, a great inventor, announced that, at a height of four thousand feet, he could disconnect an air ship from the laws of gravitation, and cause it to stand still in space till the earth had turned over. Fancy what must have been that immortal genius' feelings when he stood in space and saw the earth for the first time whirling beneath him!"

They walked on for some distance across the park till they

came to a great instrument made to magnify the music in light. Here they paused and seated themselves.

"It will soon be night," said the old man. "The tones are those of bleeding sunset. I came here last evening to listen to the musical struggle between the light of dying day and that of the coming stars. The sunlight had been playing a powerful solo; but the gentle chorus of the stars, led by the moon, was inexplicably touching. Light is the voice of immortality; it speaks in all things."

An hour passed. It was growing dark.

"Tell me what immortality is," said the boy. "What does life lead to?"

"We do not know," replied the old man. "If we knew we would be infinite. Immortality is increasing happiness for all time; it is"—

A meteor shot across the sky. There was a burst of musical laughter among the singing stars. The old man bent over the boy's face and kissed it. "Immortality," said he—"immortality must be love immortal."

THE PRESENT PERFECT

As we look at a past vision of the future, what we see is the past, and, in reflection, ourselves. This view may disclose how much one time may be composed of its visions of other times, how a view of the future may place the past in time or constitute the present, how the mirrors of time reflect upon each other so that we, standing in the midst of them, can see ourselves coming and going.